Tipping Point
The World in 2050

Book One

George Alfred Kennedy

SETAF Publishing

Dedication

To the next generation of earth's protectors.

Published Books by Author

Memoir

Cottonfields To Summits - The View from Contested Ground, A Memoir, Vol. I
The Rest of It, A Memoir, Vol. II

Crosshairs Series (Fiction)

CROSSHAIRS
Attack On A Principal
In Her Own Right - A Political Biography
VEEP - The Principal Becomes Personal - A Political Memoir
Beyond 1600 - From The Inside To The Outside - A Political Memoir
Democracy At The Brink - A Political Memoir | Co-Author Yvonne D. Merrill

Fiction

Dirty Commodities-Tricked, Trapped, and Terrified | Co-Author Yvonne D. Merrill

---

SETAF Publishing
Marana, Arizona

Copyright Notice

Contents

Prologue

Tipping Point - The World in 2050 is a fictionalized account of acclaimed American climatologist, author, and advocate Dr. Tracie Hinton's efforts to persuade an American president and the leadership of Russia and China (PRC) to rethink the geopolitics of a changing global climate to avoid worldwide famine, drought, and mass migration; perhaps a shooting war that no one wants.

In the year 2050, the world population has reached ten billion, a billion of whom are migrants brought about by the effects of a changing global climate. The looming, unanswered question is, "Can that many people be fed without destroying the planet?" The leadership of the world's larger powers is caught between ideological 'hawks' and their corporate/industry allies and financial donors who insist 'climate change' is a hoax and the existential threat of populations demanding food, potable water, clean air, and a sustainable source of energy to sustain life. No one doubts that regional, ethnic, religious, and even racial conflicts are inevitable under these conditions.

The unwillingness of President Harwood and his Chinese counterpart to act with greater urgency to dramatically reduce carbon emissions (CO_2) to net zero, has subjected planet Earth to irreversible damage.

Frustrated by a White House team that excludes the scientific community from public policy discussions, Tracie Hinton and an intrepid band of American, Chinese, Italian, and Nigerian environmentalists and sustainability experts plan to host a series of symposia to be broadcast worldwide. A key collaborator on this project is Hinton's friend of long-standing Professor Wiley Mitchell. Hinton declares that her friend's involvement in this project is essential to its success.

Mitchell had spent the last 18 of his 43 years in Southern California, New Mexico, and Washington State. He spent his early childhood in Detroit, Michigan, where he developed a strong interest in learning more about the effects of wind and weather on Lake Ontario. Temperatures so severe that they could turn a lake into a vast expanse of ice and break concrete structures fascinated him as a child. His questions, even as a child, were endless. Aspiring to become a climatologist came as natural to him, perhaps more so, than the basketball his playmates constantly thrust into his hands. At 6'5" in height, he was the tallest kid in his cohort. His Pershing High School coaches pressured him to pursue a career in professional sports, but their pressure could not compete with Wiley's desire to spend hours in the high school library and the library at Wayne State University on W. Warren Avenue in Detroit. When Wiley was not at home, his working-class parents, John and Louise Mitchell, never feared their child would be lost to the allure of the streets. They knew he was in a library somewhere in the city.

Decades earlier, the Climate Change Summit held in Tucson at the Tucson Convention Center, sponsored by over 40 international organizations, identified the desert Southwest as the most climatically vulnerable place in North America. Wiley was curious about that. That region had all the vulnerabilities: drought-caused food insecurity, wildfires, decreasing water supplies, flash floods, and climate-driven disease vectors for West Nile Virus, Dengue Virus, Malaria, Zika Microcephaly, and Lyme disease.

The presenters at that same conference, Wiley learned, predicted that the population of the desert Southwest would exceed 100 million by 2050. Their prophecies came true, but well before 2050. Years later, upon obtaining his doctorate, Wiley set out for New Mexico. A changing climate had decimated the population, as well as the flora and fauna indigenous to the Southwest. The Southwest had become the Arid Zone.

The content of the symposia Tracie Hinton and her intrepid team would develop would foil the White House's strategy to control the narrative about the issues and the consequences of a changing climate before the national elections in November 2052. President Harwood was convinced a second term was at stake. Moreover, his ambitious Vice President, Jackson Hewlett, believed his chances to capture the presidential nomination four years hence would be improved if his benefactor, the President, could secure a second term.

Upon learning of the planned symposia from an inside source within Hinton's organization, an enraged Vice President Hewlett and his political allies in the House of Representatives and the influential fossil fuel industry threaten to silence Tracie - permanently, if necessary - and block transmission of the symposia. Dr. Wilson Ojukwe, a senior World Health Organization official and Tracie's finance, temporarily relocates Tracie to his home in Northwest D.C. when unmarked vehicles begin surveilling her at home, and she receives numerous threatening calls from a member of a right-wing organization connected to the Vice President.

Meanwhile, the paranoid and erratic leadership in Pyongyang, North Korea, is confronting disease, food riots, growing civil unrest, and instability within its military ranks at home. Collectively, the North Korean civilian and military leadership fear that their Chinese patrons in Beijing may sacrifice them in any compromise negotiations with the U.S. They launch an intercontinental ballistic missile (IBM) that explodes off the California coast. The ensuing tidal wave crests over a mile inland, killing 2500 Americans. An embattled President Harwood, singularly focused on his reelection, fails to respond. Reaction from the American Joint Chiefs of Staff is swift: Harwood has to respond. The North Korean missile, Harwood reasons, did not impact American soil. In response, he kicks the problem to the UN to avoid the responsibility for unilateral action.

Closer to home, threats from the Vice President's allies against Tracie and Wiley continue to mount as the symposia stimulate debate and raise questions the White House seeks to avoid. Wilson is forced to permanently relocate Tracie to his home in Nigeria, where they marry. Her team/staff, also under threat by the Vice President, are forced to relocate as well. Now safe in Nigeria, Tracie, with support from numerous international donors and supporters, launches the Hinton Foundation in London and lays the foundation for a worldwide movement.

North Korea, misled by a Russian spy within the South Korean Government, launched a missile strike against the headquarters of the American Pacific Naval Command in Hawaii, killing the four-star commander-in-chief and incinerating 10,000 American civilian and military personnel. Also lost were seven capital ships of the U.S. fleet moored there.

President Harwood, faced with the resignation of the leadership of his Joint Chiefs of Staff and his defense secretary and an unprecedented challenge from his Vice President for the leadership of his party in the coming presidential elections, is compelled to act.

To bolster his standing on the world stage, the Russian President hosts a series of bilateral meetings in Geneva to exploit the political weakness of President Harwood at home, and the growing tension between the U.S. and the Chinese leadership.

The symposia had the intended effect of stimulating a national conversation about the quality of life here in the U.S. and the failure of President Harwood to provide direction for a national approach to dealing with the consequences of a changing climate for children and future generations.

'Climate change' is real, and only those elected officials still functioning as handmaidens of the fossil fuel industry cling to the talking points provided by industry lobbyists. The distrust of both major political parties is at historical highs. Moreover, the public demanded a real alternative. A new American ACTION 2100 Party is born with Tracie Hinton as its nominee for president in the 2052 national elections.

1

It was an unusually hot Wednesday in Los Angeles that day in March 2050 when Dr. Tracie Hinton, world-renowned climatologist, deplaned from her Delta Airlines flight at the Los Angeles International Airport (LAX). The 4-hour flight aboard one of Delta's newest acquisitions, the Boeing 797-9 LR, a wide-bodied, two engine behemoth, had been sheer joy. Service in business class was impeccable, relaxing, as advertised. She had even managed to finish the last few chapters of a novel languishing on her nightstand.

The temperature on the ground that day had soared to its average of 125 degrees Fahrenheit. Dr. Hinton had arrived from her home in Washington, D.C., two days before the conference to attend the annual, weeklong Southern California Climate Assessment Conference on the 'Desertification Status of the Southwest Region of the U.S.' hosted by the California State University Los Angeles. Dr. Hinton was, again, a regular presenter.

On Wednesday of her arrival, the heat literally took her breath away when she exited the climate-controlled terminal to take a waiting vehicle to the university just over 20 miles away. Although she had been forewarned that the temperature would feel like a furnace, and had dressed accordingly, the brief exposure between the Terminal and her vehicle reminded her of the Thanksgiving turkey her mother prepared every year. The mind takes its independence at times. The heat rendered everything lifeless along her route and, although she had just arrived, she was already thinking ahead to her departure. Gazing out the window, she couldn't help but think about those who were permanent residents here. "How do they do it?" she wondered. The heat and humidity of Washington, D.C. were preferable to life in an oven.

On Friday over lunch with Dr. Jeannette Masters, Administrator of the U.S. Environmental Protection Agency (EPA), who was also visiting from Washington, Dr. Hinton remarked, "Before we landed on Wednesday, the pilot announced that the thermometer at the airport registered 125 degrees Fahrenheit, and I wondered if that is the current normal. Friday, it was only 119°." This was one of her specializations. Los Angeles and the San Gabriel Valley were experiencing rolling blackouts and systemic power outages from outmoded generators that powered essential services. "If that level of preparedness doesn't provide a realistic backdrop for this conference, I don't know what does," Hinton remarked to Dr. Masters.

"And just imagine: it's 129 degrees in Phoenix!" replied Masters. "My colleague Jefferson Holdridge, who will be joining us this evening, is in Phoenix for another meeting. "Jeff is a senior deputy from the Bureau of Oceans and International Environmental and Scientific Affairs (OES) at the State Department. He called me just a while ago to tell me the temperature there is nothing short of Hell. I laughed and said, 'Tonight, I will welcome you to Hell's reception room.'"

Tracie responded, "Those conservative non-believers and their wealthy backers in Arizona who believed climate change was a hoax certainly became believers the hard way." She went on to add, "Sandwiched between steadily rising temperatures and the inexorable creep of the Arizona desert, they got what they deserved. In this part of the country, the Sonoran Desert is ground zero." Tracie then made another point which succinctly summarized the gravity of the challenge in much of the Southwest: "No one," she said in an almost inaudible tone, "lives in the desert. If anything lives over there, it survives only underground." Dr. Masters remarked that she would always fault the early energy providers for pushing fossil fuel when an arid Southwest has such a wealth of resources for renewable energy. Tracie went on to lament the failure of Arizona's political leadership and the state legislature to regulate the fossil fuel industry in time. The industry's voracious appetite for profit and control coupled with an equally voracious appetite from elected leadership for campaign contributions, had been at the expense of people's lives. "I'm surprised they didn't go deaf from having their heads in the sand so long."

Tracie Hinton had well-established connections with San Gabriel through a long relationship with Professor Wiley Mitchell and his vivacious wife, Roberta. She had met Wiley Mitchell many years ago at a Great Lakes Conference in Detroit. Wiley at the time was a newly-minted PhD in Biological Sciences and Urban Sustainability from Wayne State University there in Detroit. She recalled that he, too, was young, eager, and excited. The details of how they met are worth telling.

The two of them were standing in a large open space studying the lineup of meetings and breakout sessions offered that afternoon. Tracie was several feet away when she heard this guy say to himself: "Damn, the two sessions I wanted to attend most are being offered at the same time and I have to choose!" He was lamenting that he couldn't attend two key breakout sessions simultaneously. "Unbelievable!" she thought. "I have the same problem." Almost reflexively, she said to him, "I have the same problem. Why don't you attend one session and I the other. Afterward, let's meet here, have coffee and exchange notes. My name is Tracie Hinton, by the way" while extending her hand. "What's yours?" "I'm Wiley Mitchell." And for a second, they looked at each other as if to establish a connection. "Okay!" Wiley said with a friendly smile. "See you in this spot in an hour." The two of them then headed for their respective meetings.

An hour later, Tracie arrived at the designated meeting spot a couple of minutes before Wiley and was looking around when he walked up. "Hey, thanks for your suggestion," Wiley said as they headed in the direction of a coffee bar. Nearby, they were able to find a couple of comfortable chairs in a lounge to compare notes. At one point during the conversation, Tracie interjected, "So, who is Wiley Mitchell? And why this conference?" "Wow! Wiley thought to himself. She beat me to it! Okay, it's good." Wiley shifted his focus from his notes to describe growing up in Detroit with his parents John and Louise Mitchell, the challenge of being 6'-5" and resisting the pressures from friends and his coaches to pursue a career as a professional athlete. Everybody called me 'Wiles.' "I was always an outstanding student, something his guidance counselor, Dorothy Smentek, noticed early on," he explained. "She was someone I could talk to about my interest in science. Mrs. Smentek was the one who talked to me about scholarships and how to apply for them, and it was she who said that I shouldn't interrupt my education until I had my doctorate. *No one* had ever mentioned the idea of a doctorate before, ever! Not even my parents, and they were in my case all the time. Of course, Mom and Dad always said that education was the key to my future. I understood that. But Mrs. Smentek was different than any of my teachers or professors. I love Mrs. Smentek, and I'm still in touch with her to this day. She laughs and says 'I am one of her proudest accomplishments.'"

"But why science? Why climatology?" Tracie asked. "You're from the inner city. It seems an odd career choice. I would have thought education, government, and the private sector. Didn't you say that your dad worked for city government and your mom was an educator? She noticed that Wiley seemed even more animated as he began to talk about his fascination with weather phenomena: how weather and temperature affected Lake Ontario and concrete structures along the lake, and how the city responded to challenges that severe weather presented. He explained how as a child he noticed "the effect severe temperatures had on everything, e.g. people's cars, construction materials, highway and road maintenance; that a single or double-pane window was no protection against the wind. A window had to be triple-paned if you wanted any protection at all."

Wiley went on to say, "And when I learned that in Toronto, there was an entire underground economy linked to major thoroughfares in the city, that commuters from suburban communities around the lake could leave their cars at home and take a train into the city directly underground, and connect to all of the offices downtown without ever exposing themselves to the elements, I became fascinated with urban sustainability. Winters in Detroit are nothing to joke about." Laughing, he told Tracie, "A few of my close friends knew I was somewhat of a nerd, but they didn't expose me."

Continuing, Wiley said, "There is an interesting twist to this story. I asked my parents so many questions, my dad tried to find a way to deal with my incessant curiosity. His approach was to draw on his experience as a city government official and familiarity with the process of how public policy is formulated because I always asked 'why' and 'how?' of whatever the issue." And that's how Dad chose to broaden my education. As a city employee, he took me to observe a few City Council meetings on the city's budget. In those meetings, those open to the public, they discussed priorities, what policies, programs, and projects were to be funded. I, of course, as the inquisitive kid, was fascinated by the debate and how decisions were made. My dad's point was, if I wanted to understand how priorities were established, including how much was allocated for city snow removal, for example, to follow the money. That is also the issue with climate change, is it not? You acknowledge much of it is human induced and someone has to pay. Now sitting on the edge of his chair, Wiley asked, "So, what's your story? Tracie.

"My story," Tracie began, "is more complicated. Maybe not as interesting." She shared details of her life growing up with her dad, Sam Hinton, a senior official with the U.S. Agency for International Development (USAID) and Counselor to the President (of the United States).

"A changing climate was among a list of policy concerns I heard my father talk about at the family dinner table. Much of the time, my mom and I just listened because we knew the issue was important to my dad. Occasionally, when the consequences of changing climate touched on a region of the world important to my mom, she would join the conversation. Dad talked about climate change all the time because it affected his job. My mom is from the Ukraine, and she was always up on anything, and I mean *anything* happening in that part of the world." Continuing to explain, Tracie added, "I was the sponge at the table. I just listened and absorbed everything I was hearing. Some of the stuff I heard didn't always make sense, but I could Google everything. Loved the Net, even then."

"So, when did the consequences of climate change become really important to you?" Wiley asked. "Well, my high school civics class had been assigned a term project requiring each of us to write a ten-page research paper on a topic of our choosing. We had to present our papers to the teacher and the class. I didn't mind that part so much. I was finding it difficult to settle on a particular topic from a list of several. One night, lying across my bed, it occurred to me, 'why not climate change?' Dad talks about it regularly, and it could be a fun project. There is enough unclassified stuff around to get started."

"And!" Wiley interjected.

"Well, the more familiar I became with the research, important questions being raised by scientists - and ignored by policy makers everywhere - the more fascinated I became." In fact, I remember one day telling my dad how I feared that the inevitability and pace of a changing climate would affect my future and that of my generation.

At the end of that conversation between two strangers' serendipity brought together, a friendship was born that brought the two of them together as it had many times over the last 18 years. This time in San Gabriel.

The first day of the conference, Tracie missed seeing her friend Dr. Mitchell, who had said he would be late attending because he did not want to cancel a meeting with an important client. He would catch a late flight from Seattle. Tracie was in her guest accommodation preparing to go to dinner that evening with several others attending the conference when the power suddenly went out. Minutes before, Tracie had stepped out of the shower and was now partially clothed. The room was dark. Within minutes, the temperature in the room rose. She began to sweat - her panties, half-slip and bra became wet and sticky. She couldn't shed them quickly enough, thinking "I just showered!" She mumbled to herself, "I feel as though I never bothered. Hell! This doesn't bode well for being close to anyone. So, now what? How long is this blackout going to last?"

These power interruptions had been occurring for days according to some of the hosts, but somehow the university and *her* wing of the guest quarters had been spared. Until this evening. Dinner was at 7:30 p.m. It was now 6:00 p.m. "What do I do for another 90 minutes," she wondered aloud. Having shed everything, she plopped down in the center of the king-sized air mattress completely nude. Expecting some relief, she was disappointed. Tracie threw the light thermal-adjusting cover off to one side. The sheets felt damp and clammy, as if someone had taken them out of the air blower too soon. The air in the room felt heavy, oppressive and humid for the San Gabriel Valley, and just generally hard to breathe. Her impulse was to open the vents, but chose not to for fear someone on the other side would be able to see into her second level room. Opening the partition to the space next door was out of the question.

Tracie got up and went to the mini cooler. Even the fused glass insulate-over-concrete floor under her bare feet didn't feel cool because of its textured surface. The cooler was now without power. Reaching for one of the two bottles of chilled water, Tracie knew it would soon be as desirable as tap water.

"Do I drink both now? or should I save one for later?... Shit! I'm hot and uncomfortable, so why not enjoy them now? Okay! Settled." She drank one bottle slowly, savoring each mouthful while holding the other bottle against her forehead for temporary relief. She chuckled for a second thinking how reminiscent the moment was of life in some Third World countries she knew where brownouts were a common occurrence.

Tracie had planned to skim some material on desertification she'd picked up during one of their meetings that day, possibly to discuss it over dinner that evening. Well, the heat stupor had made her disinclined to read. She remembered the temperature forecast for Saturday was 122 degrees Fahrenheit. "My God!" she thought to herself. "Without power, how in the hell (no pun intended) does the university manage?" She had had a similar experience during a conference on Manila Island two years before. Only then, the temperature outside was 110 degrees Fahrenheit with over 90 percent humidity. In an air-conditioned space with humidity that high, she recalled it was like standing fully clothed under a cool sprinkler. But this was Southern California in late March *without* air conditioning. If she put something on, she might try the central cooling tower, where she hoped the dinner would be held… *if* the lights came on.

As Tracie lay there naked, her thoughts turned humorously dark. It was hot and the humidity was rising. She was lying on a bed used by countless others, and she thought of all things about dust mites; millions of eight-legged creatures fornicating, defecating, and dying in her mattress and bedding before her arrival. And now, they were keeping her company. Gross! Okay! That's it! "I've spent too much time in the Third World " she told herself. Reaching to her nightstand, she picked up her phone and pressed the image of a friend and colleague back in Washington. Wilson Ojukwe, a Nigerian official at the World Health Organization (WHO), and she had co-authored a book on desertification in Sub-Saharan Africa. She wanted to share what she was experiencing in San Gabriel with him. Tracie decided she would not bring up the subject of dust mites. She expected he would make light of her current discomfort, contrasting it with life back in Lagos, and then laugh heartily. Ojukwe loved a good laugh, and perhaps his laugh would take the edge off her present discomfort. Wilson had wanted to attend this conference, but had managed to contract a summer cold and was prohibited from flying.

On the third ring, Wilson responded: "Tracie! Is that you? How are you?" And there it was, that heavily accented, rich baritone voice of her friend Wilson. Wilson was special. They had been close friends for almost twenty years. He had always said to her, "Tracie, if I cannot marry you, I will nevah marry." He had been true to his word. They were both 42. Privately, their relationship was so special to her, she feared that if it evolved into marriage, it might not work and she would lose him and everything that made the two of them special. Her other fear was that the older they became, given his cultural tradition, the more likely it was that someone younger would come between them.

As she began to describe the events of her day, Wilson laughed, as she expected he would. "You know," she said in response to his laughter, "if there is no power tomorrow at the university, it wouldn't take much for me to get on a plane and come home."

"But you are one of the presenters; you can't do that! Besides, I'm sure the university anticipated this could happen and has spare generator parts on hand." "You're right! I couldn't leave if I wanted to. My friend Wiley Mitchell will be arriving this evening and he's bringing his wife, Roberta, with him. I haven't seen her in a while and we've got a lot of catching up to do. I really like her. Beyond my parents, I've never met a more perfectly matched couple. This is only a temporary hardship," Tracie added.

"Yeah, you're good," Wilson responded. "Remember Manila! We had air-conditioning, but we were uncomfortable, nonetheless. The temperature reached 105 degrees here in Washington today with humidity so dense you could cut it with a knife. And the air quality was what you would expect. In fact, I didn't go in today. I'm just saying you haven't adjusted to being in that part of the country again."

"You're right about everything. This isn't the worst thing that's happened to me. I just needed to vent. I'll call you when I get back. Perhaps we can have dinner, and I can bring you up to date on this stuff."

"Good! See you next week."

Before she hung up, Tracie glanced at the clock beside the bed and saw it was 6:25 p.m. She laid back and tried to close her eyes.

2

The power returned before 7:30 p.m., and Tracie assumed her dinner companions would be joining her. None of them had called to cancel because of the power failure. She was looking forward to dinner because one of the guests would be Bradford Taylor, the current Director of Environmental Quality Research and Development for the State of Colorado. He had read several of her articles and the book she coauthored with Wilson. As Taylor put it to her, "Didn't people read your material? It's all here! What the hell happened?"

Half in jest, Tracie had responded, "Remember the proverbial ostrich? They even tried to raise those in Arizona!"

"I'll be damned!" was about the only response Taylor could muster at that moment. "Well, *I'm* listening," he went on to say. And that brief exchange had led to the decision to share dinner that Friday night. Taylor was young - mid-thirties- earnest and relatively new to the field. Tracie's first impression had been that he was a problem-solver, and she saw an opening to build a new ally. Taylor had an open mind - rare in itself. She also wanted to tell anyone who might be interested that her longtime friend, Wiley Mitchell would be coming down from Seattle that evening in case they wanted to talk to him.

The other dinner guest would be Virgilio Sanchez, Director of Commerce for the State of California. Sanchez's experience had included a stint as the U.S. Trade Representative (USTR). Tracie assumed Taylor and Sanchez were acquainted with each other.

Tracie was particularly sensitive to the plight of former states on the West Coast. California had been one of the world's principal agricultural producers and exporters until rising ocean levels destroyed the Central Valley, one of the most productive agricultural regions on earth. San Gabriel was 532 miles further south. The coastal communities of San Diego and San Francisco, former major trade hubs to and from the U.S., were under water. Also under water was San Francisco International Airport because it was built on reclaimed land. Los Angeles would have been under water had the city's leadership not had the foresight to implement a gargantuan, expensive project to protect much of the city from flooding. The project had not been perfect, but it did prevent the complete loss of one of the country's principal capital cities.

Agriculture as an industry had been destroyed. California's economy, once the fifth largest in the world, had taken a major hit. Unemployment had increased dramatically, and it had become increasingly difficult to feed over 40 million people in the state. Sanchez was a lawyer with considerable experience as a trade negotiator, and it was now his charge, working with the state's agricultural commissioner, to replenish the state's seed banks, likely from former international partners.

That task would be delicate, and probably costly. He told Tracie, "I don't know that California will ever become a key agricultural producer and exporter again. My immediate concern, however, is food security - guaranteeing our ability to feed our people." Sanchez went on to describe how difficult it had been for his predecessors to convince the technology, aerospace, and manufacturing sectors and major exporters to prepare for what researchers had warned the future *would* bring. "Well, it's here, and I'm just one of those trying to figure out how we adapt. You're the climatologist, Tracie! What are you advising coastal communities? More importantly, what are those communities prepared to do? They can't continue to ignore reality."

"Well, I'm having dinner tonight with a state official from Colorado. Why don't you join us?"

"Who is it? if you don't mind my asking."

"Someone you may know: Bradford Taylor."

"Yes! I know him well. At least our conversation won't go off the rails."

Tracie arrived at dinner ten minutes early and chose a table directly under the cooling tower. As she sat, she looked around and saw Bradford, caught his eye, and waved him over. Virgilio was the next to arrive. Surprisingly, he placed a chilled bottle of synthesized wine on the table beside the one already warm that had been there as part of the dinner setting. He smiled and unscrewed the top, pointing to the wine glasses set out at their places. Tracie and Bradford immediately offered theirs.

"How is it that yours is cold?" Tracie asked, having noticed the moist ring that had quickly formed around its base. He winked mischievously.

"It's a trade!" he said as he poured the last glass for himself." "Cheers! Here's to great conference sessions to come."

"Cheers! Cheers! Cheers!" they all toasted and clinked their fused-glass stemware.

Bradford opened the conversation, but he had no sooner done so when Tracie, out of the corner of her eye, saw Wiley and Roberta. Excited, she practically jumped out of her chair saying, "They're here! They're here! I'll be right back!" Of course, Bradford stopped in mid-sentence looking around to see who Tracie was referring to. Tracie had left the table and was heading in the direction of a young couple who, having acknowledged her, were coming to greet her. Tracie embraced and kissed both of them and was now leading them to the table. "Virgilio, Bradford, this is my friend of many years, Dr. Wiley Mitchell and his beautiful wife, Roberta. They just arrived from Seattle."

Virgilio was first on his feet: "Welcome Dr. Mitchell and Mrs. Mitchell. Please join us!" He extended his hand in welcome. Bradford followed suit. "When did you arrive?" Tracie asked. "Earlier this evening," Roberta responded. We checked in, dropped our bags, and washed our faces to freshen up a little. We figured we'd find you at dinner."

Wiley added, "We would have arrived earlier, but a client I have been working with was only available this morning, and neither of us could cancel. I have been looking forward to seeing you, Tracie, and attending this conference. I'm pleased we're finally here. I'm also hungry!" Everyone laughed. "Also, please, just call me Wiley. I sense I'm among friends."

"Well, you're just in time," Bradford responded. "We're about to attack the buffet." "So, what are we talking about?" Wiley asked. Bradford picked up the conversation saying, "I'm working on a new project which looks promising. In brief, it is new technology that will improve air quality for people living in confined spaces. I'm conducting tests now and I like the results. Soon, I'll be releasing more details. "That's terrific, Bradford," toasted Tracie raising her wine glass again. "We'll look forward to the details."

The buffet was announced by the evenings M.C., the University Provost for Research, Dr. Harland Hightower. While making their way to a quickly-lengthening line, Tracie noted to Virgilio that the cooler in *her* quarters was off. "Like I said-a trade. I just came from a happy hour sponsored by the Colorado dried ice manufacturers from your state," he grinned at Bradford, "and guess what they were trading for just about anything! I gave them my web address and told them they could use my services to find trade partners.

As the small group approached the buffet tables, everyone noticed the preferred choices were fresh vegetables and salad. The collapse of California's agriculture was on full display. Well, that was certainly going to be a topic of conversation. Everyone followed suit selecting generous portions of vegetables, salad, and the limited offerings of seafood that were available. Settling in for dinner and conversation, Tracie asked Wiley to talk about his activities in Seattle.

For the benefit of Bradford and Virgilio, a little history will be useful" Wiley began. "Almost a decade ago, several partners and I founded *Marine Solutions International*." He went on to explain that they conduct research into the effects of a changing climate on ocean temperatures, the fact that almost half of the planet's oceans are experiencing a marine heatwave. Continuing, he pointed out that "the Mediterranean Sea, for example, is experiencing unusually high temperatures-the highest ever." For example, "off the coast of Newfoundland, according to reports I have seen, the water temperature is almost 20 degrees Fahrenheit above normal. And, here at home, South of Miami, water surface temperatures were above 100 degrees Fahrenheit."

"The obvious question," he asked, is "what is the impact on coral reefs, fisheries, and marine ecosystems worldwide. Everyone understands the problem; it's the solutions that are in play." Wiley shared with them that most of the planet's ten billion people depend upon the oceans as their principal source of daily protein. In most coastal societies, fishing is a local, village enterprise. Fishermen are independent and their 'economy' is off the government's political and social radar. When coral reefs die, marine ecosystems die, and there are no fish, people starve; they die, and now we have a political and an economic problem.

The floating fish processing plants of China, Japan, and others are depleting fish stocks in deep waters [Near Seas and Distant Seas]. Limited stocks made available to the market are priced beyond the means of smaller coastal communities. Governments need practical solutions as they search for balance between the larger commercial marine industry, and the requirements of millions of coastal dwellers who are now experiencing famine, starvation. Social instability, civil cohesion are at risk.

My team and I, Wiley continued, work with everyone involved to achieve a balance of interests. Profits, even greed, are arrayed against those with limited resources and seek to survive or maintain traditions as fishermen. Also, there are myriad and complex legal (national and international) issues and, to help us navigate those, we have Roberta and her team of legal experts. "That's the thumbnail sketch of our operation. Our client list is international, and we are growing. I should note: everyone appears focused on the loss of California's agricultural sector. Well, imagine the loss of marine life in our oceans! What are the alternative sources of protein for the billions who depend on coastal waters for protein and livelihoods?"

Roberta Benevento was the second child of Anthony and Cristine Benevento, born in June 2010 in Lyon, France. As a child in school, Roberta became the favorite of an American exchange teacher from Kansas on a Fulbright teaching scholarship in France. Roberta was bright, possessed of a sunny disposition, and a voracious consumer of information, the more complex, the better. She was beyond the normal curiosity of most kids her age. As a child, Roberta demonstrated an early fascination for things American and constantly peppered her American teacher with questions about the U.S., e.g. "Where is Kansas? What is it like to live there? Would it be possible for me to visit one day?"

Roberta's American instructor, Janelle Sanderson, a PhD candidate from the University of Kansas, the state's flagship institution in Lawrence, Kansas, indulged young Roberta because she saw a lot of herself in her. When Janelle returned to Kansas a year later, Roberta asked if she could write to her. Thus began a long-distance exchange that evolved into a real friendship. Roberta's parents encouraged the exchange of correspondence and the friendship because it kept their daughter grounded in her studies and fueled Roberta's determination to master the English language. Roberta told her parents that "One day, I will study in the United States." In her second year at the prestigious Université Claude Bernard Lyon 1 in Lyon, with assistance from her parents, Roberta gained admission to the Wayne State University College of Law in Detroit to pursue an American Juris Doctorate. To

Roberta, this was the fulfillment of a dream. She shared her good fortune with her old friend, Janelle Sanderson, now married and living in Chicago.

Roberta loved the pace of urban living even though she spent most of her time in the law library. One Saturday in late October, Roberta decided to change her routine and visit a local Starbucks, have a caffe latte and catch up on her reading. The reading requirements were heavy and there was never enough time during the week. The din of so many conversations was too distracting and she headed for the main library. While searching through the stacks for a particular book, she noticed a tall, good-looking, young African American male retrieving several books from one of the upper shelves. Roberta had located the book she sought, but it was further along that aisle, also beyond her reach. "Pardon me, but could you help me?" she politely asked this tall stranger.

Wiley turned to his right in the direction of the voice. At 6'-5", he instinctively looked down. The only females he ever encountered who met his gaze were several members of the lady's basketball team he had met on campus at a social event. One member of that team actually looked down on him. For Wiley, that was a first. Looking down, Wiley saw this beautiful woman with soft, kind eyes. He estimated she was about 5'-8" tall. Pointing above him, she asked "Would you please hand me that book just above you? The one with the blue and white cover." Wiley had been an exchange student the second semester of his junior year in college living in Berlin [Germany], the crossroads of exchange students in Europe. In this moment, he could not recall anyone during that experience having made the distinct impression this beautiful stranger did.

Looking up, Wiley saw the book she was pointing to saying, "This one?"

"Yes, thank you. You're so kind." Handing the book to this enchanting stranger, Wiley asked her, "Your accent, what is it? if I may ask" (smiling). He knew it was French, but that was the only conversation opener that came to mind.

"I'm French," she said. "I'm a law student here. My name is Roberta. And yours?"

"My name is Wiley, Wiley Mitchell, and I'm a doctoral student. What brings you to *this* library?" Law students generally hung out at the Law Library.

Roberta then explained briefly her earlier decision to study at Starbucks, but left because of the noise coming to the general library instead.

"Thank goodness for a noisy Starbucks, Wiley said to himself.

"What was that?" Roberta asked.

"Oh nothing. Well, Roberta, I'm pleased to meet you!"

"I'm sitting over there," Roberta said, pointing to a table in a distant corner. Do you want to join me?"

"Thanks, I will."

When they sat down, Wiley asked how long she had been in the library.

Looking at her watch, Roberta responded, "Just over an hour."

"Well, I know a more quiet place to have coffee if you'd like to. It's walking distance. I'm from Detroit - you're safe with me" he said smiling.

Roberta felt at ease with this tall, dark stranger responding, "All right."

As they got up to leave, Wiley helped Roberta with her coat. His eye roamed from her brown hair coiffed into a loose French roll with a few wisps of hair hanging over her ears, to the bulky knit sweater, to the form-fitting, knee-length brown skirt and calf-length Italian boots. But who was paying attention to details?

Wiley, true to his personality, was serious about his program of study and, apart from a social welcoming of new students in early September, had avoided any social life. He planned to complete his program in three years, not the four-to-five years which was the norm for many doctoral students, he had learned.

This Roberta was different from anyone he'd ever met. He instantly felt a connection and wanted to know more about her. Fifteen minutes later, they arrived at a small place, entered and sat at an empty table. There were others there, but the atmosphere was different. It was more congenial, conducive to conversation without having to raise your voice if you were trying to talk to someone.

"What would you like?" Wiley asked.

"A caffe latte, please."

For the next two hours, Wiley and Roberta talked, laughed, and talked some more as the two strangers got to know each other. Wiley was drawn to Roberta and he planned to let her know it. Later, Roberta would admit the attraction was mutual. "It was fate that Starbucks didn't work for me that morning," she told her parents. Over the next three years, they became very close. She spent major holidays with Wiley and his family. They were both three years from graduation and, although they became inseparable, they promised each other, for graduation, they would marry at that time - and not before.

Roberta added, "Unless you can anchor coastal residents where they are, they will migrate. That is already happening. Food insecurity is another major consequence of a changing climate. Governments cannot engage local populations on a broader political, economic, or social agenda if people don't have enough to eat. It's that simple."

Bradford was the first to speak up, saying, "You know, Wiley, Roberta, I'm almost embarrassed to say this, but, you and others have been telling us for some time now that the debate surrounding our changing climate is broader than it is presented. If I may, let me tell you what part of the problem is. It is how the debate is framed for public consumption. What do I mean by that?" Bradford then went on to explain that there are those heavily invested in how any public discussion on the effect of a changing climate is framed to build consensus for a particular point of view - pro or con. Although three-quarters of our planet is water, people are tactile and, of necessity, relate to the land. They have a relationship with it. They have history with the land. They live on it, cultivate it, rearrange it, bequeath it, go to war over it, and even despoil it.

They understand poor air quality and its harmful effects on our health. They understand that water is life, and when that resource becomes scarce or non-potable, the consequences are dire. Life as the average individual knows it changes.

Those who shape the debate, who frame the key issues, are invested in outcomes. And outcomes are determined by public understanding and consensus. We don't live on three-quarters of the earth's surface: water. We traverse bodies of water; we explore bodies of water. Closer to shore, we recreate on water. We take for granted the bounty of our rivers, lakes, seas and oceans. Why else would we allow floating islands of garbage the size of the State of Texas to exist miles from our coastlines? So, when the debate shifts to the warming of the planet and the subsequent warming of our oceans, the issues become more esoteric, but also to a smaller audience of listeners.

"What I'm saying, Wiley, and what I imagine frustrates you frequently, is that we aren't listening until scarcity of fish stocks becomes a reality at the supermarket with the resultant price increases. And then there is the issue of quality given mercury levels in the ocean. As you said, 'marine ecosystems around the world are being devastated' and then we look to our elected officials or the private sector for solutions."

They are responsible for having framed the issues for our consumption.

Virgilio then asked, "So what brings you here, Wiley? The theme is 'The Desertification Status of the Southwest." "Everything is connected, Virgilio. Everything is connected," Wiley responded. "Oceans are warming, oceans levels are rising, coastlines are being eroded. Rivers as sources of food, commerce, and transportation are drying up. I'm thinking specifically of the Po River in Italy. Moreover, our polar ice caps are melting at an alarming rate. At the same time, deserts are encroaching on living space, and rising temperatures are forcing us to make hard decisions about how we structure life above ground. There are a couple of seminars we'd like to attend. And, then, of course, we wanted to see our good friend, Tracie. That's why we're here."

For several hours - until well beyond 10 p.m., the group of friends shared experiences and perspectives on the state of the planet, our collective failure as a country to unite with other countries to fight the crisis, preferring to fight each other. Everyone agreed the future now looked grim for everyone. The world already is increasingly unhealthy and many regions are uninhabitable. The question that drew the most impassioned critiques from each of them was, 'could areas of the U.S. become uninhabitable?'

"Had we reached the limits of American technology, inventiveness, industriousness?" Virgilio asked. Bradford wondered if we, as a society, were capable of launching a 21st century Renaissance to save this country and the planet's 10-billion inhabitants from destruction? Tracie opined we would ultimately bear the responsibility for our own demise as a species.

Over the next several days, principal divisions of the University, including the School of Agriculture, the School of Technology, and the School of Earth Sciences, showcased experts to talk about current research, new material discovery, even the fragility of our environment. "Damn," Tracie, mentioned to Wiley at dinner the second night, "the University missed a golden opportunity to develop more cohesive presentations this year rather than a disparate collection of talking heads. We have a global crisis on our hands and what I'm seeing resembles competition for a Nobel Prize."

She went on to lament that each year, records for the hottest year on record are broken right here in California. Smoke from wildfires in Canada is now a common occurrence in U.S. cities and around the world, causing a continuation of unhealthy air quality. Flooding on both American coasts is up including in Hawaii. "I wanted to hear more about cooperation and less about individual technological break-throughs by the various schools on campus," Tracie pointed out. "I seriously doubt I will be here next year."

Tracie didn't sleep well that last night for a lot of reasons even though dinner with her new friends had offered a blend of light humor fueled by great wine and serious conversation. The humor early in their conversation had helped, but on the other hand, the tenor of the conference this year reflected what everyone felt: pervasive doom and gloom - to put it simply. The image that haunted her sleep was mankind at the precipice of the abyss – an abyss of its own making. She mouthed the words to herself out loud: "We have wielded the instruments of our own self-destruction as a conscious choice. This is a first in the four-and-a-half-billion-year history of this planet!" Just hearing herself mouth these words brought her out of bed and onto her feet. And then, she chuckled to herself because, at the worst moments in our evolution as a species, someone always questioned how *they* had gotten here?

As a climatologist who had spent years inveighing against those who denied the effects of a changing climate - evidence notwithstanding - Tracie *knew* how they had gotten here: indifference, disinterest, misinformation, demagoguery, greed, and the perennial political focus on exercising power and the present.

This was 2050, and the issues discussed at this conference would include survival - survival of communities in the first instance, and then whatever lay over the horizon for entire states, regions, nations, and civilizations itself. She had seen this phenomenon play out hundreds of times. You put a group of people in a room talking about survival, and the discussion becomes parochial very quickly: "How do *I* survive and protect those dear to *me*?" Tracie had observed that happening even when she and her friends were enjoying dinner. "What can *I* trade for *myself*, *my* family, *my* community, those who depend upon me.

Tracy had often heard her father comment about men and women in life-and-death situations during combat. Survival tends to focus the mind, channel one's energy, and fine tune the impulses. One's life was in the hands of the person to his/her left or right, just as theirs was in his/hers. The buddy system was often the key to survival under such circumstances. Your buddy in 2050 is likely your neighbor and those living on your street. Survival to 2050 had induced that level of tunnel vision. "Okay!" Tracie said, taking a deep breath staring out the window. "That's where we are." But then, she thought, "Don't I have a larger fiduciary responsibility given the threats this country will face from other nations under greater threat? If so, to whom?"

Before the conference this year, she couldn't recall having confronted this moral quandary. She had always focused on her research, data, publishing, establishing her bona fides in the field. Hell, she had earned a double doctorate from MIT in Climate Sustainability Technology and Atmospheric Sciences and Meteorology, in addition to a Juris Doctorate from Yale Law. Her legal background had been particularly useful when she testified before Congressional committees whose members were often prosecutorial when questioning witnesses - especially on matters of 'climate change'. She had not intended to be dismissed as another egghead with an opinion.

But a remembered factoid niggled in Tracie's subconscious. When she was still in college, nine million people were dying from air and water pollution. That information was in the public domain even though short-lived by major cable news organizations. But, why hadn't that registered with relevant Congressional committees. She also knew that several members of those committees were major recipients of funds from the Koch Brothers, but not all of them.

The one person she knew she could call was Wilson, so she picked up her phone. Wilson had always told her never to look at the clock when she called him. So, she didn't.

It was 2:00 a.m. when the phone rang beside his bed. Wilson was a light sleeper. He'd trained himself as a student because he always felt he couldn't afford the luxury of eight or more hours of sleep. "Relax, breathe deeply, and zero out your mind," he had told himself. As he reached for the phone, he prepared himself for an emergency - or a call from Tracie. He hoped for the latter.

When he heard Tracie's voice, he sat up: "Tracie, how are you? Where are you? Are you okay?"

"It's me! I'm okay! Well, no I'm not. I have a lot on my mind, and I can't sleep."

"Okay, talk to me!"

Tracie was now sitting in the middle of her bed. "It's this conference," she began. "I have so many questions, questions that seem more important now than before. Listen, I'm going to leave here tomorrow. You don't need to pick me up, but, can we have dinner? Preferably at home? I'm not in the mood for a restaurant.

"Yes! I will cook. Don't worry. Just let me know when you're back."

Wilson could settle Tracie as no one else could. Although she would not admit it to him, Wilson was a soulmate. Tracie feared that if she revealed her personal feelings toward him, she might jeopardize their relationship. Her friend was also a fabulous cook who specialized in his native dishes, which Tracie loved.

Although she was comfortable in the kitchen, she was not in Wilson's league. She had once said to a girlfriend, "The man can burn!" Wilson had learned to cook when he had lived with his family. His culinary skills had been so well known when he was a student that many of the other students often visited his room, ostensibly for reasons other than he was cooking. Eventually, he told them if they were going to eat his food, they had to contribute to his budget. They willingly did so, and dinner hours often evolved into seminars, debates, and occasionally, the all-night political discussion.

Tracie hung up and stretched out to stare into the darkness. She was ready to go home. She would stay in touch with Wiley and Roberta and her two new-found friends, Bradford and Virgilio. Otherwise, she wanted to leave. The others still had a day of tours and presentations by various of the other University programs, but she felt an urgency to get back to work.

3

P eople woke up early and gradually one at a time, trying not to wake the others. But eventually, everyone was listening to the news, stretching, yawning, and waiting to hear whether the fans had been repaired. It was about 5:45 a.m., and the world news wasn't pretty! Russia and North Korea were both rattling their nuclear sabers. They were obviously hurting because of all the sanctions, and people were starving. Of course, that was of interest to everyone there, and they were wondering what the rest of the world was going to do about it before some nut pushed the nuclear button or marched an army across a neighbor's border.

Someone on the public address system announced that the fans had been repaired. "Relief" everyone said almost excitedly. Some headed for the gym, others to the shower, and others to breakfast. The aroma of the breakfast buffet filled the air and many lined up. The gym and the shower could wait.

That afternoon having made her farewells, Tracie returned to her room for her bags, checked out, and headed for the airport. She was flying east, so she would need to rest if she could. An unfinished book was usually her companion on most flights, but not this time. She scrunched her pillow against the window, put her bag firmly under her right arm against the arm rest and tucked her legs up on the middle seat. Lucky for her, the middle seat was unoccupied.

Four hours later, almost 10:00 p.m. in Washington, D.C., her flight taxied to the gate. Feeling refreshed, Tracie picked up her personal items and headed for the exit. She used her ride-hailing app and was shortly watching D.C.'s night crowd swirling in every direction through the windows of her cab. The city never slept. "Who are all these people?" Tracie asked herself and then laughed. "They're probably looking at me and wondering the same thing."

Home was a three-bedroom, two-story brick Colonial in the city's famed Gold Coast, a swanky neighborhood in upper Northwest D.C. along the Maryland border that she had purchased with help from Mom and Dad over a decade ago. It had taken all the climate sustainability upgrades she could afford over the years to keep it livable: extra insulation in walls and triple-paned windows, water condensation domes, sonic showers, insulation-reinforced roof covered by solar tiles, passive radiant heating and cooling, everything that had been on the drawing board when she was in school - and more. Many of the trees had died for lack of precious water, even though she used effluent household wastewater. The lawns were gone, replaced by air-filtering and water permeable tiles. The toilets were composting, and the compost fed the remaining trees. Every bit of tree cover that could survive the extreme winters had been encouraged.

It felt good to raise her garage door and have her cab leave her off inside. Then she lowered it and disabled the security system with her phone. Like other people in big cities, D.C. residents and its environs no longer owned personal vehicles. Transportation was much more efficient through ride-hail cabs. Tracie entered the kitchen, opened the refrigerator and pulled out a chilled glass thermal of water. The United States had banned plastic containers of any kind by 2030, which had drastically lowered the demand for petroleum, and had sanctioned other countries who were still manufacturing them.

Tracie's dad had always instructed her that whenever she returned from a trip to check out her house before undressing. He'd warned, "Make sure you're alone and the house is as you left it. You're vulnerable when you're in the shower or lying in bed." It also occurred to her, "Before I forget I better text Wilson and let him know I'm home. I don't want to wake him, but he'll call me first thing in the morning to ask why I didn't call if I don't." Thoughts of him always restored her sense of well-being.

Tracie kept a taser in a lower kitchen drawer. Light stick in one hand and the taser in the other, she checked each room and the basement. She had settled on a taser since D.C. law had long since prohibited privately-owned firearms. Her *real* preference, and that of her dad, would have been a taser *and* a nine-millimeter.

Sam Hinton loved his daughter and had never wanted her to become a victim. Conservatives had completely rendered women helpless with their insidious anti-abortion laws, so women like Tracie *had* to protect themselves from assault. But if any man believed Tracie Hinton was an easy mark, "Hell!" would be his last conscious thought! She'd taken every new self-defense class offered and was a proficient kick boxer. She also knew the exact pressure points where to apply her thumb or forefinger to disable someone twice her size.

She took a quick shower, slipped into a comfortable nightgown and got into her artificial ice pack air bed. "OMG! I forgot to text Mom and Dad to let them know I'm back." That was another part of the ritual. Sam Hinton was now 65, and if he had not heard from his daughter, he would have been on the phone in the morning, or more likely on her doorstep. Sam liked Wilson for the simple reason they were cut from the same cloth. Wilson saw Tracie the same way Sam saw Ericka.

For Sam, Ericka had been the love of his life for over 40 years. He understood that Tracie didn't *need* Wilson to take care of her. But Wilson complemented her; he understood her strengths and weaknesses and was committed to her. He could be the sounding board she needed after a frustrating appearance before a Congressional committee, or a meeting with a K-Street lobbyist for a major oil company, a public utility company, or the conservative U.S. Chamber of Commerce. Wilson *always* had Tracie's back.

The next morning, Thursday, Tracie was anxious to get to her office on Dupont Circle in the City. About the time she'd bought her home, she had founded a non-profit company *Climate Solutions International*. Although her father was not retired at the time, her mom had joined her immediately. The understanding she had with her daughter was that she'd work with Tracie for free - doing research, drafting articles, speeches, and congressional testimony until Sam retired. Sunday dinner at her parents' home now had a different power dynamic: it was egalitarian. Tracie was no longer the sponge, so Sam would periodically play devil's advocate and pit himself against his two favorite women in argument. When Wilson was a dinner guest, the meal became secondary, and the conversation around the table began to resemble a mini-UN session.

Tracie's company had flourished and now had a dozen full-time staff and hosted six volunteer interns from D.C.'s Consortium of Universities, who received credits for their work. The work product, primarily research, was proprietary. One of their projects was recovery of essential materials from discarded or obsolete goods - everything from aircraft graveyards to plastic microbeads in the oceans that were polluting sea life, various chemical wastes, and gasses from manufacturing processes.

Tracie called Wilson. "You got my text this morning?"

"Yes, I did! I guess you're in your office."

"So, are we still on for dinner?"

"When?"

"Give me today to catch up; I've been away for almost a week. Since tomorrow is Friday and I don't plan to be in here on Saturday, how about tomorrow evening?"

"Good! Bring your appetite and your favorite bottle of non-alcoholic wine - preferably white." He was anticipating the conversation. "We're having fish."

"Good! I love that. I'll call you later." "Glad you're back, but you know that."

Tracie didn't respond, but he was right. He always missed her when she traveled, just as she missed him when he was in Geneva, Paris, or some other destination. Often, he'd have to prolong his trips abroad, and she always lamented that she couldn't accompany him. But, he told her, "You have the solution to that problem." She knew it involved her left-hand ring finger. Tracie, of course, also traveled extensively, so they could never coordinate their schedules to meet, for example, a weekend in Paris, London, or Brussels.

———

At 7:30 p.m. on Friday, Tracie arrived at Wilson's address in the 800 block of Longfellow Street, N.W. in the District through Wilson's garage. When he opened the garage door to the kitchen, the aroma beckoned. He had embraced her as soon as the garage door was down, kissed her on both cheeks, and then lightly on the lips. The kitchen awaited.

"So...how was your day?" From Wilson, that was a serious question. That was his way of saying, "The floor is yours. Tell me what's on your mind." He opened her bottle of wine, poured each of them a glass and then returned to his cooking. Under one of the stools was a pair of soft slippers. She kicked off her heels, put on the slippers, took a sip of the wine, and inhaled deeply letting it out slowly.

At that moment, Wilson turned to face her with a piece of fish on a fork and held it up to her mouth: "Taste this and tell me what it needs." Tracie closed her eyes and savored the fish as it melted in her mouth.

"Nothing! It's good." She knew it would be perfect, but that habit endeared him to her. She had been the center of his world and had been since their days in school.

"If we could only be on the same continent at the same time," she sighed wistfully. That was the closest she had ever come to a declaration before. But her recent experience in perhaps the most climatically adapted zone on the planet had made her realize how precarious life was, and a world without Wilson was unthinkable, especially if people were to survive as she understood they would in the American Southwest, and increasingly so on areas along the Pacific coastline. It wasn't better in D.C. It was just different in that, so far, living resembled more what it had been before many states in the western part of the country became increasingly uninhabitable.

Without looking directly at Tracie, his attention being focused on the stove and the meal he was preparing, Wilson again asked, "So what was it that had you up and, on your phone, so early in the morning?" Tracie slipped off her stool, walked around the kitchen, glass still in hand and said, "It was the *mood* of the conference. If I had to guess, I think I felt a little schizophrenic." Before she could elaborate, Wilson faced her, his expression implying "explain that, please."

"I know that face. I'll explain!" Wilson smiled and picked up his glass. So, Tracie began.

"I spent a great deal of time with several people I've come to admire, with whom I will be sure to remain in contact. One is my age, Wiley Mitchell, I'm sure I told you about him. He and I met many years ago as newly-minted PhDs at a conference in Detroit. Each of these conferees is committed to the survival and sustainability of their communities, both locally and extended. They live with climate urgency every day. I admire that. If severely affected regions in this country - like the Pacific Coast and the neighboring states - are to survive and create a future for the current generation of children and young adults, it will be due largely to the efforts of people like those I get to know at these conventions."

"Okay! I'm with you.

"But then, we hear that Russia and North Korea are posturing, threatening to use their nuclear capabilities in response to Western-demanded sanctions. Neither of these two countries - both heartless dictatorships - places the welfare and lives of its citizens high among its national priorities. That was true before the effects of a changing climate engulfed all of us. Anyway, their leadership, when confronted with serious challenges, resorts to form - threats and aggression. I find myself torn between loyalty to my family, my friends, my community, and a higher responsibility to be part of mitigating the threats that could render all of us extinct. Is it an *either/or* commitment? Or must I consider both - equally? Am I making sense…or just being dramatic?"

"Tracie, you're now asking what my friends and I have been asking ourselves for quite some time."

"So, I'm not losing it?" Her laugh sounded relieved.

"Set the table while I try *my* perspective on *you*. Your focus for over a decade has been on developing research, compiling data, and making your findings available to those with leadership responsibility, those the country and many around the world assume will show the rest of us what is being done to keep the climate wolf from our doorstep. Our collective faith has been they would use the data to develop the technologies, forge the partnerships, and promote unity around common purposes. Nothing of any consequence, however, has emerged for reasons clear to everyone now. To be truthful, the warning signs were there earlier, but we continued to exhort, debate, deny, and wait. And our elected officials dithered and postured - focused on staying in power. Now we're in the abyss, and everyone, including your friends who meet in Southern California, is focused on survival. Unfortunately, *human nature hasn't* changed.

"We're still a country and are still a target of others who see no escape from the abyss and are looking to blame someone. We *do*, unfortunately, bear major responsibility for the crisis that consumes us. So, until such time as we cease to exist as the United States, someone must come forward to show global leadership - if such a role still exists. I'm being simplistic I know, but only to make the point that your concern is real. You now have to choose your place and define your role - as the American Marines like to say to "get it done!"

"So, what's the next step for me?"

"Your next step is to sit down at this table and eat! But not to worry; you're in a good place." Tracie dug in and savored every mouthful while trying to continue their conversation. Wilson loved her at moments like this because they were so revealing of her personality: mouth full, laughing, hands in motion, and then she'd catch herself and put one of her hands over her mouth.

Later, while sitting there and draining the contents of a second bottle of wine, this one, full octane, Tracie said, "You cooked. I'll clean the dishes." She busied herself by loading the dirty dishes into the dishwasher and starting it. That chore behind them, Tracie returned to their unfinished conversation. "I have a business team and an organization," she began, "and I can keep them busy. But now it *has* to be more than that. I want what I do, what we do, to *matter*. I think *we* need to be a driver in the debate about how this country confronts the challenges of a changing climate. Yeah, I know that sounds presumptuous, but my dad was never one to think small. 'Think big or go home!' he would say.

"He always expected more of me than other parents. He'd give me more to read than I thought it possible to handle, and he always quizzed me on all manner of subjects. That was his way of stretching me. If I didn't know something, it meant 'look it up!' My obligation from childhood has been schooling, hence my doctorates and law degree. You know what he said to me after I received my Juris Doctorate! You see, I knew you could do it!' He and Mom were always there - and still are. I know he's at home right now wondering what I intend to do to help shape the future. I guess I'm feeling the pressure."

"Welcome to the club, Tracie."

"Yeah, you mentioned that you and some of your friends have been dealing with a similar quandary. How so?"

"One of the reasons I like your dad so much is he is a lot like *my* dad - demanding, with high expectations. Mine admonished me constantly, '*Anyone* can be average, but not you!' His family were descended from Nigerian royalty, and to him, *that* conferred not only status but, more importantly, accountability. He preached responsibility as often as he took in oxygen.

"Since I, too, was an only child, there was no escape - except at school. Areas in Africa, as you know, suffered from extended drought long before a changing climate became a concern to the rest of the world. My dad used to ask me questions like, "If you were a policy advisor to the President of Nigeria, and he asked you for advice to offer the President of the South Sudan on the drought in his country, what would you suggest to him?" I didn't have a satisfactory response, but my father was forcing me to think about the larger issues early on. I love him for that. I may have been going to school in Geneva or London, but it was all books, research, and study for me, too. From the beginning, I thought about politics for solving big problems.

"Droughts in Africa were causing famine, hunger, poverty, forced migration, tribal conflicts, and poor health. I could have chosen the UN instead, as did many of my friends who became less than enamored with the reputations of many African leaders, dictators actually. But I didn't want to engage in endless polemics. *I wanted to DO something!* That is why I chose the World Health Organization. There we get to accomplish something with the resources we have. It's ironic, but the rest of the world is finally catching up to what many in North Africa, Sub-Saharan Africa and South Africa experienced decades ago."

"True, and I have always been more interested in those experts who emphasized ethical politics and global marketing," Tracie rejoined. "I shared their view that we need to be talking about building global unity around shared practical solutions," she sighed.

"Your dilemma, if I interpret it correctly," Wilson suggested, "is to choose between a path that hews more toward publishing, research, and public education, or more toward public policy, program development and management in the best tradition of your father. More hands-on if you will. I'm thinking particularly of this trip to California. Or did I miss something?"

"No, you're spot on. I've spent years beating the drums before Congressional committees and in public conferences, symposia, and debates around the world. No one listens! The threats from China, North Korea, and Russia are real, and a conference with reams of data won't mollify them. Hunger, of course, motivates them, but how to get them to lay down their weapons so the rest of us are inclined to share food resources before they blow us into oblivion!

"I think I've got to get some people into the fray, not just here, but in the hotspots on the frontlines. Wiley and Roberta, beyond their business, have a larger sense of mission. Virgilio and Bradford both told me they want to be involved. Also, my dad has been out there for decades exposing himself in some hairy and dangerous situations. That said, he would lie in front of a tank to prevent me from going as far as he and others have gone. He'd want me to be engaged, but in a different way. The different way is what I'm seeking.

"Well, let me suggest something. WHO supports vital public health programs worldwide to assist governments control pandemics, for example. North Korea is a member of the nuclear club, and our Administration *must* deal with it as a national security imperative. That makes North Korea uniquely important. Perhaps your organization could evaluate WHO's support for North Korea's program to improve the public health of its people - in this instance, their preparedness for dealing with the health effects of a changing climate."

"If history serves as a guide, I doubt the leadership of that country has developed such a plan."

"That may be true, but you understand what I am suggesting: a more functional hands-on role that gets you into the conversation. This Administration is not going to recommend a kinetic response to the North Korean threat. It is going to look at the range of program resources available to meet that country's needs to walk them back from the brink, and that review will include the WHO."

"Knowing you, you have a plan."

"I do!" Wilson responded, grinning.

4

Wilson now had Tracie's full attention. She was elbows on the table, both hands under her chin. And so he continued. The thrust of his argument was that impoverished members of the nuclear club, e.g. North Korea - had to be treated differently because their leaders' prescriptions for dealing with pandemics and other major crises were limited without external assistance. "This White House will have to get creative," Wilson went on. "For example, the U.S. does not have a bilateral trade agreement with North Korea for a variety of reasons. Perhaps the effects of a changing climate on both countries necessitates a review of that policy. We should put it on the table!"

"Be more specific! What would North Korea have to trade - nuclear missiles?" Tracie laughs.

"Nothing! Let me back up a little. Putting it bluntly, the average citizen of that country doesn't consume enough calories to be healthy by western standards. They're a basket case - without the bread! I'm thinking broadly of a 21st century version of former President Franklin Roosevelt's Lend-Lease Program. The difference is there would be no lending nor any leasing, just a give-a-way with specific conditions

40

attached. If the DPRK can't feed its people or improve its public health programs, they won't have a country. They *will* have riots and instability. China won't allow that on its border. Millions of starving North Koreans would be seeking to cross into China. Neither country wants that."

Wilson is now up and pacing around the kitchen as he spins his plan. Tracie likes him in this mode because, again, he reminds her of her dad at their dinner table, so she reverts to her sponge mode.

"Arizona and the states of the Southwest, for example, are our worst hot spots, and we have had to reevaluate our trade relationship with Mexico, formerly our largest bilateral trade partner."

"But as you said, 'We don't have a trade relationship with the Democratic Peoples of the Republic of Korea.'"

"No! But a changing climate has changed the rules. Nothing short of war should be off the list of probable policy solutions today - including a trade relationship."

"You are aware that such a recommendation will bring China to the table. Any material change in our relationship with North Korea affects them as well."

"Exactly! Perhaps even the Russians will take a step back to see how the Chinese will respond. The threats from all three would likely subside and real horse trading begin. So, on trade, what did you observe when you were in California? What did you think of the state of agriculture in California? Now that I think about it, Tracie, that may be the wrong question? That state's agricultural economy has been devastated. I may be wrong, but maybe we're talking about the Pacific Northwest as the new agricultural sector in that part of the country - at least for certain crops. My sense is that North Korea's agriculture is in a perilous state. We would have to look at trade volumes in the Pacific Northwest. Agriculture has to factor into any trade relationship with North Korea. Your friend, Wiley Mitchell, has to be brought into this discussion.

"Formerly, the Southwest traded in a lot of things. They were basically the inspiration for seed banks, and Arizona has really expanded the reach of its solar distribution network." Wilson interjected to suggest that the North Koreans would need to be interested in establishing a seed bank. Tracie raised her eyebrows as if to say "Yes, absolutely!" but added, "I don't even remember how Arizona, and later California, started passive heating and cooling systems. They revived that native technology in the first years of the century. The Southwest has also been the most energy connected all along - even Texas had to get off its capitalistic high horse and join." Tracie went on to add, "My company had a hand in formulating several trade accords along the border. They've been using my MIT D-Lab fellowship research to continue refining soil and air temperature measurement and trading the new technology coming out of the Tech Park."

Wilson had really gotten wound up on the idea of more trade with North Korea when he finally stopped, telling Tracie, "You want to play on a larger stage? Get involved with helping us to bring about a more productive relationship with North Korea. It won't be easy. It is, however, necessary for a more stable Pacific region. Everyone benefits!"

Tracie understood North Korea was one of the more fragile states with the ability to tip the tenuous balance of power among the big three: Russia, China, and the U.S. If she were going to shift her focus from research and public advocacy to influencing policy, North Korea presented the perfect entry point. That country's authoritarian leadership was, after all, the most clear and present danger to everyone.

Over the weekend, Tracie had a long conversation with her dad, and he agreed with her shift in emphasis. Between the two of them, they decided she should review WHO's programs in North Korea over the previous decade and then, for comparison, with a region with similar problems by looking at the effectiveness of WHO programs in Sub-Saharan Africa. Which programs were particularly effective, and why? What were the obstacles to implementation? What new programs were introduced, and how sustainable were they? Was there an improvement in relations with their neighbors - people flowing across orders to escape drought, disease, starvation, lack of employment, conflict?

The following morning, Tracie assigned several members of her staff and two interns to conduct an in-depth analysis of WHO programs in North Korea and Sub-Saharan Africa. Her North Korea Task Force now in motion, Tracie got on the phone to her contacts at the U.S. Department of State and within the Administration. She also called allies at *The New York Times*, *The Washington Post*, and *The Council on Foreign Relations* in New York City. Tracie wanted an assessment of the threat from North Korea based on current reporting from media organizations and opinions from the policy experts on the Council.

Each of her contacts stated with certainty, the key to understanding the threat from North Korea was China. For decades, China had been North Korea's biggest aid provider and foreign trade partner and, therefore, exerted a measure of leverage in Pyongyang. The PRC, too, had limits, especially regarding North Korea's indiscriminate, long-range missile launches into the Pacific. Stolen technology had improved the DPRK's long-range capability. The regime in North Korea now had the ability to fire an ICBM - a new and more deadly version of the Hwasong-17 missile - to the West Coast of the United States, a distance of over 9,300 miles.

Another key concern was how unstable the current leadership was in Pyongyang and its tenuous grip on power. Unrest was growing, riots were increasing, and tensions within the ranks of the powerful military were escalating. People were starving, and defections in some military units were on the rise. The country's multi-million-man army was being reduced to a paper tiger. The likelihood of a missile strike against American bases in the Pacific or against the West Coast was real.

Tracie asked, "What is our likely response in the event of a missile strike against the U.S. or our allies?" The response most frequently offered was...*limits:* China was the big unknown. Then, there were U.S. security agreements with South Korea and Japan. Everyone Tracie talked to pointed out that the White House would have to get creative, because a unilateral policy of restraint following a ballistic strike against an ally, or our homeland, would not satisfy public opinion, nor the hawks in Congress and the Defense establishment.

5

The climatologist in Tracie had, in fact, compelled her to focus on the holes in the ozone and a collective failure to achieve net zero emissions by 2050. However, the immediacy of the threat from North Korea and her interest in shifting her focus - at least temporarily - pulled her in that direction. Members of her team were fielding dozens of calls about the ozone from clients and subscribers to the organization's newsletter. Her organization was their North Star, and they were looking for answers.

Turning to North Korea, Tracie asked aloud, "Why in hell would they launch another missile now? This is fucking madness! Did the Chinese know about this? The sanctions were biting, but what had changed recently? Has there been a natural disaster, a flood, or monsoon rains recently?" More importantly, she wondered if the North Koreans had made a calculated guess about the American response. And then, there was the unthinkable: a rogue faction within the military hierarchy making a bid for control.

Tracie knew the WHO had cooperative agreements with the DPRK, but that was a secondary issue. Someone at State, Defense, or one of the myriad intelligence agencies had to know something. Who better to call than Washington's media insiders?

Andrew "Andy" Hillyard at *The Washington Post* was a friend of more than a decade - Pulitzer Prize winner for his penetrating analyses of America's imperfect leadership in the Pacific; a discreet veteran of assignments in Seoul, Tokyo, and Beijing. If anyone could stitch the threads of the 'Asian' mindset into anything coherent, Andy could. He held an MA from Columbia U in Asian Studies and was conversationally fluent in Japanese and Chinese and comfortable in Korean - the quintessential Asian polyglot. Moreover, Andy was plugged into official Washington.

Short of a briefing from the White House National Security Advisor - which would be notable for what it omitted - her friend was the next best thing. When Tracie called Andy, they agreed to meet at the Foreign Press Center on 14th Street N.W. after the White House press briefing that day. The fact that he could meet within hours of her call was a testament to their relationship.

That afternoon, Tracie explained that she and her team were evaluating WHO's efforts to help North Korea manage the public health effects of a changing climate, but had not seen anything specific enough to justify launching a nuclear missile at the West Coast. "What did we miss?" Tracie asked.

"With North Korea, you're always working with imperfect information," Andy responded. "Whatever data they release, I've learned to compound by a factor of five to ten. Anything you hear is never what it appears at face value. They take inscrutability to depths we don't begin to understand."

"So, what prompted them to launch a missile? What have you picked up?"

"My sources tell me the effects of a changing climate have practically broken what remains of their social structure. You referred to the WHO. The truth is, WHO programs are overwhelmed; they simply cannot meet the need."

"That was one of our early conclusions from the material we have."

The number of orphaned children on the streets dying of starvation is estimated to be in the hundreds of thousands. Hard numbers are difficult to come by. The kids are transported to the countryside to keep them out of sight of visitors. The lack of medicine and essential supplies has accelerated the spread of typhoid fever and other infectious diseases. Food, medicines and potable water are the critical shortages.

"North Korea is among the list of countries most vulnerable to global warming because it has a limited area for growing crops. The western coastline is the country's historical breadbasket - and it's gone. Natural disasters visit frequently and destroy crop yields. Over the past several decades, the average temperature there has increased by over 4 degrees Celsius. Factor that in if you will.

"Their leadership cannot solve their problems on its own, and that - my sources tell me - is what led to this catastrophe."

"And the Chinese saw this disaster unfolding and decided to ignore it!"

"The Chinese are well aware of the shortcomings of North Korea's leadership, but decided against more direct intervention. China has major problems of its own. No, the thinking was to let the West deal with it, and they would continue to use North Korea as a proxy in their dispute with the U.S. What they did *not* anticipate was an attack against the U.S. Yeah! They're okay with the bellicose rhetoric the North Koreans direct against us, but this time, the boys in Beijing miscalculated."

"Did they ever! So, what is the thinking over at the White House?"

"Frankly, I believe they don't know what to do. They're not an imaginative bunch on foreign policy. I talked to an inside source this morning and was told they're more focused on China than on North Korea. Despite China's growing internal problems, including a faltering economy, they're still capable of rattling us. And then there is that Beijing-Moscow axis poking the Russian bear *and* the Chinese Panda. Sorry, I couldn't resist that one."

"And what about the loss of life in San Francisco? The evacuations."

"The missile exploded about a mile offshore creating a tidal wave that crested over a mile inland killing about 2,500 people, and that number isn't final. Thousands had to evacuate and relocate. The gang over in the White House hasn't decided what to do beyond assisting in the evacuation and organizing relocation assistance to the victims. This administration fears a likely Chinese response to a direct attack on North Korea. China is still capable of provoking military conflict in the South China Sea and increasing trade tensions with Pacific nations in alliance with us.

"Secondly, the Russians are taking a wait-and-see posture to assess our response. They did not take Ukraine the last time, but Vladimir Putin's successors have never given up on the idea of re-establishing the old Soviet Empire. NATO almost fractured under Russian pressure on Sweden, Finland, the Baltic States, and Poland. If the Russians conclude we're indecisive in responding to North Korea because of Chinese pressure, they'll ramp up pressure on Western Europe and everywhere we have important interests."

"So our perennial response is the tug of war between the hawks and the pragmatists. Meanwhile, the world watches while the President and his advisors sit in a room with a platoon of lawyers. I find it almost laughable that we didn't foresee this."

"That's about it. Many in Congress have punted on this one, because no one wants to take a public position that could damage their reelections, especially if we launch a limited strike against North Korea. People still haven't forgotten Afghanistan."

"What's your best guess on a likely response?"

"We're likely to kick the matter to the UN, spread the responsibility for a solution, and frame the issue as 'an attack on the international community'."

"The Chinese will veto any Security Council proposal that calls for a military response, and we *know* that. We avoid that outcome, find a way to mollify public opinion here, and then shift everyone's focus to humanitarian efforts to help the victims. Can you see the next presidential campaign shaping up?"

"Political cowardice elevated to an American art form - avoiding direct accountability, and directing blame elsewhere, preferably to the opponents and their past party policies as the underlying causes for North Korea's aggression."

Tracie then shifted the conversation. "You know, Andy, power politics alone cannot drive our response-or fears of China."

"What do you mean?"

"I'm a climatologist, and I know that China's internal problems are massive. Water availability, for example, is a major problem in North China because the water table has been falling throughout that region. Look at the Yellow River. In South China, flooding decimates densely populated areas displacing tens of millions of people. Three of the country's seven major river systems have their headwaters and much of their length in western China." Tracie went on to explain that "The problem is that power demand is concentrated in central and coastal China. The scale of China's water problem is staggering, and that opens the door to opportunities for U.S. - China cooperation and discussions of measures to stabilize North Korea - especially now when the shroud of a changing climate has enveloped the globe, and many look to the major contributors to ozone pollution to come up with solutions."

"Well, we've talked about that very idea for decades, but nothing significant came of it."

"The times have changed. We're all in the shit now."

The White House concentrated its energies on bringing relief to the families of the victims of the nuclear blast off the coast of northern California, including tens of thousands of evacuees. Media coverage was extensive, and it included images of the American President in blue jeans and a casual shirt delivering relief supplies, driving a van with bottled water, and even filling sandbags. Tracie understood the political importance of projecting a vital image of this President. The presidential election was only two years away, and the focus was on raising his poll numbers among those who had voted against his party in the midterms.

However, questions continued to arise about an official response to the missile attack. Many veteran media analysts and former elected officials, now political commentators, accused the President of failing his primary responsibility: protecting the American homeland. The baying opposition, including several likely contenders for the presidential nomination, suggested the President was the present-day equivalent of Nero. The caricature of the President on the front cover of a popular weekly magazine playing a fiddle against the backdrop of a mushroom cloud, rattled the White House and the President's party.

While Washington politics continued to dominate the news, China's aging leadership took a step back from the raging debate going on in the U.S. about next steps while downplaying their threat to veto any proposal to attack North Korea. China's leaders were in a quandary. A country of 1.3 billion, it was on the verge of open revolt by its 500 million middle-class citizens accustomed to consumption practices beyond the reach of most of the population, including preferred access to inexpensive potable water. In exchange for their political support, the middle-class had been promised stability and sustained economic growth to support Western lifestyles, which wasn't in America's interest either. The point was now an obsession with Sam Hinton, dismayed by a lack of a broader administration emphasis on cooperation with China.

Tracie channeled her dad, but she was also part of a growing chorus of influential critics who feared the likelihood of destabilizing regional conflicts around the world created by a vacuum of leadership. During a call with Wilson, she dubbed this an "inertia of leadership." Tracie went on to express her concern that North Korea's misguided attack on the U.S. West Coast may have represented the onset of a series of disasters, or conflicts, in response to the effects of a changing climate on countries everywhere. Her other point was that the risks of doing nothing would only embolden authoritarian regimes willing to exploit domestic economic disaster for political gain to remain in power. The actions of despots on thrones, Tracie feared, would become the model for leadership, against which the good intentions of others would be unjustly contrasted.

Tracie reached out to another friend and colleague, Dr. Chin Tan Wu, head of the prestigious Environmental Sciences Institute in Beijing. He, of course, was pleasantly surprised to hear from her.

"Dr. Hinton, I have been thinking about you and imagining what you might be involved in these days," he laughed.

"Well, I called to ask you that very question," Tracie also laughed. "In fact, I would like to know the first item on your list of concerns, a list I imagine is within your reach now!"

"Okay! You're correct. I carry it with me. That list and I have more than our share of one-way conversations! Later, you will have to share your primary concern with me. Agreed!"

"Yes!"

"Corrupt water management and its unequal distribution is threatening the coherence of China, to state the problem simply. Control of water has been central to governance in China for millennia, and we have lost that ability with the worst consequences imaginable."

"Well, we, too, are living a similar nightmare albeit on a smaller scale. We have one-fifth your population. But that's not at the top of my list of concerns because we have adapted well, especially in the Southwest and on our Pacific coast, our hottest regions susceptible to the worst aspects of a changing climate. You would do well to study the innovations we have here to sustain life while maximizing our use of scarce resources, human ingenuity, and new technologies for everyone. And we are getting better! The enormity of the problems you confront are beyond the comprehension of many here and elsewhere who have a similar responsibility."

"Thank you for your understanding. I am at home so rarely these days, my wife does not recognize my voice when I call. So, Dr. Hinton, what's at the top of your list?"

"What I see as a catastrophe is the direct result of our failure to lead, a catastrophe that could plunge the world into global conflict - or a series of regional conflicts at a minimum."

"Dr. Hinton, sadly, I'll have to leave conflict avoidance and management to others. I'd like to learn more about what you're doing in your Southwest and what you're doing about rising ocean levels and the erosion of your Pacific and Atlantic coastlines. I have read about how rising water levels have weakened infrastructure in Boston, New Orleans, and Nantucket and Martha's Vineyard in Massachusetts, for example. I'm sure there are those you can refer me to."

"One person in particular comes to mind, someone I highly recommend. His name is Dr. Wiley Mitchell. Beyond his qualifications, he is also a good friend and valued colleague of almost two decades. He and his lovely wife, Roberta, currently live in Seattle, Washington, and I'm going to put you together with the two of them. I should caution you, he is energetic, as well as competent, innovative, and experienced. What I have always admired about him is he has an idea a minute and is undeterred by naysayers. Our survival depends on people like him, and the work that he and his partners do for state governments, private companies, and national governments around the world. You just need to listen to his ideas and decide what works best for your unique circumstances.

"Please understand, Dr. Hinton. When I said I would leave conflict avoidance and management to others, I did *not* mean to suggest I did not share your concerns. I do! You understand the nature of our system. As you Americans say, 'I have to stay in my lane.'"

"And I was not suggesting that you shouldn't, believe me. I understand your constraints. I'm venturing out of *my* lane because I can. I have no guarantees my voice will be heard where it matters. But I do have to try. The missile attack on our West Coast is a harbinger of worse to come because of who we are. I could be mistaken, though I doubt it."

"Thank you for your call, Dr. Hinton! It is always a pleasure even under the circumstances. I shall look forward to a conversation with your colleague Dr. Mitchell."

6

The call with Dr. Chin buoyed Tracie spirit's spirits. That conversation also provided much-needed perspective on the frustration she and others felt about the inconsistent leadership from the President occupying 1600 Pennsylvania Avenue in Washington, D.C. Imagine, Tracie said to herself, if the American President had the daily concerns of Dr. Chin - planning for the survival of the most populous country on earth! He'd probably curl up into a fetal position. The next thing on her agenda was to call Wiley. Dr. Chin needed a lifeline, and Wiley was the closest source that qualified. Before calling Wiley, Tracie called Wilson to give him a readout on her conversation with her friend in Beijing.

Okay! Now where was Wiley's number?

"Wiley, my friend, how the hell are you?"

"Busy, always hopeful, and always pleased to hear from a friend. You likely have a lot to say, so why don't I take a break and sit down."

Wiley closed the door to his office, propped his feet on his desk, and touched the screen on her phone so he and his Tracie could see each other. "Should I call Roberta?" Wiley asked. "If she's available, yes!" In the background, Tracie could hear Wiley calling Roberta. "It's Tracie… she's on the phone…are you busy?" A few seconds later, Tracie could hear what sounded like Roberta entering the room. "Tracie, how are you? Where are you? Listen, just wanted to say how great it was to see you recently. It had been too long. So, what's up?"

"Well, the two of you look healthy. I'm here in Washington. Here's why I called. I just spoke to my friend, Dr. Chin Tan Wu, head of the Environmental Sciences Institute in Beijing, and he really needs some help getting around the powers that be to start some kind of infrastructure to meet the drastic needs in China created by a changing climate. Naturally, it will involve rules' changes, policy initiatives, and an unprecedented level of cooperation between the Central Committee and his Institute. You know, the kind of stuff you are accustomed to negotiating. The scale of the multiple calamities there defies imagination. I recommended he talk to you since this is in your wheelhouse.

"Well, that's very flattering, Tracie. China is huge, enormously complex with problems that defy conventional definition. Their issues are not unique, just presented on a different scale. Do you want to get us started with a three-way telecom? At some point, we may have to offer the negotiation services of Virgilio if he needs to make some trade concessions for our technological help. Just a thought. What do you think?"

"Why don't I contact him again, give Virgilio a heads up, and get back to you?"

"Just give me a date and time that works for both Beijing and us, and we'll confer."

"That's great! I really appreciate you agreeing to this, Wiley, because over here in swamp land, we could get in a real mess unless someone less political took the lead in getting China back to neutral at least. If we can accomplish that, that would leave North Korea unsupported, and perhaps more tractable about not starting a nuclear conflict - a conflict in which they would be the principal loser, by the way."

"Oh! Before I forget," Wiley asked, "has there been any news from the Florence seed bank? We will need to secure it from Russia and its allies in North Korea, West Africa, and the other non-committal countries run by dictators or oligarchs. We may have to back them in allowing trade with China for seeds at some point if this partnership we're trying to build is successful."

"Glad you brought that up," Tracie rejoined. "Wilson has been concerned about that, among other things, because the WHO is trying to provide food security assistance and clean water in so many devastated areas, particularly in Africa."

"Okay! We'll talk soon. Again, thanks!"

When Wiley hung up, he sat there for some time talking to Roberta about what they might be able to share with Dr. Chin and the political repercussions of doing so. He was going to have to bring others into the conversation to cover his political bases. First, though, talk to Dr. Chin to understand his needs, what he felt he could deliver, the political parameters, and then determine who he would have to bring into the process. He trusted Tracie. He knew she would not have approached him if she felt the risks were untenable. She, too, was a pragmatist and wanted to get something done.

Tracie contacted Wiley several days later with a time for the three-way telecom meeting - 5:00 p.m. the following Saturday for Wiley, 8:00 p.m. her time, and 8:00 a.m. for Dr. Chin.

Things moved quickly for everyone concerned. Tracie was ready to bring in Virgilio at 4:00 p.m. Saturday, if they were ready for him. Wiley, meanwhile, pulled material from his files on the situation in China, i.e. areas most heavily impacted by rising ocean levels and coastal erosion, declining volume of potable water in major cities, poor air quality, rivers that had dried up due to declining snowfall in the Himalayas, and impact on local farming and major agriculture. And then, there were the losses in international trade. China was in trouble. The question Wiley pondered was, how much impact could he have? Well, he would soon know.

Tracie understood that the initial call was to be the first of several; that more conversations would follow. Dr. Chin would familiarize everyone with his needs, the scope of his authority, and areas in which he felt he might have some flexibility. He would then respond to questions Wiley might have. Wiley would discuss specific strategies he felt confident could work, and then everyone would decide where there were points of convergence. Tracie would also know if she would have to expand the circle of those involved, specifically, people she could trust.

Saturday arrived for the Americans, and Tracie initiated the meeting. Wiley and Roberta were waiting in Wiley's office.

"Hello, everyone," Tracie began, then turned to her colleagues for introductions. After that she spoke to Dr. Chin.

"Dr. Chin, now that you have met my colleagues, how can we help you?"

"Thank you, Dr. Hinton. I really appreciate the cooperation from you Americans. As I see it, this is not a political problem capable of solution solely by political processes. To our great misfortune, China has not prepared, administratively or psychologically, to address widespread hunger, air and water pollution, coastal erosion, drought, and our ongoing need to sustain trade relationships. We're internationally isolated by policy. To survive, we need ideas and assistance."

"Dr. Chin, we're here to help, however we can," responded Tracie. "Tell us what you are most interested in hearing from us. Perhaps that is the best place to begin."

"Thank you also for Dr. Mitchell's assistance. He has sent me a list of topics that I may consult him and his team on. So I should begin by telling you what we need most right now: food and clean drinking water. So, I would like to hear about local or community responses to gardening, food production, and water harvesting. Also, manufacturing on a small scale and, local, or, in your case, regional or State-sponsored programs to purify air. You Americans are known for your ingeniousness."

Wiley knew that some of those topics he would be able to discuss during this tele-conversation, but he would prefer to have engineers who installed and maintained water condensation equipment from Washington State's technology sector to talk to Dr. Chin. But only if Virgilio Sanchez thought it advisable to share certain technologies with China.

"Tracie, can you bring in Virgilio?"

"Yes! Wiley. Hold on a second."

Tracie continued. "Dr. Chin, I've asked Virgilio Sanchez, a former U.S. trade representative, to join us so we can get his advice regarding the legalities of sharing certain technologies with you. We have developed breakthrough technologies in a variety of sectors that are helping us to sustain life in both urban, rural, and even isolated communities.

"My problem is the sheer size and geographic diversity of our country. I don't know where to begin," said Dr. Chin with a sigh.

"I've been considering that," Tracie noted in response, "and since I understand you need to circumvent much of the political surveillance and control in China, I recommend that you identify at least six settlements in different climatic regions where the needs are greatest, including several of your high-rise condominium complexes on the outskirts of your largest cities." She went on to explain that her idea is to use these locations as cooperatives, if you will, to experiment with various methods that would be most suited to your environmental realities. Here, we call this approach, 'identifying low-hanging fruit.' We could then help you chart critical information about the climate, the weather, and the particular environmental conditions in those specific areas. Collaborating with local authorities and the residents, you should be able to collect data you can forward to us. We can, then, make recommendations.

Dr. Chin interjected, "Dr. Hinton, I like that expression 'low-hanging fruit.' In the context of this discussion, it makes perfect sense. I will see if there is an appropriate Chinese equivalent," chuckling to himself.

Trying to maximize this first discussion, Tracie explained, "All of this may sound daunting, Dr. Chin, but I could also put you in touch with several Sub-Saharan experts on creating artificial oases in your desert settlements." She then brought into the conversation Virgilio Sanchez to discuss proprietary rights to some of the technology that will be involved. Virgilio briefed Dr. Chin on a range of technologies developed in the American Southwest that enabled people to remain largely where they were as opposed to migrating in significant numbers to other parts of the country, including water condensation projects, artificial growing, and purifying systems. Virgilio was aware that large-scale composting was extensively used in China. Toward the end of his comments, Virgilio said, "If you have not developed a seed bank, DO SO! Ordinarily, I would suggest a national seed bank. Since China is so vast, I would suggest a series of regional seed banks throughout the country. The government is likely to want to establish a national seed bank for purposes of control. The two approaches could co-exist provided information about regional seed banks remained scarce - if you follow me, Dr. Chin."

"I do, Dr. Sanchez. I do." He then added, "Dr. Sanchez, it sounds to me as though you are suggesting that we create informal trade networks across our country based on bartering or cooperation."

"Yes, I believe so. I'm concerned that your federal administrative system doesn't allow your citizens much personal mobility. People would need to move freely among those regions cooperating with the scheme we are proposing. I am thinking government restrictions on individual movement would have to be loosened, would they not?"

"That's entirely possible. My fear always has been that the external and internal isolationist practices of my country will eventually lead to the collapse of the central government, which to this point has been our one national strength - our tight central control. But, the high population concentration in our industrial and coastal cities has created several ozone holes over them, and the government has moved rapidly to relocate our industries, but little to clean their waste."

Before signing off, Dr. Chin thanked Tracie and her colleagues for their willingness to share important information outside official channels. China was in the throes of its own disintegration, but its relatively young and ideologically rigid leadership clung tenaciously to old habits whose primary purpose was central control of everything, especially vital information. Dr. Chin told Tracie, "I have to exercise caution in how I share what I have learned and with whom, to avoid arousing unnecessary scrutiny. I know you understand."

"Yes, I do! I have several other contacts I plan to approach on your behalf who could get in touch through *official* channels. That will give you some needed political cover."

"Excellent!"

The weekend was just two days away, and that included Friday dinner with Wilson. WHO had regional and country specialists he could recommend for her friend in Beijing. Dr. Chin might be known to some of them, but if not, they would also be a valuable resource. Dr. Chin's primary portfolio did not include health management, but the world was living through extraordinary times, and his interest was the survival of the Chinese people. Wilson knew everyone needed to be connected to everyone else. All of the existing rules had to change.

Tracie wanted to bring someone else into this dialogue with Dr. Chin, and that was Barbara Keesport, former Governor of Oregon, now the Special Representative for Global Partnerships at the State Department. Keesport had replaced the Special Envoy on Climate Change of previous administrations. Her mandate from the White House was to promote collaboration between the United States and foreign-based organizations-businesses; non-profits; state, municipal and tribal governments; and academic institutions to support the President's foreign policy objectives to combat the effects of a changing climate, corruption, and global migration. Corruption permeated all levels of Chinese society, the reason penalties for those convicted were so severe. Dr. Chin was preoccupied with each of these areas. A conversation between Chin and Keesport would give Chin much-needed, high-profile cover with the paranoid leadership in Beijing.

During any conversation with Keesport, Chin could then openly ask about programs in the American Southwest developed by major universities in direct response to a changing climate. The Southwest and sections of California were the epicenter for drought, ozone depletion, agricultural degradation, coastal erosion, and cross-border migration - problems well known to Chinese authorities. Chin could play another angle his American interlocutor would immediately support: intellectual exchanges. Exchanges represented an approach favored by academic/research entities because exchange programs fostered mutual learning and respect for research and partnerships.

With Wilson's blessing, Tracie put the final pieces of her plan into motion. She had been her father's willing young apprentice when he used to tell her, "You don't need to do everything yourself. Sometimes, the most important contribution you can make is putting the right people together at the right time on the right problem." Tracie wanted to move on, but first she wanted to establish an official contact between Keesport and Dr. Chin, one government entity to another. Her plan was to call Keesport the next day following a meeting with two of her senior climatologists working on North Korea. During the meeting, her assistant interrupted to tell her a Governor Keesport was on the line. Keesport preferred the title governor. It carried more cachet than *special representative*. Tracie came on the line. "Good morning, Governor! How are you?"

"I am well, Dr. Hinton. Thank you for taking my call."

"I should tell you that I planned to call you later this morning. So your timing is perfect. How can I help you?"

"You may have heard that the South Korean Minister for the Environment will be here later this week as part of a high-level delegation for bi-lateral discussions. He and I are scheduled to meet to talk about 'climate change,' particularly problems related to the impact of a changing climate on North Korea. His office has asked for a list of those attending from my side. I would very much appreciate it if you were available to participate."

"Thank you for the invitation, Governor. What day and time are we talking?"

"Thursday at 9:30 a.m. here in my conference room. And by the way, I appreciated the role you played in our symposium last year. I am still receiving feedback from several participants, especially about your presentation 'Are We Beyond Recovery?' I have to tell you, Dr. Hinton, there are days when I do grapple with that question."

"Thursday morning will work for me. And if I may, perhaps we can set aside some time then to talk about something I had planned to discuss with you during our call today. It can wait until Thursday. It's important to me, but it's not urgent."

"Very well, Dr. Hinton. Until Thursday morning. And thank you!"

"That worked out well!" Tracie congratulated herself. She had heard a delegation of South Koreans would be in D.C., but had not focused on it - too much else on her plate. She felt confident she understood what the agenda would be for the bilateral talks in general, but particularly with Keesport. Tracie's team had been paying special attention to North Korea since their recent nuclear missile attack off the California coast. A changing climate and the country's downtrodden and starving populations had driven North Korea's erratic leader to new heights of unpredictability, and to take risks without apparent regard for public safety. Most notably, thousands of desperate North Koreans were launching themselves in crafts into the open sea in a desperate attempt to reach South Korean waters, regardless of the mines planted by North Korea's military to prevent flight or foreign naval vessels patrolling offshore. Interviews of several North Korean fishermen and their families who had actually made it to the South underscored the prevailing opinion of the ones desperate enough to attempt the perilous journey: "Better to die trying to escape than die of disease, starvation, and the government's indifference at home."

Apart from its humanitarian interests, the South Korean government was rightly vigilant that North Korean agents could be among this wave of immigrants, and it wanted to avoid American and world condemnation should they have to reject many of them. The South's concerns were real because the North historically had been imaginative in its efforts to insert intelligence agents into the South to foster confusion and instability. An early primary objective of the North's leadership had been to assassinate the South Korean President. Tracie was fairly confident this topic would be on the agenda with Keesport. Therefore, her request to the Governor to make contact with Dr. Chin would be benign in contrast to the gravity of any requests the South Koreans might make of their American partners.

On Thursday, following their meeting with the South Koreans, Tracie and Governor Keesport met in the latter's office at the State Department. Tracie spoke of her special relationship with Dr. Chin, and the considerable challenges he confronted at home. She also shared details of the exchange she'd had with him and Wiley's team out in Seattle, what Chin's specific needs were, and why Tracie was asking Keesport to contact him. At the end of their conversation, Keesport told Tracie she would be willing to contact Dr. Chin, adding, "One of the reasons I enjoy this job is that, occasionally, I can make a difference with the Chins of this world."

7

S everal days after her meeting with Barbara Keesport, Tracie was at her desk enjoying a morning cup of chai lemon tea when she got a beep on her phone and saw it was from her friend Andy Hillyard of *The Washington Post*. Hmm, Andy, this early in the morning - something was up! Glancing at her watch, she saw it was 7:30 a.m. Still holding the cup in her left hand, she answered, "This is Tracie!"

"Tracie, this is Andy!"

"Yeah! Hi, Andy. It's a little early, even for you. What's up?"

"I took a chance that you might be in. If you're like me, you come in early to avoid the rush and have a few moments to yourself. Listen, didn't you meet with several members of the South Korean delegation in town for bilateral talks a few days ago?"

"Yes, I did. Why do you ask?"

"I'm following up on a rumor from a trusted source about a possible rupture in our relationship with South Korea over our failure to respond to the nuclear missile attack off the coast of California. Have you heard anything? Did that topic come up in your conversation?"

"No, not at all. I'm sure I would have picked up on it had I sensed something amiss."

"Well, that's not the worst of it! I'm also hearing about a budding mutiny among the members of the Joint Chiefs over at the Pentagon. To be more specific, I'm hearing from an inside source at the Pentagon that the Chairman and all the service chiefs have told the Defense Secretary they will resign en masse unless there is an official response. They feel uniformly that because of our non-response posture, they have lost all credibility as a reliable partner with our NATO allies and other treaty partners worldwide."

"Whoa! Is this real, Andy? Where is the Vice President on this? The Chief of Staff? The National Security Advisor?"

"They remain loyal to the President. I'm trying to get to the bottom of it. As you can imagine, people are reluctant to talk since no one is authorized to speak on the record. The President is obviously shaken, and the word is that key members of his Cabinet are backing the service chiefs. The consensus *appears to be* that we have to call the Chinese out. We need to invoke Article 5 of the North Atlantic Treaty - an attack against one member is an attack against all members. NATO has an obligation to respond."

"It's gotten *that* far? So what are the South Koreans saying!?"

"Again, according to my source, the Chiefs have told the White House and SecDef they are prepared to launch a preemptive strike against nuclear facilities in the North, justified by reasoning that, if the North can attack the U.S. with impunity, what is to prevent them from attacking Seoul, followed by a massive land invasion?"

"Wait a minute, Andy! Take a step back. If what you're hearing is accurate, South Korea makes a valid point. Let's run this out. If the Japanese were to hear about this, wouldn't they feel the same sense of vulnerability?"

"With regard to the South Koreans, yes, they do feel exposed! Which is why the Chiefs are up in arms. They are being beaten up by the commanders of U.S. Forces Korea, the Eighth Army, and CINCPAC

(Commander-in-Chief, Pacific). And, the Japanese. Yeah! I imagine the Chairman has gotten more than a few calls from his Japanese counterpart.

"Andy, we've had this discussion. Everyone understands that the leadership of the North is crying out for help to deal with the climate crisis, aren't they? We all know how desperate their situation is." Moreover, I hear people are fleeing in unseaworthy craft to the South, thousands of children and young people are dying on the streets, millions are starving, and there is dissension within the ranks of the North's military. Hell, they can't even feed their troops, who have been taking everything from farmers and peasants. I mean, this is the worst-kept open secret *ever* in the Hermit Kingdom.

Continuing, Tracie said, "Asking for help, especially from the West, is anathema to them. It casts them as supplicants with the resultant loss of face. And then, of course, there are the sanctions. If we understand anything about their mentality, they'd rather go to war than lose face. Their leadership wants any interaction to be perceived as between equals negotiating a solution to a common problem. Yeah, I know it's all bullshit, but that's what we're dealing with. I believe we have been presented with an opportunity to force the North to the table - if the Chinese back our play. The question is whether they want to cede that much leverage to us with the North?"

"I'm with you, Tracie."

"The internal situation in China may compel them to work with us. Our side has to step it up. It might take the public resignation of the Chiefs for the President to act, although I'd hate to see it become that drastic. Andy, somebody in *this* White House must be standing on the President's chest! Who is it?"

"I assume he is getting it from all sides! My fear is, unless we take a giant step in the near term, the North Koreans may just pull the plug on this one, and we could find ourselves in a nuclear-albeit limited-war! I'm serious!"

"Yeah, that's what scares the hell out of me!"

When Andy hung up, Tracie sat there wondering, "Why did Andy call me with this? What did he expect me to do with this information?" Maybe he was thinking about our last conversation when I expressed an interest in broadening my involvement on policy issues. Maybe the midterms were too close for comfort for the President. Tracie got up and began to pace, looking out the window. Early morning traffic on Dupont Circle was already dense. "Who do I call?" she wondered.

Almost instinctively, she was on the phone to Wilson. Tracie knew he always arrived early to make a cup of sweet African tea and scan the morning news' feeds. "I need to see you—NOW!" When Tracie took that tone, Wilson's usual response was, "Where are you?"

"On my way!" he replied, instead, noting the number.

Thirty minutes later, Wilson entered her office. "Tracie, I haven't had my tea yet. What's going on?"

"Close the door!" Tracie trusted Wilson, and although he was a senior official at WHO with a portfolio a world apart from what she was about to share with him, he had finely tuned political antennae. He was the soul of *savoir faire*.

Tracie told him what she had heard without attribution. Wilson didn't expect her to name her source. It was enough that she trusted whoever it was. For a few moments he sat looking at her, and she could see his wheels turning. "Okay! I listened. Can I at least get a cup of coffee if you don't have tea handy?"

"Yes! Of course. How about some decaf. Does that work?"

"Yes!" While Tracie busied herself preparing a cup of coffee, Wilson asked, "How close is Barbara Keesport to the President?"

"I can only tell you what I've learned, and what she shared with me during our lengthy private conversation in her office. She and the President are close, in fact, their families are close. They are former classmates and married mutual friends. She was one of the President's major campaign fundraisers, raising millions. He offered her a Cabinet position, which she declined, preferring the position she currently has at State."

"Hmm, that's odd…turning down a Cabinet position. Historically, the President's campaign finance chairman, or the biggest contributor, is offered the position at Commerce. All of us know that, and everyone tries to leverage the incumbent's relationship to the President."

"I voiced the same opinion when she shared that decision with me. Her rationale was simple: she wanted to preserve her *voice* with him, unfiltered through the Washington noise and the taint of congressional hearings." The Commerce Department is one of the largest bureaucracies in the Executive branch with over 38,000 employees, multiple agencies, *and* a management nightmare. As she put it, "Imagine the number of congressional committee chairman I'd be reporting to! That job is not me."

"Smart woman. She has an unusual portfolio, which is why I asked about her relationship with the President. If your instincts are right about the North Korean leadership - and I don't doubt they are - perhaps she might call the President and seek a private meeting with him. The meeting would be unfiltered through the Vice President, the chief of staff, his legal counsel, or National Security Advisor." Wilson continued, "she should share with the President her view - provided she agrees with you that the effects of a changing climate are what's fueling the behavior from the North Koreans - advising him he may be wasting a unique opportunity for leadership. She can offer that degree of candor, but only in private. Only she would know that. It might be worth a shot. We may hear from the North again. Only this time, it may be too late."

"Damn, Wilson, why didn't I think of that earlier? I was in the room!"

"Well, you were focused on other things. If Keesport's relationship with the President has the history she says, she owes it to him to be a voice of reason through the cacophony of strategy noise bombarding him at every turn. I think she'll regret not having done so if this situation with North Korea takes a turn for the worse. By the way, it's your turn to prepare dinner this Friday."

Smiling, Tracie faced her friend, got up from her desk and walked over and kissed him saying, "Okay." Her reaction at that moment in that place caught Wilson off guard. For a few seconds, he just stood there smiling. "I'll call Keesport today," Tracie told him. "What do you want for dinner on Friday? I may have to shop."

"I'll leave it up to you. Just let me know if I need to bring red wine or white."

When Wilson left, Tracie sat down feeling momentarily distracted. Her spontaneous reaction with him had felt good, different. Yes, they were close, but they had managed to preserve enough emotional distance to maintain the unique relationship foundational to them both. Neither of them wanted to do anything that could harm the friendship. Wilson would date on occasion, but nothing serious enough to suggest romantic interest. With him, dates were more social or professional than an expression of amorous intent. Tracie didn't date, nor was she that interested in doing so. As she confided to her dad, "I'm just not attracted to the kind of male Washington breeds. I'm better off alone." Quietly, he didn't disagree with his daughter. He himself had once told Ericka that, had he not met her, it was unlikely he would have married as early as he did. Washington also breeds a unique strain of female.

Tracie's staff had come in by this time and were assembling in the conference room for the early morning staff meeting. Before the meeting, she scribbled a note to herself to call Keesport. It was close to noon before Tracie had a moment to think about her early morning call with Andy, followed by the hasty meeting with Wilson. She shut her door telling her assistant to hold all calls unless urgent.

In a more ordered, less chaotic world, Wilson's suggestion made sense. You know someone close to the President. We're in a crisis that calls for presidential leadership. Ask that person to intervene, to encourage your friend to step up. Right! No! That was too neat. This President had to be receiving more advice than he could possibly absorb. How could she know Keesport was *not* among those whispering in the President's ear? She didn't know!

Keesport and she were well known to each other, but only professionally. Trading on that to suggest she offer advice to the President about the North Korean threat could seem presumptuous. This was first tier national security stuff, for heaven's sake! No, she couldn't make that call yet. Talking to Wilson initially allowed her to bounce the issue against someone whose advice and instincts she trusted. That took the urgency out of it. She needed to talk to her dad. And *now* it was time to bring him into the picture.

8

When Tracie asked her father if he were available that evening, the only explanation she offered was, "It's vitally important, Daddy; so important that I cannot discuss it by phone." Sam didn't need to hear more other than to ask what time she would be at home.

"7:30 this evening would be great, if you can make it." At that hour, Sam would need to leave home shortly after 6:00 p.m. to be on time. Ericka decided not to accompany him. On these occasions, she understood Tracie needed to talk to her father.

At 6:00 p.m., the quickest route to Tracie's home in upper Northwest Washington was the Capital Beltway, with its eight lanes of commuter traffic. Only on rare occasions would Tracie invoke the *urgency rule,* knowing the distance her father would have to travel. Sam kissed his wife and headed out the door. Unless his daughter indicated the nature of the urgency, Sam chose not to preoccupy himself with trying to recall anything previous that might provide a clue. His daughter would fill in the details when he arrived. Sam had a key to her house, but discreetly chose not to walk in unannounced when she was at home. His daughter often admonished him, "Daddy, why didn't you use your key?" To which he'd dutifully respond, "You're a grown woman deserving of your privacy." Tracie loved that 'old school' quality in her dad.

Father and daughter settled at the kitchen table, Sam with a cool glass of lemonade and Tracie with a glass of non-alcoholic white wine. "So, Sweetie, why did you rush your father halfway across the region at this hour?"

Tracie recounted her day, beginning with the call from Andy Hillyard and her subsequent conversation with Wilson. She shared with her dad Wilson's suggestion that she call Barbara Keesport. Moreover, she described her relationship with Keesport and highlights of their recent meeting with a South Korean delegation in town for bilateral talks.

"Daddy, national security, especially an issue as current as the missile attack off the California coast, is not my natural lane in this city. I only learned that Keesport is a family friend of the President because Keesport felt comfortable sharing that with me. In good conscience, I couldn't assume I had the bona fides to suggest she approach the President with an interpretation of North Korea's motives for the attack. Imagine this scene!" she laughed. Keesport suggesting to the President that a climatologist she knows professionally, believes he, the President of the United States, now has an opportunity to show real leadership on an issue vital to national security. Talk about chutzpah! I just couldn't go that far. Were our relationship different, long-standing or more personal...perhaps. Am I right, Dad?"

Sam continued to listen as Tracie paced the kitchen, describing the North Korea she understood. The dire economic and social conditions within the country and the effects of a changing climate, exacerbated by sanctions, had been largely responsible for the country's decision to attack. As she sat down, she said, "Dad, what frightens me is I don't think we've heard the last from the people in Pyongyang. I think the worst is yet to come!"

As Tracie spoke, Sam understood why Wilson proffered the advice he had. His daughter was at the moment looking for something, any responsible way she could use the information she had been given. Wilson also knew Tracie well enough to know she was deliberative, not inclined to impulsiveness when important decisions were at stake. Wilson would not be surprised to learn Tracie had consulted her father.

"Your instincts serve you well," Sam told Tracie. "You're right. It would have been presumptuous to approach Keesport and offer advice in this instance. I am as concerned as you are and frustrated that the President fails to lead. If anything, his miscalculation *will* probably open the door for a second attack. Our representative in the House, Janice Boland, is a friend. She is also the Chairman of the House Foreign Affairs Committee. Boland and I speak often, and she informs me that the situation with the President is worse than it appears publicly. He has dug in against a military response, fearing it will provoke the Chinese to attack our naval forces in the Pacific and accelerate their expansion into the Indo-Pacific. And then, there is always the flashpoint that Taiwan represents.

"Now, about your theory that the effects of a changing climate are at play...Boland and Keesport are close. Keesport, too, believes as you do, and she has shared her beliefs with Boland *and* the President. He is beyond discussion of motives for the attack and focused solely on the prospect of a wider war should he attack North Korea."

"So, what you're saying, Daddy, is we're screwed."

"In a word, yes!"

Sam went on to explain that NATO was not unified in believing that the North's attack warranted a unified response. What several key NATO members believed was that an attack against the North would prompt Russia, in solidarity with China and North Korea, to attack Poland and other states on Europe's eastern border, including Finland and Sweden in the North. The Joint Chiefs felt humiliated and were threatening to resign. The Defense Secretary was holding them off, but conceded it was unlikely he would prevail in the short term. "What I've given you," Sam told Tracie, "is a thumbnail sketch of the hours of shouting matches, threats of resignation, and Doom's Day scenarios that could determine the outcome of the next presidential election."

"I'm feeling what I felt this morning after the call with Andy. What do I do now?" Tracie asked rhetorically.

"Sweetie, there is nothing you can do. *Now* you understand my frustration and that of many others. What we're seeing is not new. Previously, a failure of American leadership led to the Russian invasion of the Crimea, a destructive invasion of Ukraine, and a blockage of Ukraine's ports. This time, it could lead to a nuclear exchange."

"Does Boland suggest that we will be able to contain South Korea?" Tracie asked.

"That's the wild card. In a word, she believes they will act independently. Privately, she says the South has no choice. And if they do, that unilateral act will shred our Asia security policy. I can share with you as much detail as I know, but that will not change the fundamentals as they are now. Of course, everything could change tomorrow."

"Daddy, you know a changing climate has altered life on this planet. Add to that the fallout from a nuclear exchange, even a limited one, and you have to wonder who and what would survive, and would it resemble civilization?"

"Sweetie, don't focus on how powerless you feel. Rather, consider the options you have to help frame the public's understanding of the stakes. You must be more agile, more fleet of foot. What I mean is, you have a voice. Use it! Become a burr under the saddle of this White House. Become a frequent commentator in the major media. *National Public Radio (NPR)* has a large, well-educated audience you can tap into. Become a useful source on the politics of a changing climate for the members of the Foreign Press Club here in Washington, and that will give you a voice in foreign media markets.

Call up your friend Wiley Mitchell and round up some of the experts from the former Climate Assessment Convention in Tucson and your recent conference in San Gabriel, California. Host a symposium through your company and invite thoughtful voices from the Consortium of Colleges and Universities in this region as well – including students. And then, of course, continue to author monographs, articles, and opinion pieces for *The Washington Post, The New York Times,* and *Foreign Policy.* Work on another book! You may not be able to contribute to the policy debate inside this White House, but you sure as hell can inform the American public better. Build a narrative the public can tap into!"

"Just how much time do you think we have, Daddy, before all this blows sky high?" Tracie almost wailed. "I can make good use of the media and try to move attention away from a shooting war. Perhaps you need to help me get Keesport and Boland in front of the big cameras with me. I need to contact Wiley and Sanchez, like NOW! Can you help me orchestrate these other people? I'll get my public relations department on the press releases as soon as we have some commitments. It will take a steady stream of climate crisis news linking the incident off California and North Korea's dire public health situation.

"We can acknowledge that North Korea has made us listen up and has the arms to wreak considerable havoc on us. But rather than address that threat, we must change the argument to the global humanitarian crisis suffered by many countries, *including* both Koreas and the West, and offer to pool our resources for our mutual benefit. If nothing else, it might help us isolate North Korea and deal with the aftermath of the midterms. If we depict the situation so that North Koreans appear to be equal partners with us in solving a global problem, they won't lose face.

After calculating the time difference the following day, Tracie picked up her phone and called Wiley, who would be in his office by then.

"Tracie! I didn't expect to hear from you so soon after our conversation with Dr. Chin, given what I imagine you have on your plate. What's up?"

"I do! And you and Roberta can help me work on a big one! How much time do you have?"

"I can spare some time. I'm meeting with a client but, first, I have to finish some paperwork on a project we just completed with a group from the Bay Area."

"Thanks, Wiley. I'll get right to it. As you know, this White House seems paralyzed over an appropriate response to the missile blast off our western coast. I've been talking to any number of people here, including, of course, Wilson and my dad. Politically, Dad said there's nothing we can do, and anything military would be disastrous. But, he implanted the idea that we *could* do a massive media campaign to foreground the global crisis we confront regarding a changing climate; a crisis that's creating motives for warfare as happened with North Korea. What I want to do is get together a whole lot of experts on sustainability in the global climate crisis. Dad is helping with people he knows, and I wanted to bring the two of you and some of the people we had at the recent convention in San Gabriel. I want to do a public awareness blitz turning the focus onto mutual survival using pooled resources, technology, and the American experience."

"Wow! That could be huge! Are you thinking of some national telecoms on major media? That's about the most effective way to bring together enough people to make the project worthwhile."

"Yes! I agree. As soon as I have enough commitments for a panel or two, I'll get press releases to *NPR, CBS, NBC,* to begin, and to the major media in Canada, Mexico, Europe, Japan, and North and South Africa. We'll have autotrans systems so we can do simultaneous audio-visual broadcasts. The idea is to do a series of them. The final one focusing on international collaboration through resource trade agreements and collaborative sustainability programs. I'm thinking you and Sanchez could jointly moderate that one. Sustainability is critical, and I can't think of a more appropriate conclusion to this project than how we sustain whatever all of us can agree is the key to survival of this planet."

"Okay, I'll get my team together and we'll develop a roster of experts we recommend. I can think of several right here in Seattle, an environmentalist from San Francisco, and, of course Bradford. You're going to rattle some cages but, if we're going to do this, we have to go big! Desperate times call for desperate measures."

"One more thing, Wiley!"

"Yeah, what's that?"

"What do you think about sending Roberta to Florence to explore some exchanges and help us assess the politics of controlling that seed bank? Seed banks, more importantly, who controls them, will determine global politics in the future. Wilson is especially afraid that seed banks in the hands of the Russians and the Chinese will lead to conflict. It is just that simple. You can fill in the blanks when it comes to a combined response from us and the West. You and Roberta talk it over. We'll talk soon."

When Wiley got off the phone with Tracie, he sat there for a moment thinking about her suggestion of sending Roberta to Florence. "Again, she beat me to it!" he said to himself. He thought about their initial meeting at the conference in Detroit years ago and how she had suggested they attend separate breakout sessions and meet afterwards to share notes. Frankly, he liked the idea of Roberta going to Florence. She was European, spoke French and Italian. Later, she added German and Russian. Had the two of them not met, Roberta's plan following graduation was to return to Europe and work for the European Parliament in Strasburg, the International Court of Justice in the Hague, or, perhaps the Organization for Economic Cooperation and Development (OECD) in Paris. Roberta was a brilliant negotiator, comfortable in both public and private sector settings. One of her strengths was the ability to take the most arcane and synthesize it to a level of simplicity that brought competing, or warring, parties to agreement in a shorter period of time. Roberta had no patience for lengthy, protracted debate when it was obvious that none of the parties around the table was prepared to compromise or reach agreement.

Wiley also remembered how difficult it had been for him and Roberta to wait three years until after graduation to marry. Their commitment to each other was strong. Without it, they likely would have drifted apart.

Florence would not be a particularly difficult assignment but the seed bank there was important to Europe and the Middle East. If Tracie's media campaign took off, that success could serve as either a deterrent or an incentive to warfare over Florence.

9

Fifty-five hundred miles East of Seattle, Italian agronomist Dr. Giuseppe Nuzzi, the permanent head of the combined branches of the Istituto di Genetica Vegetale (IGV) in Florence, Italy, was becoming increasingly anxious over world events, i.e., the increased tensions between the major powers and their contrasting approaches to handling the all-too-familiar consequences of a changing global climate. Heading his list of geographic nightmares and their impact on his organization was a development closer to home: the loss of the Po River in his own country and the threat it represented to Italian manufacturing and agriculture.

The Po Valley had provided 40 percent of Italy's GDP, and its loss reverberated from Turin in the West through Milan to Comacchio on the Adriatic. The effect on Italy's balance of payments was incalculable. Moreover, a weakened manufacturing base threatened Italy's standing in NATO. Would Italy meet its defense requirements to safeguard NATO's southern flank? And a substantial reduction in its agricultural output threatened the country's standing in the EU.

A textbook blend of Florentine bureaucrat-politician, the cultivated and urbane Nuzzi was the embodiment of Mediterranean charm.

Although originally from Milan, he preferred the pace of Florence. The common element in the global events he observed regularly was the threat to the sustainability of life on the planet. That spoke to the purpose and mission of his organization and its branches in Portici, Palermo, and Perugia.

During a recent meeting with his board of directors, the University of Milan-educated board chairman shared his concerns and directed his board to pay particular attention to collaborative efforts of communities in the states of the Arid Zone in the American Southwest and California. "Study coastal erosion in California; their experience may have some salience for the future of this country," he advised the board. "I worry," Nuzzi told his people, "about the erratic behavior of North Korea's leadership; the impact of a changing climate on the Peoples' Republic of China, most notably the prolonged drought and the failure of its agricultural sector. We should be concerned about the growing likelihood of a nuclear exchange involving the U.S., China, and North Korea from drought, famine, and loss of arable farmland." "Our world," he continued, "has been defined by a changing climate, and we have to focus on survival. That means the ready availability of potable water and food. We must revive traditional agriculture - farming rice, fruits, nuts, and, yes, trees and forests. The basis for everything is seeds. The world's food systems are in peril, and that places our organization squarely in everyone's crosshairs."

Nuzzi took a moment to remind his board members of the obvious, something he insisted was easily forgotten during periods of prosperity. Civilizations flourished - and withered - because of agriculture, organized and improved farming techniques, and the availability of water. Drought and famine have always led to conflict, mass migration, and cultural disintegration.

To employ a well-known American colloquialism, Nuzzi remarked, "We are about to become everyone's flavor of the month. We better be ready for it!"

Istituto di Genetica Vegetale is home to the largest inventory of climate-adapted hybrids, to which all of Europe, the Middle East, the Americas, and Africa contribute. Every contributing country has a stake in it - unfortunately. Fortunately, the seed library upon which it was modeled continues to provide new arid land and underground strains.

The more Wiley and Roberta discussed Tracie's suggestion to send Roberta to Florence, the more the idea appealed to them. Roberta had not met Dr. Nuzzi, but she welcomed the idea of a meeting. In a follow-up conversation with Wiley and Roberta, Tracie told Roberta, "Dr. Nuzzi is personable, curious, and flattering as only an Italian can be. Trust me, you'll love him." Roberta laughed, responding, "This ought to be fun."

"Just so you know," Tracie went on to say, "Nuzzi has visited the U.S. before, primarily in the Southwest, meeting with project directors of several of the more sustainability projects in Arizona and New Mexico. I'm not aware that he has visited California or the Pacific Northwest. He and I did meet briefly, but circumstances did not allow for any real conversation between us."

Before Tracie hung up, Roberta said, "Tracie, I have an idea!"

"Okay!

"You and Wiley are organizing several panel discussions and it occurs to me you may be considering Dr. Nuzzi as a prospective panelist."

"Yes, that's true. We haven't extended the invitation yet. What are you thinking?"

"Well, perhaps I might invite him as a way of introducing myself before my trip. He would probably have to participate long-distance, but having his voice, especially someone of his stature, would surely help reach a broader viewing audience. What do you think?"

"I like it, Roberta. I like it a lot! Here's what I'll do. He may remember, or he may not, that he and I met briefly. I'll give him a call, reintroduce myself, talk about the panel discussions we're organizing, and explore his interest in becoming involved. If he responds favorably, I'll tell him that I would be pleased if he would receive my representative, Roberta Mitchell, and also that he will be receiving a call from you by way of introduction.

"Okay!"

The next morning, Tracie calculated the six-hour time difference between Washington, D.C., and Florence, hoping to reach Dr. Nuzzi at an opportune time in the early afternoon.

"Dr. Nuzzi, this is Dr. Tracie Hinton in Washington, D.C. You may recall that we met several years ago at a convention in Tucson."

"Yes, Dr. Hinton, you are the noted climatologist, and yes, I do recall our meeting. To what do I owe the pleasure of your call?"

"Dr. Nuzzi, you are undoubtedly a busy man, so that I will come right to the point. I hope you will consider being on a panel for an internationally broadcast conference on the topic of sustainable food supplies to address hunger."

"That sounds interesting. Can you tell me more?"

"Yes! I want to produce a series of climate disaster mitigations to as many people as possible. My hope is to shift our attention away from increasing world tensions over resources and the possibility of military confrontation toward cooperation and mutual assistance. There is a more productive role the rest of us can play than bystanders - and possibly victims - to conflict. I find it ironic that the most bellicose actors threatening military conflict are simultaneously among the most needy."

"I would agree with your latter characterization and would be happy to contribute what we have been undertaking here in Florence."

"Excellent! Dr. Nuzzi. I am grateful for your cooperation. If I may, have you been sharing duplicates of your most valuable seeds with other seed vaults?"

"Yes, I have, as a matter of fact."

"May I suggest that you not do that - at least for the moment."

"I take it you have concerns."

"As you and the rest of the civilized world are aware, we have recently had a nuclear attack from North Korea, whose people are in desperate straits. If any of the facilities with whom you are sharing seeds are within easy missile range of Russia, who, by the way, is almost equally desperate thanks to its ongoing military aggression, they may become a target for Russian aggression."

"I see. You have a point, Dr. Hinton. We should discuss this at length when we can be sure of not being overheard."

"One of my trusted colleagues, Roberta Mitchell, will be traveling to Florence, and I am hoping that you would be open to discussing this issue as well as your participation in the panel discussion. I will have her contact you shortly."

"I will welcome your colleague's visit. She may also wish to visit our facilities in Perugia and Portici, as well. Those two facilities specialize in seeds that would have greater global applicability."

"Dr. Nuzzi, thank you for your support, and I do hope our paths cross in the near future."

"Dr. Hinton, I am fairly certain they will."

Tracie hung up and pumped her fist vigorously, saying to herself, "I love it when a plan comes together! Nuzzi will command the attention we seek from certain quarters. If anyone is focused on the question of how we sustain life today, tomorrow, and in the future, he is!" She then called Wiley and Roberta to share the good news. Once they were on the line, she said, "Guys, Dr. Nuzzi is a Go! We need to talk about your agenda, Roberta, and a timetable. I say the earlier you can travel, the better."

Roberta suggested to Tracie her message would reflect something she and Wiley confront regularly, and that is, "If the global community continued to die through war and starvation, life on the planet would remain in imminent danger. The attack on California was a stark reminder of the worst impulses a leader can give in to. The loss of California's agricultural industry through drought and coastal erosion contributed to hunger here and around the globe." My hope," Roberta went on to add, "is that Dr. Nuzzi and others on his panel would persuade the world that a free exchange of agricultural resources and knowledge would begin to remedy the underlying causes of global migration, thereby reducing tensions. Those who *had* couldn't horde and those who *had not* couldn't be allowed to perish when there was so much Earth repair and recovery to be done."

Public frustration in the country over the Administration's non-response to the North Korean missile attack off the West Coast continued to mount, prompting, among other things, late-night conversations between congressional leaders, senior advisors to the President, and President Harwood himself. Several major donors in the President's party expressed fear and anger - that he was a drag on reelection prospects for some of their candidates in the upcoming midterms. Ironically, opinion polls commissioned by both parties and Independents showed a steady decline in support for the President more than an interest in understanding the causes of the attack. The governor of a major Midwest state and someone seen as a likely candidate for the Democratic presidential nomination in 2052 commented that the President could likely face a challenger for the nomination.

Harwood had become an enigma to many in his party. Here was someone groomed for a sterling political career since his election as a member of the House of Representatives at the age of twenty-six, who was now treading on political quicksand. He resigned his House seat after three terms to accept the presidency of a major non-profit organization in Washington, D.C. A career still in its ascendancy, Harwood was approached by his party to run for a U.S. Senate seat from his home state of Wisconsin because the incumbent had chosen to retire due to her husband's declining health. Harwood was popular among his Senate colleagues. Approaching his third term - now an important committee chairman - Harwood, again, succumbed to entreaties from his party, this time to make a run for the White House. Repeatedly, he was told, "We can win! It's your time!" And so he did.

Although Harwood was well-liked, he had never been tested in the level of trench politics Washington can visit on the unsuspecting. Harwood got along because he went along - a familiar Washington route to political survival and success. The surprise attack from North Korea off the West Coast was his first real baptism of fire, and he was failing. For the first time, questions arose regarding his ability to handle the pressures of the presidency, and he found himself alone. He had been a White knight for his party until he faltered. Rumors among his Senate colleagues - anonymous, of course - began to circulate that he was an isolationist, unprepared to defend this country's territorial integrity. Donors and colleagues returned his calls. He was still the President. However, the wagons did not circle to protect him.

The world under threats from a changing climate had changed fundamentally, but popular sentiment focused on the attack - the geopolitics and the prospects of war. *That* storyline was easier to develop than conflicting attitudes regarding a changing climate. The attack had the requisite emotional content, i.e., fear, frustration, anger, and ignorance. It also exacerbated the ideological and partisan divide in the country, and it was good for the corporate bottom line. Crises capture public attention.

As the debate on this issue raged within the narrow parameters defined by the popular media, Tracie focused on the impact her symposia could have. Initially, she hadn't settled on a theme, which media organizations might want to cover the event, the specific topics, or the desirable participants. During one of her frequent conversations with Wilson on this project and a variety of other topics, he told her somewhat excitedly, "There's your theme! You just said it!"

Puzzled, Tracie replied, "What are you talking about? What theme?"

"Sometimes, you don't hear yourself; you get so caught up in the moment!"

"Okay! I get that, but I was off on my habitual rant."

"Exactly! You were describing mankind against itself, you know - us, the Chinese, the North Koreans - and how our instincts seem increasingly pulled in the direction of destruction, not survival. So, here's your theme: *'Mankind Against Itself - Instinct for Destruction.'*"

Tracie paused, stood with both hands clasped behind her head, looking at Wilson. "You know what? I like that! Imagine the conversation with a worldwide audience, especially in those countries suffering the worst effects of a changing climate, and looking to the U.S. for leadership to address a problem largely of our own making."

"You mean Sub-Saharan Africa, island states in the Southwest Pacific, and coastal states in South America?" Wilson suggested.

"Well, *yeah!*"

"If you raise the right questions, I can almost guarantee you a reaction from this White House. You implicate them as well. No! You are *indicting* them! The degree to which the theme resonates will determine *who* responds: the White House Press Secretary or a Cabinet-level official. You are going to be asking a lot of uncomfortable questions, not just about our leadership but of leadership elsewhere, including the World Bank and the International Monetary Fund (IMF). You will be questioning past and current national priorities. You challenge the decisions of an ultra-conservative and activist Supreme Court, the allocation of increasingly scarce resources, and the effects of a changing climate that has no man-made or natural boundaries. These are all effects that reduce everyone to our basic humanity and desire to survive. What you're saying to the elected leadership is, 'turn off the self-destruction switch, and let's talk about how we can live together on this planet.'"

"Yeah...because at the rate we're going, we're in a race to the end of life!"

On that note, Tracie decided she should check in with Wiley to see how his panel was shaping up.

"Wiley, this is Tracie. I hope this isn't a bad time."

When Wiley saw the call was from Tracie, he thought she might be following up on the Florence trip. "Tracie, how are you?"

"I'm fine, thanks. Listen, I wanted to see how your panel is coming together and to let you know what I have been working on. Also, I wanted to bounce Wilson's idea for our series theme off you and see what you guys think: "Mankind Against Itself: Instinct for Self-Destruction. How do you like it?"

"Very effective! The theme has the right degree of urgency - almost understated given the circumstances."

"I've been working with our big media outlets to find out how we can simulcast into places that typically jam our signals - Russia, China, North Korea. Radio Free Europe and streaming U.S. media use *New York Times* and *Washington Post* strategies. To get around blocking, they use various mirroring devices out of Riga, Latvia, for redirecting websites to new URLs as they get jammed, and Telegram's as-yet-unbanned social media and messaging apps can get the content distributed. Virtual Private Network architecture gurus at the major stations can locate audiences using the apps that are currently circulating out there. I'm Lining up moderators for the panels on clean air, ozone reconstruction, oceanographic stabilization, and sustainable water sources. I will have them bring in their own panelists."

"Before you go, Tracie, Roberta has made her plans to travel to Florence; she's spoken to Dr. Nuzzi, and everything seems to be coming together well. We recognize the political sensitivity of the trip, given its proximity to the symposium and the coming midterms. We need to fly under the radar on this one because when the symposium discussions begin, the Administration, their supporters on the Hill, and the fossil fuel industry will coalesce immediately and come after us with threats of investigation and prosecution to shut us down."

"Wiley, you're spot on. I knew I didn't have to go into all of the background on this to you two. It is for that reason that I have only shared information about Roberta's trip with Wilson and Dr. Nuzzi. We don't want Roberta in anyone's crosshairs. All of us will be soon enough."

The outcome of the 2050 mid-term elections cast a pall over this White House. The President's team miscalculated their losses in the House by five, giving them only a four-vote majority. The Senate majority was a razor-thin, two-seat majority that included the Vice President. The Administration's achievements in the last two years have not strengthened the Party's position in the Senate since the last general election. Privately, the Vice President fretted. He hoped he could beat the President in the next nominating convention. The Party's political fortunes now hung by a thread making a challenge to a sitting President politically perilous. If the past was prologue, the Vice President had no reason to be optimistic. Everything would depend on the President's mood and actions going forward.

10

The theme for Tracie's media project, *"Mankind Against Itself - Instinct for Destruction,"* was sure to attract the attention of media organizations, students, academics, elected officials, and activists - especially in countries slammed by the worst effects of a changing climate. In Sub-Saharan Africa, those countries bordering the southern edge of the Saharan Desert have been grappling with drought, desertification, degradation of scarce water resources, migration, and tribal conflict. Yet their more prosperous but distant European and American neighbors were still struggling to acknowledge that a changing climate was real and human-caused. Steadfastly, these deniers continued pursuing aggressive economic and energy policies that bloated corporate profits, degraded the ozone layer, warmed the polar regions, raised sea levels, destroyed the most productive agricultural land, and hastened the likelihood of worldwide conflict.

Wilson told Tracie during dinner on Friday night after the election, "I'm hearing a range of sentiment expressed around the office and from friends about the outcome of the midterms."

"So am I! What are you hearing?"

"There are a lot of very unhappy people. In fact, everyone I talk to predicts that the partisan divide in the country, and within and among elected officials, will only widen. Important legislation will stall in committees because no one will want to be portrayed as 'cooperating with the other side.' That does not bode well for future international cooperation on climate change proposals."

"Well, I'm not surprised," Tracie rejoined. She then asked Wilson about reactions at home in Nigeria to the global conversation she was organizing. Friday dinners had become a ritual for these two, an event signaling the end of another week. The dinner represented a moment to catch their breaths, savor a home-cooked meal and a glass of wine, and make sense of events shaping their lives and the lives of everyone they cared about.

"Many Africans are mystified, others mortified, by the American refusal to confront a crisis decades in the making and largely of their creation," Wilson said. He added, "They recall with a mix of humor and contempt the efforts by the rich donor countries to the World Bank and the International Monetary Fund (IMF) to set aside economic development and poverty reduction priorities in favor of focusing on reducing carbon emissions in Africa and the regions that contribute the least to ozone depletion."

Wilson went on to tell Tracie that many Africans were also unsympathetic to the U.S. and its current problem with North Korea. "Several well-connected African ambassadors here in Washington believe the U.S. is standing on the precipice of conflict they may not have anticipated, with fewer allies than they can reasonably depend upon to assist them. The missile attack by North Korea is a harbinger of worse things to come. The next time, the Chinese and the Russians will be involved. The question is, will they align against the U.S., or will the three of them square off against each other with North Korea as a catalyst?"

"So, Africans would support the dialogue we're trying to have in lieu of a conflict, perhaps even a world war."

"Yes, they would! Some countries view it as too little too late, but they would support it, nonetheless. However, a good number believe conflict is unavoidable given that the U.S., the Russians, and the Chinese are bound by histories of complex power-sharing relationships. None of them is prepared to abandon entrenched policies for reasons of national pride and global standing. Even the UN will be sidelined."

"So where does that leave the rest of us?" Tracie wondered aloud.

"Essentially, trying to have a dialogue on the margins of the war many think is inevitable. We have been telling ourselves that the UN has kept us out of a third world war since the end of World War II. That was never true! Talk to the Iraqis, Afghans, and Ukrainians. And then, of course, there was that decade-long American misadventure in South Vietnam. We avoided a global war because the three superpowers *chose* not to go to war. Who and what could have prevented any one of them from declaring war against the other - or the rest of us, for that matter?"

Wilson noticed Tracie's expression change. Her shoulders momentarily slumped, and she looked dejected. He got up, walked over, and put his arms around her, holding her for a moment. She appeared small in his embrace, confused and resigned. For Wilson, this was not the Tracie he loved, admired, and still hoped to marry.

"Listen," he soothed, "you have to play the cards you're dealt when you're in the game. You wanted to do something to fill the gap our lack of leadership has created. Well, you're in the game now! War is inevitable, and there is no magic wand you can wave to avoid that. That is what Africans are saying." He went on to add, "When it comes, war will not be waged on the African Continent, although we, too, will feel the effects of it. The worst of it, the missile strikes will be in North America, Europe, or the Central and Northern Pacific. Hundreds of thousands, maybe even millions, will die. India, the largest country between Russia and China, will also experience the fallout.

"Africans are thinking about the future. They *are* the future of humanity, and they know it. They have been adapting to the shifting winds of major-power politics for centuries. Africans are flexible and adaptable but also resolute about the role they intend to play to save the planet from future depredations by the major powers - perhaps *former* major powers. The future is going to be shaped by those with control over natural resources, not necessarily by those who field the largest army, navy, or air force. The future must be about cooperation and shared interests, not hegemony, which is what has defined the West's relations with the rest of the globe for over a century. The emphasis now has to be on preventing war, not threatening it as an expression of national will. I'll put it another way, in language Western corporate interests understand: Africa is an opportunity they *will not* ignore!"

"You're right," Tracie opined, "but it's not going to be easy! Breaking their behavioral mold, especially for the U.S., will involve a period of protracted tension. The U.S. is unaccustomed to dealing with others as equals in any sphere of interest, *especially* Africans. And when their survival or prosperity depends upon it...!"

"I hear you, Tracie, and you make a good point! But, look at it this way. This next conflict most likely will have one unintended consequence for the Americans and the Chinese: it will unify Sub-Saharan Africa. Our survival and the planet's will depend largely upon Africans' ability to work together rather than continue to work at cross purposes, as the Americans, Europeans, and the Chinese have conditioned us to do. For centuries, we and our leaders allowed our resources to be exploited for the major powers' gain and not ours. Hell, they have defined us to ourselves - to the point many of us have forgotten who we were!"

"They enslaved and murdered our people. They wrote our history; we didn't. They will fight a war over who gets to control us and our resources - to ensure their *survival.* If we allow that to happen again, almost two billion Africans will deserve whatever future they get. But Africa has one more major asset: the majority of them are young, under the age of 40. They are educated and trained at some of the world's finest universities. They are innovative, hungry for change, and determined to be treated as equals by the rest of the world. The old is being forced to make way for the new, and they *will* be establishing different criteria for alliances."

"For the sake of all of us, I hope you're right," Tracie sighed. "At times, I've felt like a hamster on a wheel, running in place and feeling no closer to a goal."

Perhaps it was these times they were living in, but Tracie and Wilson had grown closer. Their comfortable behavior now belied the fear that a deeper connection might threaten the friendship central to both. They spoke more frequently during the week and were spending more time together. Tracie told her mom, "The next time Wilson tells me I am the reason he is still single, I'm going to call him on it."

Ericka, hearing this wondered if Tracie was just being glib, as she generally was when speaking of her relationship with Wilson, or had something changed? "Sweetie, if you're serious, be prepared for how he might respond! If there is anything I have come to understand about Wilson, he loves you to his very core. I recognize that in him because I have that with your father, even after more than forty years. My marriage and our family are everything to your father and me, and we have allowed nothing and no one to threaten it. Wilson has waited twenty years for you! How many men have you known with that kind of commitment?"

"You're right, Mom. I know that, and at my age, I can't afford to ignore that any longer. So, the next time Wilson throws that in my face - which he will - I'm going to put my left hand in his face and point to this finger."

Around midday on Thanksgiving Saturday, Andy Hillyard was able to reach Tracie at home.

"Hi, Andy! You just caught me. I was on my way out. What's up?"

"I won't keep you but a minute. Your project is what's up! It's creating ripples in some interesting - no, sensitive - circles. Can we carve out some time early next week to talk?"

"Yeah, why not! But who are we talking about in particular?"

"Oh, your friends in the White House, for starters. Maybe unrelated, but I'm also hearing that some of the President's major donors are threatening to withhold their support next time. I have more on that."

"Whoa! Okay. I'll contact you early Monday. Thanks for the heads up."

Tracie stopped for a moment and returned to her kitchen. She was planning to run some errands, but that could wait. Her project was rattling some cages, some rather large and important cages. It was odd that no one had spoken to her. She was thinking specifically of Barbara Keesport over at State. Was she still in the loop, or had she, too, been temporarily marginalized by the gatekeepers around the President?

Tracie was intrigued by Andy's call and could not help but wonder who in the White House was interested in her. She also decided not to say anything to Wilson or to her father until after her meeting with Andy. Both men would only raise questions she was unprepared to answer. Wilson had been spot-on when he suggested that someone from within the administration might be in touch once the participant list had been completed and the discussion topics settled. Andy just got to her first. Early Monday morning, Tracie called Andy. He responded on the second buzz, which meant he was primed for her call.

"All right, Andy, I admit I was intrigued by your call on Saturday, as you guessed I would be. So, I'm thinking sandwiches in the park or my office. Or a salad if you prefer. I'm hosting. Today, tomorrow, or Wednesday."

"I like tomorrow. Chicken salad sandwiches in your office at 11:45 a.m. Bottled water works for me."

"See you then."

Tracie spent much of the next morning securing final commitments from moderators and reviewing the lists of panelists and discussion topics. It was 11:15 a.m. before she looked at her watch. Andy would arrive in less than 30 minutes, and she had not picked up the sandwiches for lunch. Grabbing her purse, she headed for the elevator. Pam's Deli was on the first level and offered sandwiches prepared fresh early each morning. Pam was at the far end and saw Tracie come through the door. "Two chicken salad sandwiches on rye to go, Pam!" Seconds later, lunches in hand, Tracie headed back to her office, stopping just long enough to put them in the office refrigerator. Minutes later, she looked up to see Andy approach her door.

"You're early, but that's okay. Come on in; I'll get lunch." Andy settled on the sofa. "Thanks for the invite." With a mouth full of chicken salad sandwiches, Andy asked about preparations for the symposium.

"We're tying down final details," Tracie responded. The response has been gratifying. I think we're going to have a real impact."

"You've already had an impact, from what my sources tell me. That is the least of your problems."

"Oh! Is that so?"

"Come on, Tracie. I don't think you're surprised."

"Well, yes and no." I expected some of the names we've attracted wouldn't go unnoticed, but I did *not* expect to hear from someone in the White House. I am surprised not to have heard from Barbara Keesport at the State Department. She is the *only* person from within the administration who I thought might call me."

"Well, let's begin there. She's a fan of yours, so much so that some of the President's senior staff felt she might persuade him to modify his position on 'climate change' before the elections. But the Vice President, a rigid ideologue if ever there was one, is in frequent contact with the big-money types, and they are in full-throated denial of human-caused climate change - even today, if you can fathom that. He's trying to keep Keesport at bay without trampling on her relationship with the President. Keesport is in a delicate position. She enjoys her position at State, feels she is making a difference, and is unwilling to make an enemy as powerful as the Vice President."

"So how and where do I come into this?"

My source at the White House tells me that more than a few American ambassadors abroad are being queried about a major media symposium being organized to discuss human-caused climate change. Some foreign media organizations want to carry it live. The topic here is the equivalent of the political football no one wants to carry. In many parts of the world, however, the effects and causes of a changing climate are real. At any rate, our ambassadors were not aware of the project and asked local officials about the source of their information.

"And?"

"Foreign ambassadors here have been reporting to their governments at home, suggesting their media carry your event live. Our ambassadors are picking up on this in their routine conversations and reporting back to the State Department. The volume of the reporting from our missions abroad warranted inclusion in the President's Daily Brief (PDF). The VEEP's effort at containment fell short, and he backed off Keesport. That man is none too happy these days. He's trying to keep a changing climate as a domestic security issue off the President's desk, at least until after the mid-term elections.

"There is something else. Among your moderators and panelists, those I have heard about are prominent critics of the President and his administration's policies on a changing climate. That has unnerved some of the President's senior advisors and a goodly number within the Cabinet. You, Tracie, are not popular with that crowd - not that you give a tinker's damn."

"I'll hazard a guess that Keesport is aware of reporting by our foreign missions and no longer finds it necessary to raise her profile at the White House on the issue. There is no need for her to do so. Our ambassadors became proxies. Wow! Talk about timing. No wonder she hasn't called me!"

"You're going to hear from someone close to the President. Who? I don't know. It won't be threatening, whoever it is. The contact will be more an expression of interest, perhaps a request that someone representing the administration be invited."

"That's fucking laughable, Andy. I contacted those bastards early in the process. I wanted to give them the chance to join us, and no one would return my calls. They wanted to see if I could get this thing off the ground, and now that I have, their absence would be too noticeable. Well, they'll have to call me because my invitations have dried up! The *Post* signed on early."

"Yes, it's news, and coverage will be extensive both here and abroad."

They had been talking for close to an hour when Andy told Tracie how much he valued her efforts to broaden the debate on finding workable solutions to human-caused climate change. He let her know she had a legion of supporters who trusted her as an authority on the subject and was thus an important catalyst to engage others. "You may not hear from many of them on a regular basis, myself included, but you and your team occupy a niche only you are willing to fill.

Stay in the game!"

That comment caught Tracie momentarily off guard, and for a few seconds, she just looked at him before responding. "Thank you, Andy. Thanks for that. My team needs to hear that."

When Andy left close to one o'clock that afternoon, Tracie looked around the office and did a quick head count. Everyone was there, and she asked them to join her for a quick meeting in the conference room. She saw puzzled expressions because no meeting had been scheduled.

"Thanks, everyone," Tracie began. "In today's hyper-partisan atmosphere leading up to the midterms, some of you have undoubtedly asked, does anyone really care about the issues we care about? Are we making a difference? Well, I'm here to reassure you, we *are* making a difference. What we do matters to a *lot* of people out there, especially now." She went on to tell her team that they did more than earn a paycheck; she attached great value to their professionalism and their commitment.

Tracie then shifted her focus to the symposium. "Have any of you been contacted by anyone in the administration about our media project?" Two hands went up. Tracie smiled and asked who had called and the reasons for the calls. "We're on the radar at 1600 Pennsylvania Avenue. We're the proverbial burr under the saddle."

"Yeah! All right! About time!" several staff responded.

"I'd like to know whenever anyone from the administration reaches out to us. By all means, take the calls. Just let me know who it is and what they want. While we're all here, let's spend a few minutes on where we are - our outstanding commitments, the budget, and any unanswered questions."

"I have a question before we leave," said her cyber specialist.

"Okay, I think we do need to think about how and when our message goes into the closed societies we need to reach. We certainly have to watch our timing and monitor when we go public. As you know, our first broadcast will be on providing sustainable food supplies around the globe. So we have to break through the cyber walls particularly into Russia, China, and North Korea. Those governments will want strict control of that information."

"Yes, since much of my job has been trying to monitor the underground social media and getting access to blocked data, we need to reverse the messaging as well. I've been researching D. (D Dot), about which the cyber security team in the Pentagon has been skeptical ever since the old Wikileaks scandal, but it is much more circumspect, doesn't leak unvetted data, and is careful where they publish it. The most reliable hacking companies have long used LimeWire and The Pirate Bay. When we're ready to go public, we could broadcast our message to places we most need to target."

"Okay! We'll do it. My job will be to find out if we can do it with the White House blessing or not. And I really don't want to leak any information about our content and timing until Roberta Mitchell returns from her visit abroad after the first of the year. If her name or the nature of her visit gets out, the people we don't want to be alerted will be. I haven't heard yet from Wiley or Roberta, and I don't expect to, at least until Roberta arrives at her destination. Let's cover all our security bases before our launch, which depends on the broadcast of Wiley's panel discussion. Does anyone have anything further?"

Tracie looked around the room. Since everyone seemed satisfied for the moment, they returned to their respective tasks.

11

I n Seattle, Roberta and Wiley were wrapping up final details for her flight to Florence the next day. They were no strangers to Italy, having spent several weeks there on vacation a few years ago. A week in Taormina followed by a week in February on the Adriatic Coast in Comacchio, a town often referred to as little Venice in the Emilia-Romagna region. Comacchio allowed them to recharge their batteries. Roberta, European by birth, had heard about the town's well-known Water Parade (Carnevale sull'Acqua) and wanted to time their vacation to take it in. While there, they would divide their time between playing tourist and binging out on local cuisine interspersed with trips along the coast in both directions. For Wiley, he was able to get a little work done. He was able to compare data he had compiled on the effects of coastal erosion along the Adriatic with what he could observe. The data he had compiled from independent sources was, he concluded, accurate.

For this trip, Roberta would travel to Florence and then home. She, too, had developed a profile well enough to be recognized. On this occasion, everyone agreed she should fly under the radar and avoid Rome, for example, where there was a greater likelihood of being recognized.

She carefully set aside the material that would guide her discussions with Dr. Nuzzi.

She awoke at 4:30 a.m. Seattle time. Wiley was already up, a cup of hot tea in hand, and downstairs in the kitchen, waiting for Roberta to call him about her baggage. When she did, the bags were at the top of the stairs, and she was standing right behind them. "You didn't forget anything, did you?" Wiley asked. "I don't want to get a call later," he said, laughing. "No, Babe. I'm good." It was downstairs, out the door, and heading toward the Seattle-Tacoma (Sea-Tac) International Airport. The 20-mile drive at that hour in the morning wouldn't take more than 30 minutes, more than enough time to arrive and check-in. At 8:00 a.m., she boarded her Lufthansa flight for the 15-hour flight to Bologna. From there, she would be met and escorted to Florence. A flight of this duration in economy class would be exhausting, even in 2050. Executive-business class offered the privacy and comfort she required.

Captain Koenigen welcomed everyone aboard while describing his route and weather conditions across the U.S., southern Canada, and the North Atlantic. "Air currents above the North Atlantic can be a little turbulent in January, so we'll fly south of them, along the coast of northern Portugal and Spain, and land in Bologna. Our flight crew will now demonstrate in-flight safety procedures." They were now at their cruising altitude of 35,000 feet, and Roberta had settled comfortably into her private pod. She pushed the button to summon the stewardess. "May I have a cup of hot tea? Roberta asked. I missed breakfast, and I need to stay awake for a while."

"Would you like a warm croissant with that and some cheese?"

"That sounds great! It'll hold me until lunch."

Several minutes later, the stewardess returned with a tray in hand. While going through her briefcase, looking for two reports from a particular Korean client, she saw an envelope that resembled Wiley's personal stationary. "That's odd," she thought to herself. "What is his stationary doing in my briefcase? And then she smiled to herself. Quickly tearing it open, there it was, a note from the man she had loved practically since their first meeting on campus years ago: "Hey, Sweetie! Have a safe flight. I hope all goes well for you. I would love to have accompanied you on this one, but we'll plan something later. See you when you return. Call me when you arrive. Love until that final trip, Wiley." He had done this before; she just forgot and should not have been surprised to see his stationary in her briefcase. They made a promise when they married, one they always honored: never spend more than five days apart, circumstances be damned. They anticipated their professional lives could become complex, requiring individual travel that could separate them. As their marriage matured and success followed each of them, it would have been too easy to drift into a pattern of frequent and individualized travel. They vowed to avoid that. Both of them would make the point, "We married each other, not our careers."

Bringing her thoughts back to her mission, she began to jot down some questions she planned to ask Dr. Nuzzi about the political composition of his board, the demands on his organization from countries in North and Sub-Saharan Africa, and the division of program activities among the other branches of the Istituto. And then there was his participation on the panel that would surely heighten his profile among both critics and supporters worldwide. Nuzzi had shared his comment about becoming the flavor of the month with both Tracie and Alberta. They knew the pressure he would face from Russia via the Communists on his board. Roberta had to assess the ability of Dr. Nuzzi to withstand this pressure and remain an ally of the Director of the American Seed Bank in Tucson. The objective now was to strengthen - and sustain - trust with Dr. Nuzzi and his counterparts to share resources.

They agreed Dr. Nuzzi would not meet her on arrival in Bologna. He would send his personal representative to greet her, someone with whom Roberta could speak the Italian language as though she were just another Italian national returning home.

Roberta finished her tea and that great buttered croissant with the French cheese set her materials aside and drifted off for a quick nap. Lunch would be served in a few hours, and that would be her main meal of the day. She had selected a channel with easy-listening music and had drifted somewhere between consciousness and semi-consciousness when she heard a pleasant voice say, "Ladies and gentlemen, lunch will be served in a few minutes. Please bring your seats to an upright position and stow your personal belongings in the overhead storage space provided for you or underneath the seat in front of you." For Roberta, she had only to remove the materials from her individual table across her lap and wait for her meal to arrive.

After lunch, Roberta selected the recline position on her seat and settled down to enjoy the sleep she had interrupted earlier that morning. This was a lengthy flight, and she wanted to arrive fully acclimated. This trip was not the lengthy vacation she and Wiley would have made it had he accompanied her. This was a 72-hour in-and-out. Upon arrival at the Guglielmo Marconi Airport in Bologna, she stood in the international travelers' line waiting to clear customs and immigration. With that out of the way, Roberta headed for baggage claim. Ten minutes later, baggage in hand, she emerged into the terminal and was approached by a pleasant-looking, well-dressed young man who asked, "Are you Dr. Roberta Mitchell?"

"Yes, I am."

"My name is Franco Barbieri from the Istituto. Dr. Nuzzi asked that I accompany you to the Istituto." To put her mind at ease, Barbieri reached into his inside pocket and produced his official identity card as well as a note from Dr. Nuzzi introducing Barbieri. "Why don't you call Dr. Nuzzi while I load your baggage? He will be expecting your call." Roberta immediately tapped in the number Dr. Nuzzi had given her to use when she arrived.

Dr. Nuzzi came on: "Dr. Mitchell, how was your flight? Did Franco find you?"

"Yes, he did, Dr. Nuzzi. My flight was uneventful, just the way I like it. We'll be on our way momentarily. See you soon!" Now strapped into the rear seat of a comfortable, spacious FIAT sedan, Franco told her the drive time to Florence of 117 kilometers would take about an hour and twenty minutes, barring any accidents. "We drive pretty fast here, and when there is an accident, it generally involves a lot of vehicles. "Io faccio del mio meglio." Translated, it means, "I will do my best." Roberta understood and settled back. The rest was in Franco's hands.

Roberta's first call was to Wiley to let him know she had arrived, without incident, and was en route to the Istituto. "Hey, Babe! I'm here. Good flight. Now, on my way to meet Dr. Nuzzi.... Yeah!... Okay. Good.... I'll call you later on tonight... Love you... Bye." Her next call was to Tracie. It was late in Washington when the phone rang beside Tracie's bed. Tracie hadn't fallen asleep because she was expecting a call from Roberta, nothing extensive, just to let her know she had arrived safely. She picked up, noticing the image of Roberta on the screen.

"Hey! Good to hear from you. You're safe and on the ground?"

"Yes! The flight was perfect. Lufthansa is still my preferred airline for ground service, on-time flights, passenger service, and meal selection." She went on to tell Tracie that she was on the road headed to the Istituto. "I've spoken to Dr. Nuzzi, and he is waiting for me. I'll call you tomorrow with an update on our discussions."

"Okay, thanks for the update. Talk tomorrow." And with that, Tracie was soon asleep.

The next day, Tracie was consumed with calls to prospective panelists, ironing out details of presentations, and meeting with her communications team. They were sharing with her how they planned to make use of covert hacking abilities to get their message out, especially to those nations likely to block their transmission. "Timing is critical," her team informed her. "There are time blocks when we are more likely to avoid jamming and when we can optimize our opportunity. We enjoy this challenge." Tracie had full confidence in her people and their technical skills. She knew they were up to the challenge, and for that reason, she anticipated her symposium would achieve a degree of success that would surely rattle this White House and its supporters.

By the end of the day, Tracie was exhausted and just wanted to get home and sit in a tub of hot water then her phone rang again. She didn't recognize the number, and the caller's name was not displayed.

"Should I ignore this?" she asked herself. "I've talked to so many people today; my head feels as though it will explode." "If it's important, they'll go to voicemail. Oh, what the hell! I'm here. 'This is Tracie Hinton.'"

"Are you *Dr.* Tracie Hinton?"

"Yes, this is she. How may I help you?"

"My name is Jethroe Campbell, President of the Committee for a Free America."

"Committee for a Free America?"

Tracie was puzzled to herself. I've never heard of them. They couldn't be local.

"Yes, Mr. Campbell, how may I help you?" The caller's accent was thick - southern, maybe Texan, perhaps.

"Dr. Hinton, I'm calling about a symposium your organization is planning. We understand that several of the panelists will be unfairly critical of this President and his administration's stance on climate change." From the tone of Campbell's voice, Tracie sensed an unmistakable threat, but she felt it wise to glean as much information as she could from her caller. Moreover, she knew there was a broadly entrenched community of climate-change deniers firmly supportive of the President, and once informed of her project, they would make themselves known.

Responding to Campbell's accusation and striving to lower the confrontation level, Tracie patiently explained that her purpose was to share with Americans and the world the realities of a changing climate, the hardships, and the looming possibility of conflict over societies' means of survival across the globe.

"Our purpose," she went on to inform Campbell, "is not to criticize this administration as much as it is to have a broader conversation about the need for more domestic and international collaboration. I am sure you are aware, Mr. Campbell, that we're one of the major contributors to human-caused climate change, and that means our policies and practices must be subject to review. We have responsibilities that cannot be avoided that devolve uniquely on the United States." Tracie sensed this particular caller would take issue with her last point.

"Dr. Hinton, the members of my organization, and I feel you have a larger political agenda to smear the President and portray him at home and around the world as weak and indecisive on climate change because he doesn't support your liberal views. We find that unacceptable, and my members insisted that I raise our concerns with you directly." Campbell wasn't through. "You used the issue to weaken him in the midterms and will try to defeat him in the general elections in two years."

Before Tracie could respond, Campbell added, "Dr. Hinton, we know who you are. In fact, we know a lot about you. If you persist in this effort, you *will* hear from us. Consider this call an advisory." Then he hung up. Tracie sat at her desk staring at her phone, still processing the call from this Campbell person. "Have I just been threatened? What is this Committee?" She delayed leaving, opened her computer to her search engine, and began to read: "Founded in 2040 by Jethroe Campbell with headquarters in the Dallas-Fort Worth Metroplex, the Committee for a Free America is a non-profit organization of citizen-activists: Warriors For Faith, Unity, and Freedom, dedicated to uniting America. Its membership is largely in the Southwest, and it supports a far-right political-cultural agenda, financed by wealthy benefactors in the fossil fuel industry."

Campbell, Tracie learned, was born and raised in Oklahoma and was educated at the University of Texas at Austin, where he earned an undergraduate degree in political science and a law degree. He was a product of Texas politics, having been elected to serve on a local school board in Dallas County, the city council, and the Texas State Legislature. He had opened a private law practice in Dallas and founded the Committee for a Free America in 2040.

The Dallas-Fort Worth Metroplex was the Texas 4th Congressional District, currently represented by Charlene Randleman (R.-TX). Randleman was a member of the House Energy Committee. Moreover,

Randleman was certainly aware of Tracie's project. Could she have prompted Campbell to contact Tracie? Is it likely she was, in turn, prompted by the White House? "I sound like a conspiracy theorist," Tracie laughed to herself, "but then, how can I rule anything out unless I have some answers. People play for keeps in this town, and I don't intend to be an unwitting victim."

Tracie knew she had to know more than was immediately available. But the one thing she was sure about and that was a connection between Campbell and Randleman. Which panelists had Campbell been referring to? She'd just been threatened, but who could she talk to? She also knew she was not going to cancel her media project. The imperative now was to assess the credibility of the threat and how to prepare for it. Campbell said he knew a lot about her. Did that mean her family, Wilson, friends, or her staff? What the hell did he mean? Were any of them in his crosshairs? How much should she share with them? There were too many questions and no answers beyond what she had learned in her brief search.

Tracie got up from her desk and stood staring out the window at DuPont Circle below. She felt stiff in her shoulders and lower back. Perhaps it was fatigue, or maybe the stress of the call from Campbell combined with the pressures of ensuring her media project came to fruition. The stakes in this project were increasing daily. It was now the end of another day. Several of her staff were still at their desks; others had left. For at least two of her team, the office was more home than where they lived. Looking down, she saw the sidewalks were crowded, and traffic was heavy, especially in the Circle. Too late to get out there now. The forecast had been for evening showers, and it was beginning to rain. She rubbed her eyes, kicked off her shoes, and stretched out on her sofa. She let out a low, audible sigh and closed her eyes.

The weather in Bologna was cold and overcast when Roberta landed. They had been on the road for almost 90 minutes when Franco stopped at a security gate. The guard entered a code, and the gate slid open. They followed a curving cypress-bordered drive for about fifty yards and pulled into the carriageway of a lovely white villa. Standing there waiting for her was Dr. Nuzzi. As soon as she stepped out of the car, Nuzzi embraced her.

"Welcome to Florence! I'm pleased that we are finally meeting. Come inside." Roberta's first impression of Nuzzi was positive. He reminded her of home, being back in France. Once inside, Nuzzi said, "First, I'll show you to your room. You can unpack and then join me down here for some refreshment." If this is his home, it is beautiful, she said to herself. Roberta quickly unpacked and hung her clothes in a tall, wooden armoire, the type her parents had at home. Looking around, she had flashbacks of the room she shared with two of her siblings back in Lyon. And suddenly, she had an appetite.

She went downstairs, followed a hallway, and found herself in a spacious, pleasant kitchen floored with green arabesque Italian tiles. Seattle seemed so far away at this moment. The floor tiles were veined with gold and black. There was hanging cookware over a butcher table near the sink. The house looked old, but then, that did not surprise her. There were homes in Florence with a history that preceded the founding of the U.S. This could very well be one of them. Nuzzi pulled out a wooden chair from the worn, lovingly polished wooden table, gesturing for her to sit. She put her bag on the floor and relaxed as he busied himself at the sink with his back to her.

When he turned around, he was holding a sweating glass of cold, pinkish fruit drink. He pulled out another chair and turned it to join her. "I'm flattered that you have brought me to your home. It's lovely and reminds me of home back in Lyon."

"Yes, you're French. Right!"

"Yes, I am."

Looking around, Roberta looked at the small octagonal Roman-tiled counter, the wooden shelves laden with jars of dried pasta and herbs, seeds and beans, spices, olives, oil, preserves, and various serving and prep dishes. Fresh vegetables were soaking in one side of the double sink, and a jar of what looked like anchovies sat on the counter. There was no cook present. That meant Nuzzi did a lot of his own cooking. "Wow! Just like my dad used to do to give Mom a break." Sipping the fresh juice, which turned out to be pomegranate and maybe something else - quince - perhaps she wondered briefly how he kept it so cold. He had to have refrigeration capabilities both here and at the institute. And like her home in Seattle, Nuzzi's home was probably passively cooled and heated with radiant water lines under the floor or in the solid walls.

"You probably want to rest now," Nuzzi suggested, standing up. "When you've done so, I will have a special meal prepared for you. There's a carafe of water in your room and a stone wash basin and water pitcher if you want to rinse off before lying down."

Genuinely grateful for such hospitality, Roberta rose, picked up her bag, and put her glass on the counter. Nuzzi also rose and led her back through an archway toward the stairs. This house had a full second story, and as her heels clicked on the tiled hallway, she noted a few modifications the house had undergone: the filtered air vents, the return drafts and the air movement, the long, heavy, heat-prevention draperies over what must be windows to the outside grounds. None of these modifications did anything to detract from the charm of the house.

The canopied bed in the center of the room, with mosquito netting pulled aside and fastened to the posts, looked inviting. Sitting on it, it was soft! On the left wall were the marble vessel basin and pitcher. On the right side of the bed was the drinking water with slices of cucumber in it. Standing almost in the center of the room at the foot of the bed, the only thing missing was the sound of her mom bidding her goodnight. "Dr. Nuzzi," Roberta sighed, "my husband is going to be jealous when I tell him about your home. It will be difficult to leave here."

Nuzzi smiled and quietly slipped out of the room, pulling the door closed behind him. Roberta dropped her bag beside the bed and flopped on her back, not wanting to move to do anything. Out of respect for the cleanliness of her surroundings, she pulled off her clothing, hung them in the armoire, and availed herself of the water pitcher and basin. Feeling refreshed, she crawled between the sheets and fell asleep.

It was late morning when Roberta finally awoke. The house was eerily silent. Putting on a loose robe, she brushed her teeth in the bathroom sink and opened the hall door. It was bright and cheerful, and she found that the heavy draperies were pulled aside, revealing a lush garden of food plants - some banana plants, fruit, and olive trees. The ground sloped, and she realized the house must be built on a rise. She saw what looked to be a sun-facing greenhouse built into the hill. All of this was possible in areas of Washington State, and it could be sustained. Downstairs, she found her way back to the kitchen. The smell of fresh coffee invited her to sit down. "This is luxury!" she said to herself.

Nuzzi looked up from the table as she entered. In addition to the screen he had been studying, the table held a large bowl full of grapes, pomegranates, and peaches beside a platter of vegetable-meal sausage and boiled eggs. A place was set for her. She saw some muesli-like cereal and a pitcher of milk on the counter. She could see raisins in the cereal. Enjoying her wonderstruck expression, Nuzzi smiled. "Of course, I also have bread and some preserves to go with it. It wouldn't be Italy without bread!"

"I think I want everything, but I'll start with some cereal and fruit for the moment - with an egg," Roberta answered.

"In case you're wondering," Nuzzi interjected, "the milk is made from African Almonds. Would you like some of my home-cultivated honey for your cereal?"

"Perfect," she said as she picked a bowl up from her plate and went to the counter.

"Help yourself!" he offered as she served herself a healthy bowlful and returned to the table with the milk. He got up and brought a jar of honey from a shelf above the counter. When he was seated again, and she was slicing a peach into her cereal, Nuzzi said, "I was reading the news when you walked in - none of it encouraging." Swallowing a mouthful of peach, Roberta replied, "That is not surprising. Do you want us to have most of our conversations here or at the institute?"

"I prefer it here. I have had the house and grounds scanned for listening devices, and I have a blocking perimeter. This is safer. I will take you to the institute later." The rest of the meal was conducted in silence as Roberta savored the food and Nuzzi pursued his reading.

When they had finished eating, Nuzzi became more serious. "Dr. Mitchell (Nuzzi accorded Roberta the honorific of Doctor, or Dottore because she did have a Juris Doctorate degree), would you prefer we talk in the living room where it's more comfortable?"

In response, Roberta rejoined, "Dr. Nuzzi, most serious conversations in the U.S. take place around the kitchen table. It is at kitchen tables after the kids have gone to bed, that husbands and wives make the difficult, often painful, decisions that determine the well-being of the family, i.e., Can we afford a larger home? Can we afford to send a child to college? Can we afford the prescription drugs the doctor prescribed? Can we afford to get the roof repaired? Can we afford an emergency if something happened to one of the kids? That's why politicians and economists refer to 'kitchen-table issues' during campaigns or briefings. So, if you're comfortable, we can sit here while I enjoy some more of your delicious coffee."

"Va bene, allora!" (Very well, then). "Madam, the kitchen it is," smiling. Dr. Nuzzi began with some background. Roberta, coffee cup in hand, sat back in her chair as Nuzzi began.

"Dr. Mitchell, I know the big question on everyone's mind, including Tracie and the director of the seed bank in Tucson, is, how vulnerable are we to a possible attack from Russia, Eastern Europe, or the Middle East? I suppose you could say the threat is real because we are the resource everyone requires to sustain life - even beyond potable water: seeds. It is true, my organization and its three branches are everyone's target." Continuing, Nuzzi explained, "Anything I do to safeguard the seeds or transport them to another secure location would require the approval of my board. You wonder about the Communists on the board. Our Communists are steeped in theology, but they prefer life here in Italy to life in Russia. They're not ideologically hardcore to the point of violence. Would they cooperate on a non-violent level? Yes! No question!"

"Dr. Nuzzi, talk about your staff. How do they align politically?"

"My staff is young, well-educated, and highly professional. Politically, I'd say they were more progressive. Here in Italy, that makes them more centrist. They are alarmed at the impact a changing global climate is having on Italy; the loss of the Po River, for example. Many of them are old enough and young enough to remember the Italy their parents speak of, and they know their children will experience a different country." Continuing, Nuzzi offered, "My staff rarely interacts with the board simply because they do not trust several of them. And yes, they are convinced that the Russians, or a Russian proxy, will attack us. They support my participation in Dr. Hinton's symposium and have given me suggestions for others I might ask to appear with me."

"So, what is your plan to safeguard your seeds?" Roberta asked.

"I have identified some secure destination sites and, with support, we would be able to relocate some of them under cover of darkness, of course. We have safe shipping containers stored off-site at the Institute just for this purpose," Nuzzi responded. "I would never discuss this plan in my office for fear the details would leak. Possible destinations include Norway, Greenland, Canada, and the U.S., of course."

12

Six hours earlier in the U.S., Tracie had suddenly sat up on her sofa and looked at her watch. She saw it was almost eight o'clock at night. Realizing she had been asleep for almost two hours; she got up and looked out onto the street below. It was raining steadily, traffic was manageable, and there were fewer people in the streets. Looking at her watch, she saw that Wilson had called over an hour ago. Nothing urgent. He was just checking in and would call her later that night. Picking up her personal belongings, she looked around. Everyone had finally gone home, including the two who regularly worked late into the evening. The hallway was quiet except for the tap of her shoes on the granite floor. While walking to the elevator to the underground garage, she remembered the threatening call from Jethro Campbell.

"Campbell is going to be a problem," she told herself, "And we're going to have to have a full security presence to ensure the safety of our symposium guests." The garage was well lit, but she hadn't gone down until the ride-hail app showed her car was waiting. Shifting her bag to her left shoulder, laser stunner in her right hand, she looked warily all around as the app showed her car was now available. While there had not been any incidents recently, she did not plan to become the first. With practiced efficiency she was swiftly inside the vehicle with the doors locked, and the cab left.

Her commute home took her up 16th Street N.W. The air was cool and crisp, given the rain. Tracie lowered the windows enough to enjoy the night air. Twenty minutes later, she glided into her garage. Entering through the kitchen, she went through her ritual of making sure she was alone before going up to her bedroom to prepare for the evening. By 9:30, she was down in the kitchen looking through the refrigerator for a snack to enjoy with her glass of Chardonnay. She would call Wilson, but later, after she had spoken to her dad. Sam Hinton picked up. "Hi, Sweetie! Just getting home, or are you pulling one of your late nights?"

"It's been a day, Dad."

Sam could read Tracie's tone of voice as clearly as he could blueprints, which prompted him to respond, "That bad, huh."

"You always could read me, Dad. Saves a lot of explaining," she laughed.

"I was just about to join your mom upstairs, but talk to me."

Tracie sat down to describe her conversation, first with Roberta in Italy, and then with Jethro Campbell and his implied threat. "His organization was such a complete unknown, I had to do a quick search. Its headquarters are in the Dallas-Fort Worth Metroplex - 4th Congressional District. Its representative is Charlene Randleman. That's why I'm calling, Dad. Call me psychic or crazy, but I see a connection between Campbell and Randleman. If I start calling around about her, word will get back to her if I have to deal with her before I'm ready."

"Campbell doesn't sound familiar, but Randleman does. Her name came up in a conversation I had recently with Janice Boland, *our* representative. I check in with Janice periodically. Randleman, to be indelicate, is one of the Vice President's cutouts, a spear thrower when he wants to keep his hands clean. You'll recall that series of attacks against the governors of California and Colorado several years ago, one in which both came close to being assassinated?"

"Yeah."

"Randleman's name surfaced as one of the planners, but there was not enough direct evidence to establish her guilt. She is high-profile in right-wing causes, loved by her constituents, and supported by deep-pocket corporate benefactors. You should assume Campbell's call was not out of the blue. He is just the first at bat to persuade you to go easy on the President. Randleman is waiting in the wings. The Vice President is calling the shots." Sam could hear Tracie exhale. "Sweetie, you knew going in this these people would surface. They're violent, inflexible, and politically bent. So, watch your back."

"Yeah, Dad, I will. I also must ensure the safety of all those who have signed on to support us. I'll do what I have to do. Thanks, Dad! I'll keep you informed. Please don't tell Mom just yet. She'll be down here blocking my doorway."

"You know your mom. Good night, Sweetie."

Despite the threat from Campbell, Tracie felt relieved because she knew more than she had a few hours ago. Another enemy with a face. Her project was creating ripples that were reaching her shores. She debated calling Wilson. It was ten o'clock at night. He would be up because she had not returned his call, so it was better to call him. Tracie also planned to request information about Randleman's campaign contributors. She was betting Jethro Campbell was among them.

Several hours into their discussion, Nuzzi set his notes aside and said to Roberta, "Why don't we take a break and let me show you the rest of this place and some of the grounds. I think it will remind you of home."

"Okay, great idea!"

They went into the beautiful living room of the villa, whose arched windows were uncovered to reveal the property on the other side of the house. They were facing the corner of the spacious room with views through big windows in the two adjoining walls, which were shaded by an arched arcade outside the house on both sides. From there, Roberta could see that her host had grapevines growing in terraces on the hillside. Chickens roamed freely on the lush grounds. Franco, the driver from last night, was apparently patrolling the property. She wondered if that was his real function or, just for the duration of her visit.

Other than Franco, the view was so serene Roberta might have been enjoying a particularly wonderful Italian holiday.

"Dr. Nuzzi–"

"No *dottore*, dear Roberta. We are friends and colleagues. Please call me Giuseppe."

"Thank you! I will. This is so pleasant; do you mind if we continue our conversation? My husband and Tracie are going to ask me so many questions when I return, I just have to take advantage of you."

"I rarely have guests as young, delightful, and charming as you are, Roberta, so, yes, go ahead."

" I can't get the Russians out of my head and, what I think you're telling me is, tensions between them and the West are only going to worsen. I sense you and your colleagues are in real danger here."

"It is true we have Communist sympathizers here who do not want U.S. interference, particularly in the Mediterranean, where the Russians have direct access from Ukraine and influence in Turkey. Then, of course, I have had saboteurs try to get into the facilities at the institute, presumably for desperately needed seed and food plants."

"I was afraid of that. It puts the U.S. in a tight diplomatic spot, and my friend Tracie has reason to believe this White House is becoming more and more isolationist and under the control of right-wing extremists. Rescuing the planet will be much more difficult with such strong resistance from all sides."

"You are right. We will have to conduct much of our activity under our opponents' noses and speed up our efforts at the same time as the situation of so many countries becomes more desperate."

The two of them sat in comfortable silence for a few minutes while Roberta collected her thoughts. Giuseppe stood and said, "I am going to start our mid-day meal. While I am doing that, you are welcome to walk the grounds with Franco if you like, or take the time to do other things you want to do."

"Thank you, Giuseppe. How about we take a walk this evening?"

"Then I will accompany you and show you my greenhouse."

Roberta got up and went back up the stairs, carrying her shoes. Once behind her closed door, she stripped bare, took the caftan and some sandals from her bag into the bathroom, and without closing the bathroom door, she had a long bath. Following that, she did some personal grooming, brushing her long hair thoroughly. She combed it into a low ponytail and wound it into a neat chignon at the base of her neck. Then she tackled her nails. When she had the polish removed and they were shaped, she put on the caftan. Then she pulled the chair by the hall door up to the bedside table and applied a fresh coat of pearlescent lavender gel to both her fingers and toes. What a luxury!

Just as her stomach began to growl, she heard a bell ringing from the kitchen. She immediately put her bag on the bed, opened it and unfolded a blue dress that wasn't too wrinkled. She slipped it on, and went downstairs, where her host had set a lavish mid-day meal on the formal dining table in the living room. "Wow!" She thought. Water and wine glasses sat at two places facing the windows, and a water carafe and wine decanter were in front of the place at the end of the table. Giuseppe stood waiting for her, his hands on the chair back of the other place on the side of the table. He smiled as he pulled out her chair. When she was seated, he filled their water glasses and then poured a white wine from the decanter into two heavy crystal wine glasses, heirlooms probably.

The china dishes looked old and precious, of almost translucent ivory porcelain with gold around the rims. She had seen the sparkling glass and hollowware behind the glass doors of a sideboard in the kitchen. But she had her back to it and hadn't given it a real look until now. The meal took almost two hours - and the entire decanter of San Gimignano. They spoke of everything except business, sharing mundane details of their daily lives. Nuzzi, by now, was so comfortable with his guest, he did most of the talking. Roberta, delighted at his company because Giuseppe reminded her of mealtimes back in Lyon.

When they finished their meal, Nuzzi proposed he and Roberta take their walk outside, partially because it offered them additional privacy. Roberta helped him clear the table. The sun was low in the sky, and the shadows were long and inviting. They left through the kitchen, and Nuzzi headed for his underground greenhouse. He seemed to take particular delight in showing her the chard, arugula, zucchini, eggplant, and tomato hybrids. He explained that these vegetables adapted best and he used them in his kitchen. Following this, they strolled up the hillside and around the house to the grapevines. Little grapes were appearing. He had alternated rows of red and white plants. They spoke of places where it might be safe to move the plants and seeds from the institute and from the Spitsbergen vault.

"Giuseppe, previously, you explained that you are considering Greenland, Canada, and the U.S. as possible sites to relocate plants and seeds. What about France, Germany, or Holland, or West Africa? Are they secure enough?" Roberta asked.

"When we return to the house, I will pull up a map, and we can list the pros and cons of the various locations that might work. I don't see much of Africa becoming a combatant in the event of a war, and some of the countries formerly devastated by internal warfare, drought, and starvation have begun to work collaboratively to go back to older survival methods and share resources and expertise. Many Africans living in Europe have returned to their home countries."

Lying in bed fully awake, Tracie understood the connective tissue that bound the politically supine posture of the White House about the

North Korean missile attack off northern California, the effects of a changing global climate, and now, the not-so-subtle threat from Jethro Campbell. It all made sense, and that was rare in a Washington that on an average day little seemed to make sense. Jethro Campbell was the final piece of the puzzle. For the first time, Tracie felt a palpable sense of dread that she or someone she knew could be seriously harmed in the days ahead. Jethro laid that threat on the table.

The effects of human-caused climate change had descended like a dark cloud over much of the planet, yet hide-bound corporate egos held elected officials in a vise grip to prevent change, reduction in corporate profits, and their power to maintain the status quo. Even at this late stage of the debate, leaders in the fossil-fuel industry and their allies in the Middle East were still insisting that science did not support the assertion that climate change was caused by man. "We will have to match their level of determination," Tracie told herself, "Fortified with a counter narrative." Tracie had learned from her dad that it is the narrative that moves public opinion, not just facts, especially on a subject as controversial as the effects of human-caused climate change. She was anxious for Roberta to return because strategy was one of her strengths. Roberta was also a warrior who did not shrink from a fight. Roberta had commented to her once that "Wiley and I have each other's back; as long as he's got me, I'm good to go."

The two people in her world - beyond her parents - who understood the physical, psychological, and emotional rigor of extreme and prolonged stress were two of her dad's best friends, Shelley and Henry Carson. They were both in their early seventies, but they were in great health, mentally alert, and still read at least one book a week. If anyone could help her prepare for what the current tea leaves might portend, Shelley could.

About a decade ago, after the U.S. had reopened the American Embassy in Mogadishu, Shelley had been assigned there as the American Cultural Attaché. Henry, the other half of the tandem couple, was the Chief of the embassy's Consular Section. Life was not as precarious as it had been the previous decade. The Somalian Government had beefed up security for the resident diplomatic community. Travel after dark could be dangerous, and most western diplomats were encouraged to avoid being out without an armed escort.

Warlords still employed bands of thugs to attack shipping in the Gulf of Aden, especially vessels with American flags. Their owners refused to arm their vessels, preferring to negotiate the release of captured crews along with the payment of a ransom. One such attempt failed miserably and the warlord decided to retaliate against the U.S. In a brazen, daylight attack, Shelley, along with her driver, were abducted while enroute to the embassy. The driver was murdered as he attempted to outrun his abductors. When overtaken, Shelley's American assistant was wounded, and she was forcibly abducted.

During her 45-day captivity, during which her captors changed her location almost daily, Shelley was brutalized at least once, and subjected to the most inhumane living and sanitary conditions. Her fear was that she would be sold to a slaver or, if the ransom of five-million dollars was not paid, she would be murdered and her body left in the desert. "Every moment of every day, you lived in fear it would be your last. I resolved that I would survive, and that the worst that could happen, short of death, was that my captors would abuse me when they were not high on a local stimulant drug found in parts of the Middle East and in Eastern Africa, such as Somalia, called Khat. That's how I came through." Tracie wanted to talk to Shelley and Henry, but not before Roberta returned from Europe. Her friends were going to have questions about the nature of the threat she anticipated and she wanted to be prepared. Roberta may have learned something from Dr. Nuzzi's assessment of the threats directed against his organization.

The next morning when Tracie got to her office, she was still thinking about the challenge of bringing the symposium to fruition, its disparate parts, threats, Jethro Campbell, and the big unknown - White House reaction. Her assistant asked, "Do we have a target date for starting the broadcasts yet? The Sustainable Food one is supposed to be first."

"No, not until Roberta returns from Europe. I want to be sure that when I do, I have everything in place." Turning to her tech team, she said, "We're not there yet on the technology, are we?" They nodded in agreement. "Each moderator will give us a coded signal when they want to broadcast. Then we'll keep our detractors chasing their tails trying to find where our signal is coming from by bouncing it around as soon as we know we have intruders. We can do that, right?"

"Yes." "Sure!" "Right, boss!" "On it!" came the chorus of responses. That's what Tracie wanted to hear and they knew what was expected of them.

Tracie's inner circle of support was ironclad. Every one of them was committed to remain in the trenches with her, and that bolstered her confidence. The stakes were high and becoming greater each day. The likelihood of a personal attack was real, as was the possibility that someone could die. The thought that *anyone* could lose their life was frightening enough - but that someone could be *her*! Wilson knew it, her parents knew it, and Andy knew it. The subject just didn't come up. Now was the right time to have a talk with Shelley and Henry Carson. If anyone could have *that* conversation with her, who was more qualified than Shelley Carson?

Shelley and Henry were at home when Tracie called; they were most days. Tracie didn't see them as often as she would have liked, but everyone understood the demands of an active life, especially those two. "Come out this weekend," Henry told her. "We'd love to see you." She thought of inviting Wilson but decided against it. She had to fly solo on this one because speaking about life and death - her death - around Wilson was difficult. The protective side of him would surface, and if the subject was her safety, he was immovable.

Early on Saturday morning, Tracie rang the doorbell. Henry opened the door. Although in his early seventies, he looked good. Still with hair, he stood erect. "Come in here, girl!" It has been a while." His embrace was strong. Tracie didn't know it, but Henry worked out regularly and was still a fitness buff. Shelley was sitting on the sofa in the family room. Wow! Tracie thought to herself - a picture of grace, her hair immaculate. Shelley always said that, following her harrowing abduction, she would never go without her hair being washed and fashionable coiffed or her makeup perfectly applied. Tracie quickly approached her, crouching down, almost on her knees, to kiss the woman she admired most beyond her mom. "Baby, it's been too long!" Shelley mock chided her.

"I know, I know! and I'm so sorry. There's so much going on in my life sometimes I feel like an observer watching myself in motion."

"Henry chimed in: "We hear from your mom and dad that you're quite popular with a certain crowd." He laughed.

"Yes! I'm the current flavor, but you know what? The world has changed, and it's not that we and everyone else did not see it coming. People are starving-dying-and looking for solutions and leadership! Taking my life would be easy, but it won't solve anything. Many other voices want to be heard. Those who seek to silence me must know they can't silence all of us. People vote! And I think they will turn out in numbers in 2052 that will astound everyone."

"Baby, you sound like me a few years ago," Shelley said looking up at Henry. "Once you understand and accept what you are willing to lose, it gets easier after that. It's that level of awareness and commitment that makes you a formidable adversary. But, first, let's have some breakfast. We were waiting for you."

Over a breakfast of granola, vanilla yogurt, strawberries, and multi-grain toast, Tracie shared her plans for the symposium and the people she had invited as moderators and panelists. She talked about her themes; her various attempts to reach this White House; Roberta's trip to Florence; and her conversations with Andy Hillyard at the Post, Barbara Keesport at State, Dr. Nuzzi in Italy, and Dr. Chin in China. Tracie also talked about the threat from Jethroe Campbell of the Committee for a Free America.

"Quite simply, Baby, you're shaping public opinion and that makes you as dangerous as someone with a weapon. I was abducted not because I was dangerous, but because I was a symbol, an American white female in the hands of a brutal African warlord. My captor knew this White House could not withstand the public pressure of not securing my release. Not a day passes that I don't think about my ordeal, and that was several decades ago. My assistant died as did several members of the team sent to rescue me. I survived because I had Henry, friends, colleagues, and a government determined to secure my release. I try not to think about how easily I could have disappeared." As Shelley spoke, Tracie saw that steely determination in her eyes; it was still there.

It was Shelley's last comment that resonated deeply with Tracie: the knowledge that she could disappear. That was precisely Jethro Campbell's threat when he told her, "We know about you." Henry then spoke up.

"You know, Tracie, there is really not much you can do except always to be prudent. I'm not suggesting that you are weak or helpless. People like this Jethro Campbell will play head games with you. At the moment, he is the designated hitter. Conquer, or control, the pictures in your head that others try to plant. Pay acute attention to your whereabouts at all times. Always, always let someone know your schedule and where you are. Never be out of touch! If possible, always be accompanied, especially if it's at night. In fact, avoid working late in the office; work from home. Avoid underground parking garages at night. A great deal of awareness with a little paranoia will go a long way to ensuring your survival. You are the center of the universe for a great many people right now, and that is a huge responsibility. You wanted to make a difference! Well, now you're on the cusp of accomplishing just that."

Shelley added, "The worst thing is, anyone could be your enemy, Sweetie, from the administration and supporters of the President, industries opposed to changing our federal policies, or the zealous lone wolf. And then there are foreign actors you don't know, and haven't met, but are threatened by the change your symposium portends. Know who your supporters are, and stay close to them. They will be your lifeline in the event you need one. To be honest, the lone wolf scares me the most because they're invisible, faceless."

The day with two of her favorite people passed quickly, but Tracie was where she needed to be. Shelley and Henry were survivors who refused to be victims, and that made them a special and valued presence in her life. Driving home that afternoon, Tracie told herself, "They may come for me. I can't prevent that, but I won't be the easy target they're hoping for. She had also shared with her friends the larger role she envisioned for her friend, Roberta, and the likelihood that she, too, will be in someone's crosshairs.

"From what you've told us today about your friend, Roberta, it is obvious she, too, shares your passion and commitment to the work you're doing. She understands and accepts the same risks you do. Otherwise, she would not be in Italy right now! At the end of the day, have each other's back! But do not weaken your resolve!"

13

"Seventy-two, in and out; seventy-two, in and out, that's what this visit is," Roberta said to herself: "a quick three days, in and out," Tracie asked me to assess the vulnerability of Nuzzi's institute to the likelihood of pressure from the Russians. Second, to talk to him about his participation in a panel discussion. "Well, he and his organization are very vulnerable, and that concerns me," Roberta wrote in her notes. "He is excited about his participation as a panelist, which will only heighten his visibility and, unfortunately, the vulnerability of his staff, resources, and organization."

Roberta was on the second day of her visit, and Giuseppe Nuzzi could not have been a more gracious host. He was, as the saying goes, pulling out all the stops for his guest. Although this was a business trip, the pace and tenor of this visit resembled more a working vacation - emphasis on vacation - than trips she had taken on behalf of her organization. This trip had a distinctly European feel, replete with extended conversation mixed with details about home and family, home-cooked meals, great wine, and gracious surroundings with an escort. As Roberta would later share with Wiley and Tracie, "I believe Dr. Nuzzi would not have objected had I expressed a desire to extend my visit."

. . .

The previous evening, Nuzzi showed Roberta his maps and suggested where he thought the seeds from his institute should go and how they should be transported. The logistics of transporting the seeds, however, was beyond the purpose of her visit. She and Nuzzi had not discussed logistics during their initial conversation. Roberta could only hope that the business of transporting the seeds was part of a larger conversation Nuzzi had had with Tracie. Moreover, Roberta was satisfied that Nuzzi had a plan for transporting his seeds securely. Now, on the second day of her visit, Roberta felt the need to call Tracie. She would do so that evening. She had brought with her a mobile scrambler device to scramble their conversations as a precaution against the possibility her calls were being monitored. Late that afternoon, Roberta caught Tracie as she was arriving home.

"Tracie, this is Roberta."

"Hey! I was hoping to hear from you. Fill me in!"

"Well, our friend is looking forward to his panel discussion. He told me he has a couple of others he'd like to have with him."

"Did he say who?"

"No, but I suggested he take that up with you."

Good!"

"Now - the serious stuff. I will provide some texture for this next part. I do not believe Nuzzi's organization ranks as a priority in the event of a national emergency. We talked at length about the lack of security protocols one would expect from the regional and national government in the event of an attack, for example. The security of the seeds deposited here is entirely his responsibility and it is for that reason he is anxious to relocate them. He needs help!"

"I'm not entirely surprised, Roberta. But I needed to hear from you first. I have had conversations with the director of the seed bank in Tucson along the lines you suggested. She is prepared to travel to

Florence to assist Nuzzi to redistribute the seeds. You've confirmed what we long suspected."

"I would suggest sooner than later. Tensions between us and the Russians and the Chinese are escalating, and I am convinced the Russians intend to attack Italy. The leadership in Moscow seeks to avoid more internal dissent and the likelihood of more social instability. Although the population in that country has declined from slightly above 148 million over the past several decades to around 121 million, unrest is significant; millions are hungry, angry, and jobless, and the leadership is nervous. Using the military to contain any significant unrest is a non-starter because of dissent within the military ranks. Those seed banks in Italy could buy them sometime," Roberta added.

"And, if I interpret you correctly, Roberta, Italian authorities have other national priorities in the event of hostilities. This is what Nuzzi is telling us without telling us. He needs help NOW! Okay, I'll make those calls tonight. What else?"

"I plan to wrap up tomorrow and head back. The longer I am here, the more likely a staff member could inadvertently mention to someone that I am here. The question then becomes, 'Who is Roberta Mitchell? and what brings her to the IGV?' Someone will quickly establish my relationship with Wiley and our business. You and Wiley have been friends forever, and that connection will become obvious as well. An enterprising conspiracist like Jethroe Campbell will put the pieces together. That information in the wrong hands will quickly establish links to you, Tracie, and the symposium. We may as well paint a target on Nuzzi and his team and effectively eliminate the possibility of relocating his seeds. I plan to return as originally scheduled."

"Nuzzi, then, will conclude the negotiations once he's decided where the seeds will be relocated?"

"Yes, he will."

"Good!"

When Roberta hung up with Tracie, she went down to brief Giuseppe. He was in his study. Knocking, she entered and closed the door behind her. She explained to him that he should direct trustworthy members of his staff to begin to pack seeds in each of his four facilities and get them ready for shipping. Also, the director of the seed bank in Tucson will visit with him within a week or ten days to help facilitate the logistics and, if required, travel with seeds destined for those locations that may require secrecy. Roberta thanked her new friend, Giuseppe, for his warm and gracious hospitality. Her prolonged presence at his facilities could present difficulties for him, perhaps compromising his participation in the symposium. "That has to be avoided," she explained to Nuzzi. He agreed and told her that she and her husband would welcome guests should they decide to make a personal trip to Italy on some future date. The two friends embraced, and Nuzzi told her, "Franco will escort you to the airport tomorrow."

Before going to bed, she sent Wiley a text: "Sweetie, flight schedule unchanged. See you upon arrival. All is well." The following morning, Roberta thought she would slip out quietly to avoid disturbing Nuzzi. They had said farewell the evening before. As she came down the stairs, who would greet her but her beaming host: "Roberta, you have time for a quick Florentine breakfast. It's on the table. Vieni! Vieni!" Before her was a small glass of orange juice, toast and marmalade, and hot coffee. Ten minutes later, they embraced again, and Roberta was out the door. Franco had warmed up the car and they were soon on the Autostrada for Bologna.

This had been a successful visit, Roberta thought to herself. Nuzzi confronts the daunting challenge of redistributing the seeds without interference from his board. She could not help but believe someone within his organization would throw a spanner into the works. This was Europe! She also began to revisit another idea that had its genesis in this visit: Tracie is overextended, and she needs help. Wiley and I are going to have to find more time for her. The symposium will be a success, but what then? Tracie will have enemies seen and unseen coming for her. Her staff have roles and jobs, and their demands will also increase. No, she will need a few people whose judgment she trusts and with whom she can set in motion, knowing they are committed to the same outcomes. One of the first people she will turn to is Wiley, so we may as well be prepared for it. "I'm comfortable with that," she told herself. "I know Wiley will be as well."

Several hours later, Roberta boarded her Lufthansa flight for Seattle. Once airborne, she reached into her bag and pulled out a book she had wanted to finish on this trip. She felt time wouldn't permit once she resumed the pace of her life. Two films, several delicious meals, and hours of rest later, the pilot announced they would be landing shortly at SeaTac Airport. "Home!" she said to herself quietly. The trip had been purposeful, but she missed Wiley, especially at night. The bed in Nuzzi's guest bedroom was comfortable, but without Wiley, it was cold and lonely. "Gotta see my man!" she chuckled to herself.

Roberta processed as quickly as possible through customs and immigration and practically ran to Baggage Claim as though that would make her luggage arrive earlier. The baggage carousel was not moving and she could not will it to do so. Minutes later, the buzzer sounded, the red light flashed, and the carousel began to move. And then she spotted it, her bag with the bright yellow rope around the handle. Reaching over someone, she grabbed it and walked quickly to the exits. Emerging, her eyes scanning left to right, she saw him, all 6'-5" inches of him, waving his right arm. "He doesn't need to wave," she thought to herself. "I can't miss him," as she started to run. Now, in his arms, she said to herself, "NOW, I'm home."

14

"Do not weaken your resolve!" That admonition from Shelley Carson had been imprinted in Tracie's consciousness long after her meeting with Shelley and Henry. That meeting and her friends' counsel had reinforced what she'd heard from her dad throughout her life whenever she confronted a major challenge. She thought it laughably ironic that the one thing the leadership in this White House lacked was the resolve to address human-caused climate disasters. A changing global climate presented transnational challenges that the President refused to accept, yet his leadership possessed the resolve to shut down those who were trying to suggest public-private partnerships and more international cooperation to adapt to the climate crises.

Collaboration and cooperation offered the best approach to building a sustainable future, the only approach to avoiding conflict that could quickly make our world increasingly unhealthy and uninhabitable. "As a private citizen, I never thought I could be singled out for retribution by my own government, but that is where we are," Tracie told herself. "So, what's next?"

What was next was the launch of her symposium now that Roberta had returned. While having lunch with a journalist from *The Wall Street Journal* at the Foreign Press Club, Tracie spotted her friend, Andy Hillyard, of *The Washington Post*. She was able to attract his attention. To Andy, that meant not to leave before the two of them could speak. The *WSJ*, she was told, planned to run a series of articles describing the outcome of a two-day seminar hosted by the Washington, D.C.-based U.S. Chamber of Commerce with CEOs of the energy, technology, and manufacturing giants and their Washington representatives on the impact of a changing climate on American competitiveness.

The Chamber conveniently and strategically linked American competitiveness to national security to tamp down criticism they expected from climatologists and environmentalists like her. The *WSJ* and the National Chamber of Commerce are pro-business, and as Tracie's journalist friend told her, "Your community should not be surprised by the thrust of our reporting: these guys are bottom-line types, motivated by profit. They feel the competition across the board from the Chinese *laissez-faire* attitude toward regulation. That is despite the debilitating effects of a changing climate in their most populated cities - like running out of water or water that's too dirty to drink."

Each of the CEOs, Tracie learned, reminded the President's people attending the seminar that during visits to this country and our visits to plants in China, the Chinese made no secret of their economic war against the U.S. The Chinese did not use the term *war*, but that is how those CEOs interpreted what they heard. Besides, a CEO who read and spoke Chinese told the attendees a major Chinese daily reported that a senior ministry official in Beijing, speaking on the condition of anonymity during an interview with a German reporter, declared that China *would* become the world's dominant economy in this century. As the Chinese ministry official put it, "We know how to do it!" That last comment was carried out by major media in Germany.

Following her luncheon with the WSJ reporter, Tracie found Andy at the bar.

"Andy, thanks for waiting."

"You were having lunch with the WSJ. What's up?"

"I was getting a readout on the recent two-day seminar hosted by the U.S. Chamber for CEOs. I've been so preoccupied that I'd forgotten about it. Were you there?"

"Personally, no! But we did cover it."

"The *WSJ* is going to run a series on it. And I suppose the recommendations the Chamber will propose to the administration will be consistent with the *Journal's* reporting and further complicate the task for those like me."

"In a word, yes. But then, you're surely not surprised!"

"I suppose not. I feel the urgency of the threat - *not* how to balance the demands of the private oil companies with the country's survival."

"Hey, I'm feeling you. What are you drinking? You look like you could use something," Andy suggested.

"I've still got to get through the rest of the afternoon. A non-alcoholic light beer will do for me."

"Maybe I should have had one myself. Okay, about our meeting. Our person reported that those CEOs took non-negotiable positions on the administration's energy policy and, by extension, boxed the White House in on climate change strategies."

"Andy, we've known each other a long time. I know that private oil companies, with support from allies on Capitol Hill and Presidents from both political parties, have been dictating our energy policy for decades. That's why the planet is in jeopardy. These companies *never* take responsibility for the consequences of their decisions because they are captives of their business model and their shareholders. It is rare for a president to demand accountability from them without flaming out politically.

"But yet, you remain hopeful that somewhere in this morass of cynicism lies hope for the survival of our species and the habitability of our planet?"

"Without hope, Andy, what is there? Why not just find a retreat somewhere and forget all this shit! I have thought about it."

"Someone once said, 'Hope is not a bad thing.' You know, we've been dangling our feet over the cliff on the climate crisis for so long that many consider that posture normal. Awkward, but normal."

"That is infuriatingly tragic commentary, Andy. We'd rather threaten the health of the planet and life itself than change. How fucked up is that? Think of the legacy we are bequeathing our children - which, by the way, I'm delighted not to have. It's funny; my mom and dad pestered me for years about grandchildren. Now, they don't. I don't ask them why."

"My son and daughter remind me often enough how irresponsible our generation has been in stewarding the environment. And you know what my son's favorite question is when we get into these discussions? 'What am I to tell *my* children?' My daughter has let me know she does not plan to marry, nor would she want to bring a child into this world. So yeah, I get it!"

"Andy, let's shift to another subject for a moment. The last time we talked, you mentioned the likelihood, or possibility, that the South Koreans might take out a nuclear facility in the North because they feared an invasion. You also said the Joint Chiefs at the Pentagon were threatening to resign en masse because of our failure to respond to the North Koreans' attack on our West Coast. Where do we stand on those two fronts?"

"The two are connected in a complicated way. The Chiefs feel the South Koreans have legitimate cause for concern, yet the President of South Korea and his defense team do not want to be singled out as the cause for a mass resignation at the Pentagon. At home, our President would suffer major embarrassment, and NATO could rupture permanently - a principal Russian objective. That alliance is more fragile than is reported publicly. If the Chiefs walk, South Korea could lose the support of its principal defense partner, exposing themselves to greater pressure from the Chinese to become their economic partner under the Chinese military umbrella."

"South Korea," Andy continued, "was colonized for 45 years by the Japanese, and they do not plan to become a ward of the Chinese. Moreover, our defense posture in the Western Pacific could collapse and force Australia into China's economic orbit - more than it already is. At the moment, everyone has taken a step back. They seem to be waiting for what North Korea does next. The South firmly believes the North will attack again."

"If we don't engage North Korea on climate change stuff, I, too, believe they will attack, but this time, they'll take out Hawaii or hit us here on the mainland. Either way, it'll be too late then."

"So you believe China is orchestrating this!"

"I absolutely do!" Tracie responded. "They would see advantages in sacrificing the North, expecting an American counterattack. We would be a weakened presence in the Pacific and considered an unreliable ally in Europe. In the event of a limited nuclear exchange, China would absorb its losses. Politically, could *we*?" Tracie finished her beer, took a deep breath, and looked her friend in the eye.

As she stood to walk away, Andy said somewhat ruefully, "Take care, my friend. There are dark days ahead."

Tracie felt her head would explode and decided to walk back to her office. She needed time to decompress. An hour later, she arrived at the office and called Wilson. She needed to hear his voice, his humor, anything he might say to counter the overwhelming sense of futility she was feeling. "I think I'm going home a little early today. My head is cracking."

"I made a big pot of peanut butter soup with fish and FUFU. Shall I bring you some?"

"Yes." She knew that Wilson was reading her mood, and the dish he had prepared was one of her favorites among all the West African dishes he had cooked for her.

At 4 o'clock that afternoon, Tracie told her assistant she was leaving.

"You can reach me at home, but only if it's urgent. Otherwise, I'll call whoever it is in the morning."

It was close to 5 o'clock when Tracie arrived home. As her hailed ride pulled into her garage, she noticed a vehicle parked directly across the street in front of her house. She thought that was odd. Since few people in dense metropolitan areas owned their own vehicles, none would have been on the street. This was particularly true in the Washington Metropolitan Area, where traffic density in certain city sectors exceeded that in LA.

In her "burb," it has been much less expensive and more efficient to hail a public ride since petroleum-fuel vehicles had been outlawed by 2040. What she saw parked in front of her house was an undistinguished vehicle, perhaps government? Law enforcement? After closing the garage, she conducted a thorough check of her house and then went upstairs to look out the front bedroom window. The vehicle's windows were sun-tinted, making it difficult to make out the figure she saw.

"Who is this?" she asked aloud, "and why are they parked in front of *my* house?" She wondered if the occupant had been on her property, taken any photographs, or tried the windows. She quickly activated her perimeter security system because whoever was in that car had seen her arrive. They might conclude she was alone and therefore vulnerable. Wilson would not arrive before 7 o'clock. To call him before that without telling him it was an emergency would indicate she was feeling threatened. She decided to keep an eye on the unwelcome visitor. Perhaps he, if it was a "he," was there for reasons unrelated to her; she didn't know. Approaching the vehicle was out of the question, so why not take a walk in the neighborhood and get the identification number? Cowering in her home was a nonstarter.

Tracie put on her jogging clothes and a bright jacket. In the right pocket, she had her taser. In the left pocket, she had a whistle. Her phone was strapped to her wrist to get a picture of the vehicle and its number. After jogging around the block, she re-entered her front door as the mysterious vehicle pulled away. Minutes later, Tracie went out her back door and walked around her house, looking for footprints in the soft dirt under the windows or other signs that someone may have been on her property. She kept thinking that prudence and paranoia, in this case, made good sense.

A few minutes before 7 p.m., she heard the front doorbell. She knew it was Wilson and would have opened the door without question. Today, however, she glanced at the security monitor in the kitchen before opening the door. Yes, it was Wilson, but it could have been the unwelcome visitor sitting across from her home earlier. When Wilson entered, Tracie embraced him before either of them said a word, and she held onto him. Wilson felt her heart racing and knew something was amiss. Still holding the insulated bag containing her favorite dish, he whispered in her ear, "Baby, what's wrong?" He whispered because he didn't know if someone might be hiding in the house and she couldn't talk.

"I'm fine, now you're here." Tracie released her embrace while kissing Wilson lightly. Letting her lead him into the kitchen, Wilson set the insulated bag on the center island.

"What's going on?" Wilson asked.

Before responding, Tracie reached into the refrigerator, pulled out a bottle of wine, and poured two glasses of chilled Chardonnay, handing him one. Taking a sip of hers, she recounted events since her arrival two hours earlier. Wilson put his glass on the counter, walked back to the front door, and looked out. The vehicle had returned and appeared to be parked where Tracie said it had been. "Do you mean *that* vehicle?" he asked, motioning Tracie to look out the window.

"Yes! That's the same one!" The identification number was clearly visible. Tracie reiterated that it had pulled away when she returned from her jog in the neighborhood. Now it was back! She went on to explain, again, that vehicles were rarely parked on her street; her neighbors didn't own vehicles like the one outside. She asked without expecting an answer, "Why is it sitting in front of my house? I'm nobody, and I don't work for the government. Who is this" What do they want?"

"Since we don't know who it is, I suggest we contact the MPD (Metropolitan Police Department) to report a strange vehicle parked in front of this address the second time within several hours and tell them we'd like them to check it out. You have given the dispatcher the ID number, right? Now, *I'm* curious."

Tracie nodded, "In *this* neighborhood, they'll be here within minutes." Tracie dialed 911, and almost before she could pick up her wine glass, she heard the wail of a police siren. Rushing to the front door, they saw an officer on either side of the vehicle conversing with the occupants. They could see the driver pass some documents to the officer on the driver's side, who then returned to her cruiser to confirm the rider's identity. Minutes later, the officer returned and handed the driver the documents. She and her partner then engaged what were apparently two people inside in a brief conversation, and then the vehicle pulled away again. The officers came to Tracie's front door and rang the bell.

When Tracie opened the door, the officers identified themselves and told her they were responding to a call from her address. She invited them in and told them what she had experienced since she arrived home at 5:00 p.m. She showed her phone photos with the identification number to the officers. They admonished her that she had taken a chance going out by herself, not knowing who was in the vehicle or their purpose for being there. "Can you tell me who they were or why they were there?" Tracie asked. One officer responded, saying, "For privacy reasons, we can't give you their names. They had Maryland Driver's Licenses and said they were looking for the address of someone living in this neighborhood. They said they returned because they were advised to - that they must have gotten lost."

That explanation didn't pass the smell test with Tracie, and she let the officers know it hadn't. They agreed with her but said they had no legal basis for detaining them. They told her to keep an eye out, and if they returned, to call again. After the officers left, Tracie told Wilson she didn't believe that story. She was sure she was being surveilled, and it had something to do with the threat from Jethro Campbell.

Tracie forgot she had not told Wilson about the call from Jethro, so he naturally asked, "Who is Jethro Campbell?" She also knew that once she shared the subject of her telephone conversation with Campbell, Wilson's demeanor would change.

"Let's eat first," Tracie replied. Wilson gave her a look she could not mistake. "Okay! Okay! I'm going to tell you. The food must be cold by now, so let's talk while we eat. C'mon, Honey, sit down, please!" Her eyes glistened as she began to heat the food, so he said, "No! Let me do it!" Tracie knew that meant he had to distract himself because the suspense was gnawing at him. Wilson never, ever disguised his feelings for her. She loved that about him. She just had to manage him in moments like this. He was her rock, her port in any storm.

The aroma of the soup filled the kitchen. Tracie was hungry and feeling less anxious, and she sensed that Wilson was as well. She held up her wine glass as if to propose a toast. He did, also. "To us," she said. Wilson smiled broadly, repeating, "To us." That was a first, and he liked the sound of it. Tracie liked the promise of it. She also knew the time was right for them to take the next step.

That comforting thought was interrupted by, "So, what do you have to tell me?" Tracie took a deep breath and another sip from her glass.

"A few days ago," she began, "I got a call from a Jethro Campbell from Dallas."

"Jethro Campbell from Dallas. You've never mentioned *that* name before."

"I know. It came out of the blue. And when he mentioned the name of his organization, I had to look it up." Tracie recounted her conversation with him, more a threat than a conversation. She spoke of her subsequent meeting with her dad, what they learned about Campbell's connection with Congresswoman Charlene Randleman of Texas, and her relationship with the Vice President.

"I now believe," Tracie told Wilson, "That the vehicle outside my door had something to do with Campbell, Randleman, and possibly even the Vice President. The message was unmistakable: 'Suspend the symposium on a changing climate and avoid any direct criticism of the President's approach to managing the climate crisis.'"

Wilson listened, slowly sipping from his glass. When Tracie finished, she asked, "So, what are you thinking?" For a moment, Wilson sat silently, without expression, without emotion. Every fiber of his being was primed to gather Tracie in his arms and reassure her she was safe and everything would be all right. As comforting as that gesture may have been, it could also have conveyed how precarious he felt her situation was and the real danger she was in. At that moment, it was important that he not say or do anything to heighten the obvious anxiety Tracie was feeling. No, there would be time for that later. She *was*, however, in danger.

His first words were, "Whoever these people are, *they are serious*. You are going to need security if you remain here."

"Seriously! You believe that!" Tracie responded ironically.

"Yes, I'm concerned about you being here alone. He was careful to say *concerned*, not *afraid*. Tonight, someone had sent a message: 'We know where you are, and we can get to you.'"

Tracie sat, eyes fixed on him, looking for a sign, an expression, anything that suggested just maybe Wilson was possibly, or deliberately, overstating her situation. Nothing! She knew what she had to do. It was late in the evening. They had finished dinner, and the two of them sat in the living room. Tracie went upstairs to her hall closet and brought out two pieces of luggage, one large, took them to her bedroom, and opened them on her bed. She stood there momentarily feeling alone, looking down at the luggage spread across her bed. She thought about Shelley's abduction. Henry was alone at home, wondering where Shelley was, how she must have been feeling, and how helpless he was to do anything. She would never want to put Wilson in a position where he felt powerless to come to her aid, especially if her distress could be attributed to a decision she had made. She also felt a twinge of anger at being temporarily forced to leave her home. Wilson, however, was adamant. Later that night, they looked out the front bedroom window again. The vehicle was gone, but would it return during the night? A time when she would be asleep and vulnerable.

Her bags packed, Tracie quietly left her home and moved in with Wilson. The next morning, she called her mom and dad with the news. When Sam and Ericka hung up from speaking with Tracie, they looked at each other. "I knew this was coming," Ericka told Sam. "Keep an eye on her."

15

Tracie's resolve stiffened that night. This was the ultimate indignity - being driven from my own home by people whose only allegiance was to the exercise of power at the expense of the country and, perhaps, humanity itself. Her dad had spent the better part of a career fighting to prevail against similar entrenched attitudes and had to accept the rare success he managed to achieve.

The silence between her and Wilson en route to his house was deafening, at least for Wilson. He could read Tracie's moods as well as her parents, and he knew she was digging in for the duration. She would prevail if it ultimately cost her her life. That was too high a price, but he knew there was no talking her down. "I have to remain one of the constants in her life," he told himself.

Later that night, lying in bed with Wilson next to her, Tracie was emotionally restless and struggling to bring some order to the myriad thoughts crowding her brain. At first, she tried breathing exercises: exhale, inhale slowly, hold it for four seconds, and repeat. "Try to clear my head," she told herself. "I will not get up because if I do…" She glanced at the clock on her side of the bed, and it read 3:00 a.m. "I need help! Tomorrow, I'll call Roberta."

The next morning, Tracie struggled to appear in control, calm and prepared for another day. "Wilson can see right through me," she told herself, "but that's okay. He knows I have to work through my issues. He did what he needed to do, and that was to take me out of harm's way. It's now up to me."

When Tracie arrived in the office that morning, she sensed something, the lull before the storm; nothing she could pinpoint. Her assistant greeted her with a cup of decaf as she settled in. The phone rang, and when Tracie heard it, she said to herself, "This is it!" "Dr. Hinton, a call from Tucson."

"This is Dr. Hinton."

"Dr. Hinton, my name is Candace Verdugo, the assistant to the director of the Seed Bank here."

"Yes, Ms. Verdugo, how may I help you?"

"Dr. Hinton, I would have called you last night, but I wanted to be sure of something before I did."

"Go on!"

"Yesterday, the director seemed to suffer a memory loss here in the office, and we weren't quite sure what to make of it. She didn't seem to know who she was or where she was. We were able to keep her here in the office while we looked for the number of her personal physician. Her physician arrived and recommended she be transported to the hospital. They kept her overnight for further tests and observation. A few minutes ago, the physician called."

"And what was the diagnosis?"

"The director has Meningitis."

"Did you say, Meningitis?"

"Is it permanent or temporary?"

"We don't know yet. She will inform us with more details later. I know that you and she had talked about her traveling to Europe soon. You need to know that she will be unable to travel for the foreseeable future. I thought I should tell you immediately once we had a diagnosis. I will keep you informed."

"Thank you, Ms. Verdugo, and please do keep me informed. Your director is a friend of mine."

"Yes Ma'am, I know."

Well, there it was. The feeling that something was about to break. "Time to go into crisis mode," Tracie told herself. Dr. Nuzzi was expecting logistical assistance from the director of the Tucson Seed Bank. That plan could not be shelved because his need was urgent. Those seeds had to be relocated from Italy and stored in locations that were still being negotiated. Someone had to take this on and quickly. Greenland and Canada were possibilities, as were Germany, Holland and France. The only person I can call is Roberta. She knows Dr. Nuzzi, is European by birth, culture and education, and is a skilled negotiator and European linguist. "She would be perfect" Tracie told herself, but, "is she available? on such notice?"

As Tracie reached for the phone, she glanced at her watch. It was 5:00 a.m. in Seattle. A call at that hour would suggest a family emergency and, while her call was important, it could also wait until they were up. Tracie told herself, "I can't call Nuzzi without a solution to his problem. That is what we led him to believe we could offer."

Meanwhile, she called home and, this time, Ericka picked up. "Hi, Mom, it's me!... I'm fine, really. You know me, I was really pissed last night... I'm good now, just trying to juggle too many balls at once. My friend out in Tucson was diagnosed with Meningitis yesterday so I'm scrambling to salvage a project she and I were coordinating... Wilson? he's good. I'll be staying with him until *HE* decides (laughing) it is safe for me to return home.... No, I will not argue with him, wouldn't do any good. He'd lock me in the house! Tell Dad everything's fine... Bye Mom. Love you!" Sam had been standing next to Ericka when she took Tracie's call and could hear their conversation. When Ericka motioned to Sam about talking to her, he said no, he was satisfied. Wilson had her.

At 10:00 a.m., Washington time, Tracie called Roberta.

Roberta picked up because Wiley was still in the shower. She wondered who her first call of the morning was until she looked down and saw Tracie's image.

"Tracie, you don't usually call this early. Has to be important" - laughing.

"Interesting you say that because it is."

"Oh! What's up?"

"Well, it's about our friend in Florence and the situation there."

"Has something happened? Is he well?"

You remember I told you my friend out in Tucson, the director of the Seed Bank, was going to be traveling to Florence to assist Dr. Nuzzi in negotiating sites for the redistribution of the seeds and plants from the Institute?"

"Yes? When will she be traveling? or is she already there?"

"A little over an hour ago, I received a call from the director's assistant informing me the director was diagnosed with Meningitis just yesterday. She has lost her memory and cannot recall who she is or where she is. As you can imagine, she cannot travel anytime soon. The situation in Italy is urgent and I don't have options. That's why I'm calling."

"All right, Tracie, let's cut to the chase! Are you asking what I think you're asking?"

"Yes, Roberta, I am. You just returned from Italy; you understand the situation there; you know Europe, speak the languages; and you are a skilled negotiator. I literally do not have anyone else I can ask. This is a tough one, and I'm asking a lot of you two. Can you help me?"

"You won't believe me when I tell you what I'm about to, Tracie. Wiley and I well understand the importance of your symposium project, and the many balls you're juggling simultaneously trying to keep everything on track. I thought about this while flying back from Italy - how Wiley and I can help you manage some of the load you're carrying."

"Roberta, are you serious? Are you *really* serious?"

"Yeah, Tracie, I am - we are. Wiley will be down in a few minutes. Let me talk to him. Give me a day or two. We'll need to sort some things out. And I'll get back to you."

"OMG! Roberta. You guys are a Godsend. I was thinking how I could do this while keeping things on track here."

"No, Tracie, you're the hub of this wheel and you need to be here!"

When Tracie hung up, she was practically in tears, overjoyed. "It's going to work," she told herself pumping her fist. "It's going to work!" She got up from her desk, walked over to the window, and silently thanked God for good friends.

When Wiley walked into the kitchen, Roberta handed him a cup of tea and suggested he sit down: "Sit down, Babe." Wiley looked at his wife and wondered what could have come up so early. Their day had not yet begun.

"Remember we were talking about how we could free up some time to help Tracie, about how overextended she was these days?"

"Yeah, okay."

"Well, someone must have overheard us."

"What do you mean 'Someone must have overheard us?'"

Just before you came down this morning, I received a call from Tracie and she's in a real jam. And she asked for our help."

Wiley, still sipping on his tea, responded, "I suppose you're going to fill me in."

Roberta then explained the situation with Tracie's friend in Tucson, the one who was planning to travel to Florence to assist Dr. Nuzzi in packing and shipping select seeds to new locations in Europe and North Africa. "She was diagnosed with Meningitis and will be unable to travel - and she has no one else to turn to. She apologized for the timing and the inconvenience, but asked me if I could help. "What's the timing on this?" Wiley asked. "I told Tracie to give us a day or two to get back to her since I'd just returned from Italy."

"So, what do you think?" Roberta asked. "Tracie has been there for us; she's among my oldest and dearest friends, and if we can help her, I'd like to," Wiley said. "The team and I can manage things here. When would you have to leave, and how long do you think you would be away?"

"I'm thinking maybe two-weeks, maybe less. I really won't know until I talk to Tracie. This trip may involve some travel outside Italy, to escort some seeds, or to meet with officials in countries that agree to store the seeds. I'll have details later. Right now, we need to let Tracie know what our decision is. Let's take the rest of the day to think through what adjustments we need to make here and I'll call her tomorrow. Okay?"

For the first several days after moving in with him, Wilson noticed Tracie appeared less anxious and was concentrating her energies on launching her symposium. He knew that part of the reason for this was Roberta having agreed to return to Italy to work with Dr. Nuzzi. He was pleased with the new arrangement because he and Roberta had bonded quickly over the three days they spent together. Culturally, linguistically, they spoke 'the same language.' The three of them understood the imperative of packing, transporting, and storing the seeds from the Institute's four locations because time was not on their side.

Tracie's Mom and Dad called daily, but their anxiety levels were more tempered. Sam took great comfort in Wilson's moving quickly to get his only child out of harm's way, and as long as she was with him, the less precarious her situation became. Sam and Wilson also understood something else: Tracie would not be driven from her home for any extended period of time, have her independence stripped from her, and be reduced to a less confident version of herself. As Sam put it to Wilson, "I can tell you sure as hell that ain't gonna happen!"

In response, Wilson laughed, concurring with him and responding, "I know, but at least for the moment, she is safe. It's just a matter of time before she insists on going back home." Approaching a week with Wilson, as comfortable and as secure as she was with him, he was nevertheless not surprised when their Friday night dinner conversation came to the source of the threat they both knew was still out there. "I have to know," she told Wilson, "who is behind the threat. I'm confident I know what they hope to achieve. That is not the question for me. I need a name. *I want a damn name!* she exclaimed, slamming her open hand on the table. The old Tracie was back.

Late in the evenings, they would drive to her house to collect her mail, walk around her property, and check for footprints below the windows at the rear of the house. Physically inspecting the area around the house and the backyard was something Tracie insisted upon. They couldn't tell if anyone had been surveilling her house. And no strange vehicles were on the street during their visits. When they drove away following each visit, Tracie looked over her shoulder as if she expected someone to be observing them.

The following Monday, Tracie called her old friend Andy Hillyard and asked to meet. He suggested her office. "Okay," she responded. "Lunch is on me." Two days later, Andy appeared in her doorway. Plopping down on her sofa with his classic friendly smile, he asked, "So, why am I here?"

"Someone is stalking me hoping to intimidate me, and I need to know who it is. You're the only one with the connections who can help me find out. I can't walk around every day looking over my shoulder."

That was enough information for Andy to sit upright on the sofa with a you-got-my-attention expression.

"Damn, that's the shits! You've got me intrigued. What's going on?"

"Sure, but first, I'll get the salads from the refrigerator. I also have chilled non-alcoholic beer. You know me, I have to stay awake."

Andy dug into his salad while Tracie revealed her recent experience with the visibly unmarked hired vehicle outside her home and the police responding to her call, but refusing to provide any information about the occupants of the vehicle. For context, Tracie explained what she felt was a connection between the call from Jethro Campbell, his possible relationship with Charlene Randleman, and their presumed connection to the Vice President.

"As Campbell told me himself, this is all about their fear that my symposium will focus criticism of the President's leadership on a changing climate, or lack thereof, including our non-response to the North Korean missile attack. It's all related. You know me, Andy. I'm no woolly-headed conspiracy theorist." She went on to reiterate that she was sure the intent was to shut her down.

"Well, I know that's not happening. So how can I help?"

"Andy, you have connections within the MPD (Metropolitan Police Department). Is there a way you can discreetly find out who those people were in that car the night the MPD responded to my call?" Andy looked for a moment as though scrolling through a mental directory.

"I'm not sure. Let me think about it. If I can, you know I will."

Tracie understood that Andy was one of the most connected reporters in the city, and she did not want to jeopardize his ability to maintain those connections, especially with the MPD for what could be perceived as a frivolous request. Connections are lifeblood to a reporter, and they'd rather risk incarceration than divulging the name of a source. For the moment, she was satisfied to let the question rest with Andy. At least she had done something further to diminish the threat she felt. Two days later, Andy called while she was speaking with Wiley. "Wiley, let me get back to you… I just received a call I have to take. Okay?"

"Sure, but make it this evening. I'm heading into a meeting that could last over an hour, and then after that, I'll be tied up. So, let's talk this evening." The demands on Wiley's time given Roberta's imminent departure, were crushing, and Tracie felt reassured at her friend's stamina and ability to meet them.

"So, Andy, what's going on now? she wondered as she reconnected with him. "Hi, Andy. I didn't expect to hear from you so quickly, but I'm always pleased."

"After our lunch the other day, I talked to a good contact in the MPD who happened to be friendly with one of the officers responding to the incident at your home. I thought it best to be direct and honest with her about my interest in who was sitting outside your house. You know I wanted to make it a woman-about women's security kind of thing - a woman home alone at night. Told her you took the precaution to stay with a friend for a few nights while finding out who those people were." Andy explained that he was not shown the police report, but did have the names of the two occupants in the vehicle.

"Take these two names, Tracie: Amanda Swarthmore and Timothy Milton." A few seconds later, he asked, "Did you get that?"

"Did you say '*Swarthmore*?'" Tracie responded.

"Yes, Swarthmore S-w-a-r-t-h-m-o-r-e."

"Thanks, Andy. I do appreciate this."

Tracie sat there for a moment, her face reflecting momentary shock, disbelief. Swarthmore was an unusual name, and the only person she knew, or had ever known, by that name was her executive assistant - Alicia Swarthmore. "Could they be related?" she wondered. "Fuck!" she muttered under her breath. Alicia had been with her for two years - congenial, competent, loyal, a quasi-confidante - not on everything - but someone Tracie felt she would confide in occasionally. If this

Amanda and Alicia were related, that would explain how the occupants of that vehicle had her address. "In my own shop!" she screamed reflexively. Alicia must have heard her and entered her office asking, "Is everything all right?"

"Yeah, I'm good. Listen, I've got to run out for a moment. Something came up. I'll be right back. Don't forward any calls. I'll take them when I return."

"All right. See you soon."

Tracie was seeing blood, her pulse had quickened instantly, her throat felt parched, and it took masterful restraint to keep from blurting out, "Do you have a relative named Amanda Swarthmore?" But an inner voice told her, had she done so, it might have tipped off Alicia. Alicia never spoke of her family except to say on one occasion she was glad to have left home when she did. While that may be, Tracie had to know whether Alicia was related to Amanda Swarthmore. If so, Alicia was the Trojan Horse. The question was how to deal with this situation. Her larger concern was Alicia's motivation. Why would she betray her? Compromise her security? Alicia would have to know what these people might be about.

Downstairs now, Tracie entered the Dupont Circle Bookstore, ordered a cup of Chai tea and picked up a magazine. She wasn't interested in reading the magazine as much as she needed to have something else in her hands besides the tea. While she sat there, she talked herself out of firing Alicia. Better to use her assistant's presence to her advantage, she reasoned, and only at the appropriate time, confront her. If her staff knew what she suspected, they would want Alicia's head on a pike. Twenty-minutes later, feeling more in control, Tracie returned to her office. When she walked past her assistant's desk, Alicia asked again, "Is everything Okay?" Tracie nodded affirmatively and entered her office. She also decided against sharing this development with Wilson. He, too, would want Alicia terminated forthwith.

When Alicia left for the day, Tracie did something totally out of character and quietly went through Alicia's contact list and her desk. In a bottom drawer under some supplies, she found an envelope with A.S as the sender postmarked from Easton, Maryland. The envelope was empty with a date stamp several months old. She was careful to replace everything as she had found it. Okay, mystery solved. A.S. had to be Amanda Swarthmore. On second thought, Tracie decided to remove the envelope and then observe Alicia's actions. If Amanda was an active contact and not someone with whom she only had infrequent contact, she would notice the missing envelope.

Quietly, unobtrusively, Tracie monitored Alicia's body attitude at work for any departure from her normal behavior. She had not confirmed that Amanda and Alicia were related, nor had she confirmed that the A.S. on the envelope was Amanda Swarthmore. Observing Alicia was thus an opportunity to discover anything that might be suspicious, or warranted additional scrutiny. Alicia did not disappoint. For several days, she seemed more tense, tethered to her desk almost protectively. Late one afternoon, she emptied every drawer appearing to organize the contents of each. It was obvious, at least to Tracie, that she was searching for something she may have thought she misplaced. As Tracie watched Alicia, it appeared that Alicia suspected someone had gone through her desk. She must be wondering why that particular envelope was missing. What did that someone know? And what were the implications for her?

Tracie continued her routine in the office, but prudence dictated a few changes since her physical security, perhaps her life, was at stake. She closed her door during the day - a change everyone noticed immediately but shrugged off. After all, she was the boss. Tracie also spent more time in her office and circulated less. Interactions with staff, Alicia in particular, were now issue - or project- related. Previously, she had visited on occasion, enjoyed a social moment, or had invited staff to join her for lunch in the conference room. Tracie was now more restrained. Alicia sensed a growing estrangement from her boss, but could not recall an incident or a particular conversation with Tracie that may have precipitated the change in behavior. Of course, she could not have known Tracie had intended this very outcome. The first panel discussion of the symposium was already in the works. If Alicia was sharing information with Jethro Campbell and his people through

A.S., there could be violence at any moment, and she would be help-less. The next step in Tracie's plan was to prompt a reaction from Alicia.

The following day, one of the contract couriers delivered a brown envelope to reception from an A. Swarthmore to Alicia Swarthmore marked personal. Alicia had stepped away from her desk momentarily. The receptionist placed it on Alicia's desk in plain view. Minutes later, Alicia returned. When she saw the envelope, her face became ashen. Furtively, she looked around as though she expected someone was watching her. She sat down, hunching forward with both palms on the desk to look at the envelope. Alicia hesitated, then reached into a drawer, extracted a letter opener, and opened it. Setting the opener aside, she looked inside and saw the missing white envelope. Someone had drawn a line through the initials A.S. and written Amanda Swarthmore above them.

Tracie was watching to observe how her subterfuge played out. Alicia nervously placed the larger envelope in her bag under her desk and sat there. She then went to the ladies' room where she undoubtedly placed a call. Any call she made to Amanda would have caught the latter off guard, raising the other woman's suspicion that someone was onto them. But who!? Back at her desk, Alicia could only play a guessing game and wonder what to expect next. Strangely, she did not ask reception about who had delivered the envelope. Tracie, again, chose not to confront her, but was now convinced Alicia was Aman-da's connection to Jethro Campbell. She would release Alicia - and soon.

Early the next morning, Tracie asked Alicia to come into her office. Alicia was visibly ill at ease. Tracie asked if she'd like something to drink. When Alicia declined, she began to explain the staff reorganiza-tion she was planning. Tracie claimed she had less need for an assistant but a great need to bring on another IT professional familiar with the universe of a changing global climate. She would, of course, give her two weeks to seek other opportunities including time away should she need it during the day. "If you prefer not to come in, I'll understand," Tracie told her.

Alicia asked if her performance had been an issue. Tracie thought for a moment before responding. "No, Alicia, that is not the issue. We are growing rapidly, and that necessitates a review of current and projected staff requirements. Another consideration is the requirement for enhanced physical security. I have a responsibility to my staff, to our consultants, and to our contributors. You and I work closely, and you know there are people out there who would shut us down if they could." That last comment was a direct signal to Alicia that Tracie was onto her. Alicia understood she was being offered a way out - with two weeks' pay, a reference, and no ugly confrontation and abrupt termination. Tracie later told her parents that the reasons for terminating her assistant the way she had were simple: "Why deepen the resolve of someone already aligned against you? Maybe, just maybe, Alicia may have been a victim herself. I don't know. I have a symposium to launch and an immediate problem to solve with the least impact on me psychologically. Believe me, I wanted to thrash her for my immediate gratification. But I can live with this outcome."

Tracie's tech team had decided on the combination of covert communication channels that would be most effective and least likely to be traced. She had told the team that the first panel was ready to go and she expected to hear from the water panel soon. Once they had two in the can, so to speak, they needed to decide the timing between broadcasts. What amount of time should lapse, and would a longer or shorter time interval make succeeding broadcasts more likely to be intercepted? Tracie told her tech team, "all of our adversaries will employ their latest technologies to monitor our broadcasts. Simultaneously, they will also try to implement a blackout of our transmission to prevent the dissemination of information. Information in the hands of informed and angry populations is tantamount to making loaded weapons available." She continued: "Concurrent with efforts to contain social unrest, the Russians may just move quickly to seize and control the seed banks in Italy. Moreover, they may have inside information regarding the likelihood of Greenland and Canada as possible recipients of seeds from Italy. I don't know! What I am saying is, 'once we go live, anything could happen.'"

Another member of her staff, the Asia specialist, intoned, "Don't forget the North Koreans. They are erratic, a wild card, and in a position to attack us. They will be monitoring our broadcasts as well."

16

It was still dark when Wiley returned from Seattle-Tacoma International Airport that Saturday morning. There was water ponding on the roads, and traffic was dense. Roberta did not want to find herself at the tail end of a lengthy line of passengers, and so they left home earlier than usual. Her Lufthansa flight was still listed online as an *on-time departure*, even with severe thunderstorms forecast until midday.

Standing in the kitchen at the far end of the island, cradling his coffee cup in both hands, Wiley noticed Roberta's cup a few feet from where he was standing. She loved that cup, a gift from him. It said "THE BOSS!" in large letters. "If you don't believe it, ASK ME! Looking at the cup, there was the faint imprint of her lipstick. Next to it was the small plate containing a piece of half-eaten, 7-grain, buttered toast. Normally, this early morning hour was a shared moment at the beginning of each day: a conversation about whatever was on their minds when they woke up, a review of the day's schedule, important appointments, dinner out with clients, or the two of them at home. Their preference was always the latter. Years into a successful marriage, they still preferred each other's company at the end of the day. To Wiley, standing there looking around, the kitchen seemed unusually large, not that anything had changed. His thoughts seemed to be reverberating off the walls and the cabinets. He placed his cup in the sink but left Roberta's cup on the island - as if it shouldn't be moved - at least not at that moment.

He went upstairs to their bedroom and began to undress; it was still early. Across the foot of the bed was his wife's nightgown, something he rarely took notice of. This morning, for some reason, he did. Her slippers on the floor just below it. He hung the nightgown in the closet, as she would have done before coming downstairs - the slippers just below the gown. Habitually, after undressing in the closet, she reached for her gown while slipping her feet into the slippers. It was in those moments when she was preparing for bed that he would come up behind her, throw his arms around her, and draw her into him while playfully chewing on her ear. Missing from the counter in the bath-room was her hairbrush, makeup, toothpaste, and perfume. *Missing was the scent of her.*

He decided against going back to bed and went downstairs to their shared office. Wiley felt off his rhythm; something was missing from his emotional framework, and he knew what it was. Whenever one of them traveled, in the kitchen, the bedroom, or their office, or on their phone, was a copy of the flight schedule - the all-important arrival time. You scheduled your day around the arrival time of the other. Today, that was the missing piece. *He did not know when she would return!* Wiley understood why, but for the first time in their long and happy marriage, they did not know when she would return from a trip: a week, ten days, or more. When the project with Nuzzi was completed, it was about the best they could figure. He valued the trust he and Tracie had formed, but, on this occasion, that trust came with a price tag. He and Roberta were all in. And so now, while Roberta was away when his phone rang, there would be the emotional urgency to pick it up more quickly than usual. A phone call was not just a part of his day. She might call, and he might miss it. He had to think about that possibility.

Thirty-five thousand feet above sea level, comfortably ensconced in her semi-private, business-class accommodations, Roberta sat wistfully looking out the window, her right hand fingering the wedding ring on her left hand. She, too, felt off. She had just returned from a trip to Italy, and now she was going back, but for an indefinite period. Nothing interminable, just indefinite. She thought to herself, "Only for you, Tracie. Only for you."

As expected, Franco was on hand to greet Roberta when she arrived in Bologna. "Piacere di rivederla così presto, Dottoressa Mitchell." ("Great to see you again so soon, Dr. Mitchell.")

"Grazie, Franco."

While Franco loaded her bags, Roberta settled into the back seat for the long drive to Florence. What adventure lay ahead, she wondered. This experience, just might be worth publishing, was another fleeting thought.

Dr. Nuzzi was up and waiting for her when the car pulled up to his villa. "Roberta, I was not expecting you, but I am delighted that you were able to return so quickly. We have a lot to do! But, first, let's get you settled." Roberta went upstairs, but before unpacking, she called Wiley. "I'm here, Babe. The flight seemed longer this time; I think I know why." "Yes, I miss you, too! I plan to tell Tracie she owes us one." Laughing. "Giuseppe told me to tell you how much he appreciates our assistance. He feels very vulnerable and, having been here so recently, I understand." … "Okay! Go back to bed. Love you, too." She unpacked and went back down to join Giuseppe in the kitchen.

"So, Giuseppe, where do we begin!" Roberta asked, sitting down at the kitchen table.

"I had begun to formulate a plan before you left," Nuzzi began. "When Dr. Hinton launches her broadcasts, the situation here, or our reality, could change quickly. My greatest fear is a visit from our friends in Moscow. We have four locations, two of which are accessible by water: Palermo and Portici." He went on to explain the ease and feasibility of a water-borne, night attack on those two sites, attacks facilitated by a member of the staff ideologically committed and willing to assist in the relocation of select seeds. A highly-trained team could be in and out before morning with minimal or no loss of life.

"And, what is your plan?"

"I know who I can trust in both locations, and my plan is to pack and transport seeds in both locations over land to Florence. Franco will fly to Palermo the day the seeds are packed and pick up a truck that will have been rented and prepositioned. When he receives a call from my person there, he will drive over in the early evening, pick up the containers, and begin the 12-hour drive back here. He can make the entire 1,170-kilometer drive under the cover of darkness. That's phase one. Phase two begins in Portici when the seeds are packed and ready for transport. A friend of mine in the city has agreed to rent a vehicle and will supply a driver to do essentially the same: pick up the containers at a prearranged time and drive the 474 kilometers to an address here in Florence. I don't want two deliveries on the same day; it might appear suspicious."

"So, you would have the bulk of the seeds here in Florence. Then what?"

"Then we begin phase three, and that's where you come in. And I'd like your candid thoughts."

"I have been living on the telephone since before, and subsequent to, your recent visit. Holland and France have agreed to store some of the seeds, but the bulk would be shipped by air to Greenland and Canada. You would be accompanying both shipments. I've done business with ministry officials in both countries. They share my concern about the harm that would accrue should the Russians attack and gain control of our inventory. I know that you have consulted in both countries and, therefore, your presence would not be out of the ordinary. The crates would be listed as soil samples."

"Giuseppe, I am feeling relieved!

"I thought you might. The better decision is for me to remain here in the short term, visible to all who might be watching, at least until the symposium. They will see you come and, at some point, see you depart. We can work out the schedule from here. So, what do you think?"

"You didn't mention Perugia!"

"Perugia is more inland and only 151 kilometers away - a 90-minute drive. These two locations - Perugia and Florence - are, in my view, lesser priorities for an attack than Palermo and Portici. I could be wrong but, if I were planning an attack, that is how I would proceed."

"How would you prioritize seeds for each location?"

"I'm glad you asked. Seeds for the Mediterranean and North Africa would be stored in France. That seemed appropriate, given the country's historical relationship to both regions. Holland is a logical destination for both West and Eastern Europe, including Scandinavia and the Baltics. And Canada would house seeds for the Americas, both North and South; and Greenland, also, the Indo-Pacific."

"The challenge is to schedule travel to Greenland and Canada - one trip or two."

"Is it possible then to have seeds from the other three locations here in Florence within this week?"

"Absolutely! I plan to call everyone on Monday. We will package the seeds for France and Holland to be ready for shipment next week. When I call on Monday, I will request customs documents for all locations. I don't want to prevail upon you any longer than is necessary to get this done. I am also well aware of the sacrifice you are making. It's just that there is so much at stake."

"It is, Giuseppe, and all of us are indebted to you. None of us wanted to leave you isolated in this moment of global crisis."

Nuzzi then shifted his focus to Greenland and Canada. "Before we talk about Greenland and Canada, you should know, Roberta, that everyone who has agreed to store seeds worries about the Russians and their lack of respect for norms and international law. But we all agreed that the geography of France and Holland, more so than Italy, would complicate any attempts by the Russians to seize the seeds stored in both countries.

Now, Greenland and Canada. Greenlanders and Danes control the country and share responsibility for its defense. The U.S. formerly had an air base there until they were expelled. As I understand it, between the Danes, the Greenlanders, and the Americans, they couldn't sustain a working agreement on U.S. overflights within and around Greenland's airspace. I share that in case you were wondering why we could not get the Americans to handle this request for us. You would have to accompany the seeds to both countries. This week, I will also work on arranging a flight via SAS (Scandinavian Airlines) from Milan's Malpensa Airport to Nuuk Airport in Greenland. I'm thinking of a departure date of early-to-mid next week. Our people in Greenland will need a few days to prepare the customs documents and get them to me. That particular flight will take just over 17 hours. "I know all of this sounds exhausting, Roberta, and I wish I could make it more palatable for you. I would gladly undertake this task if I were physically up to it."

"Just a thought, Giuseppe, but would it be possible for me to bring the seeds for Canada on the same flight? Say, if I were to spend a day or two in Greenland, the seeds for Canada could be held in secure storage and then placed on my ongoing flight to Canada. I avoid the necessity to make two flights."

"Yes, that is what we are trying to arrange. In both countries, you will want to know the security arrangements for where the seeds are stored and how they can be accessed.

Wiley decided to work from home that morning, at least until around mid-day. It was too early to call his assistant, so he flipped on cable news to catch any overnight developments. Nothing new or of any consequence, especially out of Washington, D.C. He changed to local news to track the weather. Thunderstorms could paralyze local traffic, and he wasn't in the mood to deal with that.

Around 7:30 a.m., before he called his assistant, his phone rang. While picking it up, he noticed it was a 645-area code. He didn't recognize the area code, but it was early, and the call could have been important.

"Wiley Mitchell, Good Morning!"

"Dr. Wiley Mitchell of Marine Solutions International?"

"Yes, this is he."

"Dr. Mitchell, my name is Sergio Hernandez, the Director of the EPA in Miami."

"And how may I help you, Mr. Hernandez?"

"Well, I was referred to you by Lester Charles, my counterpart in Boston. We were attending a meeting in New York City a week ago. I was sharing with him some issues I was dealing with, and your name came up."

"Yes, I know Lester. He is originally from Detroit, as I am. How is he these days? I haven't seen him in a while."

"He's got his hands full, as many of us along the Atlantic Coast do. I'm calling because I can use your help, Dr. Mitchell."

"Okay, I'm listening."

"I've done some research on you and your company. You're familiar with rising ocean levels along the Atlantic Coast and the impact higher water levels have had on many communities. Our data reveals an accelerated rate of erosion around Miami, which, when combined with the impact of a longer and more destructive hurricane season and the impact of atmospheric rivers redistributing water to other latitudes, forces us to revisit our five-year plans in several key areas. Tourism, international banking, and trade are the three pillars of our economy, and rising water levels impact all three. Tourism across the board is decreasing by double digits, fears of more accelerated erosion threaten our infrastructure, and investors seek alternative locations. Economics and politics are intertwined and can be a corrosive mix. Frankly, we need help. Would you be available to meet with a group I'm putting together within the next ten days?"

"Give me a moment, Mr. Hernandez." Seconds later, Wiley comes back on. "Yes, I'd be available. To help me prepare for our meeting, please forward copies of your most recent Emergency Action Plans, your Five-Year Economic Development Plan, and any other data that would be helpful. I want to be able to contribute to the conversation."

"You should plan on spending two to three days, Dr. Mitchell, if that would not be an inconvenience. I'll have my assistant be in touch regarding the materials you requested and travel arrangements."

"Thank you, Mr. Hernandez. We'll be in touch."

Wiley sat there for a moment as though he were trying to recall something. And then it hit him: a conversation he'd had seven years ago at a meeting in Atlanta. The occasion was a meeting of The American Planning Association at the Atlanta Marriott. He was in town to meet with a client who had invited him to join him at the bar in the Marriott. While sitting together, his guest motioned to Jessica Montalvo, the then EPA Director in Miami and also a guest at the hotel, to join them. Invariably, the topics were economic development, urban planning and resource management, and the effects of human-induced climate change on planning. As Wiley remembered, Jessica was an engaged and unforgiving conversationalist when challenged, perhaps because many of her interlocutors were male. Or, that may have been her personality. For example, her opinions on the subject of climate change and the necessity to factor in climate change as a variable for planning purposes were narrow and less science-based than Wiley was comfortable with.

When he suggested data-driven models could be a useful tool for planning purposes when attempting to measure degrees of erosion, she took a narrower line of reasoning. She believed that in Miami, for example, several of the models presented for consideration by the political leadership may have been politically motivated. Wiley recalled asking her the basis for that conclusion. Her response was to the effect that the rate of erosion was being overstated to undercut the model city officials and the business community preferred. He had enough experience to know that the proclivity among many elected officials was to reject facts and data when facts and data contradicted their preferred political positions, especially on climate change matters.

When Wiley returned home, he was sharing his experience with Roberta. To satisfy himself, Wiley did some research only to discover that the model Jessica and the Miami city officials preferred - and adopted - did understate the gravity of the problem to gain the support of the Miami business community. Jessica did move on from Miami several years later and was succeeded by Sergio Hernandez. Wiley concluded Hernandez inherited a political problem for which he was now charged with correcting, especially considering the current state of Miami's economy.

17

erminating Alicia was just the first step in Tracie's complex process to identify those attempting to silence a voice they feared and preserve the political future of a sitting President and a Machiavellian Vice President. A Vice President who also aspired to succeed the current President. Together, the President and Vice President were a toxic duo who represented as grave a security threat to the country as its foreign enemies. They had launched a comprehensive plan to discredit and silence prominent critics like Tracie and what they feared could be a growing legion of supporters. The Vice President was overheard saying to one of their supporters, "That bitch (Tracie Hinton) has a big mouth - but we're working on silencing it."

When word filtered back to Tracie through reliable channels about the Vice President's characterization of her, she said - laughing - "He hasn't seen the best of me yet!" It was May, and that very day, she got a call from Alicia. Tracie looked at her phone half expecting the call to be a mistake. It wasn't.

"Alicia, this is Tracie. I am surprised to hear from you."

"Yes, I figured you would be. Do you have a minute? Please don't hang up."

"Yes, what's up?"

"I'd very much like to see you if you're available. There's something you need to know." Tracie thought for a minute. Alicia hadn't volunteered to tell her *what* the matter was, but she wanted a meeting. Whatever it is, it must be important. Why not meet with her? "Okay, what do you have in mind?" Tracie inquired.

Alicia correctly assumed Tracie didn't trust her and would not want to meet at night or in a location that left her feeling vulnerable.

"How about the DuPont Circle Bookstore tomorrow at 10 a.m.? And, Tracie, you can trust me. I owe you."

The *"you can trust me"* bit sounded sincere, so Tracie agreed to the time and place of the meeting. The next morning, Tracie arrived at the bookstore a few minutes early. For her own comfort, she wanted to see how many people were there and if someone looked out of place. Being a frequent customer, she had a feel for the clientele who came in, what they looked like, and how they interacted. She picked out a table close to the door. Minutes later, she spotted Alicia entering and motioned to her. Alicia was dressed casually, wearing a white jogging suit and running shoes, not like someone coming from an office. Sunglasses and a baseball cap pulled down to her ears accessorized her informal attire.

As Alicia sat down, she thanked Tracie for coming: "I know this may feel awkward for you, but as I said, I have something to tell you." Alicia appeared earnest and that eased the tension Tracie felt. "However, before I do, I also want to thank you for treating me with the respect you did on my last day in the office. That situation could have been considerably worse for me." Tracie nodded her head in acknowledgment, waiting to hear what Alicia had to say. Alicia began by admitting, "Amanda is my older sister; you may have guessed. I don't know; I suppose I should start at the beginning. Please hear me out."

For the next hour, Alicia shared details of a tragic and painful past she had felt she could never escape. She and her sister had spent their childhood in a small town in West Texas, raised by abusive, fanatically conservative, religious parents. Their parents would not tolerate any behavior or ideas that deviated from theirs and the canons of their faith. The physical and emotional abuse to conform was daily and unrelenting. They had few friends outside their cloistered community. And she and her sister could not speak of boys in the house, at least not within earshot of their parents - as most teenagers did. They were also ashamed of the clothing they were forced to wear. The other kids taunted them. At the age of sixteen, Alicia became pregnant by her clandestine boyfriend, and she had feared her father would kill her if he found out. As she shared her story, she stressed that she *actually feared her father would kill her.* As if to underscore this point, she said her mother would not have spared her from her father's wrath. "Between the two of us, Alicia was the strongest. She endured better than I did."

Amanda, the eldest by three years and still living at home, helped her terminate the pregnancy through a crude procedure that had nearly killed Alicia. "My mom," she said, "believed I was suffering from a severe case of menstrual bleeding, the reason neither of us called a doctor. I was scared to death!" Continuing, Alicia shared how Amanda black-mailed her and how she became slavishly devoted to whatever Amanda wanted from her. That included joining the ultra-conservative Committee For Free America and becoming a disciple of Jethro Campbell.

"Tell me about this Committee For Free America," Tracie interjected, hoping to learn more about the organization than she knew.

Tracie told her that Campbell modeled his ideology after his idol, Richard Nixon. For example, he, like Nixon, had an enemies' list. Select members of his organization were charged with turning the lives of their alleged enemies into living nightmares. "Campbell," she noted, "terrorized people! He was that determined, that ruthless. In fact, she and her sister participated in several of his terrorist projects."

"And you never once questioned the morality or the legitimacy of what you were doing to harm people you didn't know or would likely never meet?" Tracie asked.

"Tracie, to be honest, yes, I did! But remember, I was young, naive, and supremely grateful to my sister for saving me from a fate I considered worse than death. Had I survived punishment by my parents - and I mean that literally - I was terrified of being kicked out into the street with nothing and nowhere to go! I didn't know the streets, the world, or what my sister knew. Yeah, I knew enough about how to get pregnant from a boyfriend who left me once I became pregnant. He assured me that wouldn't happen. I was so naive I believed him. I actually believed that bastard!

Also, the people Campbell targeted on his enemies list meant nothing to me. I just did what I was told! I became a true believer, even though I could not have told you what that meant."

Alicia went on to say that Jethro liked her and had offered her a job at his headquarters. That was the beginning of her real education when she became familiar with the members of Congress like Charlene Randleman, who were major supporters. The Vice President was a corporate executive at the time and visited on numerous occasions. As Alicia recounted, "I knew everybody and everything!" She also knew, several years prior to becoming Tracie's executive assistant, that she had to leave Campbell. "I was relieved to be away from Campbell and his organization. I knew how foolish I had been."

"So when and how did you become a target for Campbell and his group?" Tracie asked, now engrossed in Alicia's story.

"The Vice President views you as a major threat. He and Campbell are determined to bring you down. They're afraid of the influence they believe you wield. They fear your symposium will bring many new voices into the conversation on human-induced climate change, particularly how we got where we are and the need for greater unity if we are to survive on this planet. Their logic is that if you weaken the President, if you contribute to denying him reelection in 2052, you jeopardize the Vice President's future prospects for capturing the presidential nomination. He needs this President's support for that to happen. My sister chose to remain with Campbell, and she and I stay in touch. She is my only sibling, and she knew, of course, that I worked for you. They decided to exploit that. The worst thing is that my parents robbed my sister and me of a normal childhood. My sister became the *real* true believer."

"Couldn't you have warned me?" Tracie asked. "Your sister and one of her colleagues surveilled my home, drove me out of it, in fact. And Campbell actually called to threaten me!" Alicia reached across the table to grasp Tracie's hand. Tracie recoiled reflexively. Both women were now visibly upset.

"Tracie, I immediately told my sister I would not provide the information Jethroe wanted. I told her I was no longer involved with the organization, that I loved my job, and that I had no reason to hurt you. My sister knew I still feared my father, so she threatened to tell him of my pregnancy and the abortion unless I helped her. That's why I gave them your home address; that's why they knew where to find you. I am truly sorry for what I've done to you, Tracie. These people are not super-smart or complicated. They are zealots. *They want to kill you!*"

Alicia's words hung in the air, suspended like the Sword of Damocles - a clear and present threat to Tracie and perhaps her family and friends. Alicia again reached for Tracie's hand and held onto it. "The worst day I have had in quite some time was being forced to leave you and the team. I loved my job. I admire and respect you, and I always will. Maybe one day you will forgive me. At least, I hope you can."

"Well, now that I know the Vice President is the force behind this threat, what's next?" Tracie asked.

"They don't know when you plan to broadcast or how. They also do not know who your panelists are. You have the advantage there. Keep it that way! I informed my sister I no longer worked for you. That I had been terminated, I also let her know she couldn't blackmail me anymore. If she wanted to tell our father about my pregnancy, I no longer cared. This last request had been one too many."

"So, I'm still a threat!"

"Yes! Absolutely! You always need to be careful. As I told you, these people are nuts. You might consider moving permanently because you're not safe in your home."

Tracie thanked Alicia for her candor and her honesty. As she rose to leave, Tracie hesitated for a moment, turned, and said softly, "Thank you, Alicia, I really mean it." Outside, she debated returning immediately to her office and stood watching the traffic in DuPont Circle. Her mind was in turmoil from Alicia's advice that she should consider permanently relocating. Tracie also reflected briefly on the contrast between her own childhood and that of Alicia and her sister. Tracie enjoyed her home, her community, and the tranquility she enjoyed there. Now comfortable with the inevitability of something more permanent with Wilson, her preference had been to make her home *their* permanent residence. Was that option now off the table? How vulnerable were her current office suite and her staff? The one non-negotiable was the symposium. Everyone was invested - including Wilson. As soon as she had decided where to "relocate" or basically fall off the public radar, she would give the signal for the first panel. Then, the projected members would have to wait to see what the fallout would be and how determined their blockers proved.

Having accepted the idea that Washington, D.C., could no longer be her permanent home, Tracie's next step was to have that conversation with Wilson. Among the options on his list was relocating to Africa. "Africa has long since evolved from being the 'Dark Continent' as the northern hemisphere has characterized it. Technology enables us to manage and grow our business from any location on the planet." Wilson usually completed that argument with "Africa is the future, not the U.S. or Western Europe." And then, with his signature deep-throated laugh, he would say, "Your centuries-long run is over. You in this country brought us to this point. It's our turn now."

Tracie had become increasingly comfortable with the idea of a life with Wilson, even if it meant moving to Africa. This threat from Jethroe Campbell and the Vice President had transformed her and in a short period of time. Her original work had been in Africa years earlier. She just hadn't shared this change in attitude with Wilson. And then there was another factor in favor of it. Her parents would make the move with her - at least for six months of the year. They would not be separated permanently from their only child. And that notion had Wilson's full concurrence.

For example, among Wilson's clan in Nigeria, Sam and Ericka Hinton would be treated like royal elders. So that would be on the table as soon as she broached the subject of relocation. Also, she could manage her business from Africa with occasional travel, not just to the U.S. but to the rest of the globe as well, minus the threats from the deranged right. But for now, Wilson's home was her new residence until that decision became firm. It was time to talk to Wilson.

The longer Roberta and Giuseppe reviewed their plan to relocate seeds from the four locations in Italy to other destinations in Europe and Canada, the more confident the two of them felt about their efforts. Over lunch, the conversation shifted in another direction: Dr. Nuzzi's personal safety. Roberta shared that she had brought Tracie up to date on their progress. In response to her question about a launch date for the first of the Symposium's panel discussions, Tracie talked about threats from Jethro Campbell and the necessity to ensure that all panelists are in safe locations before each broadcast. Roberta then asked Giuseppe about his specific plans.

He responded, "You know, Roberta, my first priority was the security of the seeds. Now that we've accomplished that, I am comfortable stepping down from the leadership of this organization." He went on to add, "Survival brings out the worst impulses in us. I assumed Tracie's Symposium would threaten those leaders - including corporate - most opposed to change not just in the United States but here in Europe, the Middle East, and China. Any of us who agreed to participate could become immediate targets for retribution, myself included. I have already made plans to stay - at least temporarily - with friends in Austria. After the Symposium, my options are open. Oh! Those who have accepted my invitation to join me on my panel have also made similar arrangements. This is no time to shrink from a larger responsibility we all feel. I am certainly not surprised to learn that Tracie will permanently locate. How can the rest of us not be willing to make a similar sacrifice?"

Tracie's tech team had prearranged signals from the first panelists indicating they were ready to go: Bradford Taylor, Virgilio Sanchez, and a member of Dr. Nuzzi's team who had quietly relocated to Taormina, Sicily. Nuzzi serves as the panel moderator. Tracie's screen went live at 3:00 p.m. Eastern Standard time. Arrayed before her were her panelists and Dr. Nuzzi. "Dr. Nuzzi will now welcome us."

"Welcome to our global viewing audience. Our purpose today is to offer practical solutions - options to some - to solve worldwide food scarcity wherever you are. My colleagues and I are strong advocates of international resource sharing. It is only by sharing resources, knowledge, and technical expertise that we can survive and prosper without global conflict, mass migration, hoarding, and starvation. I think all of us know this. The people now visible before you are specialists in specific food supply issues. As I introduce them, they will appear on your screen, or you will hear them on your audio receivers.

"First is Virgilio Sanchez, a Commerce and Trade specialist, who will speak to you about various ways to negotiate fair resource trades. Next is Bradford Taylor, a director of environmental quality research and development, who will talk to you about the benefits of microbiomes for air quality. He will also introduce his production manager, who will discuss commercial production methods. Other panelists, who may not be visible on your screens, will discuss growing staple foods artificially, commercial composting for amending depleted soil and equalizing access to healthful food supplies. Finally, I am Dr. Giuseppe Nuzzi, a seed and plant stock researcher and hybrid developer. I will talk to you about seed banking and world trade." The first of a series of panel discussions had been launched.

18

That night, Tracie told her dad, "Over the next 24-to-36 hours, we'll know if our effort was worth the threats, the intimidation, the eventual loss of my home, and the months of stress everyone has endured. Win or lose, I gave it everything I could."

Sitting across from his daughter, Sam Hinton could see that Tracie had aged just slightly. His daughter had wanted to make a difference, and this was the price he knew from long experience she would have to pay. "Sweetie, there is nothing more you can do tonight, so why not get a good night's sleep, and we'll pick up everything tomorrow." Tracie had elected to spend the night with her parents; she just needed to be home. Her mom got up from the table and walked around to Tracie. Taking her by the hand, she said, "Come on, Baby, let's go," as she pushed her playfully up the stairs to her old room. You get undressed, and I'll run your bath." For a warm, delicious moment, Tracie felt like the child she once was with her mom. Tonight, it felt good, and she was not about to say no. "Okay, Mom, I'm coming." Although she had settled in with Wilson, there was nothing like sleeping in your old bed again. Her mom actually tucked her in and kissed her before closing her bedroom door.

During breakfast the next morning, Sam turned on the morning news. The lead item on cable news was the panel discussion on the necessity for greater resource sharing. Analysts were doing their usual punditry, speculating on the source of the broadcast, delving into the backgrounds of the panelists, and attempting to frame the discussion from the administration's perspective. "Nothing new," Sam noted.

The political impact of the first-panel discussion was largely positive in the early days. Reactions among many of the world's scientists, climatologists, and researchers to the first panel also varied geographically. In Western democracies, for example, the information the panelists shared sparked broad conversations about national unity, local and regional cooperation, the necessity of sustainability, reducing tensions between philosophically divergent political parties, and the survival - of humanity, the environment, and the planet. The broader underlying message was hope - as Tracie had intended. Each panelist stressed the point, "We have to cooperate. There is no escape from planet Earth. This is our home."

In one-party states, e.g., China, Russia, North Korea, Belarus, and Iran, whose leadership's primary emphasis was on maintaining power, the conversations among the leadership took a darker, more ominous turn: how to control the quality of information as a possible precursor to more civil unrest. Somewhat muted, but not surprisingly, that was also the reaction from the administration. The concern remained that the panelists were piercing the veil of indecision - some would argue incompetence - and secrecy shrouding this presidency.

Awareness of its secrecy was, indeed, happening as the broader communications industry raised the alarm that the White House was censoring the news. When combined with word of mouth about the broadcast, Americans began investigating their news sources and querying local and national candidates for political office. Candidates not of the President's party were interrogating administration spokesmen about transparency, what was not being reported on international tensions, and their positions on human-induced climate change. One prominent White House reporter, at the first-noon press briefing following the first-panel discussion, asked, "Why does the

President fear sharing what we have to find out from other sources?" To twist the dagger a little deeper, she added, "The President should never wonder why his poll numbers are in the tank." Complacency was giving way to greater citizen engagement.

A counter-narrative coalesced in the first two weeks, primarily because of the administration's reluctance to respond to questions from an aroused, inquisitive population. It was a courageous candidate for elected office who was willing to host a community event when the most surly and loud among the audience demanded answers to "What are you hiding? And why?" Both sides wanted to know the reasons why the other might be lying. Independents accused both sides of complicity.

Tracie's tech team stayed hidden while they evaluated the effectiveness of their signal-bouncing strategies and monitored some of their target sights for signs of hacking. They knew their next broadcast signal would come from the moderator of the water panel and were troubleshooting further ways to confuse possible blockers - now that the first broadcast had successfully reached receivers across the globe. More urgently, however, they were trying to assess the extent of domestic blockers' capabilities. How sophisticated were the Vice President's supporters in the technology? What precautions need to be taken to continue hiding from them? Tracie had been the first target. Who would be next? Only the next broadcast would tell.

Out of professional fear for freedom of the press, Andy Hillyard at *The Washington Post* began having discreet conversations with his colleagues to see if any had known about the administrative news blackout or might be part of a conspiracy. All seemed above board when he asked if anyone had gotten information on the ousting of the U.S. Air Force from Thule (Greenland) and purported Russian overflights of Greenland. Most were genuinely mystified but had heard the rumors. They were putting out feelers but were unable to speak to anyone at the Pentagon or on the White House staff. This was a news blackout, circling the wagons.

Andy tried to reach Tracie without success because he wondered if the resource-sharing broadcast had anything to do with her dropping out of sight. But knowing Tracie had disappeared for a reason - most likely the clearly present threat from Jethro Campbell and the Vice President - he didn't need her enemies to become his.

Following her meeting with Alicia, the overwhelmingly positive response to the resource-sharing broadcast, and the anticipated success of the water panel, Tracie's gut told her it was only a matter of time before Jethro Campbell's thugs caught up with her. And if Alicia were to be believed - and Tracie had no reason to doubt her - there would be further threats, no appeal to reason. This time, she would be killed, perhaps Wilson as well, if they were together. The thought that she would bring harm to him had begun to haunt her. Her priorities had now changed.

Wilson listened attentively as Tracie recounted the events of the past days, including the global reaction to the resource-sharing panel and her sobering meeting with Alicia. She couldn't completely mask her fear this time. On this occasion, she didn't pound the table demanding names while proclaiming her right to be free of intimidation or refuse to be driven from her home. No, the conversation that night was different. Before he could interject, Tracie got up quickly from the kitchen table, went over to him and tried to push his chair back. As she did so, she sat on his lap and put her hand over his mouth, signaling him to listen. There was more.

"Listen," she said softly. You know everything with me is about timing. I love that you have been patient with me. It has not been easy for you. I know that. Your patience has been a source of strength for me. In fact, your strength has anchored me in my best and worst moments. Now, I'm ready to do what I have always known I would. If you still want to marry me, my answer is 'Yes!'"

For what seemed an eternity, Wilson looked at her - and said nothing. Tracie could have sworn he didn't even blink, and he registered no emotion. When Tracie could stand his silence no longer, she looked at him, thinking, "Oh My God! He's changed his mind, and I'm living in his house." "Wilson! Say something!" she burst out, now almost plaintively screaming. She stood up, tears in her eyes and her hands over her mouth.

When he felt she couldn't stand the suspense anymore, he stood up and swept her into his arms.

"It's about damn time!" He laughed, picked her up, swung her around, and kissed her.

And then she hit him with the coup de grâce: "I want to get married in Africa, and I want my parents to be there besides yours." Wilson practically collapsed, overwhelmed. He bent over as if to catch his breath. Understanding what this meant to him, Tracie caught him under his arms and held him up. If this man she had loved for practically half of her existence harbored a dream other than marrying the one woman he could imagine as his wife, it was to celebrate their union at home in Africa with their families present. "You are serious?" he gasped out.

"Yes! I am - and the sooner, the better."

For the rest of the evening, they talked about setting things in motion, beginning with the sale of her home, then shutting down her company in Washington, relocating the staff, and reestablishing in Lagos. Wilson told Tracie he would request a transfer to the World Health Organization's Regional Office for Africa. Ten years earlier, that office had been relocated from Congo Brazzaville to Lagos, Nigeria. "If they deny my request, I will leave the organization," he told Tracie. "We are leaving here." Wilson was clearly excited, beyond anything Tracie had ever seen before. For the first time, they were planning a life together. Lying in bed that night, snuggled in Wilson's arms, Tracie turned gently to lie on her back. Gazing at the ceiling, she felt a calmness, a celestial assurance that, however, the future evolved, she and the man beside her would survive it.

At various undisclosed locations, members of the water panel were awaiting word from their moderator. The most nervous among them was Jeannette Masters, Director of the EPA. She had been the one Tracie had approached to organize the water panel. The EPA Director had had an unprecedented contact from the Vice President's office inquiring if she knew the origin of the first broadcast. Of course, she could honestly say she didn't and responded by reminding the official that most on the panel could be identified if he were seriously interested in finding out. The conversation had a menacing tone that had unnerved her.

The panel was in place and, like the resource-sharing panel, had foreign nationals on it, which made Masters clearly rethink who would moderate it. That was easy enough to arrange with a coded message to her team, but if she were not on the panel, someone else would have to get the signal. Getting back to Tracie's tech team was going to be a problem. Then she thought of Wiley Mitchell and reached out to him. If anyone could connect with Tracie, he could. She needed to know who the new moderator was so the panel could go forward.

"Wiley, this is Jeannette Masters, and I'm trying to reach Tracie." Wiley knew the first-panel discussion on resource-sharing had garnered good reviews here in the U.S. and pretty much around the world. This development would only increase the pressure from Jethro Campbell and the Vice President to shut her down. He was among the few she trusted with direct access to her now. The water resources panel, one of the most anticipated, was next. Although he had been asked by Tracie to serve as backup to a Canadian, he hadn't been advised of any changes yet.

"Jeannette, I know you're organizing the water panel. I am involved as well. Tracie is working out the final details with the moderator. Is that why you're trying to reach her?"

"Yes, Wiley. We're ready to go. I have already received one somewhat threatening call from the Vice President, who is fishing for the names of those on the resource-sharing panel. I was able to fend him off. I think we should launch the water panel right away. Let me know what Tracie decides."

"I'll be in touch - soon."

Tracie was not surprised to receive a coded message from Wiley regarding the moderator for the water panel. She picked up. "Wiley, has Jeannette called you about the moderator for the water panel?"

"Yeah, just got off with her. She's nervous, and I understand that. The Vice President's putting pressure on her to disclose names, and thus far, she's holding up. She does work for him so we've got to move quickly. Where do we stand with the moderator?"

"We lost him a few minutes ago; fear, too much exposure. Are you up to it, my friend?"

"Yes! We've got to get this done. If Jethro Campbell wants to show up at *my* door, he'd better be prepared. As for political pressure from the Vice President, he can't hurt me. In fact, pressure from this White House would be good for business."

"Just between us, Wiley, this was the arrangement I really wanted. Get back to Jeannette and get this panel on the air!"

"On it."

Wiley called Jeannette with the update. "Jeannette, Wiley here. The moderator is no longer available. You know how it goes: fear of political retribution. I was back up, so let's talk about getting this panel up and on the air."

"Wiley, my interest at the moment is going forward. How do you plan to proceed?"

Wiley explained: "I understand that each of the panelists were recruited by you or Tracie to cover the widest range of issues without any overlap. Is that true?"

"Yes."

"Well then, I plan to follow that plan - water quality control, but less theoretical and more practical. We're going to take heat for this panel since it is about a scarce resource. We need to frame our discussion from a real-world perspective." Continuing, Wiley pointed out that the Canadians, and the indigenous people especially, were concerned about industrial pollution in the major waterways, which was caused by large-scale fish dying off due to warming water. Most industries had given up the various soluble gas chemicals and metals in their processes, but the paper industry still used too much water and leaching chemicals in their processing.

We have an urban planner from Michigan, someone I know well, who will discuss the effects of drinking water purification. Storm-related flooding and sinking in coastal regions would be covered by an oceanographer from the oceanography institute offshore from what remains of Miami. The Netherlands provided a specialist in preventing sewer water from contributing to toxic marshes in the lowlands and pressure on dikes from the inside. The Dutch had gradually developed drying ponds at higher elevations in which the sewage was dried and tilled constantly with organic compost and sent back to their flower farms. And an official from the World Health Organization in Washington, D.C., will round out the panel.

The panel was in place and set to go. Wiley's name was forwarded to Lester Sanford, the head of Tracie's tech team. Lester was a product of Baltimore and a PhD from MIT in advanced computer platform design. When he was satisfied the possible weaknesses in their system had been identified and addressed, he sent the signal to Wiley. After each panel discussion, Lester wanted to assess how much actual negative public sentiment had been generated. He referred to it as an old-fashioned concept called 'evidence of effectiveness.'

As Tracie and Wilson were making their plans, her office staff had discreetly disappeared. If the conspiracy were able to put pressure on Alicia Swarthmore, she could not have told them where any of them were. Even though the water panel was completely unannounced, the tech team detected significantly higher hits than from the first-panel broadcast. It seemed as though they had successfully reached behind the Southeast Asian wall, with probably an equal number of receptive listeners and those trying to block them. American panelists on the upcoming panels - soil and air - were taking precautions to protect their identities in preparation.

Plenty of biased news reporting followed the broadcast, mostly from the administration's perspective. All this White House was able to do was *attempt* to discredit the broadcasts. Jethro Campbell was almost literally patrolling the streets in Washington, D.C., looking for anyone known to be affiliated with Tracie. The Vice President's office even had a team of tech wizards tasked with locating the source of the broadcasts. It was hard for Tracie's team to imagine someone smart enough to do sophisticated Internet sleuthing as also being stupid enough to believe the falsehoods of his followers. But stupidity cannot be underestimated.

Several days after the water panel, Lester Sanford flashed a heavily encoded message to Tracie, Wiley, Masters, and to each panelist. The worldwide response had been positive and from a larger number of listeners than the first panel. Each panelist had addressed a different element of the global water crisis, but taken as a whole, experts everywhere valued the holistic approach to presenting practical solutions. If there was one country that sought solutions to every dimension of the water crisis, it was China. Tracie was hoping to hear from her friend, Dr. Chin Tan Wu, Head of the Environmental Sciences Institute in Beijing. In one of their earlier conversations, Dr. Chin had mused aloud, "How do we feed 20 percent of the world's population with only 7 percent of the world's water? And 70 percent of our rivers and lakes are polluted, with more than a quarter of our surface water unfit for human consumption. Water is the biggest environmental issue in this country, not air quality."

As she had hoped, Tracie did receive a call from Dr. Chin.

"Dr. Chin, I have been thinking about you. I am also surprised that you could contact me. How are you faring these days?"

"Dr. Hinton, I won't ask where you are, but I will express my hope that you are safe and well."

"I am, and thank you for your concern."

"I should tell you everything I have heard from my sources means the first two broadcasts were successful. I could not be more pleased."

"I'm delighted to hear that. I just hope that we have not made your task more difficult than it is."

"Do you have a few minutes? I have a story to share with you."

"Yes, by all means."

"Following one of our earlier conversations, I thought a lot about 'being in my own lane' and decided it was time to test my boundaries. In a series of discreet meetings with key Party Leaders here in Beijing, I candidly made the point that if I were realistically to address the challenge of feeding our population with inadequate resources while staving off dissent from our clamoring middle class, riots in cities and towns across the country, and disquiet within the military, I needed a free hand, no restraints, and the leadership to trust that I was acting in China's national interest." He went on to add, "After staking my position, I stood there with bated breath, not knowing what to expect. To my surprise, Dr. Hinton, they agreed, told me my loyalty was never in question. Moreover, they looked forward to my recommendations."

"Dr. Chin, good for you! I have to ask, what do you think accounted for this abrupt and drastic change in attitude? Frankly, I'm shocked. Your leadership is not known for its flexibility on policy issues."

"I have been conveying to our leaders the reports describing the impact of a changing climate on your country, Europe's loss of its major waterways, and the accelerated impact of the loss of our glaciers over the past several decades. Although the problems I presented were known, I asked the question, 'How stable do you think this country will be when our rate of water consumption surpasses water supply?'"

Dr. Chin went on to make another point. "I also reminded them that the population of our Indian neighbor now exceeds ours, and we share water resources with them in the west. Our choice is greater cooperation and collaboration or conflict." He added, "I didn't have to remind them who would be held accountable for any conflict between the two most populous countries on earth."

"Dr. Chin, I'm proud of you, but more so because your leadership is listening to your counsel. That gives me hope. Will our efforts and goodwill be enough to stave off the larger conflict I fear is over the horizon? I don't know."

"Dr. Hinton, there is more."

"Oh! And what is that?"

"I have been granted permission to travel to your country to learn more about advances you've made with condensation technology. That is critical for us. Over a third of tested wells, mostly in our Northern and Central regions, have grade 4 quality water that is only fit for industrial use. And an additional 50 percent of wells here have grade 5 quality water containing contaminants like fluoride, manganese, and compounds used in fungicides."

"Well, Dr. Wiley Mitchell and his team in Seattle will be delighted to meet with you. He is part of a network of experts in our Pacific Northwest, deploying processes and technology in that area with great results. I shall let him know of your intentions. Keep us apprised of your travel plans."

"Dr. Hinton, it is always a pleasure to speak with you, and thank you for your willingness to work with us. I know there are elements there who would prefer otherwise."

The conversation with her Chinese colleague buoyed Tracie's spirits. Dr. Chin's words were just further evidence that her decision to launch the symposium was worth the risk. Preventing global conflict had not been one of her initial goals. But bolstering confidence in the need to cooperate in a pre-and-post-conflict world was a goal worth pursuing.

19

To Tracie's surprise, her efforts to erase her entrenched presence in Washington took less time, was less expensive, and proceeded more efficiently than the time it had taken to establish herself almost two decades earlier. This time, she did have the support of her parents, unlike two decades ago when her dad was still engaged full-time with his career. Her Mom and Dad now took on what would have been the complex task of selling her home, disposing of the furniture she had leased, and storing the personal items she chose to keep. Her Northwest Washington home was on the market for less than 48 hours when a qualified buyer fleeing San Francisco contacted her father, who was acting as her agent, and offered to pay the asking price - in cash. The buyer, Grayson Thompson, was a recently retired advertising executive who wanted to move closer to his son and grandchildren living in Silver Spring, Maryland, just over the D.C. line from Tracie. Life in San Francisco posed challenges he sought to avoid in retirement.

Thompson told Sam, "I will be in Washington and am prepared to meet you at the property if that's acceptable. I know that section of the city because my son and an old college roommate live not far from the address. They both tell me your asking price is fair but said I should personally check it out." Sam assured Thompson the house had been well maintained and was in move-in condition. Once the two men completed their walk-through, shook hands on the deal, and agreed upon a settlement date, all of the parties, including Tracie, could not have been more satisfied. Without an address, untethering herself from a city so foundational to Tracie's identity was a giant step forward.

Meanwhile, Wilson was handling the logistics of their resettlement in Lagos. Tracie did not know someone could enjoy the tedium of logistics as much as Wilson seemed to. She agreed to assume the expense of their travel and to establish a temporary office in Lagos or Abuja, the official capital of Nigeria, until permanent arrangements could be made. The next item on their list was closing her Washington office. Dupont Circle is prime commercial real estate in the District of Columbia, and property bearing that location had real cachet. Tracie had been a long-term tenant in her building and was able to take advantage of a clause in her lease that allowed her to vacate with a 30-day notice. Also working in her favor was the high demand for office space in that area. The manager of the leasing company told her he would have her suite of offices occupied within days. His confidence was as close to a guarantee as one could have, and she let the matter rest.

Resettling her staff and tech team was the larger, more emotional challenge. The entire team preferred to remain with her. Tracie met individually with each staff member to discuss her vision for the organization, its staff requirements, and her desire for a more flexible and virtual global presence. This change did not come as a surprise to her team. "Technology, mobility, and flexibility are the keys to our future," she reiterated often. Now, the key variable was timing. Each permanent member of her team would be given two weeks' salary. "Give me time to get settled," she told them, "And I will be in touch." She, of course, did not divulge her permanent destination except to a select few.

The tech team was more difficult because they were already scattered around the country to confuse the origin of the symposium signals further. And Tracie had to be careful not to leave any cyber trace of her contacts with them. She decided to do chain mail. She messaged Lester

Sanford and indicated he should send the message to another member of the team with the same message - how to contact her.

Wilson and Tracie decided to lease Wilson's home on Longfellow Street, N.W., to the Nigerian Embassy. The embassy would utilize it as temporary housing for embassy staff in transition or make it available short-term to official visitors. He and Tracy would use it as a base when they were in Washington because it was more convenient than her parents' home in the Maryland suburbs.

In Lagos, Simon Okube, a family friend and owner of a recently constructed 10-storey building in a toney suburb, offered to make space available for Tracy's organization for a nominal monthly rent of U.S. $1.00. For Okube, it wasn't about the money. It was about having a tenant who was rapidly developing a reputation as an influential global environmentalist. She was also American and would soon be the wife of the only son of one of the most prominent families in the city.

Their separation from D.C. now complete, Wilson suggested they have a quiet dinner with Tracie's parents at one of the more popular seafood restaurants on the Potomac.

"We have been riding a whirlwind dodging those people who want to kill you," he told Tracie. "I want a quiet evening with just you and your parents before we board the plane tomorrow. I know they will be coming over for the wedding, but I think they would really enjoy a family evening of the four of us." That was an easy sell for Tracie. "You know, I'm actually excited about this move," she told Wilson. "I remember how excited Mom and Dad were whenever he received a new assignment. I guess that's what I'm feeling."

Tracie and Wilson spent their last night with Sam and Ericka Hinton. Lying in bed while Tracie slept the sleep of the dead, Wilson recalled the arc of his lengthy relationship with the woman sleeping peacefully next to him. He always told her she was the only woman he would ever marry - and now, finally, he would marry her. She couldn't see the tears of happiness rolling down his cheeks. He, however, was grateful beyond measure and, staring into the dimly lit room, he mouthed to himself, "Thank you!" He leaned over and kissed Tracie lightly on the forehead. She stirred slightly while moving closer to him, all without ever waking. The next morning, following breakfast, Sam and Ericka took them to Dulles International Airport in the Virginia countryside. As Tracie and Wilson disappeared into the terminal, Ericka looked at Sam telling him, "Okay! Come on before you start tearing up. We'll see them soon enough." Watching Tracie move into her own home was a major event for Sam, but she was close, only an hour away. Now, watching his only child begin life on another continent became the equivalent of crossing an emotional bridge second only in consequence to the possible loss of his beloved Ericka.

On hand to greet their United Airlines flight at Terminal 2 at Murtala Muhammed International Airport in Ikeja were the Federal Minister of Aviation and the Director of Airport Operations. Tracie was presented with a bouquet of flowers. Clearance through customs was expedited by a federal cabinet minister present, and within minutes, they were en route to Wilson's family compound. Sitting in a custom Mercedes Maybach, Tracy whispered to Wilson, "I didn't expect anything like this. I feel like royalty." To which he responded, "Baby, you are royalty! My family has been waiting a long time to meet you. The wedding will be an event you and your parents will long remember."

Within days after their arrival, Tracy was fully immersing herself in establishing her new office. Wilson and the family were planning a wedding, an actual June wedding.

When Tracie informed Wiley of her decision to relocate, he understood and reluctantly agreed with the wisdom of her decision. As one of Tracie's oldest and most trusted friends, he, too, was fearful for her safety. He doubted that Jethroe Campbell and his band of hired thugs would show up at his home because a 6'5" African American man would confront them. Terrorizing women was more Campbell's *modus operandi*. Roberta was still traveling and thus beyond the Texan's reach. Were she at home, she would not have been an easy target. Years earlier, she had taken firearms training and was licensed to carry. She did not always have her weapon with her. Wiley's concern was that she would be able to handle herself in a one-on-one situation or in the event someone tried to abduct her. There is a large Asian community in Seattle, and Tracie began training in Taekwondo - Korean martial arts that specializes in defensive tactics up close and personal.

Roberta valued her freedom with a vengeance because vestiges of racism in this country still existed in 2050. Wiley dealt with discrimination in his own way, and she did not intend to become a victim if her physical safety was at risk. Tracie, on the other hand, was more vulnerable. Wiley, too, had encouraged her to relocate - at least temporarily. Before hanging up, he said to her, "You'll be back. You don't know it yet, but you have a political future in this country."

"Me!" Tracie responded. "Never!"

To her puzzlement, Wiley just smiled. Wiley's non-response response smile lingered with Tracie. She couldn't shake the feeling that there was something yet to define her life over the horizon. "What did Wiley know? And what was he not telling her?"

Wiley had not shared with his friend something he had picked up during his recent trip to Miami. The eve of her departure was not the moment to do so. There was time.

Tracie moved quickly to get her operation up and running while remaining in frequent contact with Wiley. In her absence, he functioned as a hub, the clearing house for information that normally flowed to Tracie for reaction, decisions, and priority. Her real focus, and the reason she was reluctant to leave, was sustaining support for the symposium panel series. Support was overwhelmingly positive and growing. Within that support, however, were those suggesting she should enter politics. When she heard that, the hairs on her neck stood up because that suggestion would only unnerve a rattled White House and the Jethroe Campbells of the world. The paranoids, as she called them, might think *that* was her *real* motivation and *not* to inform a public demanding answers about how to cope with a changing climate. Was that the basis for Wiley's recent cryptic remark, she wondered. "I'll bring it up in our next conversation," she reminded herself. She also knew Wilson would weigh in on that idea simply because a foray into domestic politics would only increase the threat level. After all, the move to Nigeria was to take her *out* of the line of fire.

The next panel would discuss soil cultivation, conservation, and utilization. Tracie had selected the well-respected Under Secretary for Farm and Foreign Agricultural Services in the U.S. Department of Agriculture as her soil panel moderator. Like the other moderators, the Under Secretary had assembled a well-rounded group of soil experts from various countries as well as the U.S. She was to give an overview and graphic presentation on the changes in crops and cultivation methods in response to the changing climate. Moreover, she would talk about conserving natural resources like water, drought-resistant seeds, soil-conserving crops, and nitrogen depletion in the soil.

She had recruited her colleague, the Under Secretary for Food, Nutrition, and Consumer Services, to talk about domestic nutrition projects that deal mainly with hunger problems around the U.S. In addition to these two officials was a Mexican national from the Mexican Department of Agriculture who had worked with the USDA (U.S. Department of Agriculture) on cross-border resource collaboration. He was to speak about mutually beneficial trade agreements that allowed for easy exchange of Mexican labor for American technical and financial assistance. Mexico had ceased to be the abundant source of fresh produce for this country it had been because it, too, had suffered terribly from drought. The U.S. Labor Department, working with Immigration Services and the Canadian government had made it easier for Mexican farm workers to go farther and farther north as the Earth warmed. They brought many native growing techniques and desert food plants with them. The diets of the North American people had changed significantly.

The panel was completed by a Brazilian expert on non-toxic insect repellents that could safely be used in farm soil and a Japanese expert in seaweed cultivation to discuss changing offshore growing conditions and adapting to higher water temperature, less salinity, and more silting in the beds.

The American panelists had been forewarned about the possibility of political retribution from the Vice President's Office should they choose to participate. Each of them, after careful consideration, decided to go forward citing "civic responsibility" and the "frustrating ineptness" of this White House to share vital information with the American population, a population they swore an oath to preserve and protect.

Unfortunately, often misdirected political retribution was the order of the day from the Vice President. The Primaries were just months away, and the President's poll numbers were in the mid-twenties, numbers not seen in almost three decades for a sitting President. Political pundits and media commentators frequently mused about the targeting of populations of color for intimidation when their suffering paralleled that of the larger population, or worse, in densely populated urban areas. The leadership of Civil Rights organizations, having flexed their political muscle in past elections, mounted fierce messaging campaigns against the administration and were unstinting in their condemnation of both the President and the Vice President. In response, the White House began to circle the 'political' wagons, but the coterie of senior advisors around the President began to shrink. Rumors proliferated daily about *who* would be the next to go, and that included among the generals and admirals along the E-Ring at the Pentagon.

The centrist *CNN* regularly dissected the President's performance not only in its handling of domestic policy, e.g., the effects of global climate change, but foreign policy as well. Almost three-fourths of those polled in three recent polls disapproved of the President's handling of our relations with Russia, China, North Korea, and Iran. One media analyst on *CNN* is reported to have an inside source who claims to have heard the President say, "I can't catch a break! My numbers have been dropping consistently since these panel discussions."

By now, Wiley had a network of supporters who kept him informed about developments in Washington, most particularly reactions from this White House about the panel discussions. When this last remark, purportedly from the President, reached him, he knew Tracie was solidly in their crosshairs. It was only a matter of time before she was going to have to address the question she would dread: "Will you consider a run for elected office?" And there would be no avoiding the obvious question, "Have you ruled out a run for the White House?"

20

The annual fall meeting of the UN General Assembly in recent years represented exercises in chaos, confusion, several threats, and more than a few staged walkouts by delegates unable to reach agreement on cooperative efforts to deal with the effects of a changing climate worldwide. Countries that looked to the U.S. for leadership were particularly vociferous in their condemnation of the U.S. because of their own powerlessness. In every session, a frustrated delegate would look at the American representative, setting decorum aside, and state bluntly, "*You* are the largest and most uncompromising contributor to the warming of this planet, yet you insist the rest of us enact measures that limit our economic growth, curb immigration, and decrease greenhouse gases. You've put more carbon into the atmosphere than any other country! Where is the vaunted American leadership?"

The American chief delegate to the U.N., Ambassador Jack Cunningham, a non-career political pal of the President, had asked for the position, suggesting his lengthy experience as a successful oil industry executive equipped him to bring the kind of bold, no-nonsense leadership he claimed the organization required. Prior to his appointment, he was a frequent critic of the UN, referring to it as "that permanent debating society on the East River." He, like many of his former corporate colleagues in the current administration, was captive of "bottom-line blinders." The UN, as he realized quickly, was not structured to respond to the requirements of an annual profit-and-loss statement, quarterly goals, a corporate board, or shareholders. Cunningham was not one to accept counsel, and his frequent tirades against his career staff for, as he put it, "Their failure to perform," were so frequent that many Foreign Service officers refused assignments to New York, preferring to remain in Washington or an assignment to a hardship post abroad. Cunningham was adrift and unable to admit failure.

Unrest worldwide was growing, but also here in the U.S., and that contributed to Cunningham's frustration and feelings of impotence. Elected officials, responding to their constituents, were predicting civil war, while others decried the orchestrated, right-wing assault against democratic principles as a substitute for an unwillingness to compromise. One side viewed negotiation, compromise, and cooperation as weakness. Fistfights and shoving matches now replaced the comedic hot rhetoric for which the House of Representatives had been noted. Also, female members were unspared the wrath of their male colleagues.

Few of the 435 congressional districts escaped problems or disasters attributed to the effects of a changing global climate. Heavy, unseasonal rainfall accompanied by thunderstorms, flash floods, evacuations, hurricanes, and tornadoes overwhelmed centuries-old water and sewage systems in major urban centers along the East Coast from Maine to Florida and as far West as Chicago. Coastal erosion and the intrusion of seawater into freshwater systems created havoc on both coasts and along major inland waterways. Subways and mass transit systems were frequently shut down due to flooding. Transit systems managers were overwhelmed and complained their requests for resources to modernize were given short shrift in annual city budget allocations. Drought, soil depletion, and ferociously hot temperatures from May through September roiled the Mid- and Southwest states.

News of these developments was filtering back to Tracie, and she worried about her friends. Equally unsettling were reports, obviously sourced from this White House, that attempted to trace civil unrest to her panel discussions. This was an amusing but futile and disingenuous attempt by a flailing administration to deflect accountability. However, within this strategy was the administration's implicit acknowledgment that Tracie's political capital was increasing. "Could she be persuaded to become a presidential candidate in 2052?" was the question on the minds of many in both major parties. Around the country, underground news sources proliferated, many of them unknown to the Vice President's people tasked with identifying and shutting them down - a challenge that proved daunting.

The parallels between life as Americans were experiencing it in 2050 and the history of Germany in the 1930s were now daily topics of conversation between friends, family members, and those of an older generational cohort. Tracie's great-grandfather, for example, had passed on stories of his early life in the old Soviet Union, and she had heard them from her mom. People choose sides on issues, and one can't always be sure with whom it is safe to share an opinion or confidence. Fear, chaos, division, and targeted violence - including murder - rippled through some communities around the country. Mass shootings were a common American occurrence, only more so. The challenge for law enforcement and media analysts was to distinguish between a typical mass shooting and a targeted shooting disguised as part of a mass shooting. For example, Alicia Swarthmore's body had been found behind an apartment building on Dupont Circle. No details, no leads, just a bullet-riddled body of a young woman. That news disturbed Tracie because Alicia had once been a valued employee. Had Jethroe Campbell been responsible for her death?

News blackouts were attributed to demands from the White House, a development that infuriated the most active and informed citizens. Headlines such as *"What Are You Hiding?"* were directed at the White House. Daily White House press briefings had been discontinued, which left inquisitive White House reporters to rely exclusively on "unnamed sources" for their reporting, especially on foreign policy, e.g., relations with our northern neighbor, Canada. Earlier, CNN, MSNBC, and the three major networks - NBC, ABC, and CBS - had reported on a development that went largely unnoticed: The U.S. had been booted from Thule AFB in Greenland and advised to discontinue surveillance flights over the Arctic Circle - especially if those flights violated Greenland's air space. The service chiefs at the Pentagon and the Air Force general commanding the North American Aerospace Defense Command in Colorado (NORAD) resisted this directive mightily but were overruled by the White House.

The administration had also accomplished the impossible in its foreign relations. It had alienated, some suggested permanently, the Canadian Prime Minister. The fallout from this blunder, in pure security terms, exposed or further weakened the protective shield over the Northern Hemisphere. To be more precise, there was now a gaping hole in NORAD charged with the defense of that region. Although NORAD could not defend against ballistic missiles, a decades-long, vigorous American air presence had been vital to keeping tabs on frequent Russian overflights of the Arctic region. U.S. relations with the Canadians were now fragile and dependent upon strained cooperation with our northern neighbors. While the quality of human existence on the planet continued to deteriorate, the daily rhythm of relations between nations did not cease.

The White House was under siege and flailing. In Ottawa, the Canadians, too, were trying to maintain balance with one of its most important foreign partners - China. The Canadian Prime Minister had had a particularly hectic day in tense conversations with the truculent, Ottawa-based Chinese ambassador over the presence of Chinese spy ships and electronic surveillance platforms disguised as fishing trawlers off the Canadian West Coast. The Chinese, exploiting tensions between the U.S. and Canada on mutual defense, had become aggressive and frequently failed to heed warnings from the Canadian Navy to respect maritime boundaries. Tolerance for this continuous pattern of behavior was wearing thin, and the Commander of Canadian Maritime Forces Pacific feared a crisis. He could imagine an exhausted, stressed-out commander of a destroyer on patrol might issue an order to fire on the Chinese. The Prime Minister shared his concerns with the Chinese ambassador, who listened passively - more out of courtesy than interest. The Prime Minister wondered if the Chinese were deliberately trying to provoke a confrontation.

That night, having just showered and sitting in his private office just off his master bedroom enjoying a glass of wine, the Prime Minister happened to turn and noticed the red light blinking on the green instrument on his desk. He'd had his back to it and wondered how long the light had been flashing. At night, the audio was turned off out of his concern that it would startle his wife, who was a light sleeper. When that phone sounded at night, she could never return to sleep. A military aide was on duty in the official residence at night and was to summon the Prime Minister in the event of an emergency or an urgent call to the residence.

About the time the PM noticed the red light, he heard a soft knock at the bedroom door. "Sir! Sir! Are you awake? You have an urgent call."

"Yes! I'm awake. Just a second."

The Prime Minister stood up, grabbed his robe, and hastily put it on before reaching the door. When he opened the door, Lieutenant Chris Tally, Canadian Air Force, repeated, "Sir, you have an urgent call. Would you please come with me? NOW!" He closed the door quietly and followed the officer to a secure military communication center in the residence's basement, manned by a mixed staff of Army, Navy, and Air Force officers. Canadian Air Force Major Konrad Thurston was the senior Watch Officer on duty. Thurston stood up as the Prime Minister walked in and directed the Prime Minister's attention to a mid-sized screen on the wall just above eye level.

"All right, Major. What am I looking at? What's going on? The Prime Minister asked."

"Sir, several minutes ago, NORAD in Colorado flashed the satellite images you see on the screen. The Americans intercepted a message between Norwegian defense forces on Spitsbergen Island in the remote Arctic and Forsvaret - the Norwegian Armed Forces headquarters in Oslo. A sizable Russian military unit has invaded largely submerged Spitsbergen in what appears to be an effort to capture the secret Svalbard Global Seed Vault. A location unpublicized in most public records. What you see on the screen is satellite imagery of units of Norway's Home Guard and Army defending the Vault and trying to repel the Russian invasion."

"Major, you're telling me the Russians launched a complex operation to capture the super-secret seed vault in Spitsbergen?!"

"Yes, Sir! It appears that way."

The Prime Minister paused a second and then responded, "Now that I think about it, we should have anticipated the possibility that sympathizers in Spitsbergen would have told the Russians about the existence of the vault, its location, and the security protocols in place." Still staring at the screen, he said to himself almost inaudibly, 'Our collective naiveté never seems to amaze me. These are desperate times in Russia. A changing global climate has severely impacted that country and thrown its hardline leadership into disarray. You have a desperate population historically struggling for survival, especially in the countryside. Subsistence living has been the norm for decades, and if you can believe it, conditions have only gotten worse.' He sighed heavily, saying to himself, "Life in the largest cities is not significantly better. And then, as if abruptly brought back into the reality of the moment, he looked at the Major, "Nothing justifies invading Norway! This is madness!" "Do we know the size of the Russian force?" he asked the Major.

"The colonel in charge of the Norwegian forces estimates an invasion force of two to three hundred land and sea personnel. He advises that a larger force may be en route. He doesn't know. Thus far, he and his forces have prevented the capture of the vault. But because he has to consider the possibility of a larger invasion, the colonel has requested reinforcements. Without additional troops, they may not be able to hold the vault."

"Get me the Defense Minister!"

"SIR!"

The Defense Minister, anticipating the call, came on the line. Major Thurston projected the Defense Chief on the large screen.

"Is it true the Russians have attacked the super-secret Svalbard Seed Vault? What's missing? What other information do we have?" the Prime Minister demanded.

"As you saw from the satellite images, sir, the fighting continues. The Russian forces attacked about twenty minutes ago - without warning and without provocation. For a force that size to enter the island undetected, they had to have come in at night by sea and traveled overland. Ocean water levels have risen significantly. Also, I can't rule out the possibility some of the troops may have been prepositioned. There are Russians within the population. Moreover, there is a precedent for a military invasion of Spitsbergen back in the Fall of 1941, during World War II, when the island was German-occupied. I think it was called *Operation Gauntlet*, mounted by Canadian, British, and Free Norwegian forces."

Concluding, the Defense Minister added, "We'll have more details on the current invasion later. Thus far, we have about ten dead and at least an equal number of deaths on the Russian side. We don't have precise casualty figures yet."

"Did this attack come as a complete surprise?"

"Yes. There was nothing in the message traffic or on the threat board presaging an attack. Fortunately, their troops responded immediately."

"Have we heard anything from the Norwegians?"

"Not yet. If this becomes a broader attack, say an attempt by Moscow to occupy not only the island but other Norwegian territory as well, then we have to assume that the King will invoke Article 5 of the NATO Defense Treaty. I have no doubt you will be hearing from him and the NATO Secretary General. The Norwegians alone are not capable of defending against a major Russian invasion, although I don't doubt for a moment that they will mount an aggressive and costly defense. I mean, it won't be a walk in the park for the Russians. At the moment, I imagine the King and his foreign minister are probably engaged in a shouting match with Moscow. You might want to summon the Russian ambassador."

"Oh, I'm sure he is expecting a call from me. If the Russians' primary objective was to capture the Seed Vault, I can't imagine they would want to try for larger territorial gain. But then, we are dealing with the Russians. Keep me informed, Major." As he left his basement communication center, the Prime Minister muttered something to the effect of having "another North Korea on our hands." At least, that's what Lieutenant Tally later reported to Major Thurston.

The Prime Minister returned upstairs and called David Standholm, his foreign minister. During their conversation, Standholm confirmed that he, too, was just learning about the attack from his operations center. He reported, "I issued instructions to send an urgent message to our ambassadors in Moscow and Oslo to make appropriate inquiries." He also informed the Prime Minister he had not heard anything from Washington, although he expected he would. "My concern," he told the Prime Minister, "Is that this thing in Spitsbergen could spiral out of control quickly, and we'd have war with the Russians in the Arctic, Greenland, and possibly in Europe as well." The Prime Minister knew his foreign minister was not given to hyperbole or alarmism, and thus, his words fell on receptive ears. Standholm continued, "Our northern flank will be exposed. And if that is the case, I am unsure how Washington and the Alliance will respond. I recommend we put our people on alert."

"I agree," concurred the PM. "We're monitoring this thing, and we'll see where we are in the morning."

In Spitsbergen, the Russian commander, initially encountering stiff resistance, stepped up the tempo of his attack. He radioed his troop commanders that time was not on their side, and they had to smash through the Norwegian defense and take the Vault at all costs. "We can't give them time to bring up reinforcements."

The *Spetsnaz* contingent (Russian Special Forces) then launched a vicious attack against the Norwegian settlement closest to the Vault, killing and wounding many of the residents in hand-to-hand combat.

The remaining Norwegian troops were captured. Close-quarters combat (CQB) was a *Spetsnaz* specialty. The Russian forces then placed underwater charges against the doors and were quickly inside. Having secured the Vault, the Russian commander and specialists assigned to him conducted an inspection. To their complete surprise, everything had been removed. The commander called his radio operator and instructed him to send a message: *"Dimitri. Repeat. Dimitri."* He then gathered his dead and wounded and withdrew to U-boats waiting offshore. They left behind shock, death, and destruction.

In Oslo, public outrage manifested itself in a chorus of calls for more economic sanctions against Russia, termination of bilateral relations, and European political isolation. The question was, "Who's next?" The response to that question was days away.

In Moscow, *Dmitry* was code for an empty Vault. The seeds had been moved to another location. The likely destinations were Greenland and or Canada. Even Nuzzi had not been informed of the relocation of the seeds because he had Communists on his board. Food riots across Russia were a daily occurrence. Many prominent elected officials, pampered oligarchs, and known friends of the Russian President were being pulled from their vehicles and homes and summarily executed, their bodies left as a warning. Families of some officials were relocated, often just escaping angry mobs with torches. Fear among Russia's privileged elite was palpable. Many left the country, some with as little as one suitcase and kids with backpacks.

The Russian President and his team were cornered, still unafraid to deal with the political consequences of direct military action. Reconnaissance flights over the Arctic region - Greenland in particular - revealed new growth, new development, and likely regions to have the missing seeds - at least temporarily. Greenlanders, who had assiduously avoided becoming caught between two superpowers, were now in Russian crosshairs. They completely understood the purpose of the Russian invasion of Spitsbergen. They could be next. Their only recourse was to call on the ally they had unceremoniously kicked out of Thule - the Americans. But was it too late?

In Ottawa, the Prime Minister and his Cabinet reached similar conclusions: the Russians would not stop after Greenland. Canada also had a new seed depository the Russians would likely try to acquire at any cost. In Moscow, the calculation was that peace could be negotiated with terms but not widespread riots, murder, starvation, and famine. A general uprising in a country with 11 time zones and a diverse population of 150 million would tear it apart, perhaps permanently. That outcome had to be avoided, even if it meant war with the West.

At 2:00 a.m. on a Saturday morning in July, a Russian-made cruise missile slammed into Thule AFB rendering it inoperable. Scores of Greenland's military personnel were obliterated, aircraft destroyed, facilities flattened, and communications knocked out. The area around the base went dark, but the fireball was visible for miles. Another two missiles simultaneously hit Nuuk, the capital, destroying the Cultural Center and the National Museum and Archives. The collateral damage in human lives would have been catastrophic in a city of 19,000 had the missiles hit during the day.

Russian transport aircraft with fighter jet escorts began landing at Kangerlussuaq Airport, the country's busiest, shortly after the missile strikes, ensuring complete control of the capital, its major international airport, and what was formerly the strategic Thule AFB. Allied aircraft were now unable to land. Greenland was under Russian control, and the search was on for the seed depository. Given the recent greening of the huge island, the Russians assumed the Greenlanders had access to forestry and grass seeds. They also knew that many of those seed duplicates could have come from the Institute in Italy.

Holding the airport hostage, the Russian invasion force had coerced the prime minister to divulge a seed horde on the base. They immediately took possession of it. The Greenland leaders staunchly denied having any other such depositories. The Russians were skeptical, but the Greenlanders responded that what they were holding at Thule was intended to repay the seed reserves as soon as they knew where they would be. The Russians grumbled and began speculating about where *else* seeds might be that they could capture. Frantic residents were calling friends and family in Denmark, Iceland, and Canada. Some called the U.S. Danish and Canadian long-range patrol aircraft over the Arctic reported the Russian attack on Greenland. Those two governments placed their countries on wartime status. They knew what the Russians were after.

The response from Washington was disappointing, to say the least, suggesting the American President was unwilling to confront the Russians militarily for fear of initiating a world war. However, his administration would provide humanitarian and military assistance to its NATO partners while pressuring Russia through additional sanctions, the UN Security Council and other international organizations to negotiate.

21

"Thank you for taking time away from your families to join me on a Sunday," the Prime Minister began. "In our world these days, private lives become a rare luxury you enjoy when you can. I appreciate the sacrifice you're making. So, let's get right to it. I have read your reports and those of our defense and intelligence colleagues on the grave danger the attacks in Svalbard and Greenland represent to Canada and our allies. We all agree it's highly probable the Russians will attack our homeland. Should they do so, we will repel them!

"We also agree their goal is to capture and control one of the most valuable resources on the planet: the seed vaults strategically positioned around the globe. Given the state of their economy, their widespread internal unrest we've all heard of, and Moscow's desire to remain a dominant power, it's no secret they are willing to plunge the world into war to gain the upper hand during any post-apocalyptic negotiations. What I've just described is a desperate and despicable state of affairs, but there it is. Feel free to interrupt if I have overlooked something. But, before you do, there is one final point. One of the major seed vaults has been temporarily relocated from Florence to an undisclosed location here, and the Russians suspect that. They're coming for it, and we're going to stop them. I repeat. We will stop them!"

The Foreign Minister spoke up, adding, "We're not going to launch a preemptive strike. I think the Russians would prefer that." The Defense Minister said, "We must anticipate the time and location of a first strike and then be able to absorb it and strike back. We will then immediately request that the NATO Secretary General convene an emergency meeting of the organization's Military Committee to invoke the provisions of the Mutual Defense Treaty. That is essential if we are to repel Russia with enough force to deter them from further aggression against other NATO members. The Russians may be gambling that the American President does not have the stomach for a NATO-wide conflict, and that, for them, may be a reasonable calculation. I don't know. We can't depend on Washington at this point."

The Prime Minister then told his envoys to remind their host governments and their resident Russian colleagues of the consequences of an attack. "We would prefer to avoid war," he reminded them, "but the West will defend itself using *any* means at our disposal. *Nothing* is off the table! All of us are dealing with the consequences of a changing global climate, but waging war against each other is not the solution."

Standholm, the Foreign Minister, then addressed his colleague in Beijing. "We also know the Chinese are stepping up their efforts to exploit this latest move by the Russians. We've had to increase our naval assets on the West Coast as a show of force to the Chinese, whose vessels regularly breach our territorial limits. Their strategy may be to draw assets away from a likely confrontation with the Russians in Europe. They may also be signaling an intent to exercise control over the Pacific east of Hawaii. Washington may be reluctant to engage the Russians militarily out of fear a U.S. response will provoke Russian escalation. I consider that defeatist thinking, but that's my personal view. I am confident, however, the Americans will respond aggressively to any attempt by the Chinese to become the dominant naval power in the Pacific. We, of course, will vigorously defend this country's maritime economic interests."

Later, contemplating an inevitable invasion from Moscow, Prime Minister Pearson, in Churchillian fashion, reached for his diary. Pen in hand, bourbon glass in the other, he stared at the blank page. On this particular day, he wrote:

"A changing climate is a global phenomenon - largely of our creation. It is also an equal opportunity calamity because it spares no one region, and that is unfortunate. What will distinguish one society from another is the ability of its leadership to forge dynamic alliances to inspire the collective genius of its people to persevere and husband its resources, both human and natural, to survive and prosper and to preserve people and the planet for posterity. That is my challenge, my legacy, and hopefully, my epitaph."

At that moment, the Canadian leader also imagined a conversation with his Russian counterpart in response to his questions, "Why did you invade Norway and Greenland? Why did you not request access to the seed vault as others do?"

The Russian leader would answer in typical Russian fashion: "I represent a power whose greatness comes from our history, popular expectation, and current world standing. Throughout our history, we have sacrificed the lives of tens of millions to earn that status. Our people expect us to act as great powers do. Great powers do not queue up to request consideration. Great powers negotiate when necessary, but more often, they prefer using power and strength. They demand and choose fear over respect from others. That is our nature. The mistake you and others make is you expect us to act against our nature."

The Norwegian and Canadian permanent representatives to the UN led the charge in the General Assembly in the days following the Russian invasion of both countries to strip Russia's veto power as a founding member. Years earlier, a similar effort had been launched following Russia's invasion of Ukraine. Russia promptly vetoed the resolution in the Security Council then, and it did so again. The two delegates were conversing in the Delegates' Lounge when they were approached by their Italian colleague. As the Italian sat down, he said somewhat ruefully, "I had expected a more vocal reaction from certain of our colleagues to this latest Russian atrocity." He went on to say, "The vote, while supportive, wasn't unanimous in condemning the Russians or stripping them of their veto. It was subdued. India and China, and a lengthy list of others, abstained. Where is the passion from our Caribbean, African, and South American colleagues - or the Stentorian denunciation from our British colleague? We expected the mute posture of our American colleague and were not disappointed. They do not want to establish a precedent that could come back to haunt them one day."

The Russians, with American acquiescence, have altered the character of this institution," the Norwegian added in response to his colleague's question. "Every one of us is challenged to find a path to a survivable future. Most of us will survive only through cooperation, compromise, and collaboration. Everyone who voted recognizes the limits of our ability to act unilaterally, and that was the understanding that animated the vote earlier. Put another way, what we witnessed was 'Russia envy' - the bear in the China shop. No one of us was in a position to function as a circuit breaker on their behavior. China has maintained a tolerance for Russian behavior that the U.S. is unable or unwilling to alter. We may be witnessing the death throes of the rules-based security system that has kept us from the brink of destruction since the end of World War II. The Canadian sat silently, listening to the exchange between his colleagues, pondering what he felt could become his country's destiny.

Tracie, now Tracie Hinton-Ojukwe, sat transfixed at their dinner table by the news her husband Wilson was sharing with her: the UN position on the Russian invasions of Norway and Greenland.

"But what was the *U.S. response?*" Tracie asked. "I need to know."

"The Americans voted to condemn the invasions. They had to. You can imagine the chaos had they not done so. But what is most interesting is the reporting we've seen. *That* story, *that important story,* didn't make the headlines of *The New York Times*. The editors positioned an important UN vote "below the fold. That placement is significant in itself."

"And coverage by *The Washington Post* - anything?"

"Basically, straightforward reporting," Wilson said. "To me, that's further evidence of a White House strategy to mute direct criticism of Russia - as you and your people have been saying all along. Well, I'm relieved we are no longer in Washington, especially these days. I'd be afraid for you to be on the street."

"I am, too, Baby. I am, too." Unspoken at that moment was the feeling that she would be drawn back to Washington in the near term. Tracie knew Wilson sensed it as well. Neither one wanted to talk about that possibility until it could no longer be ignored. Tracie dreaded that conversation because she feared being torn between her marriage and the rising swell of public support back in the U.S. for her to declare her candidacy for elected office. She had ignited a movement, and it showed no sign of abating.

Climate Solutions International, LLC was becoming a local brand in Lagos, as was the presence of its important leader. Many of her former employees had obtained temporary, renewable work visas and were comfortably settled near the office. Three other employees were working from undisclosed locations outside Washington. The National Bank of Lagos handled local transactions for her organization. Barclays of London handled international transactions, including donor contributions and international membership - both of which had increased dramatically in the wake of the symposium panel discussions.

Their proprietary research - her group's primary work product - was now published and distributed from London. In the next several months, following the last panel discussion, Tracie, Wilson, and her parents would travel to London for the launch of the Hinton Foundation. Sam Hinton agreed to serve as Chairman of the Board and would aid in the search for board members. Tracie was President and CEO. Wilson was a senior advisor and counselor. But how long, she wondered, would this arrangement work? Meanwhile, she planned to talk to Roberta Mitchell about a contingency plan should she return to

Washington. If Washington were in her future, Sam would not remain in London. He would insist upon returning to the U.S. as well, knowing the danger Tracie would face from those aligned with Jethroe Campbell. Roberta's European background and connections uniquely qualified her to take over the foundation board, and she would step up if asked.

The panel discussions had elevated Tracie's visibility and the important work of her organization in the broader international community at a time when survival and sustainability were no longer easily dismissed by conservatives, their elected representatives, and researchers and scientists funded by the fossil fuel industry. Timing was everything, and more people were now listening to her. Donations poured in with "How can I help?" The Hinton Foundation was born.

"The work we and other climatologists do will be with us," she explained to her mom and dad when they were discussing the foundation. "The foundation is the vehicle through which I will be able to identify and nurture the next generation of minds, we *misfits* as everyone labels us, searching for solutions and willing to accept derision to preserve our environment. The work we do will sustain life on this planet." She went on to argue that "children were growing up in conditions that were unthinkable when she was in school. Kids were asking questions, hard questions, and the right questions. Kids today," Tracie said, "are adjusting to a variety of lifestyle adaptations because children are resilient. Their questions, however, deserve answers. Moreover, we need to encourage them to be inquisitive, to explore beyond their horizons, and to push us for more accountability. They didn't ask to be born, but they're here now, and I think we owe them." Sam and Ericka understood this, but Tracie was just adding an exclamation point as tears welled in her eyes. Her parents looked at each other as if to say, "We better get ready; we know what's coming."

Almost as if she had flipped a mental switch, Tracie said, "Mom, Dad, let's talk about the last panel discussion, the one on ozone repair. This is it, the capstone to the symposium, and it will be hard-hitting. The fossil-fuel industry has been back-pedaling aggressively from assuming any responsibility for the increase in greenhouse gas emissions." "My point," she went on to add, "is that people today are aware, angry and insisting that the fossil-fuel industry's recent investments on sustainable energy are decades overdue and may be too little too late. People have been living, breathing, and drinking the results of the decisions affecting our environment without our consent. Corporate investments fall short of the levels required to deal with the current crisis. For example, the time to have brought China, the largest carbon emitter, into a zero-sum emissions agreement is past. So, this last panel discussion will be sure to widen the gap between where the fossil-fuel industry is and the level of public support they are trying to build. All we're asking is, how much is enough? There is only one Ark for all of us.

22

D r. Maria Karpov, spouse of Russian General Arkady Karpov, fretted about the decline in her husband's health. She confessed to a trusted friend that Arkady slept very little, had gained 15 pounds, drank too much, and now smoked almost two packs of cigarettes a day. Minor irritations at home with her or their children triggered outbursts for which he would immediately apologize. Her husband confided in her because he was frequently at odds with his staunchly rigid colleagues in the defense ministry. Arkady, at age 39, one of the youngest generals in the Russian military, was chief of the planning staff and had orchestrated the military campaigns against Norway and Greenland. He was also a recent graduate of Moscow's famed Military Academy of the General Staff of the Armed Forces of Russia.

Arkady and Maria had married very young - in their early twenties. He demonstrated leadership qualities as a junior Lieutenant that marked him for greatness, much to the consternation of many of his ambitious classmates. Arkady rose rapidly through the officer corps and now bore the additional responsibility of planning the upcoming campaign against Canada. This campaign would be more complex and carry greater political risks domestically because it would be launched against America's northern neighbor. Therefore, his new breed of pragmatic general officers expected pushback from the U.S. and the West would be stronger and more coordinated.

"The U.S. and the West cannot afford to allow a military campaign of whatever scope and duration against Canada to go unanswered," Arkady opined. "Norway and Greenland were not comparable in geostrategic importance to America's security," he wrote in one of his memos to the Chief of the Defense Ministry. Several of his senior military colleagues did not share his pessimism. They were still riding high from the two prior successful campaigns, insisting that this particular White House was even more risk-averse given the upcoming national elections.

Arkady's colleagues on the planning staff argued that NATO, without American leadership, was more formidable by design than in actuality. Arkady noticed that the members of the planning staff who supported this argument never presented supporting materials, e.g., data, research, and analyses - only logic based on NATO's recent actions. These arguments only increased his stress level. Individually, many of the most robust economies in NATO were confronting economic and social challenges similar to those in Russia. And someone on the staff always made the point that the American President was too focused on his reelection and not inclined to support a military campaign against Russia - a formidable nuclear power. Arkady, a student of political/military history, countered with a reminder of a former young, first-term American President's response to Russia's attempt to install missiles in Cuba in 1961. "Canada," he reminded his colleagues, "is not 90 miles away; it is on the American border!" Usually, by this time, he was on his feet, leaning on clenched fists across the table. "Attacking Canada would be equivalent to attacking the 51st state because that is what Canada is in the eyes of many Americans." Arkady knew he was becoming increasingly unpopular among his colleagues but felt he had no choice but to be on the record. Chest thumping was a poor substitute for planning.

"If we attack Canada," he told Maria later at home, "we're going to get bloodied. We have to ensure that we keep our people's support here at home. That will be difficult, given the impact of a changing climate. People are struggling, rioting, and dying. How are they going to react when their sons, husbands, and friends are returned to them in coffins? How do you message a coffin in patriotic terms given how the average Russian feels today?"

"And there is only one proven way to do that here," Maria responded.

"Yes, that's true. News of our activities in Norway and Greenland - where our casualties were relatively light - was practically non-existent. Our cyberwall is extremely effective, and our control of the media is total."

"But our media will have to be even more so. People are better informed today through a variety of sources. For example, what if our troops get bogged down in Canada? Getting them out will be more difficult. News will leak!" Maria was a cardiopulmonary specialist in one of the largest military hospitals in Moscow. She well understood the Russian attitude toward the care and treatment of veterans. On an average day, care was uneven. Class and ethnicity influenced the quality of their treatment, even more so outside of Moscow. In some regions, care for veterans was nonexistent and became the responsibility of the immediate family, who were also dependent upon every able-bodied male in a household to earn a living.

Maria expected that a war against the Canadians and Americans would produce casualties comparable to - if not greater than - the war against Ukraine almost three decades earlier. "And," she asked her husband, "what if we are attacked by NATO members in Western Europe and possibly Greece, Turkey, and Italy from the south?" Her question was more rhetorical than actual, explained by her husband's stress, his inability to sleep, his short temper, excessive vodka drinking, and his elevated blood pressure. A well-schooled military spouse, Maria understood the old-school brand of Russian military justice meted out by political leaders against senior officers in the event of failure or major embarrassment. Retribution would be swift.

At the first hint of failure, her hotshot husband would be offered up by his more senior colleagues as a public sacrificial lamb more quickly than she could emotionally or psychologically process. Immediately, she and their children would lose their lifestyle - the large Moscow apartment, the comfortably-appointed dacha, the limousine, social access including the coveted diplomatic passports, shopping privileges, and the generous pension Arkady would have been entitled to. If she were fortunate, she would be able to continue her employment to support herself and her children. If not, she would be on her own.

Arkady considered another of his wife's questions about a broader European military response to an attack on Canada: "What would we do in the event - unlikely as you might want to believe - Europe decides to act without American military support? And before you respond, think about this. If America demurs and Europe follows suit, every country in the West will assume it is next."

"Maria, I don't disagree with you. If we attack, for whatever reason, Europe will be in an untenable position; their backs will be against the wall. A broad, coordinated attack against us from the North, the West, and the South could divide and weaken our forces. And that is apart from the conflict in Canada. We would have to threaten nuclear retaliation - and we'd better not be bluffing! If our bluff is called, not only would an all-out war destroy what may be left of our economy, but our political, diplomatic, and economic isolation would be nearly universal. A thousand years of Russian history would be obliterated. The Chinese and Americans would thwart our access throughout the Pacific, and the Americans, with some support from the British, would give us little to no important access to the Atlantic. I hate to say this, but imagine our bear's image as a landlocked eunuch. I suppose the only goal we would achieve is the [temporary] fracture of NATO."

This last conversation unnerved both Maria and Arkady. It had a tone of finality that both seemed to recognize. Lying in bed, unable to sleep, Arkady looked over at Maria. He envied her. She could sleep. He eased out of bed, slipped into his robe, and went downstairs to his study. Sitting at his desk, he switched on the lamp and unlocked the lower left desk drawer. He pulled out a metal box with a combination lock and unlocked it. Inside was a brown envelope. For a few minutes, he held the envelope in both hands and then quickly opened it, extracting a hand-written note: "Mine is a suicide mission. How do I protect Maria and the children?"

Arkady had written the note to himself at the outset of the planning for the Canadian invasion. The conversation he'd had with Maria that evening still played in his head. There was no comfortable outcome for him. Russia would lose this war, and he would be a living reminder of Russia's loss and his country's humiliation. A public trial with him as the sole defendant in Russia would be out of the question. Other reputations and careers would also be on the line. The generals would silently demand his removal, as would the new political leadership - a hero's farewell, the operative word being *farewell*. Arkady chuckled to himself, thinking, "They could offer me exile somewhere, but that was a non-starter."

He had made peace with that outcome. Arkady's focus now was on saving his family. That night, for the first time, he slept.

23

Although no longer in the Washington pressure cooker, Tracie was feeling pressure from several fronts: getting her London foundation launched and completing the final panel discussion for her symposium. And, finally, returning to the U.S. to meet with a group of organizers and financial supporters pushing her to seek the White House in 2052. Closer to home and indirectly connected to her symposium was Russia's recent efforts to resolve its internal problems through military aggression.

The timing of a Russian attack against Canada was anyone's guess. Tracie believed it would happen soon. Therefore, she would have to launch this last panel discussion before the attack from Moscow blanketed news cycles worldwide. Although the symposium and the panel broadcasts were her brainchild, she decided that for the final one, she would assume the role of moderator and officially take ownership of this enterprise. She had assembled a team from the National Oceanographic and Atmospheric Administration (NOAA), the European Environmental Agency (EEA), the Greenhouse Gases Program Area, and an expert from China's Beijing Government Office for Tracking Air Pollution Hotspots. Each panelist was a blue chip with impeccable credentials. Pushback would be largely political and not based on the merits, i.e., science, data, and analysis.

On the day of this last panel discussion, when Tracie introduced her team of experts, she again implored everyone to set aside grievances, political philosophy, and the junk science that fails to account for the deteriorating quality of our environment and the struggle each of us confronts to survive with a decent quality of life. She reminded everyone that our survival - everywhere - will be contingent upon cooperation, not conflict; sharing, not hoarding; and unity, not disintegration.

Her tech team maintained a clear signal throughout the two-hour broadcast without interruption. When Tracie thanked her panelists for appearing on the broadcast and sharing their expertise, the team shut down and disabled their connections. It was over. She looked over at Wilson, her eyes glistening, and reached for him. Standing together, he wondered aloud about how the American media will react to this broadcast and how they will analyze the effectiveness of the symposium. "I fully expect that some media will take direction from the administration and dramatically inflate the impact of the symposium by suggesting a direct link between the broadcasts and the current discontent in the country. Hopefully, more responsible reporting will show that our efforts were about informing a public hungry for more and better information. But time will tell, Sweetie," Tracie responded. "Time will tell. I did what I could, what I felt was the right thing to do."

The panelist from the EPA was still on Tracie's mind at the end of the broadcast because she was a Black woman. It was hard to forget her response when Tracie asked her if she would be willing to become a panelist. "You know, Tracie, on an average day, I am practically invisible to most of my colleagues, my background and expertise notwithstanding. There will be those who will resent my decision to share my views publicly, even though that is part of my mandate. I suspect that I will be further ignored as a signal that I should retire early or understand that I will no longer be a candidate for promotion. In any instance, my career is over, but I am willing to participate. I am also a mother and a grandmother, and each of us has to step up." Tracie thought to herself that she knew before accepting that she would be targeted. *I hope she can be safe.*

In Washington, D.C., Andy Hillyard had heard about the last panel discussion through whatever channel *The Washington Post* had set up. Meanwhile, everyone from the newsroom was waiting for a response from the administration - the White House Press Secretary or the Secretary of State - and they waited well into the morning. Finally, the White House Press Corps was notified of a White House press briefing at 10:00 a.m. Every seat in the White House Press Room was occupied. Several minutes after ten, the White House Press Secretary, accompanied by a small coterie of aides, entered the Press Room. The Press Secretary, a functionary from the presidential campaign, stepped to the podium.

"I have a brief statement to make, and I will not take any questions. The Administration has become aware of a dangerous conspiracy that is peddling misinformation to frighten the nation. We are aware of several people behind this effort and we are employing every means at our disposal to correct the record. It is unfortunate that a few individuals are trying to inflame public opinion at a time when it is important that we pull together as a nation." He then quickly left the room, followed by his aides.

Everyone at *The Post* stood momentarily in silence, looking at each other quizzically. "What was that?" Andy asked. "What the fuck was that?"

"That's it!?" someone else asked. The Editor in Chief said, "I'm not sure what the story is there." In the White House Press Room, the reaction was similar. Reporters who came with questions about issues they thought might be covered looked at notebooks and each other. No one rushed to summarize the Press Secretary's comments before cameras on the South Lawn of the White House. Analysts had been standing by in newsrooms, prepared to cut away to cover both the Press Secretary's comments and their reporter's on-camera summary. There was nothing.

Andy, surrounded by others in the newsroom, asked rhetorically, "All of us saw the last panel discussion. Right!" Everyone nodded in agreement; a few raised their hands. "Tracie Hinton served as moderator and took ownership of the panel series. This administration has long suspected her and has taken every opportunity to demonize her, accusing her of everything except treason. Why the muted response today? Why didn't they attack the credibility of the panelists? This White House is guilty of perfidy, deceit, and an organized campaign to manipulate public opinion against truth. That's the real story!"

Everyone knew the President and his team were hiding their fecklessness to formulate a national action plan on human-induced climate change. The outlines of a real story were beginning to emerge and everyone seemed to suggest it at the same time. "*Now* we know what they were hiding," everyone said at once.

Andy, one of the senior staff present, suggested that everyone reach out to their contacts in other media who viewed both the panel discussion *and* the White House press briefing: "Let's see if all of us can come out with a statement of support for the panel broadcasts and demand an explanation from the administration for the news blackouts we have been experiencing. Instead of asking what they have been hiding, let's suggest to them *what* they have been hiding and are unwilling to share with us for reasons they should now explain."

The chief editor, not to be upstaged by Andy, opined "They can't come after all of us. Andy is right. Contact the other media to see if they will cooperate with us. What we would like to see is a unified news blast to bring out as many readers as possible demanding the answers all of us want." *The Post* and *The New York Times* were hearing from their foreign correspondents about foreign reaction to the last panel broadcast. Hundreds of demonstrators were massing in the streets of every capital worldwide. Universally, they were calling for immediate climate action. Third-world countries, in addition to Russia and China, were experiencing greater protests despite crackdowns by the police. In some countries, the military used live ammunition against protestors.

Among the U.S. mainstream media, the preparation for the coordinated news blast became a much larger project. At *The Post*, *The New York Times*, and *The Wall Street Journal*, senior editors and bureau chiefs were busily coordinating foreign news coverage with U.S. based reporters. Timing was the issue: coordinating the news blast and getting it out before the administration could shut them down. In the military, when it's all hands on deck behind a project, it translates as 'a__holes and elbows.'

Tracie had moderated the last panel discussion from Lagos. Her tech staff had developed a montage of background images to disguise her current location. She was still in Lagos as word filtered back to her regarding the success of the last panel. Andy, working through a series of satellite links, reached her to share news about the planned media blast. Andy also told her about the White House press briefing. There was silence as he finished. "Tracie, are you still there?" he asked.

"Yeah, I'm here. I'm not sure what to say, Andy. I expected a fierce reaction, something to the effect that I should be arrested on sight, nothing quite so muted. What do you think it means, Andy? I know what I think."

"I think their response is evidence that their attempts to demonize you have not had the intended effect. Theirs was an attempt to condemn and convict you in the court of public opinion, and it backfired. They got nothing!"

"I think you're right, Andy. However, I also believe the Vice President and his people will only feel more emboldened to come after me. Alicia Swarthmore, my former assistant who was found murdered behind a building on Dupont Circle, told me some time ago that Jethro Campbell and the Vice President are true believers, and they not only want me out of the picture, they want me dead! And I have no reason not to believe her. The President's gambit may not have worked, but these guys are operating from a totally different game plan. What do you think?"

"I can't argue with you, Tracie. You may be right. If you don't feel safe, then you're not safe, at least not here in Washington. So, what are your plans?"

"We're working that out now. I'll be in touch. Thanks, Andy."

Later that day, Tracie shared with Wilson and her parents, her conversation with Andy. When she finished, Ericka said, "If I interpret your friend Andy correctly, there is nothing else you need to do regarding the symposium. Your message has resonated worldwide and people are responding; they are putting their lives at risk by demanding more information and more action from their government. You were the catalyst; you were what the White House feared most - the spark that could ignite an aroused public. The media blast, if it is not thwarted, is the next step. You have allies now. But you are still not out of danger. You now have to decide how you want to go forward." Sam reached across the table to grasp his wife's hand as if to say, "I agree with your mom." Wilson was silent, and Tracie knew that meant *their* conversation would come later. Wilson would support her, but he had to be clear regarding her next steps and the attendant risks.

Despite the persistent threat from the Vice President and his allies, Tracie was greatly buoyed by the current direction of her life: she married the only man she could have imagined a permanent part of her life. Her symposium had been a success and would underpin a permanent conversation about the effects of human-induced climate change for the foreseeable future. Support for the Hinton Foundation was growing daily. She had earned the love, respect, and loyalty of a small group of people prepared to suit up with her and square off against whatever challenges lay over the horizon. And, finally, her mom and dad were no more than an arm's length away. She was ready for the next thing and knew exactly what it was.

She had a brilliant idea about how to go forward. Images from signs and banners in major cities around the world calling for action on climate change sparked an idea. The Hinton Foundation had to sponsor a Global Initiative for Climate Change (GICC). To sustain the momentum generated by the symposium, she would invite co-sponsors and donors from every participating city to assist in the planning of an international convention in London to be held within 24 months. For the U.S., she envisioned something more direct, more aggressive: a movement with a political action arm - "ACTION 2100." She noted, "I need to harness the energy, the frustration, the desire of Americans to take more direct responsibility for the stewardship of the planet. We will challenge elected officials to forge a partnership with a group whose primary mission is to clean up planet Earth and bequeath future generations a legacy worthy of our best effort."

"The mission may sound trite," she told herself, "But Americans will understand the simplicity of the mission, the language, and how to organize specific projects. The genius of Americans is responsible for much of the innovation and progress the world has enjoyed over the last century-and-a-half, so why not harness that genius to save it?"

It was now late in the afternoon, and for the past hour, ideas and images flashed through her mind in rapid succession. Tracie was writing furiously, at first in complete sentences, on a yellow legal pad, flipping page after page. Her hand couldn't keep pace with the output of her brain. Easier to develop were keywords and phrases replete with little boxes with labels, flow charts, diagrams, question marks, and, most importantly, names. Her head was about to explode. She took a breath, pushed back from her desk, and looked over the results of this latest brain explosion. Okay, time to go home. "I hope Wilson is ready for this," Tracie said, chuckling to herself.

After dinner, when her mom and dad had gone out with friends, Tracie looked over at Wilson, saying, "Sweetie, I had an idea today. Would you like to hear about it?"

Wilson had noticed the change in his wife when she arrived home earlier that evening but decided not to comment. Tracie seemed different, almost electrified; something was up. He decided to let the evening play out, knowing she would want to talk later. Maybe this was it. "Yeah, Baby. Tell me."

"There is a group of supporters and donors back in the U.S. who are asking me to run for elected office."

"Yes, we have yet to talk about that."

"Well, I do not want to present myself as someone taking advantage of a moment or in search of an opportunity to run for public office. I have never sought to do so. You know this. I'm sure these people have some specific ideas, which I'm willing to listen to. What I want to do is to bring something quite specific to the table - as that old expression goes."

"All right, where are you going with this?"

"I don't want to become a candidate for any of the major political parties. The lines of aspirants for each are too long, and the parties are incapable of major change, especially on issues that most Americans care about. The party leadership will allow the campaign strategists to play at the margins on the platform and fine-tune their messaging, but that's as far as the party apparatus will allow. No, I have something different in mind." Tracie then talked at length about how she prefers to harness the energy her symposium unleashed—with the Hinton Foundation as a catalyst, launched a new Global Initiative for Climate Change (GICC), culminating in an official launch in 24 months. An offshoot of that initiative will be ACTION 2100 - the American political arm of the initiative. ACTION 2100 would be launched on a different timetable. I want to present it to that group of sponsors and donors as an alternative, a third option for the voters in 2052. In other words, I want to build a bigger, better, galvanizing movement that attracts support from both political parties.

"Okay, why ACTION 2100?"

"Great question, Sweetie," she responded, smiling. Now on her feet, hands in motion, she began, "Because I intend to involve at the outset that generation of Americans who may seek to become elected officials in the year 2100. I want them to buy in at the creation, grow with the party, and contribute ideas. In other words, invest - NOW! Not later when we will need their vote. NOW! Work with us to define a mission and craft a platform of policy objectives and priorities. And help us get on the ballot in all 50 states."

"Wow! You've really wrapped your head around this thing!"

"I have, but look at it this way: I've been at this my whole life, and now, I have enough experience, the right instruments, and the right people to pull off something worthy of the sacrifices we have made. Think about it!"

"I really like the Global Initiative; it's timely, and you have broad-based support. Get your mom and dad behind that one. There will be a lot of work to do, including occasional travel to London once the offices are established." Continuing, Wilson said, "The political party really intrigues me because you will be operating within the super-charged atmosphere of a country gearing up for national elections. When you go public, both parties will be trying to calculate how broad your support will be - on a state-by-state basis - and whose political base will be most affected by your candidacy. The issues you plan to address are popular, and strategists from both parties know that. Now, let's talk specifics. You will need to see a timeline for having the campaign infrastructure in place, most critically, security for the candidate, a plan to qualify for the ballot nationwide, a major market media strategy, field coordinators in must-win states, and a budget. What is this campaign going to cost? And can finance goals be met? And, you will need a national volunteer coordinator to coordinate phone banking, messaging, and canvassing."

"Sweetie, we're on the same page."

"Oh, one more thing! Who do you have in mind as your running mate?"

"Wiley Mitchell, I just haven't asked him yet. He would be perfect - provided, of course, he and Roberta agree to do this. One more thing, Sweetie." Wilson looked up - waiting.

"The optics. I have to be mindful that we are still a divided nation on a wide span of issues. Yet, we are the most diverse nation around the world. I see even our diversity as a strength. So, the earlier the voters see us, the sooner they can make up their minds about us. I am married to a Nigerian and Wiley is married to a French national. Both of us are happily married, and the package is what it is."

"Somehow, I don't think that will matter to a lot of voters, considering what's at stake. If it does, then the country is in much worse shape than it is. Anything else?" Wilson asked.

"No, that's pretty much all of it."

"Would you like a cup of tea?" he asked.

"Yes, I'm not sleepy. So, tomorrow, I'll talk to Mom and Dad, and I'll also call Wiley and Roberta. I think you're right about Mom and Dad being excited about the Foundation. Both of them are great organizers." Wilson chuckled to himself as he headed for the kitchen. "Those people in the White House have no idea what they've unleashed," he said to himself. Tracie followed behind him; she had worked up a late evening appetite.

24

I n his last briefing at the [Russian] Ministry of Defense, Arkady suggested that the wild card in the proposed Canadian invasion plans was North Korea. "In the mold of his predecessors," he pointed out to the generals arrayed around the table, "the current North Korean leader is paranoid and, most damning, erratic, and unpredictable. The one thing we do know about their leadership is they want to be perceived as a global nuclear power not to be ignored - especially now." Arkady explained the contingencies built into his thinking: a robust, coordinated NATO military response; a coordinated NATO military response with the U.S. and possibly France withholding their military, preferring a diplomatic campaign for a ceasefire and negotiations; or Chinese political/military intervention in support of Russia - or not."

"Should North Korea intervene, our best guess is it will be in the form of a missile attack against the U.S.," Arkady added in response to a question from the defense minister. "What we have to figure out is the American response." Someone else then interjected, "So let's play that out."

Arkady then launched into a lengthy response focused on several key points. "The American defense secretary, his service chiefs, and their theater commanders are still smarting from being told to stand down in the wake of the last attack by North Korea. This time, however, if a North Korean missile lands on American soil, the President may not be able to contain them. They will *demand* a response!" The question Arkady asked rhetorically was whether America was prepared to fight a two-front war with North Korea and China in the West and with its NATO allies in the East. "We don't know the answer to that, and neither do our people in Washington, at the UN, or in Ottawa. We can only guess."

The Russian defense minister, a hardliner and survivor of several reshuffling of senior staff, sat listening and then asked, "What if China is prepared to sacrifice North Korea?"

"What do you mean, sir?" Arkady asked.

"All right, I'll explain. North Korea is a nuisance client state, but, as you say, it's a wild card for the Chinese as well. Yes, it does serve as a buffer against the Americans at no cost to the Chinese, but times have changed. North Korea has the potential to affect all of us negatively going forward. I'm suggesting the Chinese may be willing to jettison them once and for all. So, how do we find out?"

Before the defense minister could continue, Arkady added, "A likely outcome will be a unified Korea that is more amenable to a broad trading relationship with its Chinese neighbor, which would take years, as we know from West Germany's absorption of the former GDR (German Democratic Republic). South Korea's political and economic priorities will have to change while it builds the North's economy, absorbs or scales back the North's million-man army, improves the standard of living for 30 million North Koreans, and upgrades the North's industrial, technological, and communications infrastructure. If anything, a unified Korea of 85 million would be strong enough to negotiate a balanced relationship between the U.S. and China, something China wants."

"That tips the scales in China's favor," the defense minister added. "And they are an ally. But while that outcome is favorable for the Chinese, it is not *our* primary objective," he reminded the others around the table. "If that were our principal objective," he pointed out, "we would not have invaded Norway or Greenland. Furthermore, the Chinese would not have made a similar move." He then went on to elaborate, "The Chinese play a different, longer game but always try to capitalize on the strategic moves of others." He told his generals, "Our strategy remains unchanged. Our people in Ottawa have told us where the Canadians have stored the seeds from Florence. What we capture in Canada will guarantee our long-term survival without our having to negotiate with the West. A seed vault under our control strengthens our leverage in negotiating more Western sanctions and future economic, agricultural, and trade ties with Africa, South America, and allies in the Middle East and Southeast Asia. That, comrades, is the end game. A global prosperity network."

Back in his office, Arkady reflected on the defense minister's remarks. The resources from the super-secret vault in Norway were always the raison d'être for the military campaign. Internally, Russia was increasingly unstable, and instability would shift the political terrain under the current leadership in Moscow. Moreover, Arkady was haunted by a nagging fear he could only share with Maria outside their home. The attack against Canada was imminent, but as he whispered to Maria, "How many units will respond? And if we find ourselves in a protracted war, will our troops remain unified?"

Arkady believed he was speaking rhetorically, and that is why Maria's response momentarily jarred him when she said, "A few of the other wives and I have had that conversation because someone - probably our husbands - will be held accountable if that becomes the case."

For weeks, Russian President Vasily Krupinsky had been receiving reports about ordinary Russians raiding military supply depots en masse throughout the country, the people desperate for fuel, drinking water, food, and medical supplies. His generals had been reluctant to share the extent of the problems for fear of being removed or worse. Moreover, criminal elements were stealing small arms, rocket-propelled grenades (RPGs), and machine guns. Essential supplies at these depots were dwindling at such a rapid rate the cohesion of units dependent on those supplies was weakened, as was their military effectiveness. Compounding the problem was the response of the soldiers guarding the depots. In some areas, soldiers refused to fire on local residents because the population was acting out of desperation, not animus toward the military. Krupinsky's concern was the operational readiness of select units on the eve of military action against Canada.

Secretly, Krupinsky had asked the commanding general of the country's cyber command to prepare a plan to launch a cyber-attack against Ontario, Canada's most populous province and one of the world's top ten producers of nickel and platinum group metals. Crippling Toronto, capital of Ontario and a province of 20 million residents, would send shock waves through the country's world-class economic and financial center without firing a shot. The effects would be felt in financial markets in New York City, London, Shanghai, and Tokyo. At 1 a.m. on a Sunday night in Moscow, Operation Retribution was launched. Instantly, seven thousand miles away, the Canadian province of Ontario was plunged into darkness. The attack was planned for maximum effect, 6 p.m. local time on a Sunday, an hour when families were at home having dinner or traveling in their local communities, before the following day started a new work week.

Homes were without power, streets were dark, and traffic signals ceased to function. Chaos, confusion, and fear came seconds later. Auxiliary power generators sputtered to life and quickly died. Without electricity, life came to a halt.

Prime Minister Pearson reached for his phone, but there was no signal. A military aide came running from the basement communication center to report the loss of power. The Prime Minister looked out the window to see complete darkness. Battery-powered lights came on in the residence, but how long would they last without recharging?

Communications were down. No one knew the extent of the blackout. They could only speculate. Outside, the sound of car horns and distant voices pierced the night. Uncertainty and fear were initially tempered by the belief that power would be restored quickly. Shortly, official vehicles with their titled and be-ribboned occupants arrived at the residence to brief the Prime Minister. The reports were uniform: total power and communications blackout. Essential services, including hospitals and emergency rooms, were operating on battery power, but without electricity, batteries could not be recharged. Fire departments would be operating in the dark. Defense was on full alert, but it was blind.

Military aides and staff had lit the emergency supply of candles in the Prime Minister's residence. Within an hour, he had assembled his Cabinet and national security team. He began, "If you are thinking what I'm thinking, this is Russian. It is no accident! This is an act of war! We may have been anticipating a military invasion of some sort, but this is more egregious. Lives of millions of civilians are at stake." The Prime Minister and his advisors were unaware that the cyber-attack against Ontario had been conducted as a calculated major diversion. North of Ontario on the northeast coast of the Nunatsiavut Region of Newfoundland, a force of several hundred Russian commandos had landed via helicopters in the dead of night, intending to overcome the Canadian forces near Nain who were guarding the location of the temporary seed vault. Roberta Mitchell had been the last American to visit the site when she traveled there from Florence on behalf of Dr. Nuzzi to bring the seeds the Russians now sought.

The terrified Moravian descendants living in nearby Nain had no idea what horror had dropped out of the sky. When the town found itself overwhelmingly surrounded and their town leaders taken prisoner, they gave no appearance of knowing why they had been invaded. The Russian commander could find no way to communicate with them. It had been his intelligence that the seed vault was located in a mine 35 kilometers away, which, as it turned out, didn't appear to exist. They had searched for it with the usual location instruments, expecting to find the mine. However, what they didn't know was that the area was underwater from the rising sea level, which they rather expected. But what used to be Voisey Bay was now almost cutting the region off from the rest of northwestern Newfoundland, and the mine was an old underwater nickel, copper, and cobalt operation that had been abandoned at least a decade earlier when the main vein had run out. The existence of these precious minerals had been a veiled military secret carried out without the involvement of local laborers, who were mostly farmers and fishermen. The traces of minerals disguised the seed containers, which were made of polymold and submersed essentially in water balloons. They had remained undetected.

No number of threats, torture, or sign language was getting the invaders anywhere. Fractured French was the only lingua franca they came up with, and the residents still remained completely baffled and stunned. So innocent do they appear, the Russian officers conferred in frustration, their outbursts becoming more and more colorful and angry until the commander was forced to contact his superiors and resigned to die on his sword. Unfortunately, four civic leaders who seemed in authority had been executed.

The unsuccessful invasion was humiliating for the Russians and left the townspeople traumatized. They had no idea what to do except tell the provincial government in St. Johns what had happened. News of the attack was delayed until communication links to Ottawa could be restored.

25

President Krupinsky, upon learning of the failure of the Newfoundland raid, first summoned his national security advisor and then the defense minister. The world would soon learn of their attempt to confiscate the seed vault in Newfoundland from the traumatized and bewildered residents of Nain. The Russian President was prepared to endure the consequences of his raid had he been successful. The contents of the vault, were they in his possession, would have strengthened his negotiating position to lift crippling international sanctions and alleviate domestic pressures. Failure was humiliating and would deepen his unpopularity at home. On the streets and outside retail shops, Russians no longer queued for basic necessities. They now brazenly pillaged the walled dachas of the rich, the privileged, and the elite without fear of retribution.

Moreover, military depots were now only lightly guarded, and the guards refused to fire on marauding crowds. Also, foreign media correspondents were openly sought out by Russians to inform them of conditions in the country. Neighbors no longer informed on each other. The world was now privy to news unreported by the still tightly controlled Russian media. Krupinsky would soon earn the international opprobrium heaped upon Russia by the international press and the majority of political leaders around the world. The pressure was so intense that he confided to an aide [who told his wife] about the necessity for a food taster.

Fifteen hours into the cyber-attack against Ontario, it was lifted. Only a few hours earlier did the Canadian Prime Minister and the world learn of the attack. Although the Prime Minister could not publicly attribute the attack to Russia, the world was not misled. The worst-kept political secret had been Russia's intent to launch a special military action in Canada.

Prime Minister Pearson delivered what some members considered the most incendiary rhetorical attack in the history of the UN against a member of the Permanent Five (P5): France, the United Kingdom, China, Russia, and the United States. Offering meticulous details of the attack provided by the citizens of Nain, including the colors and style of the uniforms worn by the invaders, the prime minister asked rhetorically, "Where in civilized society today is there a place for such reprehensible thuggery, behavior not even found in the bowels of Dante's Inferno?" That particular literary flourish was just one of several he employed during the hour-long speech.

The Russian delegate disconnected her earphones and sat impassively, enduring the verbal tongue-lashing. To walk out would only have compounded her country's humiliation. She would later refer to the Canadian Prime Minister's remarks as an "undignified harangue unbefitting a head of government." Upon the conclusion of Pearson's remarks, as if by pre-arranged signal, all eyes shifted to the American delegate, who also sat impassively. The British delegate later told the German delegate they had dodged a bullet *this* time, referring to the likelihood of a coordinated NATO response had Russia attacked Canada with military force. A cyber-attack was considered an act of war, but the response was different - not kinetic.

In Ottawa, following a similar tongue-lashing by the foreign minister, the Russian ambassador was declared persona non grata and ordered to leave the country within 24 hours. His Canadian counterpart in Moscow timed his departure for the exact hour of the Russian's meeting with the Canadian foreign ministry. Russia's international isolation tightened. In London, the media were reporting the strange coincidence of two Russian generals found dead. No details of their deaths were offered. In Moscow, Maria Karpov was summoned to FSB headquarters. She and Arkady prepared their children for the likelihood that one or both of their parents could be 'disappeared' and that they could find themselves alone. There was nothing novel about this phenomenon, especially in Russia.

Meanwhile, in the U.S., political party conventions were two months away, and the President and the Vice President were breathing easier following the Russian debacle in Newfoundland. The necessity of an American response to Russia's incursion into their northern neighbor had been averted. Recent polls, however, had hardened, and predictions by most media analysts for the President and his Machiavellian Vice President's second term were grim. Even *MSNBC* and *FOX* analysts were suggesting the voters were not comfortable with the White House's handling of the North Korean missile attack on the West Coast, the impact of a changing climate on the country, the Administration's persistent hands-off approach to Russian aggression, and its willingness to target private citizens. One prominent national political analyst, a university professor, noted, "To the surprise of this White House, Americans have been paying attention while coping with the complex challenges of daily survival. We'll see how that plays out next November. If the vote were held today, I believe we'd see a change in leadership."

Tracie was under pressure to schedule her return to the U.S. She preferred to wait until after the news blast from the major print and cable news organizations across the country. If she and Andy were correct, following the blast, public support for major change could intensify, thus reducing the fear factor about her proposal to launch ACTION 2100. "Call Andy," Wilson told Tracie. "Tell him you need to know the date and time of the media blast." Tracie looked at her watch and picked up her phone. Andy responded.

"Tracie, I think I know why you're calling."

"Okay, so when will you guys go live?"

"Tomorrow morning at 7:00 a.m. Eastern Standard Time. We'll catch everyone, including our journalists abroad. Each organization will sponsor its own broadcast. This is too big a deal for a single spokesman. The message may vary, but only slightly, to capture regional differences." Andy went on to explain that "each broadcast, each blast will issue a call to action because of a failure on the part of the administration to share critical information about the real effects of a changing global climate. The call will demand that we hold our elected officials accountable for the chaos around us, including the likelihood of war."

"Andy, you've touched on the major elements in that message. Americans are now savvy enough to know what they need to know, and they're not only demanding what they need but also setting forth time-lines. Am I right?"

"Yeah, you are, my friend."

"Then it is likely they are open to suggestions for change. Let's not waste the value of a good crisis to push for major, no, radical change."

"You must have something in mind if I'm reading you correctly. Care to share?"

"I do, my friend, I do. I plan on returning soon to meet with some friends. I'll let you know the date, time, and location of the meeting. I'd like for you to be there."

"Damn! What are you up to? I like it and I don't know what it is. As long as it doesn't kill me. Okay, stay tuned for the blast, and let me know your travel plans."

"Thank you, Andy, and be safe. The idiots are still out there."

"They are the least of my concerns now. We've got bigger issues to deal with."

Col. Anaya Howard, a Senior Operations Officer in the NMCC, the Pentagon command and communications center for the National Military Command Authority, was settling into her desk preparing for her eight-hour shift. Howard, a highly regarded 2038 West Point graduate, was deep selected for her promotion to Colonel. She was also considered a rising star among her academy classmates and a prime candidate for early promotion for her first star. A Pentagon polyglot, she spoke Russian, Japanese, Chinese, Korean, and Arabic fluently. She was also conversant in Greek, Turkish, German, and the Romance Languages. Her latest undertaking was learning Vietnamese.

For two months, she had been on the midnight to 8 a.m. shift, which she enjoyed. For a doctoral candidate at Georgetown University, the relative calm of the graveyard shift offered her moments to catch up on reading to complete her dissertation. The commute from her home in Northern Virginia to the Pentagon at midnight was quicker and less congested. Fortunately for her and the other members of her 20-man team, there had been fewer global crises during the graveyard shift since the Russian landing in Newfoundland.

At 2 a.m., two hours into her shift, Howard, while sipping a cup of green tea, noticed several unusual blips on her screen that fixed her attention. Some airborne objects were on a trajectory from North Korea to the eastern Pacific, and there was nothing on the Threat Board. Hmm, this is unusual, she thought to herself.

"General Hayes," Howard called out, setting her tea to one side, "I think we have something here. Look at this, Sir!" Hayes, the Deputy Director for Operations (DDO), moved quickly to look at the screen in front of Howard. "Damn!" he hissed between clenched teeth. "Those bastards have launched several missiles. Track their trajectory! he yelled. "Where are they going to hit? And when?"

"Hawaii!" Howard yelled, "In twelve minutes!"

"Get them (Admiral Grant Holmes, INDOPACOM - Commander-in-Chief, Indo-Pacific Command) on the horn, NOW! And get the White House Situation Room! Hell is about to be in session," he muttered to himself.

Seconds later, Marine Colonel Jefferson Koppenhaver picked up.

"Admiral Holmes' office."

"Colonel, this is General Hayes from the NMCC. A few seconds ago, two missiles lifted off from North Korea and are projected to hit Hawaii in just under 12 minutes. Batten down the hatches!" He hung up before hearing a response. There was no time for the usual "are you sure" authentication conversation. The next call was to the White House.

"This is General Hayes, DDO from the NMCC. I need the President - NOW!" Minutes later, the President rushed into the Situation Room. "What's going on?" he asked.

"Mr. President, this is General Hayes in the Command Center at the Pentagon. A few minutes ago, North Korea launched at least two missiles toward Hawaii. We estimate they will impact in less than ten minutes. I have alerted INDOPACOM. I don't know what they can do with so little lead time."

"We're just finding out about this?" the President asked incredulously.

"Yes, sir!"

"Do we know if the missiles have nuclear warheads?"

"No, Sir! We don't. Their launch sites in North Korea house both conventional and nuclear warheads. If they are conventional, we expect the targets to be military to cripple our naval capability in Pearl Harbor. None of the carriers are in port, but elements of the 7th Fleet are. We could easily suffer 8 to 10,000 casualties, including wounded and missing."

"And if they are low-yield nuclear?"

"The numbers of dead, wounded, and missing could increase by a factor of 2 or 3, and that includes civilians. Bear in mind, sir, I'm giving you my best guess. One more thing, sir!"

"Yes, what is it?"

"In deciding our response, sir, be aware that North Korean policy is automatic nuclear launch if their leadership or their command-and-control systems are threatened or come under attack - what they refer to as a 'decapitation strike.'"

The national security advisor and the other members of the NSC had been called and were en route to the White House. Twelve anxious minutes passed, and the first satellite reports from the NMCC flashed on the overhead screens. Joint Base Pearl Harbor Hickam on O'ahu had been obliterated, as was the Coast Guard Base on Maui. Collateral damage adjacent to those installations was also extensive. There were no estimates on loss of life.

"This makes no sense! Why would they do this?" shouted the President. Then he paused and admitted, "My mistake was not responding after the first attack. That *has* to be it!"

They must know we will respond!" the defense secretary added. And then, in a direct shot at the President, he said, "Maybe they think we won't this time either."

"That was unnecessary!" the White House chief of staff responded, his voice rising.

"Was it?" the defense secretary shot back in his own defense. "Why should they think we'd respond?" The room was quiet. Everyone knew that the Secretary of Defense and the Joint Chiefs had been at loggerheads with the White House since the first attack. The Joint Chiefs had all threatened to resign in the days following that attack, only to be talked down by the defense secretary.

"That's enough!" the Vice President interjected. "We have to respond, and we don't have a lot of time. If we don't, those bastards will hit us again, who knows where. We can't take another hit like this. We'd have an insurrection in this country!"

The national security advisor had arrived and weighed in, saying, "We must launch a decapitation strike, taking out their leadership, their command-and-control systems, and their nuclear launch sites. And then, for insurance, we have to take out their submarine base. We must eliminate their ability to launch future nuclear attacks, including from the sea. Taking out their conventional capabilities then becomes an easier objective to accomplish. And we have to do it before South Korea gets involved. If South Korean forces cross the 38th Parallel, China will engage."

"If that is our response," the Secretary of State added, "the question is, 'do we give the Chinese advance warning?' Who knows? They may agree to some parameters to our response and decide to sit this one out."

The President, speaking more forcefully than anyone had heard recently, said, "I'll give President Chen a call and suggest that he sit this one out. Get him on the phone! I'm in no mood to be jerked around."

Following the call to his Chinese counterpart, and to everyone's surprise, the President reported, "They agreed to hold their fire on one condition: South Korea's troops cannot cross the 38th Parallel into North Korea." Looking around the table for reactions, he saw everyone was in accord. "The South Koreans may object, but we can live with that," the Vice President responded, speaking for everyone in the room.

The time-lapse from the satellite photos of the strike on Hawaii had been 25 minutes. The fear was that North Korea would launch another strike preempting American retaliation. The President turned to the Chairman of the Joint Chiefs, who spoke from the MCC, "General, how do we do this?"

"We have submarines off the coast of the Korean Peninsula with

SLBMs (submarine-launched ballistic missiles). We have war-gamed this scenario for years. All our commanders need is the order."

"All right, GET IT DONE!"

The President then told his team to settle in because it would be a long night. "First, we've got to notify the Gang of Eight (the heads of the relevant committees in the House and Senate) and then seek permission from the Speaker of the House to address a joint session of Congress." Turning to his chief of staff, he directed that the process for our Continuity of Government be initiated and, to the Chairman of the JCS, he said, "Admiral, I want to know what our losses were in Hawaii." The Secretary of State spoke up, adding, "I'll notify our allies of the action we've taken. There could be blowback elsewhere. I still don't trust the Chinese, the Russians, or the Syrians not to take advantage of this situation elsewhere. The Middle East would be perfect."

No one seemed to notice, but the Vice President looked around the room smiling to himself. He was witnessing a President in command mode, an FDR moment following the Japanese attack on Pearl Harbor. If the country responds well to the President's actions, even at this late stage of his presidency, there was still a chance they might secure a second term and keep his presidential aspirations alive.

By 3 a.m., the first reports from other commands in Hawaii were coming in. As everyone feared, the numbers of dead, wounded, and missing were in the tens of thousands. The dead also included Admiral Holmes and his entire staff. Seven naval vessels were out of commission, including three destroyers, one heavy cruiser, two littoral combat ships, and a hospital ship. One large Coast Guard vessel was also damaged. Scores of sailors, marines, Coast Guard, and medical personnel were killed. The Seventh Fleet was on full alert in the Sea of Japan, as was the 8th Army in Korea. The 6th Fleet was ordered into the Mediterranean as a contingency against Syrian adventurism. NATO was also on alert status. The President was sending the rare signal that tonight was not the night to test him.

The first satellite photos of North Korea following the American strike revealed the principal command and control headquarters in

Pyongyang had been leveled, as were all the missile and rocket sites and their largest, most important nuclear facility. The South Korean Army was on full alert and prepared to engage any North Korean forces attempt to enter Seoul. The Republic of Korea (ROK) President and his chief advisors were being evacuated to Busan in the Kyongsang Nam Do Province, the country's second-largest city, home of its major port, and the heartland of the country's key industrial and shipbuilding complexes.

The next day, the American President was still asking why the North Koreans had attacked. The answer came several days later during a call from the South Korean President. The Korean Central Intelligence Agency (KCIA) had learned from one of its agents in the North that a member of Russian Intelligence had persuaded a member of North Korea's intelligence service that the American President planned to strike North Korea to improve his chances of being reelected. Further justification, of course, had been that in the earlier strike against the U.S., North Korea's dictatorial and paranoid leadership, acting on a lie, had decided to strike first. This latest crisis, resulting in a significant loss of life in North Korea and Hawaii, could have precipitated a third world war, and it would have been at Russia's instigation.

In the days following the successful response to North Korea's devastating attack on Hawaii, the President and his campaign advisors sensed a strategic moment and launched a more positive, unifying message to the country. He stressed unity, cooperation, and peace through global collaboration. In a series of highly choreographed appearances around the country, the President acknowledged the inherent challenges a changing climate presented and spoke passionately about policy initiatives for which he asked for public support.

For critics, analysts, and even supporters, the reaction to this sudden about-face was confusion, cynicism, and charges of political opportunism. A *Washington Post* headline blared, *"President Discovers Climate Change!"* The exclamation point was the ironic emphasis. *The New York Times* asked, "Mr. President, Where Have You Been?" Political cartoons began reappearing, featuring a bumbling President tripping over a footstool labeled "climate change" and searching through a garage, and weeds asked, "Climate Change, Where Are You?" If the intent of the new campaign approach was to raise the President's profile or see an uptick in his favorability rating in the polls, his latest gambit had the opposite effect.

When Tracie learned how the President's disingenuousness had been received at home, she told Wilson. "And to think he was willing to silence me by any means necessary."

26

The series of media blasts by the nation's principal media organizations had the effect hoped for by millions of voters. Americans were demanding change. Public confidence in elected officials from both major political parties was at an all-time low: below twenty percent. Frequently, people polled on the street said, "We need more and better choices than we're getting." Or, another favorite is, "They promise us one thing to get our vote and, then, when they get to Washington, the lobbyists and swamp politics buys their vote. Either way, we lose." And the worst reaction from many of those polled was, "Why vote? It doesn't matter." For Tracie, it was time to get back to the U.S. and explore her political prospects. Mom, Dad, and Wilson were solidly behind her. It was now time to call Wiley.

Tracie reached Wiley at home and told him of her plans. He agreed the timing for her return was good for their purposes; that there were no guarantees, but the prospects were favorable to introduce something radically different. He, too, was referencing polling data, media analyses, and what he was picking up from his network of contacts. "Who would I be meeting with? and where?" Tracie asked.

Wiley then refreshed Tracie's memory about his earlier trip to Miami to meet with a group of businessmen who had reached out to him. "The leader of that group was Timothy "Tim" Paar, the wealthy scion of the Paar family, founder of a vast real estate empire with holdings on both the Gulf Coast and the Atlantic (Miami, Jacksonville, Daytona, Clearwater, and Pensacola). Tim and his sister, Jana, also own at least a dozen profitable auto dealerships in the state, including Rolls Royce, Bentley, Mercedes Benz, BMW, and Lexus. In fact, many of their real estate clients purchase and lease automobiles from them."

"Okay, so, why Tim?"

"Tim was the leader of a group of businessmen who supported the governor's proposal to manage the impact of a changing climate on the state, as well as the projections for coastal erosion along the Gulf Coast and the Atlantic. The plans were formulated around faulty data, and Tim Paar found a lot of his prized real estate underwater. Prospective buyers panicked and walked. Several dealerships are also in low-lying areas state-wide and sales plummeted." Wiley continued: "When I met with Tim and his group, they were looking for realistic solutions to their current problems. They had become believers in how a changing global climate and human-induced climate change were impacting Florida, including permanently altering its coastline. Moreover, they had heard of my group from business colleagues and wanted a no-BS plan going forward. When I shared with them the background of my relationship with you, they wanted to know more about you, your activities, and your commitment to saving the planet. They have a vested interest in that. The net worth of the group I met with is billions - lots of billions. The more they learned, the more the question came up, 'Is she interested in politics?'"

"So, these are the people we would be meeting with?"

"The group you and I would be meeting with would number about 12 to 15, but they would be representing a much larger group of potential supporters. These people are networked where it matters to what we and they want to achieve. If you agree to a meeting, I propose Raleigh

(North Carolina). It's neutral, convenient, and accessible to everyone, including yourself. So, what are your travel plans?"

"Give me three days. Delta flies into Raleigh. I will need a day to rest and get my bearings. Also, after our meeting with them, I want to meet with you and Andy, so you'll have to contact Andy and have him join us. If this thing is a go, we have a lot of work to do, and it's going to be non-stop through the Primaries and our convention."

"Yeah, I know it. But first, I need to be convinced these guys are prepared to finance this effort. We've got to build and put in place an entire campaign infrastructure on the fly."

"There's something else, Wiley. I haven't had time to discuss this with the two of you."

"Oh, what's that?"

"The response to the Hinton Foundation has been really gratifying. No, that understates it. It has been explosive! If I weren't committed to this new project, getting the Foundation off the ground would occupy me full-time. If we are successful, and that is a big IF, I won't be able to manage the Foundation, and neither will you. The Foundation is important to me, as is its first major initiative, The Global Initiative for Climate Change, and I need to be able to trust whoever manages it until my life in politics is over."

"That makes sense, Tracie. So, who do you have in mind? Your dad?"

"No, Roberta. She's European; she's got the background, the energy, and the perfect image. She's strong and she knows how I think, and, most importantly, I trust her judgment. I won't need to be looking over her shoulder."

"Wow! I didn't see that coming. Tracie, the only thing I can suggest is to talk to her directly. I think you are offering a phenomenal opportunity, but that's me."

"Fair enough. I'll talk to her."

The rest of the conversation was about details and logistics.

When Tracie hung up, she sat for a moment, thinking about what lay ahead and what a run for the nomination and the presidency could mean for her and Wilson, her parents, Wilson's family, and a host of others whose support she had yet to solicit.

For Wiley, the conversation with Tracie had a different meaning: the space in his head had a different dimension. A consequence of his commitment to Tracie was that Roberta was going to be asked to assume the helm of the London-based Hinton Foundation. As exciting as the prospect was, at least to him, it meant that Roberta would be either commuting from Seattle or living in London for months at a time. That is if she accepted. She, naturally, would find the offer as intriguing as he did. She would also be influenced by how he felt about the separation. Their marriage was healthy and strong because they allowed nothing to threaten it, and they never took it for granted. Roberta's travel to Italy and, subsequently, to Greenland and Canada would pale in comparison to what this latest commitment would entail. And he, should he become Vice President, would need the support of his wife. "Whoa!" Wiley thought to himself. "This is way out there." That night, he and Roberta were going to have to talk. He also knew that Tracie and Wilson had to have had the same conversation - and they were newlyweds.

Three days later, as Tracie's Delta Flight took off for Raleigh, she left behind a Mom, Dad, and new husband, coping with yet another new chapter in her storied life. They would adapt as they always did, just as she did years earlier, whenever her dad received a new assignment. For her, that meant a new country, new language, new culture, new schools, and new friends. The large, intriguing question that would occupy her mind for at least part of the flight was, "Where do I begin?" A presidential campaign was the equivalent of managing a tsunami that would engulf many lives. Three nights earlier, Wiley and Roberta were grappling with a variation on the same question following a conversation between Tracie and Roberta: "How would she (Roberta) feel about assuming the helm of the Hinton Foundation for the next two years?" Wiley had given Roberta a heads-up, so the call was not a complete surprise. Roberta had assured Tracie she would consider her request seriously.

Lying at opposite ends of a large, maroon leather sofa in their living room, Wiley and Roberta began one of the most consequential conversations they'd had to date. The conversation focused initially on the amount of time they would have to be apart - how to manage that. "When we accepted the idea of you becoming Tracie's running mate," Roberta began, "We talked about the amount of time you'd probably be on the road. The difference is you would be in the U.S., and we could meet. If I accepted this request, I would have to be in London for months on end, managing the Foundation while orchestrating the launch of the Global Initiative on Climate Change - a full-time task in itself. How do you feel about that, Babe?"

"I feel as you do - no different. That said, there is another dimension to this. Although Tracie and Wilson have been very close for almost 20 years, they only *recently* married. Tracie and I could make history. I said *could*. Nothing is assured. The Foundation is very important, but she is willing to set that aside for a larger historical purpose. During the interim, she would be entrusting the culmination of her life's work to one of her best friends: *You!* What if we win? If we don't win, you will have launched her Foundation and laid the groundwork for their first major initiative, and she will be eternally grateful. That's only two years - or less. Maybe in that time, we might consider selling the business and moving to London. That would be an option. I know you wouldn't mind being in Europe for a while, closer to your family. And, finally, if we win, you will recruit your successor at the Foundation and come back as the Second Lady of the United States (VFLOTUS)" laughing.

"As Second Lady, I could still run our business, only from here in Washington," Roberta rejoined.

"Yes, that's true."

"So, Sweetie, it's up to you. I'll do whatever you want - seriously."

Roberta expected that response from Wiley thus making it easier to add this new adventure to their lives. "All right, I'll tell Tracie we're on board. Besides, she is counting on us, and I do not want to disappoint her. You guys better have some damn good security out there, and you know what I'm talking about!"

Roberta called Tracie before she boarded the plane for Raleigh.

Early the second day, Tracie landed in Raleigh to be met by Wiley and Tim Paar. Paar was a pleasant surprise. He could have waited until their scheduled meeting the next day; he was serious - a *very* good sign! Wiley had flown in the previous evening to have dinner with Tim. Paar was unaccompanied, which is the reason Roberta did not come. She would join them before Tracie returned to Lagos.

"Tim, thanks for meeting me. Wiley tells me you think we have a good shot at this thing."

"I do, Miss Hinton, I do."

"Tim, please call me Tracie."

"Well, I'm a Southerner, and you know how we are about our women-folk. But, Tracie, it is."

"So, I understand we're having an initial meeting over dinner this evening? Great! I don't want to waste anyone's time. Give me a few hours to freshen up, and I *will* be ready to go."

At the hotel, Wiley checked Tracie in and escorted her to her room. "Andy is here, by the way."

"Good, things seem to be coming together quickly."

"Yes! It's almost scary," Wiley replied.

Tracie understood one immutable fact regarding this visit: She was on display with some of the most wealthy and influential businessmen and women in the country. They had heard of her, and now they wanted to size her up - as the expression goes. Was she worth the investment they were prepared to make? Wiley was part of the package, but she was the main attraction. The country was in crisis, and something had to be done. Dinner was pleasant, and Tracie genuinely enjoyed being in the company of her new benefactors. When coffee was being served, Tim rose from the table and approached the podium.

"Friends, thank you for coming! We're in a crisis; each of us knows that! The country is coming apart, and our leadership is absent without leave. In the military, that's called being AWOL. The question we have been grappling with for the past several years is, 'What can be done about it? What can we do about it?' When we met with Wiley and began to talk about solutions to the problems we're having in Florida, we knew he knew what he was talking about, that perhaps the solution to some of our problems is having people like him getting to work on them. That discussion, as you know, led to our meeting here tonight. 'Wiley, I'm going to put this on you. (Everyone laughing.) You said the solution to our problem is sitting here with us.' Tracie Hinton, welcome, and the floor is yours.'"

Tracie took a deep breath as she approached the podium just beyond the dinner table. Standing there fixing the gaze of her select audience, she felt she was among friends. They were not looking for a lengthy speech, and she was not prepared to give one. Could she and they establish a connection? The next few minutes would tell.

"Good evening, friends, and thank you for the opportunity to spend some time with you. It was never my intent to promote myself as a candidate for public office. I do so reluctantly. There is a time and a season for every great cause, and I believe for us, and those like us, that time is now. We have no choice!

"For a century after the end of World War II, the United States, by persistence, accident, or expectation, had enjoyed the domestic and international reputation of being the indispensable nation in world affairs, and our leadership was respected here at home. Alliances [NATO, ASEAN, ANZUS, SEATO, UN] and global institutions [IMF, World Bank, IBRD, WHO] were conceived, funded, and launched at this country's behest. America led the way; the civilized and soon-to-be-democratic world followed in our wake in the competition against international Russian and Chinese Communism. We solved problems; we didn't create problems for others to solve. When you assume the mantle of leadership, the expectation is 'you suit up and get on the

field, not assume the posture of a spectator.' [Tracie knew this last comment would sting once it became public.]

"A failure of our leadership has resulted in the shift of the tectonic plates beneath our principal allies and trade partners in Europe regarding how we cope with the effects of a changing global climate and human-induced climate change. Some observers around the globe suggest the shift was irreversible, while others say it was inevitable. Either way, the cloak of leadership, in my view, once more devolves to us."

"So, what's at stake? Our lives; the future for our children, our families, our communities, our country, and our planet. We have proven that truth, honesty, and integrity can galvanize the most disparate of us into concerted action. Greed, avarice, and a lust for power unified to marginalize us, to persuade us that our best interests were at the heart of the policies and programs promulgated on our behalf by those we elected to lead us.

"We know better. Many have suggested it may be too late now, but it is never too late to take the next step. We have no choice!

"To continue as we are is to invite inevitable collective catastrophe. A noted South African humanitarian and statesman famously remarked; 'It always seems impossible until it's done.'

"Let's work together to navigate this period of extraordinary challenge! We have no choice!

"Let's choose hope over despair, denial, and division. We have no choice! We. Simply. Have. No. Choice!

"Thank you."

As Tracie approached her seat, Tim Paar and the other dinner guests rose to give her sustained applause. Tim leaned over and said, "I heard your message, Tracie. We may have been part of the problem in the past, but we hear your message: 'The time is now; we have no choice! We face a catastrophic future if we don't work together.'" Tracie looked around, catching Wiley's eye as if to say, "Game on, my friend, game on!"

Before returning to her room, Tim told Tracie, "Let's have breakfast in the morning. I have some materials for you." The next morning, Tim handed Tracie a binder saying, "Here are lists of names and contact information for people we know are prepared to work with you and your team to build a campaign, to raise the funds you will need, and to ensure you are on the ballot in all 50 states. You may use them or your own people; the choice is yours. We want to work with you. I will serve as your finance chairman - if that is alright with you."

"Tim, we greatly appreciate this, and yes, we are prepared to work with you. Had you not assumed the role of finance chairman, I was going to ask you." Opening the binder, Tracie saw several names recommended for campaign chairman. Quickly scanning the resumes, Tracie said, "They look good, Tim! I will be in touch with them today. We need to build and be up and running within the next several days."

"Wiley tells me you will establish your campaign headquarters in Detroit."

"Yes, in the heart of the Midwest where we see the mix of the densely populated areas with the rural and midwestern and how they are coping with climate-related disasters."

"That's smart, that's strategic, and it won't go unnoticed. Several of our supporters are making their private aircraft available as a contribution to your campaign. Fundraising is well underway. Our targets are small and individual contributors, those who are looking for an alternative come Election Day, those who need to know they have not been outspent by corporate donors."

'Tim, before you go, what is your candid assessment of our chances? We're not in this to be a spoiler."

"Tracie, my people and I are in this thing, and we honestly believe you have a good shot at winning! Both parties are coming after you because of the threat you represent to established and entrenched interests. Your symposium was proof positive of the threat they feel. However, if you stick to the message you shared with us last night, and people get to feel the depth of your commitment, they will turn out! You just need to know what to do should you win."

When Tim left, Tracie met with Andy and Wiley to talk about organization, strategy, and messaging. Andy was Tracie's first appointment: campaign communications director and press spokesman. Andy was delighted because this was the one assignment he wanted at this point in his career. He reached across the table and took Tracie's hand in his while standing to embrace her. "Thank you, my friend! Thank you! We're going to win this thing," he told her.

Turning to Wiley, Tracie mentioned she had heard from Roberta. With tears in her eyes, she said, "I owe you and Roberta a debt I will never be able to repay. Without the two of you, what we seek to do would amount to 'mission impossible.' You and Andy should come up with an organizational plan: who we need in what role and where. I want to focus on my message and a public schedule. The rest, we'll figure out as we go."

The next day, the intrepid trio were braving the bluster of a January day in Detroit to check out possible locales for their campaign headquarters. Wiley had called a contact who suggested there were several possibilities on the periphery of the Wayne State University Campus. Standing before a newly vacated, ground-level property, Tracie was the first to say, "This is perfect! I like the location, the floor space, and the visibility from the outside. And if the people in this area are anything like we were when I was in school, they'll be checking us out - exactly what we want." Everything moved at blazing speed after that. Wiley, now back in his hometown, made his "To Do" list and contacted the real estate company about a lease; phones were installed and, while sitting on the floor, arranged for a furniture leasing company to deliver desks, chairs, and tables. The *Piece de Resistance* was the sign delivered almost a week later identifying the new tenants: ACTION 2100 Campaign.

Scores of curious students were intrigued by the sign and dropped in, wanting to know more. Within 48 hours, word had spread across the campus and throughout the neighborhood that the new tenants were the organizers of the Symposium panel discussions everyone had been discussing for months, and she was now a candidate for the presidency in 2052. Volunteers lined up to offer their time and expertise in a variety of subject areas. The School of Environmental Science would offer credit for volunteers; Law students, instructors, and untenured assistant professors were other sources of valuable expertise. And, then, there were community activists and ordinary citizens volunteering for every conceivable task. The offices hummed with activity around the clock. To ensure security, Wiley and Tim secured the services of a security firm to provide on-site security and security for Tracie. Wiley was a hometown product who was always escorted by a coterie of old friends. As one of his old neighborhood chums put it to a member of the press who was curious about Wiley not being concerned about his security, "To get to Wiley, they've got to get through us, and that ain't gonna happen."

By the end of the first week, Tracie had settled on the name Mayhew Kingman as her first choice for general campaign manager. Kingman, a veteran of several successful state and national campaigns, had decided to sit out the 2052 campaign. He was just that disenchanted with the candidates of both parties. He could also afford it. When Tracie reached him, Kingman shared with her that Tim Paar mentioned her name and that she might be in touch. "Well, Mr. Kingman, now that we've been formally introduced by our mutual friend, would you be interested in trying to make history?"

"Ms. Hinton, if I may call you that, I was going to sit this one out until Tim called. I appreciate the call. You and I should have a drink. You're the candidate, so when would you be available?"

"Nothing like the present moment; only make it lunch." By that afternoon, Mayhew Kingman became the second major appointment of the ACTION 2100 campaign. And by the end of the third week, student volunteers from Wayne State had contacted friends, family members, and other students in practically all of the 50 states. Overnight, a national volunteer army was in place and prepared to knock on hundreds of thousands of doors nationwide. Kingman shared with Tracie he had never seen a volunteer effort of this magnitude come together so quickly behind any candidate. "They are critical to our success," he said. "Organizing volunteers is the most demanding part of any campaign." People, especially young people, are not that excited or interested in political candidates now.

"Let's talk about how we announce my candidacy. Wiley and I prefer here in Detroit where we have real climate-related issues. What are your thoughts?"

"Well, I agree. We have the nucleus of the campaign in place, enough for you to make the announcement. Let's look at the weather and select a date with the warmest day projected by the middle of February, preferably a Saturday. Let's get going!" The second Saturday, February 11, 2051, was selected as campaign D-Day. That would give Tracie enough time to arrange for Wilson, Roberta, and her parents to be on hand for the announcement. Volunteers printed thousands of flyers, made signs, and transformed the storefront headquarters for the occasion. Andy arranged for local and national media coverage. Private security was barely visible, but it was heavy. Jethro Campbell, or one of his people, might try to make headlines. Uniformed officers from the university augmented by officers from the Detroit Police Department handled street closures and crowd control.

Everyone arrived by Wednesday evening, several days before the announcement. The plan was to organize a large campaign-style breakfast for family members, Tim, other prominent supporters from around the country, and elected officials who practically begged to be invited. The buzz surrounding this campaign was palpable, and no one wanted to be left out. The governor, the mayor, and members of both the House and Senate were invited, but none had a speaking role. That was non-negotiable.

The smaller, more intimate breakfast in Tracie's hotel suite was limited to the immediate family of the two candidates - Tracie and Wiley. Security positioned outside the door was instructed to deny entry to anyone before the larger breakfast event unless it was an emergency. The atmosphere in the suite was joyous but more subdued. This was Tracie's big moment. Sam Hinton was beaming with pride, and Ericka just wanted to hold the baby, who was now a presidential candidate. Wilson leisurely enjoyed his breakfast, reveling in the moment. The nucleus of this micro-universe was his wife, his pride, his joy, and the love of his life. At 9 a.m., Wiley announced that it was time to go down to the ballroom. Minutes later, the small party entered the ballroom to be met by Tim, Andy, and Mayhew, and, as if on cue, the crowd erupted. The family made its way to a large reserved table at the front of the room. Seconds later, Mayhew Kingman walked to the podium to silence the boisterous crowd.

"I intend to be brief, just to thank you for being with us this morning. Everyone who wanted to be with us could not be; they are waiting outside to hear from our candidate and, dare I say it, the next President of the United States?" The applause was so deafening this time that the glasses on the tables trembled; people stood on chairs, and toward the rear of the room, someone had to be told to climb down from standing on his table. This was the setup for the main event, Tracie's announcement, from a platform constructed in front of the campaign offices. There had been a huge debate about installing bullet-proof glass around the platform. In the end, Tracie decided, despite the threats that drove her temporarily from her home and the country, she would face friends, critics, and enemies alike with no more than the thickness of the clothing protecting her from the elements. Unbeknownst to anyone outside the family, Wilson did demand that she wear a bullet-proof vest, an accommodation Tracie was happy to make.

The ballroom quickly emptied to join the thousands already positioned in the streets outside. It was now almost 10 a.m., and the temperature was 45 degrees Fahrenheit. Over the past several decades, average temperatures during the winter months in Detroit had been creeping up. Some attributed this development to a changing global climate. The sun was visible this Saturday morning and that brightened the mood among the crowd. Tracie stepped to the podium, followed by family members standing behind her. The crowd silenced itself.

"Good morning, and welcome! My name is Tracie Hinton Ojukwe. Ojukwe is my husband's name. He is that handsome fellow to my right. Today, I am announcing my candidacy for the presidency of this great country, and I'm

asking you to join me!" The crowd applauded for several minutes while TV crews captured the moment. She began again:

"Some of you know me, but to those of you who do not, I am a student of the environment, and I have been one all of my life. I attribute my early interest in the environment to my dad, the other handsome fellow to my left standing next to my mom. As a child sitting at our dinner table, I listened to my dad talk about how the confluence (yes, he used that word. I had to look it up as he knew I would) of the environment, climate, weather, and politics affected his job.

"I came to understand how drought, desertification, rising heat levels, increased ocean surface temperatures, and leveling our tropical rain forests were more than just a vocabulary. Starvation, unemployment, and human survival were outcomes and consequences, oftentimes of policy decisions. And then I heard Dad say something that really stuck with me: 'That we are not good stewards of this planet, the only place we can call home. That is a legacy my generation will bequeath yours.' When he said this, there was a sadness about him I didn't understand at the time. I had to know more.

"I became a student of the environment and our responsibility to safeguard it. That is how and why I became a climatologist. In pursuit of more information, I met my running mate, Dr. Wiley Mitchell - a local product, by the way. That is why I'm running for president.

"We have an obligation to be better stewards of our environment. I maintain we must commit to lead a cooperative, international effort to clean it up, to preserve what we can for those who become our leaders in the year 2100. I would like to involve them as intellectual investors now. Ask questions, get involved early with your teachers. The planet is changing and young people need to know why and what we can do to influence that change. This is what my dad meant when he talked about being good stewards of our environment."

"So, where are we today? We are crippled by a White House that is unwilling to confront the destabilizing effects of a changing global climate and human-induced climate change and the manifest ways some of our allies have chosen to do so. One of the most egregious differences between us and our allies and partners in regard to both the conflicts that threaten us and the privations

brought on by a changing climate was how to cope with the one billion climate-change migrants worldwide. Our allies cannot bear the burden alone, and neither can we. Unlike our current president, we have to engage because starvation, drought, unemployment, ethnic and religious conflict, and the search for food, shelter, potable water, and security propel whole populations to move. Instability ensues, and the solution to instability is leadership. President Harwood is absent.

"The absence of inspired leadership on our part has created a vacuum that Russia moved quickly to fill. We looked inward while our allies in Europe scrambled. Nature raged, economies faltered, social institutions crumbled, and elected officials struggled to keep up. Solutions proved inadequate, and it quickly became everyone for himself. You follow the news. You know this!

"When President Harwood failed to stand with Canada during the Russian cyber-attack against Ontario, itself an act of war, Prime Minister Pearson told his Cabinet and the Canadian people at the time, 'Canada stands alone.' To signal the shift in relations with its neighbor south of the 49th Parallel, Canada has hardened its border. Individual travelers, including Americans, arriving on foot, personal vehicle, rail, or air have to produce a valid passport with the appropriate visa. Existing treaties between our two countries are subject to review and, where necessary, renegotiation. This hardline approach toward the U.S. is supported by a majority of Canadians, many of whom have family members here in this country. Could this outcome have been avoided? Yes!

"The North Korean attack against Hawaii was the gut punch from which we are still recovering. Can we afford to become more isolationist when our economy, our security, and our way of life are integral parts of a global economy? To those who say yes, I ask, 'How do we accomplish that, and at what cost?' Many Americans are unwilling to invest billions of federal dollars to rebuild the military infrastructure there when the needs of the American public here on the mainland are so great. The implications for national defense are immediate.

"Were we to retreat, our allies in the Pacific would shift their alliances with us to China, our strategic competitor and enemy. That would place South Korea, Japan, and Australia in untenable positions. And, in Europe, home of our

oldest allies, the Russians become the most likely benefactors of our failure to lead. Our withdrawal would doom the Middle East to more and protracted conflict to the benefit of Russia, Iran and Syria.

"Each of these countries is confronting the challenges of a changing global climate - as are we. The difference is an absence of leadership, American leadership. We are now in mid-century, and we are experiencing the consequences of failed leadership. Friends, the time is now! We have to lead! We have no choice! Join me!

As Tracie finished her remarks, Tim turned to Kingman, asking, "Are you seeing what I'm seeing? This is a once-in-a-lifetime moment. There are few parallels in our history to this moment!" Tim struggled to contain himself. This was magic, a candidate for the times, and he would be on the right side this time. The crowd was shouting, "TRACIE! TRACIE! TRACIE! TRACIE! Sam hugged Ericka while tears rolled down his face. When Tracie turned in his direction, Wilson swept her in his arms, telling her, "You did it! Baby. You did it!" Roberta was two feet off the ground as Wiley swung her around.

Later, back in Tracie's suite, Sam said, "Let's see how the media covered the event while switching on the TV. And there it was: SPECIAL NOON COVERAGE LIVE on all major cable channels. Tracie's remarks were covered in their entirety, not excerpted with the usual annoying analysis from compensated talking heads. This was the noon coverage. The evening news also featured Tracie's full remarks, followed by a panel discussion of the implications for the current administration. The campaign was now on.

27

Tracie's speech was carried live by all major networks worldwide. As expected, every word was being parsed for meaning, nuance, and what she didn't say. Some analysts were asking if there would be policy shifts by the White House in response, given Hinton's broad popularity. Overnight polls were highly favorable, unheard of for a third-party candidate. Roberta, en route to London to resume the direction of the Hinton Foundation, would be greeted by a surge in support and financial contributions. Early holdouts to the Climate Change Initiative were now enthusiastically signing on, and the conference the Foundation planned to host in 2052 was coming together quickly.

In the days following her speech, Tracie and Wiley were on the road to be greeted by enthusiastic crowds in urban and rural communities throughout the regions hardest hit by drought, rising temperatures, depleted soil, increased ocean temperatures and coastal erosion, and food and water shortages. American resolve and ingenuity at the community level were on full display everywhere, but people were desperate. They wanted to know what their government was doing. They wanted solutions, relief, and hope that things could change. They wanted to know what could be done that they could do to make life better for their children, their families, and their communities. In town hall meetings, participants expressed appreciation for Tracie's earlier panel discussions and their information value. Someone always asked why the President refused to provide more leadership. That question was difficult for Tracie because more could have been done - and easily.

Mayhew Kingman and Tracie agreed on an unorthodox campaign strategy following a conversation with Andy a week after her speech. A well-placed source in the White House called Andy to tell him that the President, as part of his *volte-face* before the American public, called in the Director of the Secret Service. Hinton was to be offered Secret Service protection if she wanted it. "Nothing was to happen to her on his watch," was the way Andy's source put it. The Vice President had to have passed the word to Jethro Campbell. In response, Andy commented, "I guess that decision was not well received by the Vice President." Wilson and Sam Hinton urged her to accept the President's offer, although neither fully trusted Jethro Campbell. As a true believer, he may have adopted a personal agenda.

This development regarding Tracie's security changed campaign strategy, more for Tracie than Wiley. She and Wilson then decided to re-occupy his former home on Longfellow Street in NW Washington, D.C. She could now coordinate her campaign schedule from there. Moreover, her business could be transferred from Lagos to the Foundation in London, along with members of her staff. Life suddenly became easier now that she felt less threatened. Wiley campaigned from his office in Seattle, while crossing paths with Tracie in Detroit, D.C., or around the country. Every twenty days, he and Roberta would spend an extended weekend in D.C.

Tracie's campaign had stirred a hornet's nest, but that was anticipated. If she was going to succeed, she had to give voters a viable alternative. That meant traveling to Washington when necessary. That was the nature of politics. That was the American way. She was also sending a signal to our allies and adversaries alike: change could be over the horizon. The United States would remain a world leader; that considerations by our allies in Southeast Asia of balancing relations with

China, for example, should be placed on hold or reconsidered. South Korea's challenge to rebuild North Korea could become a shared responsibility with its Pacific neighbors - including China - and the United States. Tracie was sending the signal to widen the lens on international economic and trade policy issues as well as national security options.

Russia was also in Tracie's crosshairs. The leadership in Moscow struggled to have its concerns factored into the national priorities of the members of the European Union [EU] and NATO. Moscow insisted it, too, was a European power and had long sought admission to the EU. More controversially and problematic was its campaign to eliminate the Article 5 provision of the NATO Charter. It had made some headway regarding its imperatives in the Middle East with support from Turkey. The isolation of Israel was an uphill slog, given the resistance of the U.S. To signal detente with Western Europe and eventual rapprochement, Moscow offered to host a series of conferences in Geneva to create a new, expanded Europe, one not dominated by the United States. Intense lobbying by the French, the Poles, and the Turks ensured the Russian overture would not be rejected by the Alliance.

Tracie did not want to give the White House a legitimate reason to accuse her of meddling in foreign policy by commenting on specific policy initiatives. What her campaign could do with impunity was focus on the necessity for more and better international cooperation to fight the crisis of a changing global climate and not each other. Here, hers could be an effective voice in the conversation, one this White House could no longer ignore. It was their silence, their indifference on the subject that gave rise to the "Hinton phenomenon."

The 2052 national elections were 18 months away, and President Harwood could see himself being further marginalized by the Russians and the upstart Hinton presidential campaign. Responding directly to the Hinton campaign would lend further legitimacy to his rival. On the other hand, the Russian President had outflanked Harwood on the world stage, and *that* had to be addressed. Harwood had squandered goodwill he now needed. For example, during travels to Ottawa and to European capitals, his counterparts now sat mute as he implored them to remain unified in their efforts to deal with a changing global climate and what he described as the perils of mounting Russian aggression.

Tracie reached out to her friend, Dr. Chin, in Beijing for an update on developments there. The essential difference between the Russians and the Chinese was the Russian willingness to aggress neighbors and others to obtain the means to survive. Dr. Chin confirmed that the water problem there in China was severe, and many people were dying. Productivity in the industrial north had halted. To his dismay, the country was running out of food and continuing to invest too much money in military weapons and related defense systems. And, on an average day, a third of the country's population, almost 500 million people, were in transit seeking the means to survive. "I expect food and water riots any day now," he confided to Tracie.

"Dr. Chin, while I have you," Tracie continued, "have you any news about conditions in North Korea?"

"Dr. Hinton, I don't hear much, at least not through official channels. What I do hear is disturbing. Starvation is worse, if that is possible. People are risking their lives openly trying to cross into China, and others are still building rafts trying to make it to the South. Many are losing their lives, but I guess they feel they have nothing to lose." Chin went on to venture a political opinion: "I see an opportunity for the U.S. to build an international coalition in support of reunification of the Korean Peninsula. China, Japan, the U.S., and South Korea could be the nucleus of this coalition, with support from other countries in the region, such as Australia, New Zealand, and Singapore. If the Americans don't take the lead on reunification, Beijing will. The danger for the U.S. is that if South Korea accepts a deal from Beijing, the U.S. will lose its foothold on the Peninsula and possibly be locked out of the region permanently. Japan will have less incentive to expand its economic or security partnership with the U.S."

In Lagos, a world away from the growing dystopia in Washington, Tracie had become habituated to the raw energy, the potential, and the promise of her adoptive society of four hundred million in a country one-eleventh the size of the U.S. But it was time to return to the U.S. to continue what she had unwittingly set in motion: change. Her campaign had enlivened her with what she does best: plan, develop strategy, set achievable goals, and, now, mobilize a country to save itself and the planet. She and Wiley had become the face of a new political movement galvanized by a symposium and now a presidential campaign. The possibility of launching a global entity through the Hinton Foundation, whose mission was to save the planet, was intoxicating, even for a pragmatist like Tracie.

As Wilson prepared to join Tracie in Detroit for the announcement of her presidential campaign, Wilson Ojukwe, Sr., Wilson's father, mentioned to his son he'd like to talk to him before he left. Wilson and his father were close and talked often. To Wilson, his father's wanting to speak to him did not seem out of the ordinary. In fact, he had planned to have a conversation with his dad, but more along the lines that his parents might visit them now that he and Tracie were married. His parents didn't travel often beyond the African Continent and an occasional trip to London. "Sure, Dad," he responded."

That afternoon, Wilson looked for his dad and found him sitting on the rear terrace. On the small table to the right of his dad's chair was a half-finished glass of Mango tea and a book he'd been reading. "Dad, is this a good time?" he asked. "Yes, sit down. Are you all packed?"

"Yeah, pretty much. Trying to remember some things Tracie asked me to bring with me."

"You know, son, your mother and I are now in our mid-sixties..." And before his dad could complete his sentence, Wilson knew immediately what the subject was: a grandchild to continue the family legacy and royal lineage. When Wilson was in his late twenties and throughout the decade of his thirties, his father was hopeful that the family would be blessed with a grandchild, preferably a grandson. At one time, he had even mused to his son that his commitment to Tracie was not leading to marriage and that perhaps he should move on. Tracie was committed to her career and less to the idea of marriage and family. Wilson explained to his father on more than one occasion that Tracie was the only woman he had ever loved and that if he could not marry her, he doubted he ever would. Father and son had not had that particular conversation lately, and neither of them had broached it again.

Well, here it was again. "I had thought," his father continued, "that since the two of you were now living here, especially after you married, that family was more likely than ever before. The two of you are in your early forties, and while that is late for Tracie to become pregnant, it is not too late. Even here in Nigeria, women are having children later. Now, she is a presidential candidate, the two of you are moving back to the U.S., and I believe it is unlikely that she will want to become a mother within the next several years. By *that* time, she will be beyond the age of 45 when pregnancy could become dangerous for a woman her age."

Wilson knew his dad was right and he well understood his father's concerns. However, he was beyond the point where preserving family tradition was of more importance than his love for Tracie and the depth of their commitment to each other. He admired and respected his wife's passion for her causes, her long-established fears of bringing a child into *this* world, and her enduring commitment to doing what she could to make the world a better place for the two of them and those they cared about. He shared her commitment, and if foregoing the possibility of children became the price they had to pay, he was willing to do so - and Tracie knew that and loved him deeply because of it. Tracie was the heart and soul of his existence, and he had to ensure that his father understood that.

Wilson Ojukwe, Sr., was a traditional man, proud of his lineage, his son, and their status in society. Wilson reached over to grasp his dad's hand while pulling his chair closer to him. And for the rest of the afternoon, he tried to make his dad understand how he had evolved since meeting Tracie, that had he not married Tracie, the problem his dad explained would continue to exist because he would not have married anyone else. "It was always Tracie or no one, Dad. But it was the same for her. That was the strength of the bond between us. It was unbreakable! Her parents also knew that. They, too, wanted grandchildren. In the end, they accepted our commitment to each other and that it was for life."

Later, when Wilson shared this conversation with Tracie, she listened quietly, intently. When Wilson finished, her only comment was, "Not everyone will understand, Sweetie. I hope that one day, your dad will."

28

Russian President Krupinsky, learning of his American counterpart's weakened political position, moved swiftly to organize the first of several conferences in Geneva to open a dialogue with Europe's leaders in the West. Switzerland was neutral and, to preserve its neutrality, had not joined in the sanctions against Russia. The American President had been weakened, but he maintained a tenuous hold on loyalty from the British, the Germans, and some of the smaller members of the EU and NATO.

According to his foreign minister, Krupinsky told his senior advisors, "For this first meeting, we'll take whoever responds to our invitation." The Russian's strategy was straightforward: open the door to the West, drive a wedge into both the EU and NATO, and aggressively exploit it. Krupinsky gambled on the acceptance of the French, always fearing the resurgence of its most conservative wing, the National Rally - Rassemblement National; also the Turks, Russia's neighbors to the South; and the Poles, NATO's eastern flank and most likely target for a land war with Russia.

Each of them accepted Krupinsky's invitation, followed by the Italians, the Spanish, and the Greeks. The Greeks distrusted the Turks and insisted on being in the room to protect their flanks. Politics in Italy, with roots in fascism, were historically volatile. The political right throughout Italy was, again, promising stability, cultural unity, an end to inflation, and closing its eastern and southern borders to the perennial flood of immigrants from North Africa. The door to the West was ajar, and all the Russian President sought were emissaries willing to take his message of "detente for a new Europe" back to Europe's capitals. In private, he referred to this strategy as sowing the seeds of dissent. He was fighting to remain politically viable. Were he to be perceived as weak as his American counterpart, he would not survive.

Russian society was disintegrating, a fact known in Brussels, the headquarters of the EU and NATO. The question under debate in the West was whether to allow Krupinsky to fail and gamble on new leadership in Moscow or respond to someone seeking to avoid further war, continued economic isolation, and the end of his pariah status in the world community. Russia's internal condition was not unique; it was simply more chaotic and thus more dangerous because of its size and nuclear power status. Millions of climate-change migrants were fleeing west, and Poland - a favored destination - had long since signaled problems with absorption capacity. Migrants flowing toward relief posed an existential cultural, social, and economic threat to many of the countries in the European Union as it had in previous Russian aggressions.

Russia's key message at that first meeting in Geneva was, "We have to resume and accelerate trade among us." On that first day, Krupinsky stood and declared, "Russia supports a new Pan-European Trade Consortium, which could form the basis for a new Global Trade Consortium. As a global society, if we are to survive, prosper, and sustain ourselves against the ravages of a changing global climate, it can only be through collaboration, mutual trust, and an end to economic aggression. Russia is prepared to take the first steps. Will you join us?"

That rhetorical question was a shot across the bow for Europe's leaders in their forthcoming conversations with the Americans. President Harwood would be under intense pressure to respond to entreaties from his European trade and security partners to reduce the economic isolation of their Russian neighbor. The French and Germans often quietly made the point that Russia was *their* neighbor - sometimes nemesis - more than it was for the U.S., an ocean away. That last comment always rankled American officials who tired of reminding their European cousins of America's decisive involvement in World War II over a century earlier. In private and in a moment of frustration, the American secretary of state brusquely told his French counterpart, "You bastards would be speaking German, or Russian had it not been for us!" The French foreign minister, uniquely disdainful of this American remonstration, responded, "Yes, that's true, but the times have changed."

In Beijing, the focus was now on the Korean Peninsula and the reconstruction of the North. The Chinese ambassador in Seoul and their consul general in Busan had well-established relations among Korean industrialists and were aware of the schism between those who were younger, advocating greater Chinese ties with the North for new opportunities, and an older generation closer to the Korean President and the ruling Party preferring a consortium of Japanese, Australian, and American investors. In the short term, the Chinese ambassador cautioned his leadership that the American-led consortium had the upper hand, but over the long term, China could effectively counter American influence in a unified Korea.

The Chinese ambassador well understood his hosts. Korea had a young population with a median age of 20, and the two envoys advised that China focus on this younger cohort. It should expand outreach through their Confucius Institutes, their most potent mechanism for recruitment and influence at foreign universities. As an example, China's cultural footprint in Africa includes 100 Confucius Institutes in over 45 African countries. Closer to home, China's proximity offered unlimited opportunities for online learning through Korean high schools and universities.

This system was no substitute for the person-to-person direct exchange experience, but it did offer a younger generation of Koreans exposure to the Chinese language, culture, and history. And it offered unlimited access to Chinese universities. "Make China a preferred destination for Korean students from the North and the South," the ambassador advised. Build the connective tissue that could form lasting bonds with a new generation of Korean citizens. That is the future." This advice resonated in Beijing.

China, meanwhile, moved aggressively to expand its naval presence East of Hawaii, long considered the invisible demarcation line in the Pacific, while a third of its population was destitute, hungry, and occasionally riotous. Internally, the policy debate on domestic priorities required deft statesmanship by the Communist Party leadership, given the level of spontaneous violence in the Chinese countryside.

The Chinese defense ministry declared publicly that the Pacific was within China's sphere of influence and it would defend its interests by any and all means available to it. The leadership in Beijing had thrown down the gauntlet to this White House. Within weeks, Chinese warships were visible just outside U.S. territorial waters. The National Security Agency [NSA] also reported an increase in the number and sophistication of Chinese satellites.

Alarm bells were going off in the Pentagon, and the vast complex of intelligence agencies from this heightened Chinese offensive posture. President Harwood was under siege from the Russians, the Chinese, and his military establishment. Also on his radar was the growing popularity of the Hinton presidential campaign. Close to home and equally ominous, his Vice President smelled blood. Being a heartbeat from the presidency, dare he consider challenging a sitting President?

Harwood was in a serious bind as summer turned to fall in 2051. Primaries were just over five months away. Unless he could reverse his plummeting poll numbers, he feared how he might fare in the Iowa Caucuses and the New Hampshire Primary after the turn of the New Year.

The Russian overtures in Geneva had faltered due to growing international support for the Hinton Foundation's Global Initiative for Climate Change and its emphasis on trading resources. Not only was there growing enthusiasm for Hinton's ACTION 2100 presidential campaign in the U.S., but it had caught on overseas as well. Foreign media coverage of Hinton was broad-based and, worse for this White House, positive. Allies and enemies were looking past Harwood's administration to the future. The subtext of reporting by American ambassadors abroad was the question, "What might the future portend if there were new leadership in the United States?"

Everyone knew Russian motives behind their Geneva initiative were suspect. Moreover, few trusted any promises Moscow might make to secure more international support. National sustainability linked to increased trade in resources had a positive ring to it in capitals every-where. Was trade not preferable to war and threats of aggression? How would a Hinton White House deal with this question?

In their frequent conversations, Wiley had become increasingly concerned about the torrid, frenetic pace his wife maintained at the Foundation. "Babe," she would argue, "there is so much to do; there is so much support for what we're trying to accomplish, and I'm having so much fun, I rarely think about the length of my day until I return to my apartment in the evening." Wiley knew his wife was capable of that level of commitment once she immersed herself in anything she felt passionate about. It was her passion, combined with unbridled energy and competence, that helped them build a successful business. Wiley would often tell Tracie she could set aside any concerns she might have about the Foundation, her business, and the Initiative coming to fruition in 2052. Between the team she has assembled and your staff, she has everything well in hand. In one of their conversa-tions, Tracie confided to Wiley, "I knew the strength of the relationship between you two and that it could sustain demands I have made upon you. What I am attempting to do would not be possible without you and Roberta."

The mood in the White House, however, was fraught with high drama both within the administration and its relations with allies and adversaries alike. The Joint Chiefs were making forceful demands on the administration to protect their Southeast Asian presence and the right of free passage in the southern and western Pacific. This, too, was creating pressure on Harwood and threatening to divide his party. His vice president was livid. Where was the media when *he* needed them?

Sitting in his office on the Pentagon's famed E-Ring, home of the defense department's top brass, Defense Secretary Vernon Pembrooke studied the documents arrayed before him. Head down, shoulders slumped, he was confronting the nightmare scenario he had long sought to avoid: signed and dated letters of resignation from each of the four service chiefs and their boss, the Chairman of the Joint Chiefs of Staff. Minutes earlier, he had concluded an hour-long meeting with the five 4-star chiefs, during which they explained in calm, measured tones the reasons for taking this extraordinary step. Pembrooke knew what he had to do as he reached for the console on his desk.

Punching in the White House, Pembrooke identified himself and asked to speak to the President. Hearing the presidential assistant's pleasant voice, he told her it was imperative he speak to President Harwood. He said he was leaving his office en route to the White House, and he could be reached in his car in the event the President would not be available to him. Then he hung up. Pam Chasten, the President's assistant, was struck by the abrupt message from Pembrooke - contrary to his normal and courteous demeanor - and sensing an ill wind was blowing in their direction, she buzzed Harwood. "Secretary Pembrooke just called saying he was en route and could be reached in his car if necessary. He should arrive shortly."

"This can't be good," Harwood thought, wondering what was afoot - not that he needed any more bad news. Within 30 minutes, Pembrooke strode into the President's outer office, indicating he planned to continue into the Oval Office unless told to wait, which is customary. As he approached Harwood's massive oak desk, the President waved him toward one of the sofas. "Mr. President," Pembrooke began, sitting on the edge of the sofa as he reached into his briefcase, "I have just spent the past hour with the Joint Chiefs, and each of them handed me a signed and dated letter of resignation. I've feared this would happen and advised you of that possibility unless we revised our policy toward Russia and China. The death of Admiral Holmes, our INDOPACOM (Indo-Pacific Commander) during North Korea's recent strike on Hawaii did not sit well with our combat theater comman-ders." Harwood sat forward on the other sofa, staring at him.

"Are they serious, Pembrooke?" Pembrooke sat in silence for a second, thinking this man must have lost it completely. Four-star officers are not in the habit of offering their resignations on a whim.

He took a deep breath before responding to the President's question. "Adamant, Mr. President. Many of the remaining theater commanders are also threatening to follow suit. Had we not been forewarned, their behavior could be construed as an insurrection. They have been consis-tent in their recommendations, and they have been consistently ignored. They respect civilian control and leadership of the military and feel this is the only course of action available to them."

Pembrooke went on, "The Russians are on the verge of permanently fracturing NATO, and the Chinese now have a Pacific-wide presence up to and including our maritime borders. As we well know, both countries are grappling with some of the worst effects of a changing global climate, just as we are. Details are part of your PDB [Presidential Daily Brief]. What is different is our lack of response to what is obvi-ously a strategic partnership between them, the challenges they present to us worldwide, and how we are perceived by our allies and partners."

Harwood sat back on the sofa, looking intently at his defense secretary in disbelief. "I didn't believe they would do it," he said dispiritedly. He stared at Pembrooke for a moment and, rising, walked over to the window behind his desk. "I'm done!" he said, turning to Pembrooke. "When this gets out, their resignations will become the dominant narrative from now through the primaries and the election." The normally calm, reserved Pembrooke sat there with his mouth slightly agape. He quickly regained his composure. The uniformed leadership of the country's armed forces, the world's most lethal military, just resigned en masse, and all this guy could think about was how their resignations would affect his reelection prospects. "Son-of-a-bitch!" he muttered to himself. At that moment, he decided to lay everything on the table. "Mr. President, that's not the worst of it! Your own Vice President will likely challenge you for the nomination. In fact, I'm damn certain of it!"

As he rose to leave, Pembrooke reached into his briefcase and, pulled out another envelope containing *his* resignation and laid it on the President's desk. He had hoped for a different response from the Commander-in-chief. But this! "Thank you for your time, Mr. President. It has been my privilege to serve." Pembrooke turned abruptly and walked out. He had been a stalwart within Harwood's Cabinet. The effect of his loss would ripple throughout the larger defense community.

A distinguished graduate of the Naval Academy, Pembrooke had completed his initial five-year obligation, and then resigned his commission. Often critical of the institutional and cultural constraints of the uniformed services, he had been an advocate for greater reforms due to the high attrition rate among junior officers through the rank of major. He felt he could be more effective outside the institution. Pembrooke campaigned for a seat in the House of Representatives from northern Virginia. He was fortunate to be given a seat on the House Foreign Affairs Committee [HFAC] as a first-termer. Following two terms as a House Member, he joined General Dynamics Corp. in Reston, Virginia. There, over the course of the next decade, he quickly rose to become CEO before being asked to join the Harwood Administration. Pembrooke supported his commanders, agreed with their critique of the administration's strategic policies, and with the resignations of his military leadership, and could not in good faith remain as their leader.

Resource transfers, the new international currency promoted by the Hinton Foundation, resonated, and everyone sought to contribute. "Let's trade, not make war" was a loose slogan floating around. Roberta and her team developed priority lists of resources from urgent to useful and circulated them among prospective participants in the Foundation's upcoming Global Initiative for Climate Change. Russia offered to contribute natural gas, which few countries really needed, in exchange for food seeds.

While campaigning across the country, Tracie would make specific references to the Global Initiative for Climate Change, telling Americans, "This initiative is just one example of the kind of collaboration required to fight the climate crisis. We are only limited by our imaginations and our interests in saving this planet. We are not bound by culture, politics, or religion. What binds us is our hope to survive and prosper before it's too late."

The sound of the Oval Office door closing behind the Defense Secretary lingered momentarily as Harwood stood alone in silence. As he looked around the office, whose power and perks he enjoyed, it seemed cold and isolated, and he went along with it. Every object in it reflected a former occupant's past. Yes, he had selected the furniture, the art, the sculptures, even the carpet, but at that moment, he felt detached from everything except the family photos arrayed on the table behind his desk.

Pembrooke's departure represented the loss of a valued senior advisor who had stood as a bulwark against the wolves. In the solitude of the moment, and perhaps for the first time, Hardwood realized it was he who had created the gilded cage in which he now found himself. If he were to survive the duration of his presidency and remain a competitor for his party's nomination, he would have to take the initiative without the support of his hyper-ambitious vice president - Jackson Hewlett.

Hewlett, a former governor of Oklahoma, had brought the support of the South and Midwest to strengthen Harwood's nomination years earlier, and he had wanted the Veep slot. A party loyalist to his core with deep roots in the fossil fuel industry, Hewlett publicly and proudly proclaimed climate change to be a hoax, a fabrication of those who would sacrifice the world's most dynamic economy on the altar of natural global/environmental change. In his acceptance speech as his party's vice-presidential candidate, Hewlett famously pronounced, "We have to co-exist with the natural forces of nature, not take responsibility for what we cannot control."

Harwood could visualize tomorrow's headlines following the mass resignation of his service chiefs at the Pentagon and factor them into the decision he had to make to change the damaging narrative that would dog him from now through the convention. He stepped out onto the South Portico, breathed in the Fall air, and headed up to the residence.

The next morning, during the President's Daily Brief, Hardwood interrupted his briefers, saying, "Get the national security team in here! We've got work to do." He stood up and waved everyone out. Forty-five minutes later, his national security team now occupying every available seat in the Oval Office, Harwood took command. Representing defense was the deputy secretary, Georgia Braxton, former executive vice president at Boeing. She admired and respected Pembrooke and had been prepared to resign as well. Pembroke had persuaded her to remain, saying, "The President is going to need you."

"We've all seen the headlines," Harwood began, "so let's move on! We're currently in a two-front psychological war - with the Russians in Europe and the Chinese in the West. There's nothing new here." He framed the issue this way: "The Russians are the 'Bull in the China Shop.' They like breaking things, making a lot of noise to create chaos, instilling fear, and forcing submission to their demands. They'll threaten war - even nuclear war - if they have to. The Chinese, on the other hand, take the long view. War with us would defeat the long-term gains they have made and undermine their fragile hold on power. They prefer to own the China Shop and change the display once the bull has left to project their image of stability and control. We're going to counter their presence in the Pacific right up to the limit - downsize our fleet in the Atlantic and the Mediterranean and maximize our presence in the Pacific. I want a show of force, unlike anything the Chinese have seen in decades."

Doubling back to the situation in Europe, Harwood reminded everyone that "the Poles, the French, and the Turks are the weak links against the Russians, so let's buck them up!" He paused. The room was silent; he knew why. Everyone was wondering ...why *now*? The right moves too late. He had to take the initiative from Hewlett and his national security advisor, both of whom would have advised the course of action he outlined had he not done so.

Harwood had reached another conclusion the previous evening. Anything he might do at this juncture in his presidency regarding a changing climate or Russian and Chinese aggression would likely not move the needle of public opinion measurably in his favor. Now, it was damage control, warding off the possibility his Cabinet could invoke the 25th Amendment and remove him from office. He had waited too long and had lost the confidence of the party's major donors, their leadership, and the voters. Better to go out on his own terms - as personally and politically painful as that would be. He was sure Hewlett did not know he was aware of the latter's intent to challenge him for the nomination. That previous evening, he had admitted to his wife how he had squandered his presidency, giving in to his insecurities about reelection and listening to his vice president on climate change policy.

Regarding national security, catnip for Washington's voracious media, the lobbyists on K-Street, and the vultures on Capitol Hill, the Chinese would match what they would refer to as American belligerence - the enhanced American naval presence throughout the Pacific - and wait for Harwood's successor. Public opinion in China toward the U.S. was negative and the Chinese would want to build on that short of war: demonize the U.S. at the U.N. and in every bilateral meeting. More-over, accuse the American president of declining to cooperate with them to reduce carbon emissions and to make the planet more livable.

Harwood understood the greater short-term threat was that America's EU and NATO partners were unconvinced of American resolve. Even a partial defection of Europe's principal economies, and trade and secu-rity partners would have immediate and lasting effects on a broad array of American policy objectives. Harwood had to stanch the bleeding. His legacy, however meager, was at stake.

<h1 style="text-align:center">29</h1>

Celeste Hewlett, the authentically ambitious wife of Jackson Hewlett, sat across the desk from her husband in his second-floor study in their residence at the former U.S. Naval Observatory on upper Massachusetts Avenue in Northwest Washington. The observatory, built in 1893, had been the home of the Vice President since Walter Mondale, the Vice President to former President Jimmy Carter. The Hewletts were listening to a call from one of their party's major donors. It was just the latest call of many to validate Hewlett's ambition and encourage him to seek the presidential nomination. Challenging a sitting president was a serious step; one Hewlett would not have contemplated without promises of financial and political support. Harwood had been a major disappointment, and the party saw in Hewlett someone capable of countering the unprecedented third-party challenge from Tracie Hinton and ACTION 2100.

Hewlett's ambition was matched by that of his wife, the politically savvy daughter of one of Oklahoma's wealthiest oil barons and owner of the state's largest independent bank. Weaned on state party politics and watching her father rise to become a U.S. Senator, Celeste had been the wholesome, all-American high school cheerleader, president of her college sorority, and fiercely determined to become First Lady of the United States one day. She and Jackson had met at a fraternity rush party as college freshmen. She was immediately drawn to his charm, brash self-confidence, and intended pursuit of a law degree. On their third date, he told Celeste of his intention to seek the nomination for the presidency one day. They married in their senior year of college. Celeste had confided to her roommate, "I'm not letting this one get away."

Childless and unencumbered by the daily responsibilities and challenges of hearth and home, Celeste threw herself into building the right social connections and managing her husband's political career. Now, she convinced herself the endgame was in sight. She abhorred the title of Second Lady of the United States. The title was awkward, meaningless, and deferential to a President she did not respect. The only person more quickly forgotten by the average American than a vice president, she claimed, was the vice president's spouse. Celeste Hewlett coveted the second-floor residence at 1600 Pennsylvania Avenue, the position of First Lady of the land, and the size and majesty of Air Force One, the aircraft assigned to the President. A small, close-knit circle of friends kept her confidence and were a constant source of encouragement.

Jackson would announce his candidacy right after the New Year, 2052. Celeste hoped that Harwood would also announce his intention not to seek a second term and thus spare himself the ultimate humiliation of a challenge from within his administration. Of course, they would proceed without regard to Harwood's decision. Celeste paid assiduous attention to the President's shrinking popularity in the polls and confidently asserted to her husband, "Harwood will step down! He has no choice, he has no money, and he has no political backing. Best of all, he knows it." Jackson later confided thankfully to a family friend, "I'm fortunate Celeste is not my opponent." But Jackson, no novice to the game of national politics, kept a keen eye on the rising political fortunes of Tracie Hinton and her ACTION 2100 campaign.

He instinctively felt the greater challenge was this attractive, disciplined, and well-respected climatologist, a new force in American politics who had captured the country's imagination. Moreover, she had her finger on the pulse of the nation, the angst about difficulties presented by a changing global climate and Harwood's lack of response. His counsel had contributed to Harwood's lack of response - and that would not be easily disavowed. That was an albatross he would have to shoulder; the question was, how? The President had extended the offer of Secret Service protection to the Hinton campaign - which they accepted. He had also said he did not want anything to happen to Hinton while he was in office. Yet, to Jackson, this populist climatologist was the more ominous threat because, in those regions of the country most affected by a changing climate, she makes the case that the two major parties, as ideologically presented, are ill-equipped to effect consequential change. She had to be eliminated. Best to keep that one from his wife and Jethro Campbell. He needed a new plan.

Shortly after the New Year, 2052, President Harwood was feeling renewed and prepared for the final and most demanding year of his presidency. The first item on his agenda was to speak to the country. He summoned his press secretary to schedule a time for an address to the nation. He had made several key decisions, and the American people needed to know what to expect of him in his final months. Over the holidays, he had developed a framework draft of his remarks and left it to his speech writers to add the polish. Several nights later, relaxed sitting behind his desk in the Oval Office, Harwood spoke to the country:

"Good evening my fellow Americans, and thank you for hosting me in your homes tonight. We've entered a new year with new beginnings and new tasks ahead of us. I have been accused of failing to speak forthrightly with you in the past - a failing on my part. Well, tonight, I am changing that." He paused momentarily, rose from his desk and stood in front of it staring directly into the camera. Clasping his hands just below his chin, he continued.

"A changing global climate is the existential threat of our times. We know that. Inherent in any threat is the challenge to devise a strategy and then marshal the necessary means to confront the threat. I plan to devote the remainder of my presidency to working on your behalf with our allies and partners and the leaders of other nations who would join us to bring together

the best brains and the best ideas to ensure a sustainable future for all of us - friend and foe alike. I choose to believe we can still make a difference.

"No nation has escaped the effects of climate change, including those who would attack us: Russia, China, and North Korea. We shall meet their threats head-on and offer them an opportunity to join our effort or be consigned to the margins of our civilized world. That is not a threat; it is a promise I intend to keep. They have to know they cannot prevail.

"This effort will require my total commitment. Therefore, I will not be a candidate for reelection this November. It has been, and continues to be, the privilege of a lifetime to serve as your president. Thank you, and may God bless these United States of America."

Everyone in the Oval Office and throughout the administration watching the President's address was in shock. Only the speechwriters, sworn to absolute secrecy until the broadcast, had been aware of the content of the President's remarks. Phones began to ring on every desk in Washington. The question was, "Did you know about this?" The inevitable response was, "No! I did not!" followed by, "So, what now?"

Harwood had thrown a spanner in the works. He was now officially a Lame Duck, unencumbered by the herculean, fruitless task of gearing up to mount a major campaign to remain in office another four years: the endless fundraisers, a grinding travel schedule, sleepless nights too numerous to count, gallons of bad coffee and cold pizza, pleading with key supporters, sweating daily polls, making promises he knew he couldn't keep, and struggling to keep his blood pressure under control. And, of course, debate prep.

His party wanted him out, his donors had abandoned him - with good cause - and he was now above the fray and untethered to anyone's expectations. He had no promises to make or compromises to negotiate. When the staff had cleared the Oval Office, and he was alone with his wife, he said to her, "So this is what liberation feels like."

Jackson Hewlett decided the better part of discretion was not to approach the President after the address. He reasoned, "If the bastard wanted me to know, he would have told me. Someone must have tipped him that I plan to seek the nomination. No need to make an enemy." He also knew that Harwood could force him to choose between doing his job and resigning from the vice presidency to organize a campaign. The job of any vice president is what the President wants him or her to do, and that could mean spending days and weeks on countless missions to some of the world's most unwelcoming destinations, attending state funerals, national day ceremonies, or discussing issues of minor consequence with second-tier leaders.

In the period following his address, Harwood had fewer contacts with his vice president and then only on issues of minor interest to either man. Office space assigned to the vice president in the West Wing was reassigned to a senior counselor brought on board to advise Harwood through the remainder of his term. Hewlett had to make the daily commute from his formal office in the Eisenhower Executive Office Building - derisively labeled *Siberia* - to attend meetings. He was effectively sidelined with no official duties. Senior staff in the West Wing were minimally civil.

Sitting in his cavernous formal office across Executive Way, the prized avenue and parking space between the West Wing and the Eisenhower building, Hewlett was now out of the loop. He was reminded of the words of former Vice President Harry Truman, who once famously remarked the vice presidency was worth no more than a "pitcher of warm spit" - or words to that effect. The weekly luncheon between Harwood and Hewlett was canceled, and the two men rarely interacted throughout the balance of Harwood's tenure in the White House.

The news that Harwood would not seek reelection drew mixed reviews from American correspondents in major capital cities around the world. In Russia, Moscow was mute, while in Beijing, a foreign ministry spokesman told a group of foreign journalists that America's days as a world colossus were over. MSNBC's correspondent in Tel Aviv reported the loss of a "Friend in the White House." In Western European capitals, the consensus report attributed Harwood's decision to a failure to stand up to attacks by North Korea and bullying by Russia. Closer to home within the Hinton campaign, there was no public reaction. Harwood's decision was a non-event, meriting no public response. Tracie and her team agreed that Hewlett would step up, albeit from a weakened position. "Our focus remains the same," Tracie told her team. "We have proposed the most significant actions to manage the effects of global climate change ever. Those actions must remain the centerpiece, the narrative of this campaign."

Sam told his daughter that Hewlett, should he become a candidate, would throw caution to the wind. He will campaign aggressively and ruthlessly in an effort to overcome any weaknesses attributed to the President's decision. "He may not honor the President's pledge regarding your security," Sam suggested to Tracie. "Watch your back!"

"I won't run scared," she told her dad, "But we'll bring in more private security to watch out for the Jethros."

In the days following the President's announcement, Hewlett sat in his office fuming. Yes, he planned to run, but he overheard his executive secretary talking to one of her friends over in the West Wing, which changed everything. Apparently, the President was considering sending Hewlett to New Zealand as his personal representative to commemorate February 6 - the date of the initial signing of New Zealand's founding document: The Treaty of Waitangi [Te Tiriti o Waitangi] on that date in 1840. A Cabinet member sufficed for representation over the past three years. Why the Vice President this year? He wondered aloud. This was retribution and possibly a harbinger of what was to represent the balance of his time in office. Almost as if by Divine intervention, Hewlett understood the President's strategy: derail the presidential ambition of his vice president - at least in 2052 - even if it meant the possible loss of the White House for his party in November. Harwood had cards to play, and this was one of the strongest.

Hewlett felt trapped. The President had thrown a punch, but perhaps he could throw one of his own, not against Harwood, but against Hinton. She had momentum while he was mired in political mud. He got up, closed his inner office door, and opened a personal safe on the wall behind his desk. Rifling through some personal papers, he found the small address book he was looking for. He shut the safe, took his coat off the rack, and told his assistant, "I'll be back shortly." With his Secret Service detail in tow, he headed out of the building, turned north on Executive Drive, and then turned West on Pennsylvania Avenue. He hadn't planned to go very far. He needed time to make a personal call away from his office. Retrieving his personal mobile phone from his inside pocket, he called a number in Oklahoma. On the second ring, Hewlett said, "AR?"

"Yeah, this is 'AR.' You know, I was thinking about you several days ago. So, your boy screwed you, huh."

"AR, you always did get right to the point!"

"Is there any other way? What's up?"

"When will you be in town again?" Hewlett knew the question was code for "When can you be in D.C. since AR never came to D.C. unless he was asked to. "AR was the nickname for Vernon AR Coulter, President of an Oklahoma-based, right-wing group called DEFENDERS of the FAITH. AR was known to everyone because he never appeared in public without his AR-15 strapped across his back. One of the jokes was that the third person in Coulter's bed at night besides his wife was his AR-15.

"When do I need to be there?" he asked.

"Would this weekend work for you? Just let me know when you arrive and where I can find you. Good!"

"Okay, be in touch."

His call now completed, Hewlett turned around and headed back to his office. His detail didn't think much of the Vice President's behavior because this was customary for both Hewlett and his wife.

30

Mayhew Kingman, Hinton Campaign General Manager, advised Tracie that the timing was perfect for a foreign trip. Her campaign was stable, poll numbers were up and rising, fundraising was meeting goals, and media coverage was positive in all the major media markets. Moreover, the Iowa Caucuses were still days away.

"Well, I'd like to go to London. I talked to Roberta [Mitchell] several days ago, and she'd like for me to meet with the Foundation board, highlight a major fundraiser for the Global Initiative for Climate Change - which, by the way, is coming together very well - and attend a rally promoting cooperation, collaboration, and resource sharing. Project American leadership. That agenda sounded good to me."

"Something else you might consider," Mayhew suggested, "is an open forum with young people, college students, at the London School of Economics, for example. The group would be international, representing a broad range of backgrounds, opinions, and interests. But I think they will have something in common as well: Most likely, they will have knowledge of your Symposium's panel discussions and have questions about some of the processes you support. You can revisit the opportunity to share your vision of how, cooperatively, we can save this planet. Resource sharing is just one idea."

Tracie liked the idea, explaining, "I am not an elected official; thus, I am not in a position to commit resources to any policy proposal. What I do get to do is engage ideas, defend my purpose, define a mission, and suggest that nationalistic competition and the pursuit of power combined to bring us to where we are. We need to commit to a different model for cooperation going forward."

The ulterior motive behind this trip and its purpose was to engage what both Tracie and Mayhew believed would be the thrust of any 'Hewlett for President' campaign. Hewlett would be a forceful advocate for the status quo, arguing that any radical departure from our current economic policy would demonstrably weaken our national economy and thus our global leadership; that what is needed is more enlightened, focused, and committed leadership - which he is uniquely positioned to provide. "Hewlett will get personal," Tracie suggested. "He will resort to name calling, suggest that the American capitalist economic model is far superior to what he will refer to as the 'socialist' policies I advocate. He will equate collaboration and cooperation with socialism and a lack of leadership. And, there will be a segment of the population who will support that point of view. Hewlett is about survival, not international cooperation to save the planet. I get to engage his narrow worldview from London."

The first of the early 2052 caucuses and primaries were only weeks away, and Jackson Hewlett and his wife sprang into action. While Hewlett now welcomed the disconnect between himself and President Harwood, their former partnership was seen as a political millstone by some caucus candidates in Iowa - a millstone Hewlett would have to carry until he severed ties with the current President. Balancing his views on a changing global climate with those now espoused by the President would require a deft touch. Earlier, he had tried in vain to diminish the influence of Hinton's initiatives on a changing climate. The saliency of her messaging through her panel discussions resonated with millions of Americans, and they coalesced into the new ACTION 2100 party. Hinton and her ACTION 2100 movement were transforming the American political landscape in 2051 and now 2052.

Hewlett felt confident he would become his party's nominee, but could he overcome an upstart juggernaut now positioned to derail the quest of his lifetime by November? The mood in the country was shifting. In some states hardest hit by a changing climate, the mood was ugly and distrustful of Washington. Some younger voters, who saw their lives and futures diminished, were demanding "heads on pikes."

Celeste cautioned her husband against enlisting the service of Jethroe Campbell. "The time to eliminate Hinton has come and gone. Besides, any attempt on her now might backfire. 'She is damn popular!' Let's not forget, our people are enthusiastic and prepared to turn out." Celeste's reference to Jethroe reminded Hewlett of his conversation with Vernon Coulter but chose to keep that from his wife. In the context of this conversation, he admitted that he would be less effective in offering a full-throated defense of the fossil fuel industry given how Hinton had successfully persuaded many Americans that that industry had contributed to global warming and the weakening of the Ozone Layer.

"The only avenue left to me is to attack Hinton on the basis of the harm her proposals for resource sharing, for example, will do to our economy: the loss of jobs, the decline in our quality of life, the erosion of our global standing, and the eventual impotence of the leader of the Free World. That message still resonates with our base. There is no substitute for American leadership - at least not yet! Continuing, Celeste reminded her husband that his message will put him at odds with Harwood, but she went on to add, "that could work to your advantage. Challenge him on the contradiction in his policy, his 24th-hour conversion. Force him to explain what he knows now that he didn't before. That is political hypocrisy! He doesn't have enough time between now and November to make himself credible. You, on the other hand, remain the voice of constancy."

"In other words, at this point, I have nothing to lose, so take him on!"

"Okay, if you put it that way - yes!"

Andy Hillyard, now communications director and spokesman for ACTION 2100, relished his new role and the access it gave him to deliver Hinton's message. He could now distinguish Hinton, her ideas, and her supporters from the two other parties and the failed policies of *this* administration. Institutional filters previously imposed by his former employer - *The Washington Post* - no longer existed. He could advance a point of view consistent with his own views. During a press scrum following one of Tracie's speeches, he said, "Most of you know me. You know where I stand on the issues that the elections in November will ultimately decide. I reported on them; we all did. I'm just asking for a fair and thorough review of our platform. I know it's different; some would say it's unique for a presidential campaign. I also know many of you share my sense of urgency, or the lack of it, from this White House despite the late conversion of this President."

"Andy, my name is Denise Evans from the Associated Press. This is my first presidential campaign. So, what is your take on Jackson Hewlett? I'm told you know him? What kind of campaign will he run?"

"Denise, I don't have a personal relationship with the Vice President, but I have been covering him and this administration for over three years. Now, to your question: Jackson Hewlett is an acolyte of fossil fuel and big energy companies, and his policy prescriptions are unlikely to change. Phoenix, Dallas, Reno, and Fort Worth are perfect examples of major urban centers that are practically uninhabitable because of a changing climate." He went on to add, "Hewlett's beef with Harwood was that he was indecisive and too accommodating to Russia and China. North Korea was a no-brainer. Had we responded to their first attack off the coast of California, we would not now have the blood of so many Americans on our hands and the destruction of our naval assets in Hawaii. So, in many respects, we know what to expect from Hewlett's candidacy."

Hillyard, in his role as Hinton campaign spokesman, took every opportunity the campaign offered to amplify Tracie's message of survival, sustainability, cooperation, and hope for a new generation. Following interviews, small group discussions, and town hall meetings, he'd laugh wryly while making the point, "We're the grownups in the room now. Give our candidate a shot! You know what you have to lose." And then, to forestall any lingering doubt about the veracity of his claims, he'd end a press availability with, "If you don't believe me, ask your kids. Tell *them* you're prepared to gamble with what's left of *their* futures."

This last gambit always had the desired effect of spreading Hinton's narrative, swaying media analysts, and framing the question for other candidates seeking the nomination. The worst thing for any presidential candidate is to be thrown on the defensive to respond to questions posed by their political competitors. Andy had spent years perfecting his ability to pose the questions most candidates preferred to avoid. Tracie was familiar with what Andy brought to her campaign. That's why she wanted him. Timing was everything in most important matters. If Andy understood anything, it was the importance of timing. At the end of the day, sitting with Tracie, Mayhew, and Wiley when he joined them, enjoying a beer or a glass of wine, Andy would remind them he was having the time of his life."

Tracie's first international trip as a "serious" presidential candidate was just days away, and she was thrilled. " London was her favorite European capital. She embraced its energy, its rhythm, the essence of what it meant to be a Londoner. The logistics of her travel there were complicated by the "X factor," defined as reliance upon those of a foreign culture to ensure successful outcomes. Presidents and other government officials were accustomed to accommodating the "X factor" in foreign travel. She, on the other hand, was not an American official but rather someone who could become the chief of the American Executive branch. The logistics of traversing the length and breadth of the U.S. as a presidential candidate was simpler.

For her trip to London, she would be accompanied by four-armed U.S. Secret Service agents. The weapons were subject to controls. Also, among her traveling team would be several ACTION 2100 campaign staff; one to handle the press and media, and two others to coordinate travel arrangements and on-the-ground events.

Their overnight flights landed at London's Heathrow International Airport early on a crisp Monday morning in January. Upon arrival, they were met by a member of the Prime Minister's Protocol Office, an officer from London's famed Special Branch, and Roberta from the Hinton Foundation. Special Branch would provide additional protection, armored vehicles, and event security during Tracie's three days in London. Following expedited clearance through Customs and Immigration, Tracie and her group were whisked off to the London Hilton on Park Lane. This hotel had the distinction of being the first Hilton to be opened in the UK in 1963. It overlooked Hyde Park and was only a half-mile from Buckingham Palace.

Media interest in Hinton's arrival was extensive. *"HINTON IN LONDON"* was the bold headline of *THE SUN*. *"American Presidential Candidate Tracie Hinton in the U.K."* topped the headline for *THE DAILY MAIL."* Every major daily, including the *Financial Times*, featured a front-page story with extensive background material, including her Symposium's panel discussions, and her decision to locate the headquarters of her foundation in the city of London. Roberta had briefed her prior to her departure, telling her, "Media interest in your trip to London is insane, generally positive, and supportive of your efforts to save the planet." She added, "We've prepared hundreds of media kits with all the essential background about your candidacy." Roberta went on to say,

People here like to say, 'You're trying to save us from ourselves.'"

The first event that Monday morning was a meeting with the foundation's board of directors, a lineup of eleven of the city's most distinguished, pro-environment men and women from academia, the private sector, the nonprofit world, and independents. After that meeting, while en route to the next event, Roberta asked about Wilson. Tracie and Roberta were practically sisters, and she shared with Roberta a conversation she'd had with her mom, who posed a similar question.

"Wilson had decided not to accompany us on this trip. He knew London well and said, 'Sweetie, this trip is about you, the long-shot, third-party candidate for American President. It is about the mission of the Hinton Foundation. It is about sharing your message to the world from one of the most prestigious media capitals on the globe. You will be front and center on a world stage. Command it! When you've done that, you will come back to me.'"

"Roberta, I've loved this man all of my adult life, and when he described what my trip meant to him, I lost it, I lost it! I cried; I hugged him so tightly, I don't think he could breathe."

Mom said when I told her this story, "It took you two a long time, but the two of you could not be more perfect for each other." "Your mom is right," Roberta said. "To hear you talk about you and Wilson, I think of Wiley and me. That's why we have this rule about not spending too much time away from each other. What we're doing now is something we have never done!" Tracie understood what Roberta was telling her.

For three days, Tracie was a whirlwind in motion. Her agenda included conducting a Town Hall/Open Forum discussion with students from The London School of Economics, speaking before a packed rally at Piccadilly, and addressing a Joint Session of Parliament. She also met with the Board and officers of London's Carbon Trust, a non-profit organization that delivers commercially sustainable solutions and projects that can change people's lives for the better by cutting carbon emissions.

Three days later, Tracie's debut on an important world stage as an American presidential candidate was over, and although a little exhausted, she felt she had acquitted herself well. Having bid all of her hosts farewell and now sitting in her first-class cabin on an overnight flight to Washington, Tracie leafed through a compendium of press clippings of her London visit prepared by the Foundation staff. Roberta had lovingly proclaimed at Tracie's farewell to her Foundation staff, "Ya done good, girl! You came, you saw, you conquered!" to rousing applause. Now sitting alone with her thoughts, Tracie also decided that should her campaign not capture the White House that November, she and Wilson would return to London - permanently. Still too pumped to sleep, Tracie leaned back in her comfortable seat, put on her earphones to easy listening music, and closed her eyes.

31

Tracie's apparent success as a political novice in London was not lost on Jackson Hewlett. To his well-disguised distaste, Hinton had pulled off a major upset several days later in the Iowa Caucuses, the first political event of the 2052 season. She now had momentum, or what a former President referred to as the "Big Mo." Money would obviously pour into her campaign, and the media would blanket her every move, her every breath. Moreover, Hinton's popularity would spread like a disease and, as he shared with Vernon Coulter, "Disease has to be stopped, better in its early stages for best results." Coulter listened, hesitated a few seconds, responding, "You know what you're asking? dont'cha? I mean, you *know* what you askin'?" "Yeah, I do. You got a problem with this?" "No, I just wanna be clear." "Okay." "Well, it's gonna cost five million cause I'm gonna have to disappear for a while. Is *that* a problem?" "No, that can be done. I'll leave timing and details to you. Send me the account number. Half now and half when it's done." "Okay, we good. When the money's there, I'll get started."

Coulter, or 'AR' as his friends called him, was an arresting character. Coulter and his twin sister, Virginia, were raised by a single mother in Rush Springs, a small town of less than 1,000 residents in Grady

County, Oklahoma, 27 miles NE of Lawton. Their mom worked two jobs during the week and also as a cocktail waitress on the weekends at a club in nearby Lawton [OK] to feed, clothe, and house two fast-growing, boisterous kids. Eight years into single parenthood, the daily regimen was overwhelming, and Virginia was sent to live with her maternal grandmother in Oklahoma City. Vernon missed his sister and was restless without her. He evolved from an outgoing, gregarious kid into this moody, quick-tempered person ready to fight at the slightest personal transgression. At the age of 14, he began to spend more time with the White Knights, a local gang of white youth who engaged in petty crimes in the county and were under constant surveillance by local law enforcement.

A high school dropout at the age of 16, Vernon became a member of Defenders Of The Faith, a right-wing paramilitary group. Here he found the sense of belonging missing in his life, especially since the forced separation from his sister. Anti-Semitism, anti-LGBTQ, and anti-immigrant were cornerstones of their hate-filled philosophy. Lacking the ability to empathize with those from similar backgrounds or display common decency toward others, he found a comfortable, emotional niche to fill the void in his own life.

Several of their group's members, including 'AR,' had been convicted of hate crimes. The group, however, wore their convictions and time spent behind bars as badges of honor, a rite of passage. 'AR,' even as a pre-teen, was fascinated by long guns and, later, spent countless hours at a shooting range frequented by members of their organization, eventually qualifying as an expert with the AR-15 - a semi-automatic, military-style assault weapon designed to kill people. Later, he purchased his first AR-15 with money from petty thefts, and having qualified expert with it, his nickname became 'AR'.

Mexican laborers were in high demand in the state because they were cheap labor. They worked hard and mainly kept to themselves to avoid unnecessary contact with law enforcement. To 'AR' and his friends, the Mexicans were visible and easy targets to vilify. 'AR' would often say to anyone within earshot that "the most effective solution to the illegal immigrant problem is to mine the border with antipersonnel mines. Those crossing illegally who survive the minefield should be shot when they set foot on American soil." His friends also knew that, were such a barbaric policy ever adopted, 'AR' would not only volunteer to plant the mines, he would also volunteer to shoot survivors.

Coulter drifted for several years doing odd jobs until he found regular employment with a local pipe-fitting company. It was there he met his future wife, Eileen, the company secretary. Eight months later, they married. Their bond was strong because, as a survivor of parental abuse, she also shared Coulter's views on most social and cultural issues. Vernon was her first stable, personal relationship beyond the groups he had joined earlier in his life.

Coulter and Hewlett met at a political rally early in Hewlett's career when Coulter walked up to Hewlett after the rally and introduced himself. He let Hewlett know that he supported him and wanted to volunteer for his campaign. Coulter tells the story that the two of them hit it off, shook hands, and a relationship slowly evolved. Coulter liked Hewlett's conservative philosophy. He was especially supportive of Hewlett's dislike for the same people he disliked. And now, he was being asked to eliminate a political rival of his friend. This would not be the first time Coulter had accepted a similar request. On two prior occasions, he had participated in targeted killings. However, there was never enough evidence linking him to the crimes to convict him. In his right-wing community, 'AR' was viewed as untouchable, certainly reliable.

He did not lack confidence in his ability to fulfill the terms of his contract with Hewlett. Any contract, he once boasted to a close friend, is all about timing, means, and location. "Why should this latest one be any different?" he thought to himself. Timing would involve not just the attack on Hinton but also when he and his wife could leave the country. First, he needed to research which countries did not have extradition treaties with the U.S. 'AR' learned that Ecuador and Venezuela were in this hemisphere, but those two countries would be the focal points early in any investigation to locate the two of them once it was established that he was the prime suspect.

Other possible safe havens included Qatar, Saudi Arabia, Vietnam, and Indonesia. China did not appeal to him. Neither did Mongolia or Taiwan. However, several countries in Africa, especially on the eastern side of the African Continent, might also offer the haven he would be seeking given their former colonial histories, e.g., Zimbabwe and South Africa. The U.S., in all likelihood, would be seeking the death penalty if he were found to have been guilty of the attack on Hinton.

The New Hampshire Primary was the next political hurdle for Tracie. A win there, or a very strong second place, would make her competitive for the South Carolina Primary. She was also keeping an eye on the Global Initiative for Climate Change, which her Foundation was sponsoring in London in late May. She was in debt to Wilson and her father-in-law Adebiji for a masterful feat of diplomacy: uniting the members of the Maghreb Union, especially Morocco and Tunisia, behind the Foundation's first major initiative. Adebiji's stature as an African leader, combined with his son's high profile as a member of the World Health Organization and senior consultant to the Hinton Foundation, were persuasive in gaining the support of the Maghreb Union. Mutual survival, father and son argued, had to take precedence over political disagreements.

The Maghreb Union was the last political bloc on the African Continent to come on board along with the Economic Community of West African States [ECOWAS]. Africa was now a full-fledged partner. Africa's resources were vast and varied, as was the Continent's needs. The Continent's agriculture had to be redesigned to make more sustainable use of its resources to feed its people. On the other hand, Africa's southern coastlands had succumbed to the sea for several miles inland. Former coastal settlements and fishing villages had gradually moved, so most of the development now was new and modern. But Africa was not alone in this regard. Coastal settlements and their economies worldwide had suffered, and their populations were forced to relocate further inland to survive.

As the Global Initiative loomed ever closer, Tracie and Roberta talked daily. Tracie was practically ebullient when she shared with Roberta that they were no longer just a disparate group of intellectuals raising the alarm about the deteriorating condition of the planet. "People see us as worthy of their trust, an alternative, something to invest their hopes in for the future and the future of their children and grandchildren. Our values give them hope and a reason to plan, to believe that working together and sharing resources, we and our planet will survive - and without resorting to war over resources."

"Tracie," Roberta responded, "what you have achieved with the Global Initiative is nothing short of a miracle. I am already thinking about how we build on this year's event. Two years from now, we have to be able to look back and measure the progress we've made with Global Initiative Redux. I don't want anyone to think that this year's event was a one-off, a one-and-done." "I agree with you. So, what's on your mind?" "I propose that we meet again in 2054 but, this time, in Africa." "Wow! Okay. Why Africa?" Tracie asked, even though the suggestion appealed to her.

"Well, the staff and I have developed a strategic rationale which addresses that very question. Get a cup of tea, relax a little, and let me read it to you. It's a first draft, so should you have questions or modifications, let me know, and we'll incorporate them." "Okay, I need to take a break. Hold a minute while I get that cup of tea"…seconds later, "I'm back."

"Okay, here it is: 'the majority of Africans today between 18 and 35 believe they represent the future for our survival - and I agree with them. There are 2.5 billion people on the African Continent, the world's second-largest, with an average age of 19. One out of every four workers in the world is African. This suggests to me, in the final analysis, the youth of Africa are the solution. Here is what I've heard from many of them. They want to be a force for stability and dynamic growth, but that requires partnerships in order to create and seize opportunities."

"That sounds good to me. I heard essentially the same thing when I was in Lagos. Continue."

"Africa's potential is enormous. Many of the world's fastest-growing economies are African. Ask the Chinese, the Russians, and the Turks, to name a few. Now, more specifically and germane to our survival, Africa is home to some of the largest reserves of rare-earth elements and minerals vital to green technology. Cobalt, copper, and bauxite are essential in batteries and other renewable energy sources. Africa's youth prefer the U.S. and the West as partners because we are better positioned to help them achieve a more sustainable future. And that is *despite* our neglect. They value our technology, culture, and approach to entrepreneurship to transform their continent and the world into a green economy."

"I like it. Is there more?"

"Yes: 'The final point I would make is that we are in competition with China over whose global vision Africa's youth will favor. Africa's youth are watching. I offer them, and those who would partner with the Foundation, a path forward through our Global Initiative for Climate Change. That is a lengthy response to your important question. I see the Foundation establishing viable partnerships with Africa because we share a vision for the future of our planet. Thanks for the question, by the way.'"

"Roberta, and here I was beating myself up for having pulled you away from Seattle to do this thing for me. You're the right person at the right time in the right role."

"I have to admit, Tracie, I am enjoying myself. The hours are exhausting, and Wiley hears me complain all the time. Our extended weekends in D.C. take the edge off. He also knows I'm having a great time. Let's see what happens in November."

"Okay, my friend. Talk soon!"

When Tracie hung up, another plan took root in her head: If she were not successful in November, she would return to London as Chairman of the Board and President of the Foundation. Roberta would be offered the position of CEO. Just as she had moved her firm to London, perhaps Roberta and Wiley might consider following suit.

President Harwood had evolved comfortably into his role as an advocate for a more enlightened approach to dealing with a changing global climate and thus viewed Tracie Hinton's latest Global Initiative for Climate Change as less threatening and more alliance building. He, too, read polls and had recently concluded that the ACTION 2100 Party could upend American electoral politics in November. The presidential elections that year could produce the country's first 3rd party President in over two centuries.

Now that he was no longer a candidate for reelection, he had an ulterior motive - to recast his legacy. Tracie's latest project could be instrumental. So he now had no need for not approving the delegates to the London Global Initiative for Climate Change when he publicly saw no conflict with the initiatives Hinton and the other delegates would likely support. This could be a win-win if played out strategically. Sitting on the terrace outside the White House residence with its sweeping view of the South Lawn and the Washington Monument while enjoying a glass of Chardonnay with his wife, he commented that he couldn't have scripted a better outcome had he tried to do so. He added, "Hewlett will likely lose everything in November. I would not want to be in his shoes right now. He has to be shitting bricks!" His wife shared her husband's comments with her friends. Although she found her husband's language crude, she felt it acceptable to make public under the circumstances.

Jackson Hewlett, on the other hand, was apoplectic about the growing strength of the ACTION 2100 Party as he and his team read the polls and engaged in lengthy telephone conversations with their field operatives, especially in battleground states. Frequently, those conversations escalated into shouting matches with Hewlett determined to prove he was the better campaign strategist. Several veteran strategists decided against tolerating Hewlett's verbal tirades and left the campaign.

Unfortunately, they were the ones his campaign could ill afford to lose. Hewlett's message was not resonating when voters were struggling to cope with the daily challenges of survival - rising prices, food shortages, job losses, higher utility bills, and general disgust with elected officials of both major political parties. Voters rightly drew a connection between the quality of their lives and a changing climate; the X-factor Hewlett struggled to overcome. Daily media coverage included one or more items about a climatological anomaly somewhere on the globe attributed to a changing climate.

If the President was disinclined to send an alternate slate of delegates to London, Hewlett was powerless. Harwood had boxed him in at a time when he could have benefitted from offering an alternative message on strategies to manage a changing climate to a major world event. And there was no appeal with Harwood since the President and his embattled Vice President rarely saw each other. Hewlett, formerly a West Wing fixture, rarely saw the inside of the place now. He was *persona non grata*, receiving instructions only from the President's chief of staff. Hewlett's fatal mistake with Harwood had been miscalculating how much the President prized loyalty to him. Harwood understood and accepted that he and his vice president would not always agree. But for his hand-picked running mate to challenge him publicly for the nomination was *the* unpardonable sin.

When Hinton took the New Hampshire Primary and almost won in South Carolina, Hewlett was desperate. If Hinton swept Super Tuesday or, more likely, garnered a close second, her chances of capturing the nomination would improve significantly. The excitement, the momentum to nominate a true third party candidate for the first time would make history. The temptation would be irresistible. Voters like to be on the "right side" of history even if they prefer another candidate. Those voters want to be able to tell their children and grandchildren they "helped to make history." A middle-aged white guy, Hewlett reasoned, the perennial default position in American presidential politics, would fall quickly out of favor.

Conversely, Tracie was every general campaign manager's dream candidate: photogenic, media savvy, disciplined, indefatigable, and comfortable thinking on her feet. It helped that voters understood the link between their daily lives, their prospects for the future, and the rampaging effects of a changing climate. Voters and candidates were in sync on key issues, and the candidate's vast knowledge left critics resorting to tired, disproven talking points. Tracie always ended an exchange with critics with, "Set your talking points aside and do us all a favor and tell us something we don't know."

Privately, Hinton's major asset and source of strength as a candidate was there was life after the quest for the nomination. While she believed in herself and her mission, she was prepared to either assume the presidency or return to her work with her Foundation. Sam and Ericka, her parents, called their daughter "The Happy Warrior." Primaries energized Tracie. She understood that if the voters elected her, they wanted radical change. Bringing real change to Washington would be fraught with peril - serious peril, possibly even at the loss of her life. Everyone in her small inner circle understood this. There were entrenched corporate, industrial, and financial interests that feared the unknown, change. They feared a loss of power and control, the ability to influence national policy in every important sector of American life. Most importantly, these socially privileged captains of industry and finance feared a rising level of social equality and a more equitable distribution of national resources. Presidents were expendable, especially radical reformers. Hewlett was the preferred candidate for this stratum of American society.

It was now late February, with Super Tuesday just over a week away. While returning from a West Coast campaign swing, Tracie called Wilson because they'd had a previous call interrupted by a crisis in Wilson's office. "I'm thinking of spending Super Tuesday in Detroit with the team. We'll watch the results that night, and I'll fly to D.C. the next day. Are you good with that?"

"Yeah, if you win or do better than expected, you should be there." Wilson had his wife's schedule for the period leading up to Super Tuesday, and she was heavily scheduled - several stops daily, often in different states.

On that Tuesday in March when the greatest number of states held primary elections and caucuses, more than a third of all delegates to presidential nominations can be won. "What are your polls showing?" Wilson asked Tracie.

"We're better than 50 percent today," Tracie responded. "If I can keep the gap to single digits or low double digits, I'll be satisfied. A win would be phenomenal!"

"I say this all the time, Sweetie: As a long-shot, third-party candidate, you've confounded everyone, especially the odds-makers." - laughing.

"Well, without you guys - Mom, Dad, Wiley, and Roberta, the people in Detroit, I never would have attempted this. Something else, too."

"Yeah, what's that?"

"If we win or place a strong second, we should seriously look at how we might staff a new government. We can't wait until the last minute. We're going to need good, competent people who can be confirmed, especially if we don't carry the Senate. The opposition will be coming for us, and they're going to do whatever it takes to populate our administration with their people."

"No doubt. Confirmation hearings will remain unscheduled or highly partisan and contentious. The longer hearings can be delayed, the more likely the most qualified people will tire of putting their lives on hold and drop out of consideration. There is plenty of history to support this."

"Dad has been briefing me on just that likelihood. He is very familiar with who our principal antagonists could be if we don't capture the Senate or should we lose key committee chairmanships."

"One final thing, Babe. If you win, tighten security! I mean, go into full presidential mode. I can't shake the feeling that something, that some-one's out there. I think often about the threat you represent to the most powerful interests in this country. They're already organized."

Tracie paused momentarily - as if she dared not breathe. Exhaling almost inaudibly, she responded, "Yeah, Sweetie, I know. But that's who we've always been as a country, isn't it? Success and change scare those invested in maintaining the status quo, even when the planet is at risk. Maybe what we represent is what it will take to bring us together. There is no acceptable alternative to cooperation."

When she hung up with Wilson, Tracie looked out the window of her aircraft, recalling a series of conversations she'd had with representatives of this country's ski industry about the impact of a changing climate on their industry, the decline in the portions of this country covered by snow. The industry had been losing areas covered by snow equivalent to about 1900 square miles per year, an area roughly the size of the State of Delaware, for over 50 years. That trend had continued since the 1970s and was an existential threat to an industry valued at over 60 billion dollars annually. These executives supported her candidacy because the costs associated with trying to create artificial snow with increased average air temperatures were unsustainable. The U.S. was a much desired destination for winter sports enthusiasts the world over and demand for reservations had increased despite the industry's challenges.

———

Mayhew Kingman, Hinton Campaign General Manager, was poised to make American political history on Super Tuesday 2052, and he was confident he could pull it off. His candidate had performed brilliantly the past 18 months, and now it was time to deliver the first stage of the *coup de grace* he had long planned: win the majority of the delegates on Super Tuesday. Context is important for the uninitiated.

Super Tuesday primaries and caucuses in more than a dozen states its uniquely an American political phenomenon occurring every four years. Results are awaited with great anticipation by the voters, the candidates, political pundits, the media, and elected officials in the two major political parties. The outcome can be - but not always - a reliable predictor of a political party's presidential nominee in the general election that year. In 2052, Kingman's candidate, a third-party candidate for the first time, had better than an even chance to emerge the victor on that Tuesday. His success as a manager and chief strategist could tip the balance of electoral power in America away from the two-party system into uncharted waters - and, thus, political history.

Therefore, the stakes were high, not just for the U.S. but also for the billions of non-Americans worldwide whose political and economic destinies were in some measure linked to a two-party America. These non-American investors, we'll call them, could often, under a two-party system, reliably predict the policies and events that would likely shape American reactions with a global impact. There was enough history to do so. In 2052, the salient global issue was a changing climate, and the question was, "Would America lead?" It was expected to. Tracie Hinton, the third-party candidate, promised real leadership if elected. Her success on Super Tuesday would be a watershed event. She had methodically previewed a roadmap for global cooperation and sustainability that resonated with large segments of the American electorate across the political spectrum from left to right. Success on Super Tuesday *could* catapult Hinton into the White House in November. The axis of American politics will then shift permanently. In the mind of Mayhew Kingman, a win on Tuesday could represent a pivotal moment in American history where *"faith in what could be achieved"* triumphed over the bankruptcy of *"hope that things might change."*

By noon on Super Tuesday, Tracie and Wiley had arrived in Detroit and had checked into The Godfrey Detroit Curio Collection by Hilton. Later that afternoon, they would meet up at campaign headquarters to watch the returns. States from California to Vermont, Massachusetts to Texas, and Maine to Utah would be reporting throughout the evening. Between 1200 and 1300 delegates would be chosen. This was going to be a long night. Most of the southern states are Republican strongholds in the general election, and many of the others are Democratic. Kingman, however, was unfazed by this. He had received internal polls indicating major shifts in both parties in favor of a real third-party candidate the voters could believe in. A key factor in behavioral shifts was the Symposium panel discussions. People had tuned in. They choose faith over hope. In this election, few dared vote *uncommitted.*

Polls closed at 8 p.m. local time, and the results between then and early morning the next day sent shock waves through the country that also reverberated around the world. Hinton was the winner. The traditional two-party system was in its death throes, at least that night. Kingman beamed from ear to ear while Tracie and Wiley stared at each other momentarily and then screamed, "We did it! We did it! We did it!" The two of them hugged, cried, and then hugged again. Tracie then called her mom and dad and Wilson, while Wiley called Roberta in London. Wiley was so excited, Roberta, who had not heard the news, said, "Babe, what's going on?" Wiley had not recognized that he may have been a little incoherent. "Turn on the television!" he practically shouted.

At 3:00 a.m. the next morning, Kingman, Tracie, and Wiley stood on the platform in front of their staff, still somewhere between shock and jubilation. Kingman looked at Tracie, and she took the mic. When the shouts, whistling, and general mayhem subsided, she said simply: "I believe in you, I thank you! Now, let's play tonight, but tomorrow, let's get busy and deliver on the rest of it. They're coming for us, we know that. The race begins now!"

HINTON SWEEPS SUPER TUESDAY! was the headline for the early Wednesday edition of the city's largest daily, the *DETROIT NEWS*. Wiley had been on the phone practically the entire night with family, friends, former colleagues, and old classmates. Similar headlines were featured in dailies around the country. Early morning cable talk shows grappled with the question, "How could this happen?" and "Is this the end of the two-party domination of politics in America?" Phase two of Kingman's strategy would now unfold: endless reviews of Hinton's Symposium Panel discussions. Segments of each panel would be part of hourly news for the next several months. The voters would be reminded hourly, daily, about why they had voted differently this time. Party loyalty took a backseat to survival, faith that life in this country could still change.

At a White House press briefing the next day, the President was asked about his reaction to the results of Super Tuesday. He responded, "The people wanted change." He smiled and left the Press Room.

32

On Wednesday morning after breakfast, Tracie and Wiley were looking for a quiet corner in campaign headquarters, someplace they could talk. Phones were ringing, staff were huddled over charts, polling data, and myriad other conversations were competing to be heard. Waste baskets were filled with plastic cups, plates, and cutlery from the previous evening's celebration. The mood among the staff was jubilant and energized. "There's a coffee shop around the corner," Wiley told Tracie. "Let's go there. We don't want to interrupt anything that's going on here."

"Yeah! I'll tell Kingman where we'll be." Minutes later, the two stepped out into the cold, crisp morning air for the brief walk to the coffee shop around the corner. As they entered, early morning customers already populated the place, but you could have a conversation without shouting. While Tracie found a small table in the corner as far from the entrance as possible, Wiley queued to order two hot chocolates and two butter croissants. Within five minutes, he returned. "You know," he began, "Roberta and I spent many hours in this place when we were students here. We would debate endlessly. I purposefully let her do most of the talking because I loved hearing her accent. Second, she is passionate about the things she believes in, especially politics and social justice issues. Third, I wanted to spend as much time as I could with her away from the usual campus haunts."

"Your strategy worked, apparently."

"It did. It did."

"Listen, Wiley," Tracie began, while cupping her hot chocolate in both hands. "I've been thinking about next steps - yours and mine. Of course, we hoped for this day; we planned for it! Well, now it's here. What I'd like for you to do is begin transition planning in the event we actually win this thing. Campaigning is the fun stuff. I actually enjoy it. Both of us can't be out there, and I don't mean to diminish the importance of what you do. I think you know that."

"We're in sync - as usual, Tracie. I've also been thinking about some possible Cabinet choices, who we would want that are reliable, competent, and can pass muster with the Senate. Roberta and I have been kicking around some ideas regarding a draft program/policy agenda: what we want to be able to get done in the first 100 days, 180 days, the first year."

"Great! Send me a draft when it's ready. I'd like to see it."

"Yes, I will. After the first year, everyone on the Hill will be focused on the midterms. The agenda of those who oppose us - from both parties - will be simple: How to take us down, accusing us of government overreach, assaulting the capitalist economic system, and engaging in class warfare. To them, a multi-party system in this country can never be allowed to succeed. Such a beast would upend decades of carefully constructed and nurtured alliances both parties depend on for their very survival - political and financial." He continued: "There is a rhythm to American politics that governs relations between the parties, and its supporters will wage war to preserve it. Remember, there are no permanent allegiances, just permanent interests. We have to be ready for that. Also, I don't want to be on the defensive within a year of taking office. We should try to control the policy narrative for as long as possible."

"On that point," Tracie interjected, "we're going to need a first-rate politically-savvy, White House congressional liaison team to support you on the Hill."

"Yeah! Roberta and I have several candidates in mind."

"So, you're comfortable coming off the road?!"

"Yeah! At least for the time being. I should be back out there beginning late summer."

"I've got the Global Initiative for Climate Change event in London coming up in late May before the annual G-7 Summit of Industrialized Nations. You'll be in London; otherwise, Roberta will walk out on me." laughing.

Continuing, Tracie explained that she wanted to concentrate on states like Texas, Oklahoma, Missouri, and Kansas, where their current level of support may be weak but could strengthen their position by November's general election. "I'm not taking anything for granted, nor am I conceding anything. I'm going to run as though I'm the underdog. We'll have data soon. Mayhew and I will go over it, and then we'll target those areas where we may have opportunities to shore up our position. He may have some other states in addition to the four I just named. Overall, our ground game is solid nationwide, but we'll have more money to make it even more effective."

"To the four you suggested," Wiley added, "you should spend some time in West Virginia, Ohio, Kentucky, and Western Pennsylvania. That's coal country, and we're going to need their support. Political leadership in those states practices strategic autonomy, something we've proven societies can no longer afford. We've got to do a better job of educating the voters in some regions why their survival depends on being included, not excluded."

Tracie then asked Wiley about his business - Maritime Solutions International. "I talk to my partners regularly," Wiley responded. "We're doing very well! Since joining the campaign, I'm told we've picked up several new clients from West Africa and the Caribbean."

"Well, here's some food for thought, Wiley. If we don't win in November, as you know, I'll be returning to London to the Foundation. My business will have been well established there as well. You and Roberta might consider relocating your business there. I'd like her to join me at the Foundation, and she could still be involved with your business. Just think about it!"

"Okay, we will. Thanks for thinking of us!"

When they returned to campaign headquarters, and Tracie went in to talk to Kingman, Wiley remembered the one thing he and Tracie had not discussed was security arrangements after the results of Super Tuesday. He knew existing arrangements would have to be revisited; they were adequate before their campaign had pulled off a major upset. Now, Tracie, and perhaps himself, would be in the crosshairs of seriously powerful interests and lone wolves as well. Since Tracie would be focusing on the Southwest and the mid-Atlantic regions, home to some of the most extreme right-wing organizations in the country, she could be in danger. He decided to take up the matter with Kingman and the head of campaign security.

Tracie's security was very much on 'AR' Coulter's mind as well. It was public knowledge that she had accepted Secret Service protection early in her presidential campaign because of the volume and severity of the threats against her. The organization charged with protecting the American President did not have a spotless record and had earned its share of critics. How effective was her security was a question that crossed not only his mind but of others as well.

Coulter had a history of political violence, but he was viewed by many as untouchable because he was no idiot; he knew how to protect himself. The question for him was how to get to Hinton, not a fear of the U.S. Secret Service. The real challenge, as he saw it, was covering his tracks after. He didn't want to bring his wife into his planning - at least not yet. Eventually, he would have to. Their escape would have to be meticulously planned. Coulter kept his own counsel, and I imagine his thought process proceeded along the following lines:

"What is Hinton's travel schedule? Where will she be for the next several months? And when? Does she plan to return to Oklahoma? What is the best method of attack? Should I be concerned about collateral damage? How do I cover my tracks to avoid scrutiny or raise questions about our absence - my wife and myself? And, of course, timing? To begin, I should contact her campaign office here in Oklahoma and ask when she might be returning. Volunteer to do canvassing or distribute materials. Make a plan."

Over the remaining days of winter into the spring of 2052, Tracie campaigned strategically, promoting her message of cooperation, unity, and sustainability. She referred frequently to her panel discussions, solutions to specific challenges, and how, through cooperation, life can be sustained. At night, after a quick dinner, she would call Wilson, and together, they would review drafts of her opening remarks to the Global Initiative for Climate Change in late May. Those moments of her day when she could hear his voice, his laugh, his humor, she would recall later, were often the highlight of her day. Nights and weekends were the most difficult because that's when she felt the absence of his companionship. Technically, she and Wilson were still in the early years of their marriage - practically newlyweds. In her heart, especially after talking to him, Tracie wanted everything, the campaign, to be over. They had been apart too long, and whatever the outcome of this campaign, she looked forward to being together with her husband again. Brief calls to her mom and dad came earlier in the day.

Now released from the 'presidential doghouse' for having challenged a sitting president, the Vice President campaigned at a frenetic pace. There were pockets of supporters in some areas, but far too frequently, he encountered friendly and hostile questioning about President Harwood's consistent refusal to confront the effects of a changing climate earlier in their presidency. To make matters worse, the Vice President often had to agree with some of the conclusions offered by the experts on Tracie's panels. Trying to present a counter-narrative to victims struggling to survive would have made himself look too partisan and less credible. And then there were the questions about North Korea and Russia. Were he to distance himself from the President's decisions, he risked appearing disloyal, and if he agreed with the President, he, too, appeared indecisive. There was no 'sweet spot' when the issue was North Korean or Russian aggression. Americans, thousands of them, died, and we lost a critical Pacific naval base. And we sat by when our northern neighbor was not only the victim of a deadly cyberattack but was invaded by the Russians.

Securing the nomination of his party was not Hewlett's main concern. It was the odds against him overcoming Hinton in the general election. That realization enveloped him like a shroud, one he could not shake. He couldn't quit, and the odds against a win were too great. Hewlett's temperament ranged from frustration to flashes of anger on any given day. Anything could trigger an outburst: a misstep by one of his aides, unfavorable poll results, a bad interview, an unflattering article in a local daily, or a decline in donor contributions. Traveling staff were often unsure how to read the Vice President's moods or fix whatever the problem was, so they tried to give him space. His wife, Celeste, was the only one who could talk him down when he would rage about being held accountable for Harwood's decisions. As painful as it was to do so, she had to remind him that that was what he signed onto when he joined the Harwood ticket. To inject a bit of humor into the moment, she would say, "Honey, he set the menu; you just got invited to dinner. Remember, poor old Harry Truman was never invited to lunch or dinner."

Several of Hewlett's principal financial donors are reported to have advised him to just finish the race. 2052 was not his time that he should focus on 2056 when a Hinton presidency will have a record to run against - if she wins. Hewlett also feared the likelihood of a younger challenger for the nomination in 2056, perhaps someone that Harwood would endorse to further humiliate him. Harwood would not run again; therefore, the endorsement of a former President would be prized by anyone from his party seeking the nomination.

It was almost 8:30 p.m. on a Wednesday evening in late May when Tracie's armored Secret Service SUV slipped into traffic for the drive to the General Aviation Terminal at Detroit Metropolitan Wayne County Airport. No sirens, just flashing red and blue lights sufficed to facilitate the drive. Tracie sat alone except for one assistant and the two-armed agents in the front seat. Behind them was the customary trail vehicle with four armed agents. Tracie's absence from the campaign did not make news among the staff because she was rarely in Detroit. Not everyone could tell you on any given day where she was because they had other duties to occupy their time. Her schedule was not classified in the strictest sense of the word; close hold would have been a more accurate description - security considerations. On this particular evening, her destination was London in the U.K. for the opening of the Global Initiative for Climate Change.

Access to the General Aviation Terminal had been arranged by the Detroit Police liaison to the Hinton Campaign as the two SUVs proceeded through the gates without stopping for ID checks. Officials at the terminal were familiar with this particular VIP. Once in the hangar, the vehicles came to a halt a few yards from a gleaming Gulfstream G-1100. Its owner was a supporter of the Hinton campaign and had made the aircraft available to her for both domestic and international travel. The two women, accompanied by four of the six Secret Service agents, stepped out of the SUV and quickly boarded the aircraft for the seven-hour flight to London's Heathrow Airport. Departing Detroit at 9:00 p.m. meant a 9:30 a.m. arrival on Thursday morning. Tracie, dressed casually, settled comfortably into one of the recliner seats and was soon asleep. She'd had an exhausting schedule that day and looked forward to an uneventful flight. Within minutes, they were airborne. While Tracie slept peacefully, her assistant reviewed Tracie's opening remarks for the last time. She closed the folder, asked for a glass of wine, took off her shoes, and curled up to listen to music. She had heard about this particular aircraft but had never flown on it before. This was an experience she intended to thoroughly enjoy. Within 30 minutes, Jennifer, the assistant, had fallen asleep. One of the flight stewards passed, picked up Jennifer's wine glass, and dimmed the cabin lights.

Two hours from arrival in the U.K., the two passengers were awakened and offered an opportunity to take a shower, dress, and have breakfast. The agents were already awake. Tracie, feeling refreshed from a restful flight, took a quick shower, dressed, and ordered a full breakfast. Jennifer followed suit. While having breakfast, Jennifer remarked, "I could really get used to this, Tracie," as she took in the sweep of the cabin with its five distinct passenger compartments. Tracie laughed. Breakfast was a bowl of granola topped with strawberries, 5-grain toast with vanilla yogurt, green tea, and a small glass of orange juice. After breakfast, Tracie turned on her computer to check her email and to catch the international news while Jennifer was on the phone with Roberta. "We're all set!" Jennifer announced as she passed a copy of the day's schedule to Tracie.

Thirty minutes later, the wheels touched down on the runway and taxied to a stop at the General Aviation Terminal. As they rolled to a stop in the hangar away from the main terminal, Tracie looked out the window to see Wilson, her mom and dad, Wiley, and Roberta. Tears rolled down her cheeks. She knew each of them would be there, but the sight of all of the most important people in her life in one place at the same time on such a momentous occasion was overwhelming. When the attendant opened the door, she remembered taking the first two steps and was in Wilson's arms. As the two of them embraced, everyone moved in to welcome her. For an instant, everyone seemed to be speaking at once as they moved to the waiting vehicles. Sam, Ericka, and Wilson climbed in with Tracie while Roberta, Wiley, and Jennifer rode in the second vehicle. The Secret Service agents accompanying Tracie joined their colleagues from the American Embassy in London in the third vehicle. Special Branch, again, provided escort as the motorcade headed to the London Hilton on Park Lane in central city.

"Tracie," her mom remarked, "you seemed surprised to see us. You knew we would be there, didn't you?"

"Yes! I did, Mom. It was just an emotional moment for me to see all of you at once. I'm okay. The past few days have been a blur with the campaign and preparing for this trip. And now, after two years of planning and this thing is happening tomorrow! I just need a moment to catch my breath, that's all." She was gripping Wilson's hand so tightly, he glanced at his hand and then at her and she relaxed.

During the 60-minute commute from Heathrow to downtown London, Roberta and Wiley resumed their earlier conversation about moving permanently to London. Roberta loved being back on the Continent and Tracie had broached the idea separately with Wiley. Roberta had wondered how the idea would sit with Wiley. When he raised no significant opposition, she was delighted. The move was now a matter of timing and logistics. "Sweetie, you'll love this city," Roberta intoned, looking out the window. "It has everything that appeals to us, plus the Continent is just across the Channel. We can be practically anywhere on a weekend." Wiley was ready for change. Both the campaign or a move to London guaranteed a new direction for them. Their skills were not only transferable but in great demand.

Roberta had arranged a low-key arrival for Tracie at the hotel, not like the earlier visit as a pure presidential candidate. Now, Tracie preferred to slip in unnoticed until the following day when she would deliver the keynote address to the Foundation's first major global initiative. The world would be on notice! The only event on her schedule that day was an informal luncheon at 12:30 p.m. with Roberta and the Foundation board. The members were enthusiastic about the growth of the Foundation and the ever-increasing level of support it enjoyed. The balance of Tracie's day would be free. Sam and Ericka planned to host an extended family dinner at the hotel - meaning Wiley, Roberta, Jennifer, and Roberta's principal assistant.

Looking around the dinner table that evening, Tracie was momentarily reflecting on her mortality and how she missed being with the people at the table. Everyone, with the exception of Jennifer and Roberta's assistant, was in their forties; her parents were close to seventy. How much longer would she have them? They were in good health, but who knows? However, her life evolved, she would want her mom and dad closer to her, including Roberta and Wiley. They, too, were family. But as important, should she ascend to the White House, Wiley would be by her side and Roberta supporting him. Wilson was in a separate category. He had been a central feature in her life for two decades. Her future was inconceivable without him.

During dinner, Sam stood up to offer a toast and say: "Thank you for making all this possible. I don't mean just the event tomorrow. I mean the larger purpose our daughter seeks. My wife and I rest well - although sometimes anxiously - knowing that our Tracie has friends like you, friends who love and support her as we do. You smooth out the rough spots in her journey. You are part of her legacy, and we are forever grateful to each of you. A toast."

Sam's beautiful toast caught everyone by surprise, especially Ericka and Tracie - who got up and went around to embrace her dad and mom. Returning to her seat, Tracie picked up her glass, saying, "I am a daughter, a wife, and a friend, and I am enriched by all of you. Thank you! Thank you! Thank you!"

That night, while Wilson slept, Tracie slipped out of bed and walked to the window overlooking the street below. She thought to herself the debt she owed to President Harwood and Vice President Hewlett. "If only they had not tried to silence me and lock me out of the process, perhaps we would not be here today. Well, I'm here, and he and Hewlett are not. *That* is something." She had always wanted to establish a legacy for herself, but as a climatologist, she had nothing on the scale that she could now.

On a beautiful day in late May 2052, Tracie Hinton Ojukwe stepped in front of the podium to thunderous applause from international delegates, media representatives from around the globe, and billions of silent observers worldwide.

She and Wilson had awakened early that morning. While Tracie had positioned herself at the table in their suite at the London Hilton on Park Lane, Wilson prepared a pot of tea along with whole grain toast, English jam, and cheese, courtesy of the hotel. These were the quiet moments they enjoyed together in silence before their respective agendas propelled them into a new day. The fact that in a few hours, Tracie would command the world's attention that particular day had not intruded on their morning ritual.

Later, sitting with her in a comfortable holding room minutes before she headed to the podium were Sam and Ericka, Wilson, Wiley, and Roberta. Wilson was the last to leave her, and before doing so, he approached her with that expression she recognized. She stopped. He cupped her face in both hands, touched his forehead against hers, and then kissed her, saying, "This moment is what you've worked for. Knock 'em dead."

"Good morning, delegates and family. On behalf of the Hinton Foundation, thank you for joining us today." She paused. She caught her dad's eye and winked.

"The terrain we all occupy has shifted with consequences for all of us, some more harmful than others. We agreed that no one had escaped. The crisis of a changing climate, a transnational challenge, has changed the world. We are truly in this boat together. There can be no question that we have to row together - in the same direction. Starvation, mass migration, human trafficking, disease, increased crime, and violence have affected us all." She could hear murmurings of assent and see heads nodding in agreement. "Our world leaders have ignored the signs and exacerbated the causes, motivated by their avarice, greed, and desire for power over the planet. The international consequences of their failure have been tragic - and are the reason we are here today.

"In the past, on the issues of war and peace, life and death, and even a changing climate, some of us were discomfited by having to choose sides between the policies of the major Western and Eastern powers. Someone called that posture 'strategic autonomy.' But if we all go back to our roots, the resources of the Earth belonged to everyone, and community was valued over everything. Science has demonstrated that a changing climate has increased our aggressiveness - from the individual who commits crime, literally in the heat of the moment, to our arbitrary division of societies who wage war over access to and control over resources.

"Today, no one enjoys the luxury of strategic autonomy. We must adopt a new posture of strategic inclusion. Our survival and the future of our children and grandchildren depend upon what we do here in this place at this time. You would not be here if you did not believe that. Those we lead and those we represent are watching, and it is their faith in us that will determine our ultimate success. Their faith will determine the security of our world, and it is their faith that will refuse to accept conflict as a solution to disagreement.

"Each nation represented here is a donor and or a recipient. You brought something of value and a statement of need. Our obligation this week is to remember that each of us represents people who all need the resources of our planet to live, and collectively, we have a diversity of resources. So, we are here to share them to sustain life on our planet, wherever we live. You have a program before you with each nation's statements and the schedule of appointment times with the representative. But today, as the inaugural and, hopefully, first annual convocation of the Global Initiative for Climate Change, it is up to you to work collaboratively on our mission statement. The CEO of the Hinton Foundation, Roberta Mitchell, will conduct our discussion. But it must be a collaborative endeavor in which each of us feels represented.

"Tomorrow will be devoted to your individual statements and needs, and our last day will be devoted to the actual negotiations each of you needs to make. Following the conference, the Foundation will see that all of you receive the results of those negotiations, which will also be published to the rest of the world. If any of you are authorized to speak on behalf of your country to offer a location for the next convocation in two years, please tell our Foundation representatives, who will send you the date and location."

Then Tracie introduced Roberta Mitchell to begin the deliberations over the mission statement. She asked for initial wording from the delegates after a brief pause as the delegates from each country conferred. Every delegation entered its wording on an electronic device, which was instantly shown on the large, central screen.

At the end of the morning, a list of all delegations' wording had been published. The convocation broke for a sumptuous lunch buffet provided by their British hosts.

The wording offered by each country's delegates appeared on the screen. When everyone had considered the various submissions, they added, deleted, or altered words using the language translation program on their electronic devices. If a long pause ensued, the Chair called for a quick electronic vote. As the length of the pauses increased, the participants looked at each other to observe body language and facial expressions. When the Chair saw a majority of nodding heads, a final vote was taken. By the end of the afternoon, the vote was unanimous. This was the final wording of the official mission for the Global Initiative for Climate Change:

"The Mission of the Global Initiative for Climate Change is to bring about international collaboration and cooperation among societies affected by a changing climate. Members commit to developing and implementing the best national practices to ensure that resources vital to sustaining life on the planet, e.g., potable water, clean air, arable land, seeds, strategic minerals, are shared and preserved in perpetuity."

A round of applause rose from the delegates as the Chair announced the final vote. The mood relaxed as people rose from their seats, stretched, smiled, shook hands, and began to file out of the room.

The evening was free for everyone to enjoy one of the world's iconic capitals, a capital city known to most of those present. Some of the delegates had been educated there and were frequent visitors. Others owned homes in London. Those delegates with the most extensive knowledge of the city freely offered suggestions about places to visit, restaurants, and the better night spots. Tracie marveled at how quickly the delegates shifted their focus from solving global crises to more social interests.

A truly heartwarming experience for Tracie on the margins of the convocation was the number of delegates who expressed their admiration and support for her presidential campaign. Each of them felt that her candidacy offered more than hope but the real possibility of change, greater prospects for regional unity, more rather than less global cooperation, and the universal recognition that resources had to be shared if war was to be avoided.

Many of the delegates from South America, the Continent of Africa, and Southeast Asia suggested to Tracie, "Starving children die silently, but people will not starve quietly; they will not fade away. They will migrate to where they see the best chances to survive. That presents political, economic, cultural and social problems for those wealthier societies responsible for the environmental policies and programs that brought us to this point." As this message was being delivered, Tracie wished it were possible that President Harwood and his industry supporters had taken heed of this admonition at the outset of his administration. She received open invitations from most of the delegates to visit their countries, to meet with local climate experts and ordinary citizens engaged in devising creative means and methods to sustain life.

33

On the second morning of the convocation, Tracie and Roberta greeted the delegates. Roberta announced that the Foundation would take a roll call of delegations to hear their requests and offerings. As countries with severe needs spoke up, the countries with resources began to offer what they could. The U.S. had effectively offered seeds and expertise on issues related to ozone layer mitigation. The world's indigenous people asked for their voices to be included in the conversation about climate solutions, the restoration of their livelihoods, and a return to traditional methods of farming in exchange for access to science and, research and advice on living within a society's resource means. In the American Southwest, for example, that meant a return to "dry" farming in areas with scarce water resources. The Russians, to avoid being excluded from such an important world event, ceded their aggression in return for the resources to feed their people. The Chinese touted their technological expertise, specifically in exchange with Canada and the EU, for clean water consultancy.

The third day was hardball. However, after the previous day's sharing, a Foundation board member took over the logistical formalities, and the rest of the day was spent in one-to-one meetings between different delegates hoping to secure mutually beneficial contracts. Tracie and Wiley were also lobbied for their expertise.

Finally, the long day was over. All of the delegates were simultaneously relieved and hopeful. After Tracie had closed the session by promising that the Foundation would send every delegate the results of the Initiative's proceedings and the dates for the next convocation, she reminded delegates empowered to speak for their governments to volunteer the site of the next convocation and leave it with a Foundation representative. And it was over. Global Initiative for Climate Change One was now in recent history. It was time for all the participants to take their contracts, their hopes, and their commitments home. The Initiative in 2054 was the carrot that participants had before them to reinforce their determination to follow through on their agreements.

Wilson was waiting for Tracie as the last of the delegates stood patiently to congratulate her for the success of the Foundation's first major event and to express hope that she would be successful in November. The time was late afternoon; Tracie was feeling fatigued. As she approached Wilson, she leaned toward him, saying, "I just want to take my shoes off and relax. Let's go to the room." "As you wish, ma'am," he responded, laughing as he led her to the nearest bank of elevators. In the elevator, she rested her head on Wilson's shoulder. Moments later, they were back in their room. Sitting on the sofa, Wilson motioned for Tracie to pick her feet up. He began to massage her legs and feet as she let out an audible, delicious sigh of relief.

To Wilson, it was obvious his wife had something on her mind. She hadn't completely transitioned mentally from the events of the past several days. "Okay! You want to tell me what's going on up there? [pointing to her head.] "I'm just thinking about how much work remains to be done and how much time we have before the balance of nature tips away from us. We have been playing politics for so long I'm thinking we may be beyond the tipping point. Nature can be a heartless taskmaster, as history reminds us."

"You know, Babe, the idea of having reached a 'tipping point' permeates many of the internal discussions we have at the WHO and in talks with many of our poorer members who lack resources and are in dire need."

"The contrast between the world presented to us this week with the world I encounter sometimes while campaigning is so stark. I do wonder if many Americans are really prepared to accept the changes we'll have to make just to avoid, for example, the tide of humanity that will flow to our borders seeking entry. And that's just one of many issues on the agenda." Tracie continued making the point that "massive resource transfers will be required in the short term to stabilize some of the most desperate countries - especially those with highly mobile, destitute populations. Short of wartime conditions, are Americans prepared for that? Are they prepared to accept adjustments to our economic model of capitalism, growth, short-term profits, and competitive domination or superiority? Frankly, Sweetie, I doubt it."

Wilson continued to massage his wife's feet because she was feeling more relaxed and it was important that she continue her stream of consciousness. She would recall all of it later when she resumed campaigning in June.

"How do you think the media will cover this week's events?" Wilson asked. "So far, at least here in the U.K., it's been good," he added.

"Media coverage will be extensive and positive, but will it be balanced back in the U.S." Tracie wondered. "November is five months away. Americans will vote; the world will be watching. And then begins the 'expectations game.'

'Reality versus expectations. What will not change, however, is the reality presented to us this week: coastal erosion and flooding caused by atmospheric river storms, rising average temperatures, drought, hunger, disease, migration, and social instability. People are desperate for support and solutions. I've done the best job, and I am capable of presenting the choices we have if we are to survive, coexist, and sustain life as we know it."

Upon her return to the U.S., Tracie planned to mobilize an army of surrogates to stress the themes she hoped would bring the country together and support the level of collaboration the world's major powers could get behind.

Tracie lay there on the sofa, quietly reflecting on her improbable journey to that moment. What began as one citizen's call for national unity had evolved into a movement to sustain life as we lived it. She abruptly stood up, declaring, "If I'm meant to do this, I'm determined to get it done, opposition be damned." This is gonna be a roller coaster ride no one's ever gonna forget, she said to herself quietly.

"Did you say something, Babe?" Wilson asked.

"Oh, nothing."

About the Author

George Alfred Kennedy's life experiences as a senior Foreign Service officer under five presidents in seven countries have made him a keen observer of the human political animal. This career has informed his work in recent years as a political and economic analyst, social commentator, memoir writer, entrepreneur, humanitarian, and novelist. He has always loved to write.

Kennedy's historic rise as a Black man to the highest ranks of the Foreign Service occurred between 1963 and 1996. In volume I of his memoir *From Cotton Fields to Summits*, he gives much credit to the early sacrifices and encouragement of his mother, who supported him and his three siblings in New Jersey.

In volume II of his memoirs *The Rest of It*, Kennedy continues his journey chronicled in volume I. During a retirement seminar sponsored by his former employer, the U.S. Department of State, Kennedy was encouraged to focus on the future - The Rest of It - while seeking to continue a life of service, adventure, and personal enrichment.

Prior to and during his diplomatic service, George served in Italy twice, Germany, France, Belgium, Korea, the Philippines, and Canada, and he traveled to a dozen other countries. He acquired a working knowledge of the languages for his assignments.

In retirement, George and his wife, Anna, moved from the Washington, D.C. area to Arizona, where he has been actively engaged in his community, serving with the Marana Chamber of Commerce and as a volunteer on several official committees of the Marana Town Government. A former board member of The United Way of Tucson and

Southern Arizona, George also served as a public member representing Pima County on the Arizona Judicial Performance Review Commission (JPR). Since 2006, he has been a member of the Advisory Board of the College of Social and Behavioral Sciences at the University of Arizona in Tucson.